Fighting for Eden

Jeff Stilwell

For Manya,
who taught me to ride bareback

The tarmac is weeping pools of lazily dancing rainbows, or so she thinks. Snapping alert, she peers more closely at them, marveling how that could be and realizing that it is pretty much like something he would say. She looks around and, automatically, up. A dark night. Still, you can't see as many stars as you can at home. No matter how hard they try. *She wonders how green the hills are now, breaking off her thoughts as the plane's lumbering shriek grows in volume, beginning to envelop her as it backs its way toward her. Soon, she thinks, staring at the cargo bay doors.*

The plane's engines subside into a quiet ticking and, as if on cue, the crickets once again pick up their lament. She waits. Not long now.

Dark figures appear at the edges of the plane in stark relief against the runway lights. Airport personnel. And others. Just like they said. Setting about this way and that with a solemn, restrained urgency. One, holding a uniformed clipboard, turns toward her just as a car approaches. He made it. *She feels a quiet stab of pained joy, then sparks of anger at the thought of seeing him, then guilt that she should be thinking of them at such a moment. She tries to steel herself but gives up, not having the energy. Instead she begins wondering if the shimmering off the runway is coming from her own eyes, swimming at the recollection of his booming laugh, his quickly found beaming smile.* Does it matter? *Doors slam. He is coming. Both of them. She turns.*

I

Andrew clutched his duffel bag more tightly as he heard the scream. "GO HUSSKEEEEZZ!!" He chuckled. This was what he had wanted, though maybe with a little less noise. The cramped stairwell of his dorm began thumping with shouts and stomps, moving downward, moving at him. He threw himself back against the wall just in time to see a pack of hooting primates in purple and gold round the corner on the landing above, jump the six stairs en masse, and plow past him around the left. Their riot followed them, lessening only slightly it seemed, as he shook his head and moved on up the stairs.

His door opened on to a typical, if neat, student's room. "Elevator's broke again."

Andrew blinked around, sweatily gasping a wet "Yeah" through the musty light until he located his boxes sitting in the middle of the floor and then the smiling boy on one of the beds.

"Jake Van der Vaal."

"Andrew Worth." A muscular grip, he reflected. Dark eyes.

"Worth what?"

"Huh?"

"Worth what?"

"I don't know." He put his bag down with a sigh on the spare bed and stripped off his rain-spattered sweater.

"'Spect you wanna improve on that." Andrew looked at Jake, sharply.

Jake grinned. "Oh, come on. You're the newbie. You gotta expect some hazing."

"Yeah."

"So they tell me you're from back East."

"Oh, ju--just the Midwest."

"Right, back East."

"Okay."

"Where from?"

"Wisconsin."

"Ahhh, a cheesehead. Auspicious."

"If you say so."

"Grouchy, aren't we?"

"Maybe."

"Well, here. Maybe this'll make it better. I kinda saved it for you." Jake reached into the small fridge and brought out a beer. Cracking it open, he passed it over with a cheerful smile.

"Oh, thanks." Andrew took a hefty gulp and let it soothe its way down.

"You bet."

The motes swirled slowly around the two boys in the deepening sunshine as they silently regarded one another. Out in the hallway, Andrew could hear the thumps of other boxes, other suitcases being lugged to their new homes. He suddenly put down his beer with a jerk. "Isn't it illegal to have this in your dorm room?"

"It is?" Jake beamed. Andrew grinned back, slowly. Nodding, Jake opened one for himself, murmuring, "Good man," as Andrew took another swig. "We're going to get along just fine." Andrew found himself holding the beer in his mouth, feeling its cheapness turn warm, sour. He swallowed.

"So, where you from Wes-consin-ite? You're transferring, right? A junior? Where'd you go?"

"The UW."

Jake gazed at him. "You're at the UW, fool."

"Oh, right," Andrew flushed. "The Un--university of Wisconsin. At Madison."

Jake nodded slowly. "The other UW."

"Something like that. Yeah."

Andrew began unpacking his bag. Jake watched him. Finally, realizing that he was being rude, Andrew asked about Jake's home.

"Yakima Valley," he said, stretching out on his bed. Andrew waited, then continued unpacking. Jake watched him. Finishing with his duffel bag, Andrew took a key and slit open the top box from the stack on the floor. Reaching in, he took out a handful of books.

Jake sat up. "Those aren't all books, are they?"

Andrew stared at him for a moment, wondering if the boy was joking. He set the books into a bookcase, then, sizing up the boxes, shrugged, "Yeah, I guess so," and continued unpacking.

"Damn."

***

Much to his astonishment, Seattle's fall dressed the trees just as prettily as Madison's. He guessed that he had been expecting only the dark hues of wet evergreens. And wet they were, garlanded in dripping crystal beads of mist. He was coming to love the Mall, or at least what he called the Mall. Its long lines of jade-like neatness bordered by the twin tall pillars, topped with lotus buds - he had wonderingly found - and the heralding long lines of yellowing oak trees, spattered here and there with splashes of orange and brown, made him think of the Mall in Washington D.C. and then, of course, the several photographs in his father's office of the sunny demonstrations outside the Pentagon in Vietnam days. Of the crowds. Dancing, shouting, breathless with anticipation in their 60s hairstyles and clothes. Of the faceless spectre of armed troops standing in long lines of olive green, its protecting lines following the contours of the building. His father always talked about those days with a feverish sheen of excitement - a departure from his usual dry acridity - about how brave they all had been facing down "the Man" and "his helmeted hordes." Always that same description. Having heard it thousands of times, Andrew never knew a variation. Sometimes, Andrew wondered if that moment had been the highest point of his father's life, that it had been all downhill from there. He didn't like to think of such things. He looked up to his father. And if his father's life had peaked so early, what had he to look forward to?

Besides, there had been that one day when he was ten. He was still not sure why, but he had walked to the campus by himself and had found his way into his father's office. Alone, he had stepped carefully through the dust over the stacks of Tibetan and Indian tomes perched in little stupas on the floor, moving to the wall, moving past all the photographs of the demonstrators to focus on the ones of the helmeted hordes. There, he had found it. Most of the photographs had rendered the soldiers as one anonymous line of defense, almost like an olive picket fence with its uniform, long lines of shoulders broken only by rounded helmets. And the rifles of course. But one photograph had been different. Somehow, a trick of the light - perhaps the dying sunlight bouncing off someone's passing car or a shifting camera lens - had painted a smear of light across the very young and very frightened cheeks of a boy in uniform who had seemed not much older than Andrew had been himself, even then, standing there in that fusty office, peering back through time to another age. He had felt sorry for the boy soldier and

4

had wondered what the boy had been thinking about as the picture had clicked. He had felt sorry for his father. Years later, tired of the stories, he had read up on the affair and learned that Secretary of Defense Robert S. McNamara ("that slick-haired imperialist from Ford Motor Company" his father always called him, even now) had refused to allow any rifle in the lines to be loaded with ammunition, and he had confronted his father with that fact. His father had paused mid-story for a moment, then had shrugged, "As far as we knew, they were loaded; it could have easily become Kent State," and had gone back to those days at the Pentagon, when young people had stood for something.

It was fast becoming Andrew's habit to trudge the Mall when he felt restless. It was usually empty as most students preferred the other side of the campus with its views of Mt. Rainier. He liked the ever-present, ever-changing rain. Just now it was forming out of mist into spatters, suiting his mood. Northwest natives were grumbling that such weather was unusual for the fall, though he saw that the Greens were noticeably smug in their predictions of a globally warmed meltdown. Yet one more sign, they celebrated while tramping through the puddles. Noticing a couple of girls walking by in tie-dyed shirts and wet daisy braids the colors of the rainbow, he asked himself how much had really changed since his father's days.

The other UW. He brooded over that distinction. He wondered how long he would have to live that one down. His roommate. Yesterday, noticing Andrew squelching around their room in his sneakers, Jake had commented, "Tell you something about Seattle in the winter." Andrew had paused without looking at him. Jake had gone on as if not noticing. "Two things. Get yourself a good raincoat cause you'll be wearing it nine months out of the year and waterproof your shoes." Andrew had nodded and opened a book.

"Nothing worse for a man's state of mind than walking around all day in wet socks." Andrew had nodded again, mumbling a thanks. "Look for a gortex and fleece coat. Set you back a couple of hundred dollars but it's worth every penny." Andrew had glanced at him. "Just down the hill in U Village." Andrew had nodded a third time and gone back to reading.

Through the rain beginning to pelt down, he thought about the time and peered down at his shoes. As much as he hated to admit it, his roommate was right. It did suck sitting through class in wet shoes. And his coat, which had always seemed to work just fine in Madison rains, seemed to leak everywhere, the sleeves, the back of the neck, even the damn zipper. Well, maybe he'd ask around, he thought. Checking his watch, and letting in yet another cold trickle of autumn, he sighed and decided to head back to his dorm to prepare for New Testament Studies. And that girl.

***

"Eastern Mediterranean propaganda." Andrew looked down a few rows in front of him to see a spiky-haired Goth lean back with earrings so large they stretched his lobes to make holes the size of curling irons.

"Really?" Dr. Schnoebel stopped tossing her chalk to check her seating chart. She smiled at the Goth in smoky tones. "Mr...Edwards, pray tell us why."

"Well, it's obvious, isn't it?" Schnoebel waited. "All that talk at the end about sending the disciples forth to baptize the world. It's just Christian propaganda." People stirred in their seats to look at him.

"Propaganda must serve a purpose," Schnoebel tilted her head as she regarded the Goth, commenting,

6

"if it is to be effective propaganda. What is the purpose of Matthew's propaganda?"

A hand at the front shot up. "It's not propaganda. It's the truth."

Without turning her head, Schnoebel nodded. "Ah, Mr. Hegland weighs in. Güt. However..." Schnoebel began a measured pace along the table, cutting a stylish line with her attractive scarf attached - was it pinned, Andrew wondered - to her shoulder like an epaulette under wind-swept white hair. She stopped pacing, leaned back against the table and resumed meditatively tossing the chalk up and down in her thin, spidery hand. "The Truth."

"No, it's not," a voice chimed in from the front left.

Schnoebel looked over and, failing to find that statement's origin, smiled. "Well, it didn't take us long this morning. So." She sat on the table, crossing her bony legs at the ankles. "We find ourselves at our first impasse. There will be others. For the time being, let us retreat from the barricades of whether Matthew's claims are the truth and ask ourselves about the purpose of, as Mr. Edwards terms it, Matthew's propaganda."

Hegland's hand jerked up again. "But, it's not--!"

"Softly, softly, Mr. Hegland," she gently rasped. "How can we know whether it is propaganda or not? Let us examine his claims." She ran her eyes over the class. "Come cherubs, where is your wisdom? Or should I say your strong words? For out of the mouths of babes and sucklings comes no less the Hebrews promise."

Andrew made a move and the girl turned toward him. Green eyes under magnificently drawn eyebrows, the right one tapering up into a permanent sly question, waited. He shut down. Quickly. Except for the rosy heat rising in his cheeks. She watched him a moment more and then returned her attention to the professor.

"Come, cherubs. We must not let the Hebrews down."

Long auburn hair revealed no more now than sweetly rounded cheeks over a green turtleneck. And those lips. Bright red, beautifully sculpted lines, set off in profile against fair, delicate, almost alabaster skin. Vanilla, he thought.

"Nothing? Tsk, tsk, tsk. All those decades of Sunday School come to this! Perhaps our churches need to inquire into their quality control." Some nervous titters sprang up around the room. Hegland's impatient hand raised again.

"My pastor says," began a shy voice in the middle before dying.

Schnoebel snatched a glance at her chart, then back at the student, her falcon's look of hunger fading into kindness as she stood. "Ms. Lee, you were saying."

Lee began again in a quivering voice, "My pastor says that Jesus is the Son of God and the savior of all mankind."

"So much for the chicks," the Goth's voice drawled out.

"Thank you, Mr. Edwards, for your careful parsing of that faith statement." Returning her attention to Lee, she remarked, "I have no doubt of that. My question is, what does Matthew say?"

"That they should burn everyone who doesn't go along with being baptized," rang out a mocking voice from over to the far right.

Schnoebel shook her head. "You, my dear boy, have been reading graphic novels instead of this Gospel." The class chuckled. "Sorry. The Inquisition was not unleashed for over a millennium after Matthew put pen to papyrus. Any other takers?"

Schnoebel leaned back against her table and resumed tossing her chalk. "Let us return to Ms. Lee's offering. Savior. Very well. My question, and what I believe your question should be, is what kind of savior? What does Matthew tell us? What does he say?"

Feeling that old pounding in his head, Andrew began to raise his hand just as he noticed, as expected, the girl's measuring gaze return to him.

Looking up at him, the professor smiled, "Goodness! A new voice. I was beginning to worry I had over-taxed our secondary education system by assigning such a lengthy reading assignment. Yes, oh fearless cherub?"

The burning reached out again from his chest and rushed, like a flood, up his neck and over his cheeks. Andrew squeaked out, "The new emperor." Faces from all over the room turned toward him.

"Emperor? Mein Gott! What an odd thing to say, cherub! Where would you get something like that?"

"Well..." Andrew started and feeling those green eyes with their questioning eyebrow on him, he fought for his words, saying, "Well, he...he says that...he tells that..." before relapsing into frustration.

"He tells that...?" The radiator began knocking in rhythm with the pounding in his head as Schnoebel continued her long strides back and forth along her table, a little faster now, with her arms folded. "Matthew tells us that Jesus is the new emperor? You mean of Rome, of course." She gazed at him. "This peasant Jew from the sand-encrusted toenails of the Empire..."

"I thought Jesus wasn't Jewish," a girl commented.

Schnoebel paused mid-stride, glancing at the girl. "Please." Checking her chart, she then turned back up to Andrew. "Yes, cherub, you were saying."

To hell with it, Andrew thought. "He doesn't say that. Not ex--explicitly. At least I don't remember that. But he...he implies it with his stories about Jesus' life."

"His account of Jesus' life," Schnoebel corrected him with the lift of one corner of her mouth.

Andrew blinked in confusion, his thoughts swirling as he tried to remember, then responded, "His stories."

She waited, watching him. He stared back. Finally, nodding, she sighed, "Ach, cherub." Turning to the class, she said, "Alles, wir haben mit uns...," then correcting herself, continued, "We have a heretic in our midst." The class, mystified, stirred. "Stories. Implying, of course, Mr. Worth, that they are not true."

He squirmed in his seat. "Not necessarily."

Hegland's hand shot up.

"You have ruffled Herr Hegland's feathers, I see. Wünderschön. Mr. Hegland?"

"They're not just stories! They're the truth."

"Ach, that dreaded T-word, again. Mr. Worth? Rebuttal?"

The class watched him, waiting. She watched him, waiting. He could feel her, breathing next to him. Could smell her. Was it really vanilla?

"Well, Mr. Worth? You've laid down quite a charge. Can you back it up?"

"Not with spe--specific verses. No." Her eyes turned away from him, embarrassed for him. Down below, Schnoebel's smile deepened, considering.

Hegland's voice scorned, "That's because he doesn't read his Bible."

Andrew sat forward, trying to find Hegland in the rows, feeling himself flare up. "It's not that simple."

Hegland turned in his seat, a handsome boy, an air of self-assured fraternity entitlement, the kind Andrew hated on sight. "Yes, it is that simple," Hegland scoffed, turning away. "Read your Bible. Then, we'll talk."

Schnoebel found a seat and leaned with an elbow on the table, cupping her chin with a finger crossing her lips, eyes following the exchange with sparkling delight.

"I have. I can see you haven't."

Hegland turned around in his seat again, his gaze narrowing at Andrew. "All right, then, mouth. Test me."

A chorus of ooos and whispers fluttered around the room.

Andrew stared at him. He could see the boy's nostrils flaring in whiteness against his tanned, muscular cheeks. Could see amused contempt in the boy's eyes as he waited. He wondered of what circumstances such self-assurance was born. More than simply money. More than privilege. More than a lifetime of sprawling homes, private swimming pools, and sports cars changed as frequently as most people's sneakers. Why was Hegland here, anyway? Why not some eastern school of ivy-festooned royalty? But, of course, because he was northwest royalty. Hegland. The Wrights, the Kings, the Yeslers and, of course, the Gates, he had heard of all of those. But Heglands? Nevertheless, he remembered hearing somewhere that the petty duchy of the Northwest go to the University of Washington and then the biggest northwest firms because they are so proud of what they have carved out of the rain-sodden and volcanically threatened wilderness out here. Harvard, to the northwestern mind, was for the effeminate. Fair enough. But why Scripture? What? Did he grow up playing some sort of scriptural Trivial Pursuit at Sunday School or--?

"Nothing?"

Hegland's smirk, interrupting Andrew's thoughts, flashed up at him, waiting. As was the entire room. As was the held breath next to him.

"Who comes to the manger at Bethlehem? Kings or shepherds?"

"What?" Hegland sneered, "Both!"

"Maybe at the Christmas pageant, but not in Scripture," Andrew rapped out, surprising himself. "Better fetch your Bible, church boy, because it depends on which Gospel you're reading."

Hegland glared up at him, a question dawning in his eyes, then over at the professor who sat as if carved from stone, looking out the window, admiring the rainy pearl gray of this late afternoon. He mumbled something under his breath and reaching into his bag, pulled out his Bible. He flipped it open to the beginning of Matthew and scowled up at Andrew. "Well?"

"Matthew believes that Jesus was..." Andrew paused, gathering his thoughts, trying not to feel the discomfort growing more acute by the moment, "...the new emperor, even greater than the emperor of Rome. That's why he has kings - you know, the three kings of Orient are - follow a star to come bow down before Jesus when he is first born."

"Yeah, so?"

Andrew thought about going further - pointing out that Matthew's Jesus was born in a house, rather than the fabled stable - but decided it was overkill and that he always hated it when his father did that. "Mark's Jesus is different."

"No, he's--!"

"Yes, he is," Andrew cut him off. "Mark's Jesus isn't interested in the empire, he's only interested in..." Feeling her eyes resting on him, Andrew suddenly, horribly, felt his mind go blank. He tried to remember what Mark's Jesus was interested in but could only think of how nicely the green of her turtleneck went with her hair. Abruptly it came to him. "The peasants of Galilee. That's why--," he said, before noticing Schnoebel's gaze, quizzical now, was turning from the window to rest on him. "That's why there is no Bethlehem story in Mark. No King Herod, no flight to Egypt. No slaughter of the babes. No nothing. Mark's Jesus just shows up one day at the edge of the desert, fully grown, gets baptized by John and then starts shouting something about the kingdom of God being at hand and that you had better repent."

12

Hegland's hands flew through the pages of Matthew to the beginning of Mark and, while the class watched, after quickly scanning the first few pages, he snorted in disbelief, then went back to the beginning, trying to scan even faster. Feeling a certain recklessness, Andrew shot out, "You won't find it because it's not there," and prayed that it wasn't. The class waited, listening to the flipping of pages until Hegland's tightening look of embarrassment brought forth a general sigh followed by a stir. Her hands left her notebook and moved down to her school bag to pull out her Bible and search through its pages. As did other students'.

"John's even less interested in some sort of manger birth. That's way too mundane for him. He's only interested in talking about how Jesus is the logos or the fundamental logic of the universe. Our fundamental sense of order." The classroom was filled now with the sound of flipping pages, furtive glances at Andrew and subdued mutters. Hegland, bright red now, flipped through his pages faster and faster, ripping one. Schnoebel sat with her chin cupped in both hands watching Andrew and not watching Andrew, as if lost meandering the memories of other classrooms, other student debates. Captivated, Andrew hesitated a moment, then plunged on, just wanting to finish it.

"Luke's Jesus is the total party animal. Every time he gets together with the disciples, he's partying. But he's also..." he broke off trying to think of an apt metaphor. After a moment, inspired, he grinned, "Che Guevara." Most of the students had stopped checking now and were simply watching him. Andrew saw that they weren't even doubting anymore. Just earnestly staring at him, wanting to know. He felt stronger, buoyed by their trust. "He's no king. He's no otherworldly demi-god of fundamental order. He's not even the teacher of Galilee peasants, like Mark's. Luke's Jesus thinks bigger. He's a revolutionary. That's why Luke doesn't have kings coming to visit Jesus at his birth." Hegland made a half-hearted attempt to flip to Luke's Gospel, then gave up. "Instead, he brings in the lowest of the low in their society - the landless, the shepherds. And in case you missed the point, he has Mary singing the Magnificat in the very beginning of the Gospel, about raising the humble and tearing down the mighty."

He stopped speaking. He looked at his hands. She still watched him, as did the others. Finally, realizing that he had nothing more to say, they began, one by one, looking back at the professor.

"Ausgezeichnet, cherub. A little light on John, I think, but overall, a well-argued position. Ausgezeichnet. Thank you for demonstrating the value of a close reading." Looking around the room and lifting her chin to make sure that her students heard what she said next, she slowly intoned, "Those of you who have been Christians all your lives will find it hardest to give the Christian Scriptures a fair, close reading because all you will hear in your heads are those Sunday School lessons. My advice to you is to read it as if it were a car manual or a cookbook."

Chuckles and not a few guffaws broke out across the room. "You think I joke, cherubs?" She nodded. "Try it once more for Matthew. We shall see." Reaching over to grab her bag, she barely glanced at the clock. "Enough for today. Auf Wiedersehen."

With a last quick survey of Andrew, she swept out of the room. The students all began talking at once, peeking over at Andrew while packing their bags.

"That was nice."

He glanced up at her, not sure if he had imagined it.

"Did you hear what she said at the end? Ausgezeichnet means 'excellent' in German."

"Oh." How did teeth get so white, he wondered? Knowing his weren't, he closed his lips to cover them.

"My name is Amber."

"Like your hair," he stammered and then shut up.

"Yes," she smiled. "Like my hair. Say, would you like to get together to study sometime?"

He went numb. Amber watched him, waiting and then because he did nothing, said nothing, she tilted her head and smiled even more prettily. He stopped breathing, able only to stare at her.

"Well, maybe think about it, okay?"

He managed some sort of nod. She smiled again, less deeply this time, and sweeping her hair over her shoulder, she turned and left.

***

Andrew could feel the pulsating before he was halfway down the hall. Some kind of metal music, he thought, and thanked God that his roommate was not into that. The past few weeks had gone pretty well between them, he had had to admit. Drawing closer, though, he heard the pulses growing louder with each step until, in disbelief, he stood outside his dorm watching the door vibrate within the frame. From the other side of the door, he thought he could hear some shouts and whoops in between the screaming lyrics and guitar trills. Unlocking the door, he got a flash image of Jake and two other boys with jarhead cuts jerkily dancing, strumming their air guitars all over the room, between and on the beds, somehow managing to miss the empties strewn around the floor like discarded butts, just as one boy, eyes screwed up out of a bull-necked face, screamed a "HOOAH!" and kicked a beer can straight at Andrew's head. Andrew stood there, wondering what to do as it slowly turned end over end, coming closer. He closed his eyes and took it right in the temple.

"Whoa!" The music cut short.

"Petie, what the fuck you doing, fool?! You think this is your own private battery in Kabul?"

Jake walked over to Andrew who was holding his temple. "Let me see." Andrew shook his head and began turning away, trying to remember where Kabul was, finally settling on someplace in the Middle East, over toward India. "Let me see!" Jake pulled Andrew's hand away. "More a dent than a scratch. You'll live." Andrew nodded.

Gesturing over at his two friends, Jake said, "This here's Whore-hay and that other lunk, who I am definitely not going to call on for artillery support especially when my platoon is being overrun, is Petie." Jorge, a small Hispanic boy, nodded shyly behind his square-cut glasses. Petie mumbled a "Sorry" as he reached out an impossibly thick arm to shake hands. Andrew smiled foolishly after shaking it and turned to put his books down.

"Want a wet?" Andrew glanced over to see Jake offering him a beer. He hesitated. It suddenly occurred to him that Jake was ROTC. That's why the neatness, the straight, muscular bearing. Jesus, he thought, and wondered what his dad would say. He took the beer and set it down without opening it, asking himself how he could have missed it. He darted a quick peek at Jake's closet for the tell-tale camouflage uniform but saw that it, as usual, was tidily closed.

Petie sat down on Andrew's bed and changed the subject. "So, I'm in the mess the other day and this craphead comes up to me asking about LDAC. 'What's it like?' he wants to know. So, I says, 'Tougher than the birth canal. What of it?'" Jake passed a beer with delight to Jorge and sat down. Not knowing what to do, Andrew sat at his desk and listened. "'Well, what about the CWST?' he says. I shrug and tell him--'"

Jake took in Andrew's bemused expression. "It's a water test. Get your gear off while you're confused under water. Combat Water Survival Test."

Andrew nodded his thanks and Petie, anxious to continue, broke in. "'--tell him 'Weeell, let me think about that.'" He leaned back and stretched out his legs. "'First they spin you around twenty times until you're good and dizzy.'" Jake chuckled. "'Then after you're stumbling around so much they have to hold you up,' I says, 'they drop you ten meters--'"

Jorge broke in for Andrew, "It's only three." Andrew looked a question at him. "Three meters."

Petie shrugged him off, "'--ten meters,' I tell him, 'straight in.' So now this poor little craphead's starting to look all green and shit and I tell him, 'You're all confused and don't know which way is up, but you're already starting to go blind from no air.'"

Jorge shook his head laughing with Jake as he cracked open his beer. Petie continued, "'Really?' he says, 'No shit?' 'No shit,' I say. 'But you gotta do it, so you start stripping off all your gear before you sink to the bottom from all that LBE'd hundred and fifty pounds on your back." Jake and Jorge were chortling straight through.

Petie's face was red now. "'Hundred and fifty?!' this craphead shouts. 'Hundred and fifty?!' 'Hey,' I say, 'I'm telling it to you straight. You gotta get your gear off and get back to the surface which is pretty fucking difficult when you don't know which way to go.' 'How do you do it?' he asks. He's all serious now. Reeaally worried. So, I tell him..." Petie tried straightening his face, then gave it up for hooting and slapping his knee. "I tells him..." He tried again and failed, all broken up, his audience waiting, poised to guffaw on cue. "I tells him...Just watch to see which way the bubbles go." Andrew felt the air change as he saw Jake's and Jorge's smiles fade, serious now, nodding slowly, almost in unison. "And this poor little shit for brains craphead..." Petie gasped for breath between his whoops and knee slaps. "He looks up at me, as if I'm the Old Man and asks...he's thinking, right? He's thinking real hard now. 'Where do the bubbles come from if I'm holding my breath?'" Petie boomed out a big long laugh, shaking his head at all the stupidity that God put on this good green earth.

It dawned on Andrew why he had never seen the ROTC in Jake before. It was a missing quality of...what? Beefy bravado, he supposed. Seeing it in Petie, Andrew realized that he had never seen it - that characteristic military swagger - that makes you suspect, just as with the puffed up popinjay, all that volume hides a hollow core. Whatever the quality was, he thought, Jake clearly didn't possess it. His reflections were interrupted by Jake and Jorge jumping to their feet to give Petie high fives and roaring, "HOOOAH!" Then again...

All three glanced over at Andrew who sat, as before, one hand on his beer, still unopened, an expression of perfect distraction on his face. Jake grunted, "Civilian present."

Petie gave Andrew a look of perfect pity and began to explain to him in slow, loud English. "You...see...when...you're...confused...and...under...w ater--"

"Ah, knock it off, Petie. Show some respect for your friendly fire victim over there." Jake sat down and picked up his beer. "He's my roomie, after all."

Petie smiled lopsidedly, laughed, downed the rest of his beer, and smashed it against his head, letting out a huge belch.

"Pendejo!" Jorge shook his head, taking a sip.

Petie shot back, "Spook."

Jake smiled over at Andrew. "Whore-hay here's a real egghead, like...Well, anyway, his MOS is intel. Which means we're all in big doo-doo."

Andrew nodded a polite smile as Jorge threw an "Ese!" at Jake before flashing a quick grin and looking down.

"Inzzie Allah!" Jake raised his fist to Jorge.

Jorge shook his head at Jake. "I keep telling you! It's Insh' Allah.'"

"Whatever!" Petie glowered. "Fucking talk English, you wetback, not Raghead!"

"Well, I'd be--better get back to the library."

The three froze for a moment, glancing at one another. Then Jake said, "Sure you don't want to hang around? We'll keep Petie here under wraps."

Andrew hurried out, "No, it's okay. It's great. I just got to, I have to..." before trailing off under his breath.

"Snow me that again, hoss. Hanging around Petie makes me deaf after a while."

Andrew looked over at his books in confusion. "I...There's a professor in...A professor asked me to help her with something."

Jake nodded. "Ah, extra credit."

Petie leered, "Is she hot?"

"Hardly." They waited. Feeling that pounding in his head, Andrew blinked around. "She asked me to write a pr--pr--précis of one her grad students' abstracts." They waited.

"A what of what?" Petie, asked, squinting.

"A summary of...of an article."

Petie shook his head. "Well, why didn't you say so?" he grumbled and muttered something about "fancy words" and "eggheads" while opening a new beer.

"What's it on?" Jake asked.

Feeling the pride rush into his cheeks now, Andrew said, "The long ending in Mark." They gazed at him. "The Gospel. There're two endings, a sh--shorter one and a longer one. And there are clues about the author's--"

"You mean the Bible?" Petie stared at him, horror-struck. Jorge quietly crossed himself. Petie shrugged, "Well, that oughta get you some hot dates."

"Cabron!" Jorge moaned and crossed himself again.

"Yeah." Andrew quickly scooped up some books and slid them in his bag. "So, I'd better get going. Nice meeting you." He turned to go. He saw Jorge staring at him with an expression eerily like awe. Petie shook his head in disgust. Jake sat watching him, thinking.

As he was closing the door, he heard Petie drawl out, "Pr-pr-pr-precee! Dorm life!" and Jake's quick retort: "Yeah, well, when's the last time you got some in that rattrap of yours?"

***

Drums. He awoke to hear a thrombling boom-boomboom-boom shaking the earth. And to his own coughing. Smoke eddied up from all over the thick browns and mustard yellows of forest overlaying the wet stench of jungle rot. Boom-boomboom-boom. Just ahead, he could see that the scrub trees marching all and up down his front began to thin, revealing a wide space of cleared ground, tanned green in some patches with their thirsty lack, burning oranges of wide swathes of fiery ash in others, throwing up great, swaying black plumes and adding to the apocalyptica. Looking down to his lap, he realized that he was in some kind of wooden carriage, painted white and gold and sprinkled with encrusted gems of rich greens, blues and reds. Garnet, he thought? Boom-boomboom-boom, the drums continued so loud he could barely hear himself think. Amethyst? The richly embroidered robes sitting next to him shifted.

Glancing up, he saw a fierce, if strikingly beautiful and hideous, war-mask of white and gold with the same gems adorning it, turn toward him. "The drums will soon quiet."

Good, he gasped, just as a piercing trumpet of animal origins drowned out the thought. A few feet in front of him, a grayish black limb with endless furrowing of intertwining wrinkles, some deep, some shallow, rose extending out of silvered armor plating to straighten above his head. The trumpet shrieked again, this time answered by a ragged chorus of like behind him. He turned on the hard seat and saw, blinked, and saw again several, no tens, no many, many more, war elephants arrayed in long, beaded sheets of worked silver, striding toward them out of the deep jungle, crushing the man high mounds of grass bearing their name. Their mahouts, thin brown figures in dirty turbans, perched behind the ears, tapping their steeds and singing their own refrain of "hut, hut, hut!" Mounted atop all were large, wooden towers containing thin, brown archers at the ready, already slinging their bows and adjusting their feathered quivers.

Watching him, the mask conveyed much less meaning, the eyes as thin slits impenetrably less yet, than the satisfied tones coming from within it. "Nine thousand. My revered father at his peak, fielded no more than two-thirds this many." The robed shoulder hitched irritably. "When charged by my elephants, hearing their cries, Kalinga will burst their hearts in fear."

Kalinga? Andrew's world shifted horribly for a moment. Alarmed, he grabbed at the railing, bumping into the robed shoulder next to him as the world shifted the other way. Their elephant - a real war elephant! - was moving! Trying to stifle the boy's delight welling up in him, he broke off choking as they passed through a plume of foul, greasy smoke. Watching a passing branch easily twelve feet off the ground, he barely resisted the urge to snatch a leaf. Their trumpet blasted again, deafening him for good now, he was certain, as they stopped at the edge of the trees.

Spreading across the plain ahead, far in the distance, he spied a brown city with short walls of stone, topped by some sort of weaving of, were they wooden posts? If he squinted hard, he could just make out little heads running back and forth behind the fortified fence. "See? They are already beginning to panic. My revered father's teacher of great wisdom, Chanakya Kautilya, is proven right once again. This battle is already half won." The shoulders began to relax as a sigh issued forth from under the mask. Just now Andrew realized that they had been bent forward with tension.

His view of the city began to be eclipsed by the sound of hooves that he could just pick out over the drums. No. Not hooves. A stampede. Two wide milling arms of dust crept in from the sides of his vantage, carrying forth impossibly large numbers of horses and riders, racing across the plain to cross one another's paths, thousands of voices roaring in waves that rose and fell above the poundings of the hooves and drums. A few wheeled closer to them, and Andrew saw that they carried one long spear each and wore a leather tunic of some sort, all patterned with grime, smoke and sweat stains. The same tunic, peering down, that he wore underneath a wide gold breastplate circling his neck and chest.

Their crazy, wheeling patterns began to subside into some sort of order across the plain, ringing the city beyond yet leaving large gaps between them. The drums picked up their rhythm and, if possible, their volume.

"Now you will see something indeed," the mask bent, scanning forward. Out of the scrub trees and clumps of tall grass all around them, between the war elephants, shying away from the shifting hooves and swinging trunks, shadowy forms of tall, narrow shields decorated with shapes that he could not make out for the smoke, began to form on either side. Looking quickly out of both sides of the howdah, the shields and their carrying figures, stick-like, moved much as wraiths among the trees and grasses as far on either side as he could see. Glancing down at a

passing turban with flashing yellowed teeth, he saw a
long, wide bronze sword hanging down the thin,
muscular back, swinging against the buttocks,
rippling, with each step of the bare dusty feet. Slung
over the back of another he saw a long bow, cut of
bamboo, he reflected, and thought of Henry V and
Agincourt. Still another carried a javelin, cut a length
half again the warrior's height. More shields, bows,
swords, and javelins, long, thick lines of them,
proceeding endlessly, vomited from the deeps of the
scrawny trunks and ferny drip. On and on they came.

"Ashoka! Ashoka!! ASHHOOOKAAA!" the cry
rang out, ripping the throats with its power. The
drums began a faster beat, and the waves of soldiers
answered with a quick trot, pouring on to the plains,
circling the doomed city of brown stone.

"Six hundred thousand." The shoulders stretched
gleefully, their sleeves reaching out to finely shaped
hands beautifully waving their heaps of gold, silver
and gemmed rings around the devastation forming up.
"Never has such a host been seen in the annals of war.
Never shall one so large ever be seen again. It is
good that you are here to live it."

Ashoka? Andrew sat, stunned. The Ashoka? The
Great Buddhist emperor of India? This was insane.
He peeked up at the emperor, sitting next to him
adorned in all his magnificent ferocity.

"My lord, Beloved...Beloved of the Gods?" Andrew
stammered, uncertain if he was using the right
supplication.

The mask did not turn, only inclined slightly
toward him. "You may speak."

Andrew did not know what to say. This could not
be right. His Ashoka was a great apostle of
Buddhism, the first great evangelist after Buddha -
thinking of his father, he winced at the misplaced
designations - who spread the faith all across India
building stupas and monasteries. He even reconciled
the competing doctrines of nascent Buddhism at

Patna, much as Constantine had done for early
Christianity at Nicea. Ashoka, to Andrew, was
almost a god. How could this light of non-violence
be so delighted at the forces of destruction he was
unleashing?

"My lord, Beloved of the Gods, what does our Lord
Buddha teach about the making of war?" he found
himself asking.

The robes shifted in the smoke. The mask looked
off to the left, nodding at a circle of horse-borne men
wearing ornaments of their own. They bowed low
over the braided manes in response and raced off
toward the milling armies and the city.

Andrew's voice quaked, "My lord--"

"I know of your Buddha's teachings," the mask
interrupted. "I began instruction myself a few years
ago for I could see its uses. But...in war...," the robes
shrugged. "The Lord Buddha, the Enlightened One,
Lotus in the Vale of Pain, and Subduer of Naga, was
a great and wise teacher. He opposed war, it is true.
But then, he was never a king."

The mask turned to stare at him while slapping the
elephant with a staff. Andrew felt the world shift
beneath him again, rocking him up, then down, faster
now, melding into a pattern as the trumpet deafened
him with its war cry once more. Behind him, the
answering chorus began in ones and twos, then
releasing its own combined volley. Looking back, he
could see the other war elephants beginning to trot,
their silvered armor flapping out from their ears and
sides, their mahouts whipping them with the mad
frenzy he could smell, seasoning the battle like a
spice in the air.

"My lord..." Andrew began again, then stopped, not
knowing how to continue.

"I hope they remember to clear the path." Andrew
squinted through the smoke to their front and saw to
his horror that thirty or forty soldiers, beating swords
on shields, did not, or could not, with all the ferocious

din surrounding them, hear the elephants coming.
Moving faster now, he saw the distance shrinking
with each rocking thrust from below. He glanced at
Ashoka who did nothing but continue slapping their
charge with the staff. Closer and closer they came.
In agony, he thrust his thoughts as far forward of
them as he could: The soldiers must hear! They had
to! Suddenly, as if sensing the doom plowing them
into next year's crops, a few turned with wide eyes,
screamed and began to scramble. The standing ranks
of proud warriors began to dissolve wave-like,
Andrew saw with horrid fascination, into a howling,
kicking, punching mob of terror. Anything to get out
of the way. Almost on top them, he saw one
frantically stabbing another while leaping over him.
Was that a sigh, he heard? How could he? Then, he
caught it. "They never do." Screaming, Andrew
closed his eyes as he heard the sickening crunch and
wails of flesh and bone ground into the grassy
pebbles and ash beneath, the lumbering stride of their
elephant hardly a step out of place. On and on it
went, never ceasing. Or maybe he never stopped
screaming. Crunches, wails, smoke and drums.
Always drums.

"It is well that war is so terrible, else we should
grow too fond of it." Andrew opened his eyes to see
the mask lifting upon the beaming smile and
mourning eyes of Jake.

***

The Dream, as Andrew had begun calling it,
troubled him over the following weeks as autumn
made way for the dark, long nights of coming winter.
Of course he read up on it. He learned, to his relief,
that the carnage of Kalinga had become the watershed
event of Ashoka's life, that the bloody streets filled
with hundreds of thousands slain had so shaken the
emperor that he had finally embraced Buddhism with

a whole heart and had begun the reign of non-violence for which he was remembered. Or so the edicts left behind on scrawled pillars and pottery tell. That there was new scholarship questioning the sincerity of Ashoka's leaf-turning, suggesting that the emperor's Road to Damascus experience was born more of the pragmatism needed to govern a diverse territory did not trouble Andrew too much. When it came to religion, and its saints, he knew that the reality rarely added up to the script. Still, he couldn't understand why the prospect of a warrior/king Ashoka had frightened him so much. Almost as if one of the navigation markers to his universe had turned out to be false. The appearance of Jake in the dream also needled him, leading him to avoid his roommate more than ever.

Tiring of the Mall, he began walking the drizzly streets of Seattle, avoiding "the Ave" with all its student hangouts, trudging for miles throughout the night and hiding his sorry and sodden coat from Jake in his closet to pool its damning indictment each morning. On just such a night, he stood in front of a huge, rough-hewn concrete statue easily filling the overpass roofing it. He contemplated its large, bald head staring stoically out at a wet, quiet night almost overwhelming the Volkswagon it was clutching in its claw. Was it a real car, he wondered, peering closer and gauging the scale. Sure enough. What a crazy kind of statue! A testament to what, he ruminated. To Lao Tze, he finally decided, if only just for his own fancy. After all, nobody knew what the old sage had looked like. Just a story, as rough in its brush strokes as the hand-made and tool-carved furrows shaping this monstrosity here, carrying its forgotten 60s flower-power symbol from one uncaring generation to the next, much as Lao Tze must have his *Tao Te Ching* while striding up to that ancient city gate before handing it to a guard without a word and disappearing forever. Smiling at his whimsy, he bowed before the icon's towering girth and trudged off into the night, toward some city life lights that beckoned.

If only he could figure out what was bothering him, he thought. A persistent sense of lack. Once again, as so many times before, he found his eyes penetrating the facade of these dripping, modern streets, monuments in themselves to the prosaic, reaching beyond to the lanes, byways and ancient wisdoms of Chuang Tze's China. Shit! He grimaced as a dribble of rain ran down his neck, interrupting his thoughts. Maybe not. Continuing on, the lure of Chuang Tze's bell-stand maker came to mind again. If only he could do as the bell-stand maker had done. As if, in shrugging off the coming loneliness of Thanksgiving break and the rain as constant in duration as the odd, alienating stares he was daily receiving from classmates on the way to class, he could focus, much as the bell-stand maker had shrugged off the adulation of the country at being chosen for such an honor, the fame, the threats from the king if he should fail in his duty, the hunger and thirst as he had hiked for weeks among the forest searching for that perfect tree, that perfect source of wood, suitable for the stand that would hold the new bell to be cast. As if he, too, upon finding his tree, his source of untouched beauty, he could reach out his hand, with no more distracting thoughts of the inconsequential, and, finally, find the missing answer bedeviling him. Simply draw forth his bell-stand from within his tree, freeing it to become its purpose.

The rain cascading sheets now, he peered up out of his hood with surprise to see a small, attractive bridge across a narrow canal. In the window of one of the battlements defending the bridge that had to serve as the control booth, he saw a neon Rapunzel letting down her hair for all the passing cars to admire, if not to free. There! Maybe she was trapped in her tower, he thought, but at least she served a purpose. The perfect Taoist, he chuckled to himself. Unchanged in her potential. Bending before the changing needs of the world but, in essence, changed not by them. Passing under her, he gave her a thumbs up, shouting through the rain, "Keep up the good work!"

On the other side of the bridge, he saw a bright and cheerful-looking, not to mention warm and dry, tavern a block on and headed for it. Inside, he made for the bar, setting his raincoat on a nearby stool for a companion to drip away the late night's last moments before last call.

"Any northwestern beer," he asked for and was rewarded with a large pint of cloudy amber, topped by a friendly head a half inch thick. He took an experimental sip and liked it. He took another and rolled it around his mouth. Damn! Shaking his head at the thin beer of the Midwest he had grown up with, he played with the robust flavors tingling his mouth. Taking a gulp, he suddenly found it hitting his head. Okay, he thought, make that thin and weak beer.

He glanced around and noticed several pretty girls, in groups, dotting the tables here and there throughout the tavern. Not many men. He paused in thought and listened to the melodies of chatter, reflecting on the higher, softer tones of the female voice. Not unlike a group of wrens or some other songbird, he thought, numbers equaling safety. He smiled. Why were girls so pleasingly thin out here, he reflected, watching one walk by, and yet so well-stacked? He hoisted his pint to the miracle of the modern bra before taking another large gulp. Thinking of the many miles he had walked tonight, he wondered how many of the students here were from the UW. Nobody that he recognized. Feeling like a conquering adventurer then, who, braving leagues of treacherous lands and waters, had found the treasure at last, he drained his pint. Maybe it was the beer, but he suddenly felt all right with the world. For the first time since arriving out here, he thought. Could it really be? The first

time? Thinking it over, he ordered a second one.
Maybe he could fit in here, he thought. He had a pain
in the ass for a roommate, then, correcting himself, he
admitted that Jake wasn't all bad. More intriguing,
really. And maybe the other students gawked at him
like he was an alien but, truth be told, if they did a
little reading outside the syllabus on occasion, they
wouldn't be so damn ignorant. It didn't matter
anyway. He sat, feeling the bright cheeriness of the
tavern warm him. Maybe he could do this, he
thought. As the second pint came, he examined the
color more closely, admiring the cold, cloudy light
spilling through the amber, just as he heard her laugh.

Looking around, he spotted her auburn hair swept
over the shoulder of a bright orange turtleneck in one
of the booths along the wall. She was crouched over
the table animatedly talking with three other girls,
about half the distance now that she had begun sitting
from him in class since their one conversation. She
began to turn toward him, so he quickly looked away,
thinking how much the orange suited her coloring.
After a nervous gulp, he darted a second glance at
her, only to see her looking right back at him. She
smiled, those lips mouthing a "hello" and offering a
little wave. He managed a smile and waved back just
as the raven-haired girl next to her held up a cell
phone whose tiny light winked at him. "Stop it! He's
shy! Oh my god!" Amber pushed her friend's cell
phone down as the others laughed. He turned away
from their mingled hoots. Okay, maybe starlings, he
thought, took a swallow and burned.

"I'm sorry about that." He looked up to see Amber
standing next to him. "Alicia just got that for her
birthday and she's been taking pictures of everything
that moves."

He grunted, looking away.

"She didn't mean anything by it."

He took in her beauty again, feeling his breath seize up in his throat and managed to squeeze out a "It's okay."

She gestured at the empty seat next to him. "It's Andrew, isn't it?"

He froze, barely registering that she knew his name.

"Do you mind if I?"

"Sure." She sat to the applause of excited whispers and shhhs! that somehow made their way across the floor.

"It's pretty wet out tonight, isn't it? You look like you walked." Glancing at himself in the mirror over the bar, he saw bedraggled, limp locks of black hair dripping over thin cheeks, embarrassingly red now, and gray eyes.

Pushing his hair back, he resolved not to act like an ignoramus this time. "Yeah, it is."

"Did you?"

Looking askance for a moment, all at once he understood, "What? Oh, yeah. Yeah, I did. I...I like..." She waited, smiling at him. Hypnotized by her lips, he felt his mind wretchedly empty. "The rain. I like...the rain," he dribbled off.

"So do I. It's a good thing we're going to school in Seattle, isn't it?"

"Yeah."

"Are you from here?"

"No, I'm from the other..." he grimaced. "...from Wisconsin, Madison."

"Really? I'm from the Twin Cities."

Andrew blinked, uncertain if he had heard right or whether there were another twin cities out here, too. "Not Minneapolis?"

"Sure! Home of the Vikings, the Guthrie, *Prairie Home Companion*..."

"Land of Ten Thousand Lakes..." Andrew said with a smile, feeling better now.

"And ten thousand mosquitoes." He laughed. She laughed, too, a charmed laugh that thrilled him to the bones, right down to his toes. "There aren't nearly as many out here. Almost none, in fact."

"Really?" Andrew asked, interested.

"Weird, isn't it? You'd think with all the rain..."

"Yeah."

They sat a moment until Andrew suddenly remembered his Midwestern chivalry. "Say, can I buy you a beer? This is my first try at northwestern ones."

"Well, I guess we can't let that go by uncelebrated. Sure. That'd be nice," she smiled. His stomach dissolved into molten warmth.

He got the bartender's attention and pointed to his pint. "Andrew?" Amber asked, resting her hand lightly on his arm. "Do you mind if I ask you a question?"

"No, shoot," he replied, astounded, and uncomfortable, at this sudden bravado yet willing to do anything, say anything to keep her hand there.

"How did you know all that stuff about...you know...the Gospels being different and everything?"

"Oh." He looked down. "It's nothing."

She waited for him to continue for a moment, then threw her hair over her shoulder, "Well, I thought it was something. I'd never heard any of that before." Her beer arrived. She thanked the bartender with that smile, he noticed with a jolt. His smile.

"Well, I...shouldn't have done it."

"Why not? I thought it was great!"

He shrugged.

"Hegland's a jerk, anyway. It was nice to see him get taken down a peg."

His heart swelled. Yes, definitely, he thought. He could make it out here. He could do this. "Do you know him?"

"Oh, just from frat parties." She took her hand away to take a sip. "Thanks for the beer," she smiled at him.

He nodded, going blank.

"So...tell me...how'd you do it?" She placed an elbow on the bar, leaning toward him. Resting on the polished mahogany, not more than a few inches from his hand, the silken mound of her breast pushed up the sweater's knitting, dazzling him with all its promise.

Pushing his mind away, he struggled out an "Oh, it's just..."

She rested her cheek on her hand then, completing a line so immortal in refinement, he thought it must have first been etched by the gods in Egypt.

"You're kind of shy, aren't you?"

He looked at her, then away.

"I think that's sweet."

Rousing himself, he said, "Well, the thing is, it's som--something my dad does when he wants to piss off fundamentalists. It's not like I learned that all by myself or anything."

"Amber!" A clean-cut blazer leaned in for a kiss on her cheek.

"Hi, Rod!" she smiled that smile at him. "What are you doing here?"

"Slumming. Out on a dark and rainy night in search of adventure."

She laughed that charmed laugh for him. Andrew's world began collapsing inward, rooting him motionless to the stool.

"Last call!" the bartender shouted out.

Rod nodded toward the window, revealing gusts of windy rain sweeping the street in lighted torrents. "Pretty bad out. Want a lift?"

"Ummm..." She glanced at Andrew's wet coat a moment, then back at Rod, smiling, "Sure!"

Moving off the stool, she turned to Andrew and once again threw out her whore's treasure, as he abruptly named it, stunning himself with his ferocity. "Thanks for the beer, Andrew."

***

Savagely stomping his way back to the campus through the storm, he cursed the world and everyone in it. Throwing back his hood he opened his face to the tempest outside hoping to drown the one storming within. The streets were deserted. Instead, he felt the pitiless company of the streetlights staring down, one by one, racing through each to the more comforting stretches of anonymity between. His father had been right, he swore. He didn't belong here in this fucking hinterland tucked away in the remote corner of the country. He should have stayed in Madison. Maybe it was an island, beleaguered on all sides, but it was an island whose people, whose climate made sense to him.

Skipping the elevator, he stormed up the steps of his dorm, feeling his breath catch more harshly at each landing, yet pushing harder up the next one and the one after that, trying to calm the rage pounding in his head, his heart. Running, stumbling, running down the hallway, he stopped outside his door, panting, not wanting, what? To show his weakness to his GI Joe "roomie." He stood there, dripping, catching his breath. Finally, he softly opened the door. Jake snored in his bed. Andrew went over to his closet and not wanting to open it for the noise, stripped off his drenched coat and dropped it on the floor. He squeezed out of his shoes and padded over to his bed wanting to climb in and fade into the forgetfulness of sleep, yet wanting to pace out more of his anger. In the dim light through the blinds, he saw a dark form laid out flat on his bed. Drawing nearer, he saw that it was a coat. A raincoat. A nice one. Picking it up, he thought how unusual it was for Jake to leave something lying out unstowed.

"You can pay me back...," Jake's sleepy voice drawled out, "...installments if you need to...," before turning over.

Andrew stood there, holding the raincoat. "No fool like a wet fool," Jake mumbled and snored again.

Remembering, Andrew held the raincoat up to the light to see and feel some kind of soft lining zipped into the coat. Squinting at the label, he could make out something like "gortex." He carefully draped it on his chair, quietly took off his clothes and crawled into bed.

***

A face like frayed tapestry and still he scores, Andrew thought, awed. He watched Jake huddle in a far corner chatting up a breathless blonde in ponytailed lycra now pressing hard against the wall, as if hoping that the God of all gods would make Jake kiss her. There were a lot of girls at this party, Andrew had noticed. A lot of loud music. A lot of beer. He frowned at the keg, realizing that he had always perched next to the keg at house parties in Madison. In fact, substitute all the purple and gold for red and white, he might as well be back there. This was not a conclusion to savor.

Surveying the crowded room with a sudden, intense dislike, he downed the rest of his cup and poured himself another. "It's Turkey Day," Jake had beamed, startling Andrew that afternoon. "Let's go drain somebody's keg!" A week had gone by and Andrew still had not found the right words to thank Jake for the raincoat which, true to Jake's word, was keeping him snug and dry. He reached down to rub the zipped-in fleece lining. Contemplating its warm, light softness, he tried to remember how the Midwest got along without it. Much as he tried to suppress it, he felt delighted with the coat. Its several velcro straps, pouches, zips, and snaps "Even under the arms when you're on a long hike," Jake had pointed out, gave Andrew some sort of vicarious militaristic thrill every time he wore it. Andrew had only been able to mumble some sort of "Thank you" before turning away in embarrassment. Jake had slapped him on the shoulder and gone back to his homework.

Andrew was profoundly dissatisfied with himself. Probably a little drunk, too, he considered as he found his first steps wobble away from the keg. He thought he had left all this behind. Back on State Street with its picturesque shops, its cornucopia of international flavors stuck in the middle of the great Midwest, its rasta-tinted view of the Oneness of All Things, "So have a toke, mahn." Back where sad attempts to recapture the idealism of the 60s play out in the International Marijuana Harvester's Festival parade each year, marching to the state capitol, fists pumping the air, twirling foot-long braids of ganja smoke amid the steel drums and shouting "Hemp, Hemp, Hurray!" while the police in jackboots, white helmets and sardonic smiles stand in pairs off to the side watching and the Germanic farmers just sixty miles north in Joe McCarthy country mutter into their pints over the evening news about "the Communists at that goddamned university" and vow to "boot that Sodom out of the Heartland" someday.

Finding himself on the street outside, no less crowded, no less soused, he loudly toasted, to the claps of a few passersby, the Farmers and their Fidelity to the Godly Life. Back where the pseudo-Buddhism and pseudo-Taoism, his reflections continued, so fashionable among the university set these days when the Religious Right rule the White House, the Congress and the Supreme Court - hell, might as well include the whole world - were in fact, just trumped up veneers over that old, respectable strain of rabid anti-Christianity and, being set, his thoughts raced on, by fundamental self-expression, in opposition to another idea, instead of standing alone for eternal truths that exist on their own, will always be helplessly defined by that they hate most. Back where, no matter how many times he had tried, he couldn't get to--he rested the top of his head against the wall and, careful not to spot his new coat, threw up.

"What the fuck you doing, white boy?"

Andrew blinked, peering through his spinning head and trying to clear away the fumes of vomit and urine coloring the night air. It was a dark alley, he realized, but not too dark to see the group of young men wearing dark clothes and backward baseball caps pulled low, surrounding and methodically beating a young black boy, probably no older than fifteen. The largest of them, a head taller and considerably wider than Andrew scowled over at him. Andrew watched the young boy take another hit to the stomach and struggle to remain standing.

"This ain't your bidness, dorm boy. Why don't you take your sorry little college boy ass and scat outta here." The young boy gurgled out a moan as he took another hit to the face. He spat out some blood and, shaking his head, tried to glare back at the surrounding circle only to take another hit to the stomach that made him start coughing.

"Hey," Andrew slurred out. "What're you doing?" He staggered up to the leader, noticing how the night painted vivid black blues across the tall, high well-shaped eyes and cheekbones glowering at him.

"Fight!" someone called out behind him. "Fight!" He could hear a group of footsteps hurrying down the alley behind him. Thinking of his own pale, hueless skin, Andrew envied the deep ebony tones about to speak.

"What? College boy want some, too?" The leader shook his head and, without warning, grabbed Andrew and threw him inside the circle.

Glancing around, Andrew saw that there were white as well as black faces staring right back at him, hard eyes sneering with a ghastly delight as their fists smacking into hands created a crude beat for all to dance to. Swallowing hard, Andrew made his eyes meet those of the leader as the tall tough, too, entered the ring.

"College boy wants to know what this is all about." He walked up to the young boy and hitting him in the stomach, shouted into his ear, "Tell him!" The boy, eyes swollen so wide they appeared as if they might split nonetheless fluttered to cough some more. "Tell him! Tell him who you are!" the leader standing right next to the boy, screamed into his ear.

The boy shut his eyes tight and screeched out, "I'm a Hoover!"

"That's right." The leader rewarded him with a hefty slap to the face, making the boy spit up some more blood.

Andrew realized now, as sheer fright scared the fumes from his brain, that he had stupidly stumbled into some sort of ritual in which, the leader was right, he had no "bidness." Trying not to show anything, he made to leave only to find the leader grab him and turn him around.

"Not so fast, now. You want to help out and now you can." He walked over to the boy and feinting one last blow to the stomach, whacked him to the back of the head. "Come on, Hoover! Show us your stuff!"

The boy nodded tiredly, then to Andrew's horror turned a face of fear, then hatred toward him. Andrew found himself caught by the boy's eyes. He couldn't look away. Inside their meaty, bruised shininess, they grew larger, then harder, then glittered. With an effort, Andrew tore his eyes away, back at the group of students watching beyond the circle, searching for a friend, and seeing only flushed faces, captivated in revulsion, breathing faster at the prospect of the next few minutes. He was alone. All alone. Again. This sickening thought hit him just before the explosion of pain and red light flashed across his eyes and he found himself falling backward, back down into helping hands that roughly caught him, stood him up, and then threw him right back into the center of the circle.

Jake ducked under paired biceps and stepped inside the barrier. Biting her lip, his blonde friend stepped in after him as he hollered out, "Yo, man, what are you doing?"

Holding his hand up to stop the next punch, the leader squinted down at this new gnat as Jake approached them, talking in a smooth rhythm. "He's a guest, man. You oughta know better than that."

"A guest? What shit you talking about, dorm boy?"

"Yeah, an egghead, from the other UW."

"Egghead? Other UW? Shit, that about--"

Pushing off as he swept Andrew back into the girl's arms behind him, Jake reached up to sweep the leader's nose with the flat of his hand and to the sound of a splintering crunch. Gargling and gasping, the tough staggered back, bending over, reaching up to his nose. Turning on his hip, Jake brought his other elbow cracking down on the offered head, collapsing it with its body to the ground. Glancing up, he quickly scanned the circle of meat and, seizing upon a set of eyes, moved toward them just as they settled on him with a touch of that same glitter. Taking two quick steps, Jake punched them right at the base of the temple, walking through his third step as this heavy went down along Jake's side. Taking a quick second scan of the group, he relaxed and smiled. Looking over at his friend, he nodded her and Andrew through the circle breaking up in confusion and followed. Steering their way, he moved them quickly and quietly through the safety of the watching students and down the street.

***

Andrew lay on his bed still groggy and still smelling the vomit he had lost on their way back to the dorm. He tried to get up, but Jake, sitting next to him in the dim light of their room pushed him back. "Settle down, hoss. Just a second. I got something here." Twisting it up, he lifted a bundled sock and touched it gently to Andrew's temple. Andrew gasped at the cold, then lay quietly.

"Man, that little kid must pack one hell of a punch. You're swelling up like our Conk's eggs back home."

"I think I'm going to throw up again."

"Hush. Just lie there and breathe. It'll stop." It did.

"You did a good job there, Andrew. Facing down our visitors from the Rainier Valley like that." Jake smiled. "This must be one of their new things. Tell a kid a pack of lies about how dangerous the Ave is, then take him up here to test him."

Andrew lay there quietly, staring at the ceiling. Jake watched him, saying nothing and lightly patting his eye with the sock. The swirls of Friday night dorm life eddied about them out in the hallway. Whoops, hollers, bangs and laughter now rising, now falling, each the central actor of its own stage, Andrew thought, playing out its role for all the audience this night, creating some memories that will last a lifetime, some that will fade by the dawn's snores. Jake filled the sock with more ice from the bucket and watched the bars of light from the blinds slowly march their way across the ceiling as cars passed along the street below, one after another. One after another.

Andrew stirred. "I just wanted to help him." The sock, faithful to its ministerial melting, was now leaving streaks not unlike tears running down Andrew's cheek. "He didn't even want it!"

"Of course he didn't. He knew that. None of them did."

Andrew sat up and stared at him. "Well, why not?"

"You don't know?"

***

While cramming for finals one evening, Andrew abruptly asked, "Who said, 'It is well that war is so terrible, else we should grow too fond of it.'?"

Jake turned from pushing in a pin to mark the advance of some unit in Afghanistan and, after checking with a frown that Andrew wasn't joking, responded, "Only the greatest general that this country ever produced."

Andrew waited a moment then shrugged, "Okay, so I'm a bit light on my military history..."

Awed for a moment, Jake shook his head. "Robert E. Lee. At Fredericksburg." As if not wanting to witness such monumental ignorance, he turned back to admire his handiwork before continuing. He had put up his map a week earlier, with the fall of Kabul. "Just after that idget Burnsides kept ramming the Army of the Potomac into the Confederate killing zone like it was one big meat-grinder."

"Civil war..." Andrew ventured. "The South."

Jake nodded. "A general who not only repeatedly outmaneuvered his opponents but also kept his under-strength, under-provisioned army operating in the field for almost two years after they should have been shut down." With a look of expectation, he turned to stare at Andrew who only shrugged in confusion. Jake groaned and threw his hands up in the air. "Gettysburg! You know, hoss?!"

"Okay, Gettysburg." Changing the subject, he glanced over at a book spread-eagled on Jake's bed. "I thought you were cramming for German."

"Ich war studiert."

Closing the cover on Schnoebel's latest request - checking a grad's thesis about what might be known of early Christian women leaders from Paul's letters - and rubbing them in thought, Andrew replied, "Ich bin studiert, but I thought studieren was one of those haben verbs, not a sein verb."

"Who cares?" Jake snorted. He picked up his book and threw himself down on his bed. Staring up at the ceiling, he mulled, "This man says that we know from concentration camp film footage that dead bodies can't be stacked. They sprawl." He massaged his chin as Andrew watched him. "So, in battle, they only stack two or three high forcing everybody else to fight around them. It's a factor."

"Well, now we know what kind of grade you're going to get on your German final," Andrew smiled, feeling lighter. It felt good to tease someone, just once.

Jake shrugged. "It'll be fine. It's just like Dutch, anyway."

"What are you reading?"

"*Face of Battle.*" He held it up.

"What's it about?"

"Now you're talking!" Jake beamed, plumping his pillow, and sat back. "It's a review of three battles from the company level perspective: Agincourt..."

Jake broke off looking perplexed until, understanding, Andrew said, "I know about Agincourt."

"Oh, good," Jake continued, as if relieved to be on good ground again. "Waterloo and the Somme." Warming up, he went on, "Instead of writing about it from the field level perspective, you know, the general and command staff perspective, like every other military history. This one takes you right down to the mud, the trenches, the food, the sleep, or none of them in this case. Even the wounds you got if you fought there."

"Where do the bodies come in?" Jake paused. "The piled up bodies? I thought the Somme was World War I."

"Oh. He's just looking at how the French knights would have...at Agincourt...never mind." Jake crossed his hands behind his head and leaned against the wall with a happy smile.

Andrew watched him a moment. "You...," he began before breaking off.

Jake glanced at him. Andrew tried again. "You really do like this...like studying war, don't you?"

Jake gazed at him for a long moment.

"How come you don't look military?" Andrew blurted out, startling himself. Jake kept watching him, waiting. "You know...all...puffed up and everything."

Andrew looked at his hands, wishing he had stopped. Jake didn't say anything, just kept staring at him. Andrew could sense it. He'd done it again, he thought. Why did he have to blow it every time he found somebody who actually looked for a moment like he might be interested in being a friend? Why couldn't he just keep his big mouth--?

"I don't like that all that much either."

Andrew glanced up. Jake smiled, "You mean like Petie?" Andrew nodded, then quickly looked away. "Well."

Cars swished back and forth on the street below, a sound unusual to be heard at this time of the day.

Jake sat up. Andrew glanced at him, seeing a scowl of wariness in Jake's eye. "Have you ever seen Colin Powell speak?"

Andrew shook his head. "Who's he?"

"Only our Secretary of State."

"Oh."

"Well, before that he was Chairman of the Joint Chiefs of Staff and..." Jake paused a moment, looking off, then right back at Andrew. "He doesn't do that. And if the Chairman of the Joint Chiefs doesn't need it, then neither do I."

He waited, a fierceness blazing in his eyes that made Andrew look down, look for cover, until, sensing this would be the wrong thing to do, he made himself pick up his eyes and stare straight back into Jake's. Jake nodded. Andrew smiled.

They went back to their books. After much mindless page turning, Andrew threw out, "The bodies."

Jake looked up. "What about 'em?"

"Do you have to read about that?"

"Well, *Face of Battle* is on the suggested reading list for company level officers, but I admit I do tend to memorize 'em."

"Why?"

Jake scowled at him again, that same wary fire coloring his expression. Andrew, knowing better now, stared right back, holding Jake's eyes. Down the hall, a whoop followed by a large blast of music blared out, quickly shut off by a slammed door.

"Sometimes bodies rain from the skies."

Andrew turned away, ashamed. No. Confused. He remembered that day. Just last fall, though it seemed, somehow, a lifetime ago. He had been wandering the campus at Madison, eagerly anticipating what classes were going to be like in Seattle, when he had seen people running toward the student center. He had followed them, wondering what to do, what was going on. Inside, at the bank of television sets, students had stared as the footage of an airplane crashing into the World Trade Center had played over and over again, its shadow leaping over neighboring buildings just before it hit, the smoke plumes of an earlier hit, someone had said, rising above it all. And then, that most horrible moment, when some reporter pointing out the debris falling from the top floors of the towers and how that would hamper rescuers from entering the building on the ground below, had abruptly stopped mid-sentence, her stern face sliding into a cascading mosaic of disbelief, horror and grief as her professional voice had broken into choked sobs: "Oh my God! That isn't debris falling, that's people jumping!"

He came back to their dorm knowing that Jake was still watching him.

"You see why, but you still don't like it."

Andrew gaped at him, shocked. He tried to rally, to organize his thoughts. "I don't know what I...think, what I..."

"Sure you do." Jake sat back crossing his arms with a quiet smile beneath a piercing stare.

"I can tell you what my father says," Andrew reached out.

Jake waited. Then shaking his head, he said, "Okay, your father, then."

"That's it karma."

Jake blinked at him in confusion. Andrew pressed on. "The twin towers were a symbol of our..." he paused, unsure how to explain, then suddenly finding the words appearing in his head as if straight off a teleprompter, he went on. Why not? He had heard it several times before boarding his own plane for Seattle. "...our capitalistic oppression of the world...globalizing corporations enslaving the poorest of the poor so the wealthiest of the wealthy grow ever richer." He cleared his throat. "The towers were going to come down someday. It was karma."

He glanced over at Jake. "Well, that's what he says."

After a moment of quiet, Andrew asked, "That's okay, isn't it? I mean, you're not mad or anything are you?"

"No," Jake shook his head. "But it does sound like your dad, no disrespect meant here, I'm just reacting is all..."

Andrew nodded.

"It sounds like your dad didn't know anyone personally who jumped."

"His brother." Jake looked at him, quickly, sharply. "My uncle worked for American Express...he was visiting a client up there that day..." Andrew found his voice failing, then said, "They found his body in the street, holding hands with some woman we didn't know."

Jake said nothing. The afternoon sun's slow departure began to cast a shadow over the grim look deepening his features.

"We heard later that a lot of the jum--...people held hands when they jumped because there were afraid..." Andrew's voice died.

The clock ticked. Cars passed.

"Fucking A." Jake wiped a hand over his eyes. "What does your dad do?"

"Buddhist studies - Indian Buddhist studies - at the other UW," Andrew managed a wan smile.

"Is that what you're going to do?" Jake looked at him, interest dawning through incredulous eyes.

"I don't know."

***

Christmas. Snow. Garland and Tinsels. Brandy egg-nogs. Arguments.

So, how is it out there, Andrew? Just as I suspected. We do quite all right out here in the Midwest. We hold our own. And there is no argument about how the Northwest innovates in technology, but when it comes to questions of ultimate meaning, to these fields with their well established hierarchies of discoveries, they are sadly, sadly behind. They have no exposure to it. All you have to do is take a look at their research. Not even that! Read the denominational resolutions that come out of their simplistic polities. No, no! Better than that, take their electoral politics for a moment! No subtlety. No sophistication. No complexity. No nuance for God's sake! No, no, no. I told you: If you don't want the Eastern seaboard, then you should be able to muddle along pretty well out here. Even so, you would already be building obstacles into your career with that choice, let alone going way out

45

there! Come. You've spent a quarter out there. You've proven your point. Come back here. I'll call the dean right now, and we'll get it settled. I'm sure that she--

Have another eggnog, Andrew. Have three. No, just sit. Let's...let's talk now for a moment as professional to professional. How...how are the students out there? How are your classmates? How well-read are they? Basic? Missing fundamentals? Fine, then, Andrew, tell me where the pressure to excel is going to come from. Even you have to admit...For Christ's sake, in your first quarter and this Schnoebel already has you doing grad level research! What? You think that's an accomplishment? You do. Andrew, Andrew, it only serves to make my point ever more clearly. She has you doing grad work because your undergrad mind, prepared as it is according to our undergrad expectations, already functions at their grad level! Don't you see?

Andrew, I have to tell you that you're throwing your career away. What does that mean? Ever since you were a boy, you--! Rubbish! Sheer rubbish! I'm not going to accept that! Because you're acting like a child! Surely you can--! Wait. Wait! Don't go. Don't go, it's Christmas. Maybe I have been speaking out of turn here, but, surely...Andrew, it's Christmas. Your mother and I...Andrew... Fine. Fine. Fine! Go then! Run away like you always do. Stay at a friend's, stay--! Well you can stay at the bus depot for all I care! Go, then! Just tell me one thing: What the hell out there is so goddamned important to make you want to go back?

***

Andrew opened the door to their dorm to see Jake grinning complacently atop a pile of lumber in the middle of their floor. "What's this?" he laughed, delighted at how pleasurable it felt.

"Christmas, fool!" Jake threw him a plastic bag.

Catching it, Andrew heard the metallic jingle of nuts and bolts clinking together. "What?"

Shaking his head, Jake got up. "Nope. First things first." Opening the fridge, he took out two beers decorated with tinsel and handing one to Andrew, said, "Froliche Weinachtzen."

Andrew laughed. "Weinachten! Nachten. Holy night."

"Whatever." Jake cracked his open and took a swig. "That's the last time I ever let you help me with Deutsch. Egghead roomie picks up more than I do."

Andrew dumped his bag on the floor, opened his beer and took a healthy gulp, then gawked, staring at the label. "Real beer."

Jake chuckled. "It's Christmas, after all."

"Nice."

"Yeah."

"So, what gives?"

Jake swept his bottle over the wood with a flourish. "We are going to build for you, for us really, a loft."

Andrew gaped. "A loft? A real loft?" He had seen them before, of course, but had never thought... "Cool!"

"That's my man. Look, it's easy. I measured everything before I left."

"All right!"

"Besides, it's my own private salute to the Rakkasans as they drop into Kandahar."

Suddenly remembering there was a war on, Andrew asked, "The who?"

"Rakkasans. 187th regiment, the only airborne regiment to see combat in every war since airborne tactics were developed. Means 'falling umbrellas' in Japanese."

Then, realizing he had forgotten, Andrew plucked a gift out of his bag. "For you. Merry Christmas."

"Oh, hoss!" Jake took it and sat back down on the lumber, ripping it open to find a red and white knit cap, emblazoned with a UW, stretched around something else. "Wrong colors," Jake grinned. "But, what's...a book?"

"Well, open it."

Jake threw him a happy glance and took out the second package. Opening it, he found a copy of *Dummy's Guide to German*. "Oh, man!" Andrew laughed a long and cheerful chortle, delighting in the pleasure again. "Oh, hoss!" About to throw it on his bed, Jake noticed an envelope sticking out one end. "Okay, what's in here?"

"I don't know," Andrew smiled brightly and turned away.

Hearing Jake open the envelope, he turned back and leaned, resting against his desk, feeling all at one with the world. "A gift certificate?" Jake glanced up at him. "For...*The Face of War*...Is...I've heard of this!" Jake stared at him in amazement, excitement building in his widening eyes. "Asymmetric warfare, information dominance, networked platoons communicating under fire..." He jumped up. "How'd...?"

Andrew smiled in triumph. "I stopped in the other UW's ROTC office and asked the major, the uh...X...they called--."

Jake broke in. "The XO. Executive officer."

"That's right. I asked him what books coming out soon they wanted their cadets to read, and he told me about this one."

"When's it come out?"

"Sometime this spring."

"Hoss..." Jake laughed, shaking his head. "Okay, hoss. You really beat me." Shaking his head again, Jake said, "Wow." He saluted Andrew with his beer.

The loft went up easily, just as Jake had said. "Logistics," he only replied to Andrew's amazement. Just four beams, holes already drilled, bolted upright to cross beams for the upper bed, "Using inertia," Jake said, to keep it from falling down. Tightening a bolt while Andrew held the beam in place, Jake asked him how Christmas was. "White." Jake laughed. So, Andrew asked him in return. Jake grunted, "Afghanistan, Iraq and WMD." Andrew paused in amazement at what different worlds they must come from.

"Oh, and a whopping ol' Christmas ham."

When it was done, Andrew wondered for the first time who would get the upper bunk.

"I'm a dogface," Jake smiled. "Happiest in a good, deep foxhole with a strong parapet up front and a firing step for action."

Used to this by now, Andrew just smiled a "What?"

"I figured we'd put you up top so you can be closer to your heavenly meditations." Not wanting to argue, delighted at the thought, Andrew just nodded and got ready to heave.

After talking about it, they decided to leave Jake's bed where it was, giving them a small, den-like living room under Andrew's bed. They moved the chairs over to face one another under it, the fridge between them as a centerpiece, and opened some more beer to celebrate. Curious, but not wanting to pry, Andrew asked what a typical Yakima Christmas was like. "Oh..." Jake said, stretching his legs out, propping his beer on the chair arm and glancing around their little space. "We need a couple of better chairs. I know I only have two quarters left, but..."

Andrew's happiness dimmed. He kept forgetting that Jake was done this summer while he had one more year. Oh well, he thought, feeling the beer coating the inside of his head, everything is transient the Buddha teaches. Enjoy it while it lasts.

"Christmas in Yakima," Jake drawled, bringing Andrew back home. "Well, we have hayrides to carol our neighbors."

"Hayrides?!" Andrew giggled, feeling silly. "You really have hayrides?"

"Sure," Jake nodded.

"With horses and everything?"

"If Sticks has her way. Everybody else complains about how long it takes and wants to use a tractor."

"Who's...?"

"Sticks? My little sister. She's crazy about horses." Taking a swig, he smiled thoughtfully. "Matter of fact, Sticks is crazy about everything about the ranch." Andrew nodded, trying to imagine what life on a Yakima ranch was like.

"Why do you call her 'Sticks'?"

"Cause she's rail thin. Just a bundle of sticks walking around." Jake smiled, looking dreamy for a moment and murmuring, "Jardín del Paraíso." Before Andrew could ask, he said, "Tell you something, hoss. When Esmeralda de la Cruz comes along, I vote horses every time." Taking a thoughtful swig, he continued, "Anyway, this year, all you could hear in the wagon was talk about Iraq."

"Oh, yeah?"

"Oh yeah. 'Jake, we gonna go over there?' 'Jake you gonna shoot me a raghead?'"

Andrew gawked at him, horrified.

Glancing at him, Jake smiled. "Oh, that's just Old Brouchet. He always talks like that. Nobody pays any attention." He chuckled, drawling, "'Jake, you gonna find those WMDs?'...'Jake, when you get there, you tell Sodam Insane for me that...' on and on between *Jingle Bells* and *Silent Night*."

For the first time, it dawned on Andrew that Jake wasn't studying war-making for a degree. Much less a hobby. He began to feel sick.

"What?" Jake frowned at him. "Oh, not you, too?! I can duck."

Andrew felt a chill for his friend. Yes, he thought, for his friend. That thought gave him a weird feeling. He had a friend. It was a new thought. A warm thought. And, yet... "Do you really think we are going to go to war with Iraq?"

"Go to war for Iraq, don't you mean, hoss?" Andrew looked at him in confusion.

"Jorge thinks so. And, much as I give him shit about his MOS, when he talks intel, I listen." Andrew glanced around the room.

"Oh, not tomorrow," Jake laughed. "Not even next month." Andrew smiled foolishly, feeling relief, feeling very small. "Nope. Jorge puts it around a year from now."

"Why?"

"Because Hussein keeps re-arming his NBC, because he likes to use them, and--" He broke off, seeing Andrew's confusion.

Jake crossed his legs. "Nuclear/Biological/Chemical. In his war with Iran, Hussein gassed their forces. When the Kurds up north revolted, he gassed them. Hussein'll keep using them until somebody...stops him."

"But how does Jorge know...?" Andrew gestured helplessly.

"Projections. He's just looking at the facts on the ground: The climate, the Saudis, Syria...things like that."

Feeling quite out of his depth, Andrew pondered the surreality of discussing war-making with his roommate.

Jake smiled at him with genuine affection. "Oh, I know. He's just a cadet. But Jorge's got a real hard-on for stuff like this." He sat forward, his features hardening. "Okay, he's thinking it goes like this: The UN will keep rattling around trying to get Hussein to let in their WMD inspectors. He'll keep them off as long as possible because he doesn't want the rest of the world, not to mention the guys in his own backyard wanting to bump him off, knowing how much he has and how little he has. We'll keep at him and France and Russia and China will keep trying to put us off because they don't want their investments put in danger. Who would?"

Andrew nodded helpfully, still trying to follow along.

"Eventually, we'll get tired of it all and mobilize and, next thing you know, we'll have Gulf II."

Andrew barely remembered Gulf I. Mostly all his father's fulminations about "exchanging blood for oil" and "pathetic attempts to build a second term on soldiers' coffins" and other pithy remarks that did so well over academic sherries.

"Can't we just talk with him?"

Jake stared at him as if he had spoken in gibberish.

Andrew pushed on. "I'm sure if we just sat him down and talked with him, we could come to some kind of understanding."

Jake gently smiled and said, "Like we've been able to talk to Robert Mugabe, Charles Taylor, Farah Aidid, and all the other assholes that..." He stopped, seeing that Andrew was completely lost.

Jake finished his beer. "Look, you hear loudmouths around campus talk about how we fought the last war for oil and that's what this one is going to amount to."

Andrew nodded.

"I don't know about that. All I'm saying is that in this world, there are people who like to take power at the point of the gun, others who want to help them, and I don't like either very much."

Andrew felt that he should say something to refute that, but he didn't know what. Jake seemed to have all the answers, and it made him feel ignorant, a feeling that he didn't like all that much. It was like talking with his father, he thought, and squelched that idea almost as soon as it had finished forming. Gulping the rest of his beer, he got two more for them, trying to think of something intelligent to say. Finally, opening his while standing, he came out with, "Jake, you're telling me that..." Then he stopped, realizing he heard his father's pedantic tone substituted for his own. He glanced at Jake who sat there, waiting, comfortably. It irritated him.

He went on. "You're saying that you believe that there are...people that--"

Jake broke in, "'Bullies,' we usually call 'em. And their cronies."

Pausing, Andrew then nodded and continued. "You're telling me that you believe that there are bullies in this world--"

Jake broke in again, "I know that there are bullies in this world."

Andrew stopped. He didn't know how to answer that certainty. Was it the military training talking now, he wondered? Some sort of indoctrination for the impressionable seventeen year old? He didn't know how to go on. He liked having a friend, but he couldn't just let that kind of naivety go unanswered. Perplexed, he sat down. What price truth, he asked himself, as he had so frequently in the past. How many times had he alienated people by picking apart their positions, sometimes even their most cherished beliefs, using simple reason? How many times had he won the argument only to find as everyone left the table leaving him alone, he had lost the...war? He smiled.

"Go ahead."

Andrew glanced up at Jake.

"Say it."

Andrew gathered himself, hoping that this wouldn't prove yet one more of those times. "How can you tell me that there are bullies with whom we cannot reason?"

"I don't have to."

Growing angry, he darted a glance at Jake's face for signs of the sophistry his father practiced but found only honest confusion. "Why not?"

"Because you met one along with his buddies yourself. Over Thanksgiving break. Remember?"

***

Whispers and a giggle. Andrew turned over in his dream seeing the cross-hatched, narrow beams from the window playing across the ceiling. He liked sleeping this high up, he had found. It was a new experience. And it got him out of the immediate proximity of Jake's snores.

"Are you sure he won't come in?" a sweet voice whispered, giggling again.

"Nah." He heard Jake's whisper. "He had to go home, his sister is sick or something."

"Oh, that's sweet."

He heard a soft slap, followed by a muffled gasp and another giggle. Looking down, he saw Jake bathed in the cool tones of moonlight sitting down on his bed with the blonde ponytailed girl from that house party. He smiled, trying to remember her name but instead remembering the floral scent accompanying her now and the soft crush of her catch when Jake had pulled him out of the middle of that gang's beating-in ritual. He grimaced at the memory.

Watching, he saw Jake kissing her neck, slowly following the V tapering from a soft blue wash down into the deeper, indigo delights of her sweater as she threw her head back, tossing her ponytail, closing her eyes and moaning so softly, he could barely catch it. Jake was whispering something to her, and she shook her head. He whispered, caressing the delicate folds of her ear with his lips while reaching under her shirt. She shook her head again, then gasped as he abruptly, softly, lifted it right over her head. She giggled and kissed him back, pushing him down on the bed and pulling his shirt out of his pants. Bending over the muscular ridges of his belly, she sighed the triumphant moan of the penitent whose patience has finally been recompensed. Jake watched, stroking her hair.

"I love that," she cooed, kissing and licking him, pushing his shirt up to nibble his nipples. Jake kissed the top of her head and whispered to her again. She laughed softly, a deeply amorous chuckle, then began removing his belt, stripping it out of its loops one by one before dropping it on the floor.

Andrew suddenly realized that he wasn't dreaming. She pulled down Jake's zipper as he lay back, closing his eyes. Pausing a moment in her ministrations, she reached back with one hand and unclasped her bra, pulling it off to drape it softly over Jake's chest, tracing circles one way then another before, with a giggle, flinging it across the room.

Captivated, Andrew knew that he should look away but couldn't. The moon's kiss lit up the hanging mounds of her breasts, like any ripe fruit, he thought and suddenly better understood the bizarre imagery of the Song of Solomon. Jake grunted and Andrew, afraid, glanced at him but saw that Jake's eyes were safely closed. The sound of soft sucking filled the room, punctuated by Jake's grunts and moans. Her ponytail lay down her back, beautifully drawn in the night's light. Andrew suddenly wished that he were a sculptor. The contours of the small of her back gracefully tapering into the thick, dark belt she wore around her waist, blossomed up, out, reaching like two lines of sweet prayer, sung as a pleasing melody, pausing at the soft cones of her breasts, tapering neatly in agreement with the nipples, to round out at the slender shoulders before embarking on the willowy neck, topped all by that luscious hair bobbing up and down now that, reaching back to earth from heaven, began the divinely inscribed circuit once more. What contrasts, he marveled. If there was a Creator, and he often hoped there was, He must be smiling with pride and satisfaction at His handiwork.

Jake grunted as the tang of pure pleasure filled the room.

"Was that good?" she asked.

"Like heaven," Jake sighed.

"Because I have more." She chuckled throatily and began to remove her belt. Andrew pulled back from the edge of his perch and, as quietly as he could, pulled his sheet over his head.

***

"What do you think of a girl who uses the same smile to everyone?"

Jake put down his moldy copy of *Company Commander* and regarded Andrew. "Is it a pretty smile?"

"Yeah. Fantastically gorgeous."

Jake shrugged. "That maybe she's doing the best she can knowing that's all she's got."

Andrew stared at him. Jake shrugged again and picked up his book.

"But, that's impossible."

"No, hoss, it's not."

"But...everyone has...," Andrew stammered, searching for the right words, "...some sort of potential."

Jake sighed and put his book down as if he had done this before, times beyond count.

Ignoring him, Andrew went on. "They just have to develop it."

Jake smiled back. "Well, hoss, the truth is that a lot of us simply don't want to work that hard."

Andrew snorted.

"Okay?" Jake picked up his book again.

"That's pathetic!" Andrew flipped a page and continued reading.

A sigh. "Who is she?"

Andrew glanced over at Jake, mumbling a "Nobody" before looking away.

"Uh-huh." Jake closed his book and took out a WWII era bayonet that he had taken to sharpening lately.

"Do you have to do that?"

"The most overlooked weapon in an infantryman's arsenal," Jake grinned, spitting on a whetstone. To the rhythmic scrapes across the stone, Jake mused aloud, "When your platoon is being overrun, this is about the only thing standing between you and imminent..."

"I got it! All right?!" Andrew slammed his book shut. "Do you have to enjoy it so much?" He glared at Jake who sat, as before, imperturbably scraping away at his cold steel.

As if Andrew had not spoken, Jake thought out loud. "Do you know what a stammtische is?" Despite himself, Andrew shook his head. "It's a gathering of Germans at a table discussing the weighty matters of the world."

"In German?" Andrew felt a smile tugging at his lips.

Jake grunted, "Over beer when we can get it."

Andrew smiled wider.

"Anyway, last quarter, there was a girl at our weekly stammtische. Beautiful girl. Beautiful smile. Long auburn hair..."

Andrew stopped smiling.

"...who had somehow figured out that you and I are roommates." Jake stopped mid-scrape to survey Andrew's gape of astonishment, then continued. "All last fall, she would throw out these subtle hints about expanding the number of non-German speaking students to the stammtische or offering help, with her friend of course, to carry some books back to our room one time. You know, little suggestions like that. All the time looking at me with that...fantastically gorgeous...smile." Jake beamed at him.

"What happened?"

"Dunno. Somewhere around Thanksgiving, she stopped." Andrew rubbed his eyes as Jake continued. "Not a peep since."

Andrew went back to his book. Jake waited.

Finally, tired of holding his bayonet without sharpening it, he spit on the stone again. "Why don't you cut her some slack, hoss?" Andrew didn't say anything. "At least then you could stop watching Ella go down on me."

Andrew gasped, then put his head in his hands. "I'm sorry."

Jake laughed, a rich, cheery boom. "Don't worry about it. At least I know you're not gay now. Petie will be relieved."

Andrew scowled at him.

"Oh, come on, hoss. Lighten up! It's no big deal...so long as..." Jake's features slid into a mask of toughness, making Andrew's heart stop. "So long as nobody ever learns about that. That's between you and me. Right?"

All but leaping to his feet, Andrew reached out and shook Jake's hand. "Yes! And, I'm sorry...I'm so sorry...I don't know what got into me that night...I'll never, never do that again, Jake. I promise you..."

Jake waved aside his rushing apologies. "What you need, hoss, is a little sack time. And I don't mean alone."

Andrew blushed.

"Are you armed?" Andrew blinked at him, looking at the bayonet. "No, fool, are you...Never mind." Muttering "ivory towers," Jake set down his bayonet and stone, wiping his hands before reaching into his night table. He flung a strip of condoms to Andrew. "Rules of Engagement: When you're armed, get in there. When you're not, get the fuck out."

Astounded at the simple joys of Jake's life, Andrew nodded and put the condoms in his desk drawer.

"You might want to re-think that ordinance dump, hoss." Picking up his bayonet, Jake pointed with it at the desk drawer then slowly up at the bed. Andrew grinned, feeling like an idiot and said, "Sure." He tried to imagine himself in a situation where he could use a condom.

"There's a house party in Ravenna Friday night." Andrew groaned. "Some buddies from ROTC, celebrating the start of Operation Anaconda." Andrew groaned louder. "Oh, come on. If anyone asks, just raise a glass to the Screaming Eagles. Besides, if you stay in the house, even you should be able to have a good time."

Andrew shook his head, beginning, "I don't know..."

"And you, hoss," Jake rode right over him, "are in desperate need of charming a girl."

Andrew turned back to his desk and put his head under his arms.

"You hiding now, hoss?"

From under his arms, Andrew mumbled, "I don't know the first thing about charming a girl."

"Easy."

Andrew sat up and stared at Jake.

Jake leaned back. "Simple enough: Ask her a question about her life. Stare right into her eyes while you listen. Compliment her when she's finished. Repeat."

Andrew nodded and began. "Ask her a question--"

"No, fool!" Jake broke in, laughing. "What I mean is when you're finished with the three moves, you start over again."

"Oh!"

"Got it? And you keep repeating those same moves until you're holding the covers up for her to slide in next to you. See?"

Andrew stared at him with the awe reserved for pure genius.

***

Watching Jake put the moves on Ella through the countless high and tight haircuts, Andrew smirked at the question whether there was a time when she wasn't breathless. Then, remembering that night with shame, and her night-lit chuckling as she disrobed Jake with bubbling glee, he found himself contemplating the power of situational circumstances to determine one's behavior. What did Jake always call it? The COE - contemporary operating environment...urban warfare of the early twenty-first century affecting battlefield tactics just as surely as the jungle warfare of his own father's beloved Vietnam era did. Take himself for example. He was at a house party: He was blinking with pain at the ubiquitously ear-splitting thumps of metal music. He was tightly holding a cup saying nothing - it suddenly dawned on him why the music: no one could hear how stultifying everyone really was - and standing next to the keg to make sure that his cup runneth over. Now if he could just do something about that annoyingly repetitive "HOOAHH" that kept bouncing off the walls. He belched, realizing that he was getting drunk. See? That, too - behavior unusual for him - always occurred at house parties and nowhere else. He tried to calculate how much beer he and Jake had managed to put away this year. Suddenly, remembering his last house party, he nervously cast a look around for a large lunk-headed bully, like Petie, to challenge his right to stand there. Seeing no one, however, but Ella walking toward him. Ella?

"Andrew, you look lonely," she spoke into his ear. "How about if I introduce you to one of my friends." Taking in her ice-cream blonde freshness and the sweetly high tones tickling his ear, he abruptly ached for her soft yielding, then ashamed, he looked down, then back up at Jake, who nodded and gave him a thumbs up.

Gathering the shreds of his pride, he leaned into her ear, responding, "Thanks, Ella. I've already got someone picked out."

"Who?" she mouthed at him, gifting him with the tender look reserved for fragile lambs. Irritated, he glanced over at the wall and pointed at the first girl he spotted - a short, thin, tough type wearing a black beret over butch black crosses of electrician's tape covering her nipples. Ella's pouting lips pursed in an "Oh!" as she followed his glance.

She stared at the woman while framing her words very slowly. "She certainly has her own flair, Andrew. I never would have expected that she would be your type...In fact, are you sure that...?"

"Of course I am." He lurched out and brushed past Ella's vexing downiness on his way to conquer, nodding at Jorge along the way.

"What the hell do you want?" The girl scowled at him from between countless tiny pierced silver rings marching up both earlobes. Like soldiers, he thought, encouraged that they already had a connection.

"My name'ssh Andrew," he began, then rubbing his forehead, started again while leaning into her until she put up a flat hand stopping him. "My name's Andrew...." he shouted, before petering out, unsure what to do next.

"So?"

Suddenly finding his mind flooded with images of medieval courtly flourishes of chivalry, he continued, if more loudly than they would have. "Might I know your name?"

"It's Rae, and who the fuck are you?" a voice behind him bellowed.

"Some guy that wants to fuck me," Rae shouted back.

Her friend retorted, "There's isn't a cock in this world flexible enough!" They both cackled with glee and high-fived, then stared at him like he was some kind of lunatic set down in the middle of the party for their private pleasure. This wasn't going well, he thought.

Finding new spirit, however, he grasped around in his thoughts trying to remember the first of Jake's Simple Rules, then offered, "What's a couple of dykes doing at a Gestapo party?"

Rae narrowed her eyes at him, sizing him up. "What makes you think we're not ones?"

 Andrew blinked with surprise but decided it didn't matter. He leaned between them and said, "So, what about it, huh? I'm more than man enough for the--"

He suddenly found himself on his knees staring up at Rae in pain just before she bitch-slapped him into the wall. He bounced off it, then decided to simply rest there and dissolve into the music as they parted with a dismissive "Fuck-head."

"Hoss, I don't know about you sometimes." Andrew blearily stared up at Jake. "Can you stand?"

"I think so." Jake and Ella picked him up as Andrew gasped at the pain in his testicles. "Jesus."

"What? Both didn't knee you at once did they?" Andrew looked away with embarrassment. Taking either side, Ella and Jake tried to smother their giggles as they worked him through the crowd, outside to Jake's car. Leaning Andrew against it, Jake took Ella aside for a quick talk, followed by a lingering kiss and the sigh, "Goodnight."

As Ella walked away, she turned around, saying, "Call me!" Jake gave her a two-fingered salute to his temple while wrestling Andrew into the car.

***

PROST! the letters said with three foot high cheer over the door. Inside, Andrew saw long tables hewn out of some thick timber decorated with stains and steins, real steins! of beer. Maybe a liter each, Andrew guessed. Adding the finishing touches were black and white photographs dotting the walls of buxom Bavarian beauties nestling up to stern, mustachioed bullet-headed Germans in, no less, lederhosen.

"See?" Jake proudly waved both arms around the bar. "Thought this might get your mind off your...eh...lovelies." Shaking his head, Jake tried not to chuckle. "My god, hoss, Beth and Rae are going to be telling this story for weeks."

He walked over to the bar as Andrew, pissed off all over again with the world, limped over to a shorter, square table and sat.

Before long, Jake set down two tall steins with a flourish. "Straight from Der Vaterland itself!" Andrew wrapped his hand around the handle, picking it up, ready for the weight but still surprised at it, and took a gulp. Oh. So, that's where his midwestern weak beer came from, he thought. "I know," Jake smiled. "Nothing compared to northwestern beer. Still, this is where we have our stammtische, and you can't beat the atmosphere."

Andrew nodded before realizing with a shock what Jake had been saying. But, then he remembered, she hadn't been coming around to them lately. He relaxed and took another gulp.

"German beer," Jake laughed. "You can drink it for hours without getting the slightest tipsy. Good for long conversations!" His brawny arm lightly swung up his stein and, gesturing to Andrew to do the same, crashed their steins together splattering them both with foam. They laughed, Andrew feeling better by the moment. Jake filched a bowl of pretzels from another table.

"Are they really dykes?" Andrew asked. Jake smirked. "Can you be a lesbian and be in ROTC?"

Jake spread his hands. "All I know is that Rae doesn't ask me who I sleep with, so I don't ask her."

Andrew whistled. "It's really true."

"Besides," Jake went on, "her piercings come off when her battle dress comes on." Taking a swig while watching Andrew to see how this next bit was going to come across, he said, "Rae may not look it, but she regularly beats Petie in the confidence course."

"No."

"That woman is pure will." Andrew hid his embarrassment with a gulp. "At least we know you like strong women." Andrew looked up at him in astonishment. "And electrician's tape," Jake got out before dissolving into booming laughter.

Andrew, finally, had to smile at himself.

"Never mind that," Jake said raising his stein. "Here's to the Rakkasans kicking ass in Shah I Khot." They clinked and swigged.

"Do all the army units have special names?"

"Sure. Most, anyway. Builds esprit de corps. The Rakkasans, 101st Airborne brigade, were the first unit to land boots in Japan during WWII. That's why the name."

Andrew nodded, his heart warming to his friend's pride in their endeavors. Kind of like rooting for a football team, he thought, watching Jake take a long, hearty gulp of beer.

Slamming his stein down, Jake popped out, "What are you doing for summer?"

Andrew paused at the change in topic, wiped his mouth of foam and considered. It was true, winter quarter had passed in the blink of an eye, he reflected with agony, and spring break began at the end of next week, after finals, he thought unhappily. Jake was already slated for extra duty that week off, helping redesign the confidence course at Ft. Lewis to better reflect urban warfare - quite the honor, or so Petie's envy had suggested. Jake had, of course, simply smiled. So, not even wanting to broach the thought to himself of flying back to Madison, Andrew was looking forward with slumping spirits to a long week spent burning away as many of the hours as he could crawling around the library stacks. But summer and the thought of Jake leaving...

"I don't know," he shrugged. "I guess I thought I'd stay out here. Find some job for the summer. Maybe Starbucks or something."

"Better you than me, hoss."

"Yeah. Schnoebel said something about being able to use me this summer, too. But I don't know what for or how much she'd pay yet."

"Well, why not come back to Yakima with me?"

Andrew's heart leapt at the idea. Follow Jake? Anywhere. But then, he thought, Yakima meant... "To do what?"

"Work the ranch. We'd get there just in time to see the bulls mounting the cows for next spring's calving."

Andrew gaped, trying to imagine that picture. "Jake, I don't know the first thing about working a ranch."

"No problem," Jake beamed. "You've seen pictures of cows and horses, haven't you?"

Feeling foolish and not a little nettled, Andrew nodded. "Of course."

"There you go. Don't worry. I'll teach you."

Andrew considered. Jake watched him, one corner of his mouth lifting. "Come on. An egghead like you can figure this out. It's just a cow-calf outfit. Angus mostly."

"What's that?"

Jake smiled. "A breed of cattle, hoss. Black as..." He beamed now. "...as Rae's nipple tape."

Andrew choked on that, slopping some beer on his front.

"Basically raising calves, keeping them healthy while they fatten up for the buyers, either direct from us or through the feed lots, Halverson's mostly. Used to background 'em elsewhere, first, until he bought up that outfit." Andrew felt a little weird, or maybe a little sick. Jake took a swig, saying, "You do know that hamburgers aren't just harvested with the corn each fall."

Throwing a pretzel at him, Andrew glowered. "Of course!" Jake waited, smiling. "Okay, so maybe I didn't. Is it hard?"

"If you don't know what you're doing, you can easily lose your shirt at it."

Andrew was tempted. But then, tell the truth, he simply could not see himself as a cowboy, galloping around in a saddle and lassoing cattle or whatever it is cowboys did these days. He didn't even own a pair of cowboy boots. He had to laugh at himself at the very suggestion of the idea. Put an obscure passage from Ecclesiastes in his hand, and he could expound for hours. Put a branding iron in it, and... The thought that Jake would be leaving his life in about twelve or thirteen weeks made it all the harder to even...maybe it would be simply easier not to think about the future at all, he thought. Just float along in some sort of eternally present moment.

"You know, hoss, you'd be doing me a favor."

Surprised, Andrew looked up. "Why?"

"Well, my pop loved the idea of ROTC helping pay my way these four years, but now that it's time to for me to make good on their investment, he's...getting a little stingy, you might say." Andrew waited, uncertain what Jake was getting at. "He's been groaning lately about how long it's been since the ranch had a good steady hand directing things. That would be me," he said, pointing at himself, "by the way."

"But--" Andrew objected.

"This way I can bring home another set of eyes. Cover more ground, faster. Oh, don't worry," Jake waved off his coming objection. "I can show you what to look for." He leaned forward. "I trust you, hoss."

Andrew hid his burning cheeks in a hasty gulp of beer.

"You can help me look into what Pop's grousing about. Nothing probably, but you never know. Ranch'd pay you three grand for the summer."

Andrew shook his head again. "Jake, I just don't think..." he started off, hoping Jake would contradict him.

Jake tilted his head at him, squinting one eye. Then with a mock flourish, he squared off his index fingers and thumbs at Andrew as if measuring an object in the distance. "Yep, you'll do." Andrew grinned foolishly. "Really, hoss. Don't worry. BOLC doesn't start for a month and a half after graduation. That'll give me plenty of time to show you everything you need to know." He waited.

Andrew, feeling the rising of some sun just broaching an inner horizon, smiled, "Why not?"

"That's my man!" Jake laughed, delighted. "Prost!" They crashed their steins together, drawing the notice of some nearby girls, then drained them.

"My turn." Andrew jumped up, then stopping halfway, uttered a quiet groan as he tried not to grab his groin.

"You might rethink your approach with Rae, next time, hoss. Talk about attempting the impossible."

"That's me." Andrew threw him a raised eyebrow, astounding himself. "Do or die." Jake screamed out a bouncing laugh and pounded the table a couple of times as Andrew crossed to the bar.

Returning to their table, he saw Amber enter with her black-haired friend and two other girls. She stopped upon seeing him and smiled her smile. Her smile for all the world, Andrew reflected, almost pitying her, then chided himself for such an uncharitable thought. He nodded in return and sat at their table. Jake, watching all of this, said, "Ah." He took a swig, one eye still on Andrew, who busily took a swallow himself.

"What's Bulk?"

Jake snorted. "A repetition of everything we've been doing for the last four years, just ramped up." He frowned, taking a sip. "Okay, that's not fair. But that's the Army. Training repeated, endlessly, until the slowest shit for brains in the entire unit gets it. It works."

"Where do you do it?"

"Different places. It's six weeks, Basic Officer Leadership Course. Broken up at Forts Benning, Bliss, Knox, Sill..."

"Fort Knox? There really is such a place?"

"Of course, fool. Kentucky. It's all small unit leadership and tactics exercises."

"Oh."

"I know. 3.2% of our GDP goes to defense, right?" Surprised at this new direction, Andrew nodded. "That means that 96.8% of the economy has nothing to do with defense." Still wondering what this had to with Jake's next training, Andrew nodded again. "So, that means that 96.8% of the country doesn't have a clue what we do in the military. No touch points. No exposure. No nothing. It's like we're a secret society anymore..." Jake scowled.

Confused at Jake's sudden gloom, Andrew reminded him, "You said small unit leadership and tactics or something."

Waving it away, Jake smiled. "Sorry. Just trapped in a stupid argument from the other day. Small units, yeah. This idget was trying to tell me that as a soldier I was just another cog in somebody's wheel. Some drunk on power general who's going to be pushing me around on his own personal chessboard. A pawn."

Andrew's smile grew stiff as he remembered how many times he had thought precisely that about Jake's future.

"I was trying to explain to him...never mind. Small units. The future of warfare is...the days of Kitchener and Patton are over. We don't field huge armies like that who battle it out along some long front.

Trenches or otherwise. There is no front any more. Troops are too mobile now."

Andrew frowned at him, puzzling.

Jake looked at him, his hard eyes softening. "Look." He grabbed the bowl of pretzels. "Let's say that this is your army and I need to shut it down." Andrew looked at the bowl and nodded. "Oh, never mind. Suffice it to say, I'd load all my guys in Blackhawks and Chinooks and heliport them behind you or on your flank, or wherever Jorge told me you were weakest. There is no front anymore."

Mystified, Andrew watched all this, watched Jake. As the memory of his brush the other day faded, Jake's face, his whole body settled, Andrew noticed. This was the Jake that had first fooled Andrew. The Jake of the quiet, friendly, muscular handshake, the tidy room and little else. The Jake of the patient, quiet confidence rather than the noisy bluster. The Jake that had so completely assumed the role of warrior that he didn't even appear to be one. "That's what BOLC is about. Drilling into all of our heads that the warfare of the future depends on the actions of the individual platoon in the field, or on the street as it were, not on some goose-stepping general back at the TOC."

"Huh. Do you go to your unit after that?"

"Screaming Eagles? No, I gotta earn that yet. Just more school."

"More?"

Jake shrugged. "Fighting wars is a complex business these days. Airborne for three weeks. Air Assault--" Seeing Andrew's question, he slowed down. "Airborne is parachutes, without falling. Air Assault, two weeks, is rappelling out of helicopters, again without falling. After that is the big one: Ranger school." He looked off in the distance, wistfully. "Man." He took a swig.

Andrew waited.

"It's hard?"

"Yes. It's hard." Jake smiled at him. "Only 1/3 pass. I intend to be one of those 1/3."

Andrew smiled at him, proud for his friend, and clinked steins with him again. Thinking of Jake's future, he worried about his own. He had another year to think about it, of course. He wondered if it would be enough, envying Jake's certainty. He shook his head. "All your training after graduation. It's like grad school or something."

"Yeah, I suppose it is. I certainly won't have much of a future as an infantry officer without it."

"Is that what you want to do with your life?"

"Of course." Jake beamed at him. "Just don't tell my dad."

***

Spring break was not nearly as bad as he had feared, if only because he found himself making more and more excuses to stay in their little home, feet up, reading...well...everything. Jake's battered copy of the Vietnam War battle in Ia Drang Valley was particularly interesting. He found a few pages of the text outlined in the margin, as if for easy access, beginning with the judgment that some captain was the best battlefield commander the author had ever seen. Intrigued, Andrew read those pages closely, both to understand the verdict and Jake's marking of the pages. All he could see, however, was that the captain had merely done everything that the author said he should have: confirmed that all the foxholes were dug deeply enough and those that had been dug too deeply equipped with built up firing steps, that the parapets built up in front were high and stout enough, that that anti-intrusion devices were set up 300 yards out, a field of fire cleared out to 100 yards out and - though he didn't quite understand this part, he gathered that it was vital - the captain had spent time with his artillery observer before they were attacked locking in pre-set targets so that, in the confusion of combat, calling in artillery strikes turned out to be relatively simple. He delighted in his new fluency in the arcane language of this strange art and dreamed of showing off to Jake but then quickly realized Jake would guess where he had learned it. In any case, the heralded captain seemed so carefully thorough in his planning, so thoroughly Jake-like, that Andrew felt a vicarious pride for his friend in learning that the captain's preparations enabled his company to hold off a vastly superior force, killing hundreds of Vietnamese soldiers while suffering only a handful of scratches and light wounds.

The campus was charmingly deserted for the warmer, if clichéd, climes of California, Florida and the Caribbean. He wandered it with real delight, not missing anyone but Jake. Not for the first time, he heaved a large sigh of relief at the thought that his new-found friendship wouldn't die with graduation. The cold rains of winter, gradually and grudgingly, he noticed, began to give way to the warmer days and more fruitful birdsong of spring. With each day passing, his mini-vacation seemed to disappear in pieces: there a pair of students walking the campus together whereas there had only been solitary strollers like himself; here a parking lot that suddenly seemed to grow cars overnight as quickly as mushrooms; now more and more students returning, some tanned and happy, some wan and disgruntled, all set for the final quarter of the year.

***

Jake showed up one day with all his usual fanfare. Stepping quietly into their dorm one day and, finding Andrew dozing in a chair with the Lotus Sutra spread across his knees, Jake cracked open a beer next to his ear. Andrew started, smiled and got one for himself.

***

As much will as Andrew applied to slow it down, the last quarter seemed to pass even faster. Jake called his dad one night to talk about their summer plans. Nervous, Andrew made an excuse and left for the library. There, he took refuge in its Gothic arches as much as he could until, not being able to stand it any longer, he set out at a quick pace back to their dorm. Jake was studying quietly. Andrew set his bag down on his desk without making a noise and waited. Jake turned a page. Andrew cleared his throat.

"Oh, hi," Jake nodded and went back to reading. Andrew took a step toward their little den under his bed. Changing his mind, he turned and took a step back toward his desk. He stopped, not knowing which way to go, as he heard a chuckle. He looked over at Jake, who sat leaning back with a broad grin on his face.

"Well?" Andrew glared at him.

Jake shrugged. "He said, 'Jake, so long as you teach him, I give him three weeks before he's busting broncs.'"

"He did not!"

"Okay, he didn't. He actually said, 'riding herd.'"

Andrew thought for a moment. "How do you ride herd?"

Jake smiled mysteriously and went back to his reading.

Before Andrew knew it, they were halfway through the quarter and the first ominous mutters about finals began once again, this time in the full knowledge that it would be their last days spent in the room together. Jake grew tender again in a way that he had not been since that night, so long ago it seemed, when he had perched over Andrew's bunk, softly pressing the ice-sock against Andrew's bruised cheek, listening patiently to Andrew's angry tears at the unfairness of life's moments. Jake also stopped seeing Ella, a development that, from the eyes drained of all but melancholy accompanying her ponytail around campus now, Andrew gathered was not welcome. Not welcome at all. Watching her listless attempts to joke with a friend one day, he was moved for her and tried to reach out to her mind with the compassion that everything is transient. As he walked away, proud of his wisdom, it suddenly and appallingly dawned on him that were he to lose Jake, and someone had pontificated such an idea to him, he would have easily stabbed that gentle sage with a fork.

The intensity of his feelings disturbed him. If not for the frustrating ache to finally know the happiness of lightly running his hand across a flaring mini-skirted hip, tracing the line in all its rises and folds of pleasure, now sitting next to him in class, now passing him in a hallway, now leaning across some friends and laughing delightfully in those higher, softer tones of melody, he would have thought he was in love with Jake. Seeking inspiration, he searched through the Hebrew Chronicles, finding solace in the stories of David and Jonathan. That a number of gay activists he knew back in Madison took the stories as coded language for a sexual relationship rather than simply accepting it as a love of another sort - a brotherhood, really - did not disturb him too greatly. All across recorded time he knew, no matter the faith tradition, scriptures had and have been read into by readers in search of a divine approbation to justify contemporary needs. Like why he loved Jake so much, he smiled, as the brother he never had. He, too, had to be fair about the way he read Scripture, he reminded himself.

Jake's graduation and commissioning were disappointingly typical of every other such ceremony seen in movies, except for that short exchange of nods with Rae. Perhaps it was because everyone appeared distracted after the president's speech at West Point the week before. "Preemptive strike" and "the Bush Doctrine" appeared to be on the lips of everybody on campus. Students who had always seemed most interested in the latest versions of Sim City - whatever that was - now suddenly hissed at ROTC cadets as they passed by in the halls, making life harder on Andrew, it seemed, than on Jake. "They're just waking up to the COE," he shrugged when Andrew commented on it, "and realizing that they liked it better in the days when we had just won the Cold War."

Jake had been disappointed to see that Sticks couldn't make it. His father, looking about as Dutch as a man can, with a pair of faded blue eyes staring out of a round, white wrinkled head and a bulging potato sack for a belly perched on top of two "rail thin" legs that went up to Andrew's belly button, had shaken his head. "She's sorry, Jake. The plot on Evans has got its first cutting, you know, and Angel's mother taking poorly. He had to drive her into Union Gap and stay at the hospital. He's a good son." He sighed, pounding Jake on the shoulder. "Can't sell pounds if you can't feed 'em." Then fumbling around in his shirt, he held out a folded note with a gnarled hand. "She wrote you this, though."

Jake's eyes welled up - was it really tears, Andrew was astonished to ask himself - and disappeared around the corner of a pillar.

"My son tells me that you will make a fine horseman, yes?"

Wondering what lies Jake had been telling, Andrew hesitated, until, remembering how Jake dealt with such situations, he nodded his head very slowly, looked the old man in the eyes and said, "I promise you, sir, that I will work very hard for you."

"Very good." Pop slapped him on the back with a force to make Andrew cough. "Very good."

That night, their last before they headed out, Petie and Jorge joined them with a case of beer each. Good

74

beer, Andrew noticed this time. With their bars shining on their battle dress uniforms, Andrew realized that he was sitting here sharing beers - for they were certainly friendly enough, even Petie - with his country's future military leaders. Thinking of his father, he had to smile at the amount of difference that can grow between generations. Looking at them, listening to Petie's latest hazing story, he was pleased to feel a great sense of pride at being able to share time with these warriors. He felt honored. Yes, it was true, he decided. He felt honored.

Seizing the moment when Petie took a breath, he spoke up for the first time. "I was just reading the other day how pre--pre-set...pre-locked in strikes saved an entire company from getting wiped out."

Petie gawked at him. Jorge smiled. Jake waited, watching. Andrew, realizing he had created far more of an effect than he had wanted, felt the heat rise in his cheeks but pushed on. "The Blackhawks...fired co--continuously for three days, didn't they? Saving the companies, the platoons on the ground at Ia Drang Valley."

He stopped talking at the blank stare Petie gave him. Jorge peered out into the space in front of him and began blinking rapidly, reminding Andrew of the old Tibetan monks who, having memorized thousands of pages of Buddhist wisdom, grunted as they turned the page in their minds during recitations, until Jake, whose eyes had wandered over his empty bookshelves, murmured, "LZ Xray." Jorge blinked once more and nodded a friendly grin at Andrew. Petie's blankness slowly began to give way to a smirk which stopped, frozen, as he caught Jake's cold, narrowed gaze leveled at him.

Clearing his throat, he turned to Andrew, saying, "The Falcons. That's right. They're still called Falcons. The same batteries, to this day, because of their supporting fire from LZ Falcon those three days in Vietnam." He saluted Andrew with a beer.

Andrew saluted him right back.

Before very long, Jorge and Petie had packed up, shook hands with Jake a few times, shouted "HOOAH!" a few more times and, then, finally, said goodbye. Andrew glanced around their little room that had become such a happy home for - could it only have been eight or nine months? To think that they were leaving tomorrow. Over Snoqualmie Pass and on to his new life as a cowboy. He chuckled to himself. He was looking forward to a good summer.

Jake was sitting with his feet up, drinking quietly, when he said with a sudden jerk, "Oh, by the way, I told Pop that you are a Buddhist."

Andrew spun around. "Is that okay?"

Jake shrugged and smiled sadly, slurring his words. "Yeah, I don't know what got into me. All he said in response was 'Jake, so long as he's accepted Jesus Christ as his personal savior, you know he's welcome.'"

Andrew nodded. He pulled over his chair and opened a beer. Seeing all the empties, he wondered how many they had drunk tonight, then decided to worry about it tomorrow.

He looked up with a jolt to see tears at the corners of Jake's eyes. "What's wrong?" he asked.

Without blinking at the wetness, Jake stared at Andrew. "Best friend I've ever had and I can't even bring him home because he hasn't prayed the prayer."

Confused, anxious at what Jake was saying, Andrew managed, "The prayer."

Jake grunted. "The prayer inviting Jesus into your heart."

"Oh, that!" Andrew shook his head in relief. "I've done that."

Jake perked up. "You have?"

Andrew nodded.

"When? Why didn't you say so?"

Wondering what the big deal was, Andrew thought back, saying "When I was, I don't know, ten or so.

Some traveling troupe came to Madison and I was interested. So, I went. My dad doesn't know, of course. He would have grounded me if he had found out. They were, well, traveling evangelists, I suppose. You know, do the songs, preach the sermon, save a few souls and pass the plate at the end."

Jake nodded enthusiastically. "And did you? Did you go down?"

Andrew paused for a moment, registering that whatever it was that was bothering Jake, it was enough to let his unintended double entendre slip right by. "Yes," Andrew smiled, chuckling to himself. He struck a deadpan. "Yes, when they called, I went down."

Jake looked at him for a moment and then began hooting himself. "Excellent! This is excellent!" He pumped a fist in the air, cracked open another beer and sighed. His eyes looked completely normal, making Andrew wonder if it had been a trick of the light.

Still... "Jake, you know that I'm not a Christian."

"It doesn't matter, hoss. Here's all you have to do: First time at dinner, find the right moment to slip that story in, just like you told me. It'll be the only time you ever have to tell it."

"Why?" Andrew was intrigued.

"Because, fool, after that, Pop will make sure the entire town knows. They live for that kind of thing over there."

"Does it matter?"

Jake looked at him, serious now, and said, "Yes. It matters."

A bit stunned at this new turn of events, Andrew thought back to all that he had ever read about evangelists, about Fundamentalism first showing up on the prairies in the 1890s and not letting go since. Wild, he thought, just wild. "Jake."

"Yeah?"

"Does your father--?"

"Might as well get used to calling him 'Pop.' Everybody does."

Andrew nodded. "Does Pop...?" he paused, again, thinking how much he liked saying that word in that way, "...believe in Original Sin?"

Jake shook his head with pity at Andrew. "Yes. And the curse of Eve, the apple, the garden of Eden, and all of that."

"Wow." The word uttered hung above them as the single note of a cymbal struck, resonating, its soft echoes delineating the sharp boundaries separating, Andrew saw, their two very different worlds of birth. Jake watched Andrew, thinking.

Andrew stirred. "You know that's only one way to look at the Eden story."

Jake smiled. "And you can go right ahead and tell me the other one, so long as you never tell it that side of the pass. Well, at least not to Pop. Please, hoss."

A bit unnerved at how seriously Jake was taking this whole conversation, nevertheless, Andrew couldn't help himself and began. "Instead of the fruit of...the bitter fruit of death, the apple could be a Hebrew metaphor for wisdom." He looked at Jake who shrugged and gestured that Andrew continue. "That while they lived in Eden, they may have been happy as children, but they were also just as ignorant. After biting of the fruit of wisdom, they became aware of...I don't know...their ignorance, their self-absorption and, growing beyond it, began to realize how..." Andrew broke off, realizing suddenly that the stories he had heard around his father's dinner table from visiting Jewish scholars weren't...complete enough. As he pondered this thought, and why he should feel that way about an old truth that had seen the rise and fall of millennia to yet stand today, he began to sense a tiny pulse that was just now forming, just beyond the murky horizons of his mind, not seen, certainly not understood, but whose approach was undeniable. Jake watched him, the puzzled expression resting on his hand overtaken as he slowly lifted his beer to take a last sip. Wondering what that pulse might be, and where it was coming from, Andrew went on, "...how much greater, how much more mag--magnificent...in life *and* death...their world truly was and what possible...roles they could play in it." He looked at Jake again who swallowed his sip, still staring at him. Andrew hesitated, wondering how he should continue, wondering why he didn't simply go on with the old tale. Jake sighed and made as if to speak.

Suddenly, that pulse popped right over the horizon as bright as day. But it was too bright, almost bewildering in its intensity. Feeling a mounting excitement and ignoring the answering stutter and its accompanying scoring of his cheeks, Andrew rushed out, "That maybe...maybe they would have lived forever in Paradise, ig--ignorant, or maybe they would have died there, still ignorant, we don't know. The point is, the point is...that at the moment they took the bite, at the moment they took a step toward...self-knowledge, if...if we can call it that, they could not go back." Yes, he thought. That was it. Something about no possibility of return. Life in an expanding universe of possibilities, he realized, was simply too complex for the simple formulas of day to day living, either in fundamentalist places, say Yakima, if it really was all that fundamentalist, or in secular ones like Seattle, in...anywhere, really. He plunged on, "Having gained the...," but found himself again lost in the complexity of what it was he was struggling to say. Finding the passion rising in him frustrating now, he began to fight it, began to fight for clarity, for the right phrase to cut through the mounting tide of joy swelling his heart. "Having achieved the...earned the...awful grace of...wisdom...they could not give it back."

His voice stopped. He felt the tide receding, just as suddenly as it had appeared, but leaving him bereft. Empty.

Jake watched him with a small smile on his face. "You can say what you want, hoss. They're still going to like the other one better." He crunched his can in a tight fist, letting out a long, slow belch. "It's easier."

II

Jessie wrinkled her nose at the sweat trickling down, then chanced letting go of the bouncing reins with a hand and wiped it away before snatching them back. The hop field, with its tall trellises dripping its long, thin strands of young fruit, flew by as Whip thundered along, pounding stride by stride into the dry dirt, leaving little poofs of dust in their wake. Up ahead she could see the rise ending the tractor path. It was the usual ramp leading up to the canal track separating this field from the next one. She bent low under the blackness clouding her mind, of what she had seen in Pop's ledger last week and, over the brown withers rippling with the excitement of the chase, urged Whip on. She knew she shouldn't. The hands had planted the hop trellis too close to see who might be coming along that canal track when they crossed it. Much less what awaited the other side of the rise. Let 'em get out of the way, she thought, clearing her mind of everything except the feel of her knees naturally clenching more tightly around Whip's heaving belly.

Up the rise the mare pounded, her head with its clear white blaze thrown back, clearing the corner of the trellis to reveal a boy's astonished gape as he groped for his hat on the ground, then leaping across the canal bridge and down the other side where, disappointed, Jessie noted nothing lay in their path. She let Whip gallop a few more strides down the new field then began to pull her up. Whip subsided into a cheerful canter, then slowed to a walk, barely breathing. Jessie turned her around and trotted her back up the path to the canal track to see who the boy was. Like the field before, this one's trellis was planted too close to see much. Probably trying to squeeze in another couple of bushels, she snorted.

Just rounding the corner of the trellis at the top, she heard a "Sticks!" Smiling, she trotted over to Jake, mounted on Asa, watching him hold Digger's reins while the boy, now hat on head, struggled to get back up into the saddle. "Hey, Jake! Got Digger out, huh?"

"Yeah. What've you been doing with him? So fat he looks like he's going to keel over from a walk."

"Nothing. He just roams around the pasture these days. You know Pop."

"Yeah." Gesturing to the boy who, astride now, was trying to sort out the reins while holding on to his hat as if fearing another playful gust would rear up and take it, Jake beamed his usual smile. "This here's Andrew. A real egghead from the other UW."

Jessie looked him over. He sat okay at least, she thought, considering that Jake had always rode pretty well. The boy turned a bright red, then tried to move Digger over to her. Giving up, he got off his horse and walked over to her to shake her hand.

"Andrew Worth," he mumbled, not quite looking her in the eyes.

She smiled. Thinking how different it was to see a man get off his horse for her, how ridiculous he looked in his new hat, gloves and shiny boots with nary a crease on them, she shook his offered hand, saying, "Jessie Van der Vaal." Something seemed to hit him then because he suddenly froze, his mouth hanging open before he snatched a quick look at Jake, then looked down. "What?" she asked.

Looking flustered, he looked up at her, then down again, then, as if making up his mind about something, he slowly looked back up into her eyes, passing right over her breasts without a change in expression, not that they were all that much, she knew. "I think I must have been expecting someone...younger." He waited.

Wondering what he was waiting for, Jessie shrugged. "Well, now you know." Turning to Jake, she asked, "How's the pass?"

"Oh, not bad. Dry now, you know. Pretty though."

"You made good time. I thought we wouldn't see you 'til tonight."

"Couldn't wait for your cooking."

"Yeah, right." Whip began shifting her feet, so Jessie turned her away from them, thinking she'd give her another good breeze before bringing her in.

"No, really, Jessie. I was."

Surprised at the note in Jake's voice, she turned back to him. "Well...okay. Making you steaks. Thought we'd barbecue 'em on the porch."

"Right on!"

Embarrassed now, though she couldn't see why, Jessie threw them a quick wave. "At six. Pop'll be happy." Looking at Andrew, she said, "Use the lanyard. It'll keep your hat on your head." He blushed again, she was amused to see. "At six, Jake. Two kinds of people in this world," she tossed over her shoulder before trotting Whip over the bridge and back down the rise.

In the stable, rubbing down Whip, she could hear Jake and Andrew come in. Andrew was groaning about his ass hurting and Jake was chuckling. "You'll get used to it, hoss." Andrew groaned again, then noticing her in Whip's stall, quit. Going red in the face, he clambered down Digger's side and began stiffly walking toward Digger's rear.

"Not that way, Andrew!" Andrew stopped, one foot in the air still waiting to be put down. Good reflexes, she thought. "Jesus, I'd never hear the end of it if I lost you the first day out!" Andrew looked over at Jake, confused. Jake sighed. "It's all right, hoss. Just, never, ever, walk behind a horse if you can help it. Unless'n you run your hand along his side while you're doing it."

Andrew looked about him as if realizing where he was going for the first time, then turned back to Jake. "Oh. They kick, right?" At least he wasn't entirely stupid, she thought.

"Enough to kill you without another thought." Andrew swallowed foolishly then stumbled off, stiffly, the other way. "That's right. Just walk it off, a few times up and down the stable. Pretty soon you won't even have to do that."

Jessie went back to brushing Whip, smiling in spite of her mood. This was the Jake she had always loved growing up. Pop and the other hands wouldn't ever give her the time of day, but Jake had always had a moment or two for her. Not that he knew a damn about horses, she grimaced. Whip snuffled and Jessie reached up, circling her arm around Whip's neck so that she could lean against the cheek. Whip threw her head a bit, but softly, then let Jessie rest on her again. She stood there, delighting in the wet smell of horseflesh, wondering how much she would miss it next fall. She didn't like thinking about it, though, so she soon resumed her long, slow rasps of the brush across Whip's coat.

"That's right. First the halter, then the bridle. Here." Wanting to watch Jake's idea of basic horsemanship, she got some oats for Whip and moved out of the stall to watch. Andrew was fastening Digger's old blue halter of rope around the horse's neck, then tying it a stall beam. "Good. Now he won't go anywheres on you. Not that Digger would," Jake chuckled. "Okay, unbuckle the harness. That's right. Right out from underneath the halter." Andrew fumbled a bit with the buckles but got it out, smiling proudly. "Good, hoss. Now, hang that on that nail next to Digger's stall to dry."

Andrew walked with his old man's gait over to the stall and glanced at Jake. "There's already one there."

"I know it. Hang it next to that one. You're going to need both these next few weeks. Sticks here'd flay you alive if she ever caught you putting wet leather on a horse. Not that I've ever noticed a difference."

Jessie asked, "How much you gonna be riding him?"

Jake beamed while undoing Asa's bridle. "Six hours a day. To start. Two at sunup, two after lunch, and two, maybe three slow ones, at night. Plus a couple caring for the tack before dinner." Nodding at Andrew, he said, "Pop wants an entire survey of the ranch before I ship out, and I talked him into letting us do it from horseback. We'll get him into shape in no time for our Pounds Patrol. Digger, too."

"You're going to get up at sunrise?" Jessie cocked an eyebrow at him.

Jake shrugged with a grin, "I'm in the Army now."

"Better not say that around Pop."

"I know."

***

She banged out four plates around the table and threw the silverware down in the middle, then stomped back into the kitchen to see if the beans were boiling yet. Not yet. Swearing to herself, she grabbed the bag of bread and the butter dish in one hand and scooped up some glasses in the other before heading back outside. At least the coals were going good, she thought. Last thing we want to happen is dinner late. God fucking forbid, she grinned savagely before hurrying back in for the water and napkins.

Seeing that the beans had finally begun their unwilling bubbling, she grabbed the steaks out of the fridge and, not bothering to wash them, rushed

outside, unwrapping them as she went to throw them
all on the grill. Biscuit sniffed her hand hopefully,
but she irritatedly pushed him away, saying, "Git."
He moaned a protest then retreated to lie down next to
Pop's chair to begin a slow pant in the heat. She
sorted the steaks out with a pair of tongs and, feeling
a bit better now, remembered doing just this at the
Young Life booth at the fairgrounds all through
junior high. She smiled at the memory of those hot
days with all the people walking around the grounds,
gobbling down corn dogs and heaping clouds of pink
and blue cotton candy. You could always hear the
shrieks from the rides, even if Pop couldn't afford to
let them go on more than one or two. She had always
chosen the roller coaster, throwing her arms way up,
feeling the air pluck at them as they went over and
around and over again, screaming her eyes out. Jake
had always managed to get lost for an hour or so in
the haunted house, usually with one of her classmates.
Serving up thick burgers for Pastor Don and
everybody from Brickton Christian Church as they
shouted out their greetings through the smoke: "Hey
there, Jessie! Hot enough for ya?" Over and over,
the same greeting repeated throughout the day, as
regular as the sun working its way across the sky to
spray the grounds with its own warm, golden glow as
the heat finally, thankfully, slacked off.

Squinting through her own smoke, she wondered if
this blackened water tank Pop had sawn in two to
make their grill was as big as the Young Life ones.
She flipped the steaks, then stretching her arms, she
tried to measure the length. It was weird barbecuing
again, she reflected. Probably not since last summer,
when Jake went back to the UW. Then, remembering
what Jake had said about another UW, she smiled at
the pain that boy was going to be feeling these next
few weeks. He'd be snoring at night, she grinned.

"Almost done, Jessica?"

She stiffened without thinking and, turning to face him, answered, "Just about, Pop."

He grunted, looking at his watch, and sat down, Biscuit raising his nose to slip under Pop's hand. "Better get your brother, then. Two kinds of people in this world, quick and hungry."

"Yes, Pop." She flipped the steaks again, hung the tongs on the side of the tank and stepped inside hollering, "Jake!? Dinner!"

The table was full of quiet munching after Pop's reminder not to "waste what the good Lord in His wisdom has provided." Eventually, after Pop had pushed back his plate with a sigh and sipped some more water, Jake smiled over at Jessie. "It's good, Sticks. Real good." On signal, Biscuit got up from a nearby corner and began to nuzzle one of Andrew's hands who began to pet him slowly, softly, especially around the eyes, a responding shine growing in his own.

Jessie wondered how Andrew knew Biscuit liked that best, then said, "Yeah, right."

"Better than the commons at school, right hoss?"

Andrew blushed again. What now, she thought with exasperation, as he mumbled something like a "That's right." Burying his head in petting an increasingly grateful Biscuit, he then said without looking at her, "Thank you very much for cooking dinner...Jessie..." as if he wasn't sure that he could say her name. "It was very delicious." She pursed her lips and nodded brusquely, then looked out past the corner of the corrals at the valley walls to the south, looking in the late afternoon light like the soft downy folds of a golden-sage blanket heaped on itself in some places, stretched out in others, but going on and on and on out to the east. She wondered again what the world was like beyond them and, again, wondered if she gave a damn.

"Andrew," Pop cleared his throat. "Jake tells me that you have accepted Jesus as your personal savior."

Andrew stopped petting Biscuit mid-stroke and looked over at Pop, his cheeks flushing their brightest red yet, if that were possible. "Yes, sir."

"Good. I am glad to hear it."

Pop stared at Andrew, waiting. Andrew looked back, his eyes growing wider by the minute, his mouth dropping open. Jessie felt, rather than heard, Jake nudge him beneath the table. In response, Andrew's eyes changed as if they had dimmed.

"Yes, sir. It was a tr--traveling troupe that had come to town...in Madison, where I grew up...they..." He looked off over at the valley walls, too, as if trying to remember something. "They were...preaching the gospel."

"Good." Pop nodded, smiling.

"And at the end, they asked us to come down..."

"Good." Pop slapped the table with a wide beam.

"And..." He looked off again, searching, this time his eyes looking inside his head, Jessie thought. "...ask Jesus into our hearts...And I did."

"Very good!" Pop reached out, Jake leaning out of the way, and slapped Andrew on the back.

Andrew coughed, looking down, with a silly grin on his face. Pop looked on Jake with a proud smile as if to crow to the world about the good people his son befriended. Jake beamed right back. Without knowing why, though, Jessie kept her eyes on Andrew to see his mouth tighten and his eyes look up with a new shine. It was a gleam that, she could have sworn, reminded her how she felt taking Whip full out over a field neither of them knew all that well.

"Of course I was pretty young, then, only--"

"Only ten, right, hoss!" Jake boomed out. "And he's never gone back, right, hoss?"

Andrew coughed hard, suddenly, bending slightly toward Jake. Jessie watched, fascinated, as the gleam faded. "That's...right. That's right."

Pop paused, knowing he had missed something but not sure what. Finally, he shrugged and pounded Andrew on the back again. "Good. Good. Andrew, you are welcome to this table and to our church." He sat back at peace with the world.

"Great," Andrew mumbled. Then, slowly tucking his arm into his side next to Jake, he smiled up at Pop. "Great."

"Jessica, we have ice cream."

"Yes, Pop."

Pinpricks in the night. Lying back over Whip's warm haunches, she turned her head to her favorite sight in the sky and inhaled the sweet smell of cooling manure. Overhead, the sprawling dust of the Milky Way lay strewn all across her view, much like the flour of tomorrow's bread, she thought. She sighed and turned away. In the working corrals next to her, she could hear, rather than see, the lazy plodding of a few cows come to see who was visiting their fence, the anxious stumbling of their calves following them. As if they'd never seen us here before, she smiled. Helping, the moon came out from behind a cloud and spread its blue light across the pasture enough that she could see that it was Mae, recovering from her foot rot, sticking her blue black, snuffling nose through the planking, little Buff at her side, tugging away with a mewling low, as always, at Mae's teats.

Whip nickered and began a slow stroll back toward to the gate. Enjoying the ambling pace of Whip's muscles under her shoulders, Jessie could now hear Jake and that boy leading out Asa and Digger, Biscuit growling a happy bark around them. The boy was moaning. She grinned. "Why not wait until tomorrow?" he was saying.

Jake chuckled. "Because if'n we don't, you'll be hurting much worse than you are now."

"That'll be the day."

"You'll thank me in the morning. Now. Just like we practiced this afternoon."

She could hear Asa's clops coming around the corner of the stable, so, silently, she slipped off Whip's back, gave her a soft slap on the haunch to get her moving away, and stepped herself into the shadow of the stable's wall. Asa came into view with Jake astride her, looking back over his shoulder at Digger following while Andrew hopped along at his side, one foot in the stirrup, struggling in vain to jump up. She chuckled.

Jake looked right at her and smiled, though how he could have seen her, she couldn't tell.

"Pull him up sharp, hoss. Remember?"

"No," Andrew panted out an exasperated grumble.

"Here, hoss." Jake swung Asa back to them and took the reins from Andrew, pulling Digger in a sharp circle to stop as Biscuit jumped out of the way. "There. Now..."

Andrew jumped up quickly to groan again as he lay flat out over the saddle. Jessie started giggling silently at the sight of his ass poking out straight at her.

Jake shook his head. "Egghead."

Jessie could just barely hear Andrew's grousing reply. Something about "German finals." Jake laughed.

"Come on, hoss. You can do it."

With a heave and a sigh, Andrew pulled himself upright and scrambled over the saddle lip to seat himself. "There," he blew out a breath.

"Give it a few days. You'll see." Handing him the reins and nodding a "Stay" at Biscuit's whine, Jake turned Asa back down the road and began trotting. Looking all of perplexed for a moment, Andrew shook his head in irritation, grabbed up the reins and kicked Digger into a walk after them. Biscuit gave a last whine then trundled off to his spot under the porch.

God knew what good that boy was going to be this summer, she laughed quietly and softly whistled for Whip. As the sound of their clops on the gravel of the back road faded, she swung back up and relaxed into her reverie. Egghead. She wondered how smart Andrew really was. Of all Jake's nicknames for people, this was a new one.

Deciding she didn't care, she let Whip's slow rocking take her mind off into the aimless meanderings of her sky, her pasture, her horse and Pop's cattle.

Other than lunch and dinner, what with their pounds patrolling and night rides, she didn't see too much of them those first weeks, though she did notice doing the wash that the saddle sore bloodstains in the Egghead's underwear growing smaller. At lunch, if they came in for it, with Angel, Josef and the six other hungry ranch hands at the table all reaching for something, the Egghead faded into the background. At dinners, with Jake and Pop trading gossip about the weather, the difference in the price of beef using the new grid formulas, this spring's calves and just about everything they could think of to talk about except the Army, he might as well have been a fence post. One more mouth for her to feed, anyway, was about all he amounted to. One scorching afternoon, as she was finishing a light breather for Whip, she was startled to see Andrew slowly backing Digger in the yard. Jake stood nearby, hands on his hips and head tilted to one side as he called out different commands watching Andrew struggle to follow them. "Right wheel. Okay, not bad. Left wheel. No, hoss, you gotta jerk the rein. Well, better. Try backing him again. Better. Better, hoss. Left turn again."

"Won't he get tired of this?" Andrew asked.

Jake snorted. "He's got so much fat on him, this'll do him some good. He'll be thanking you sooner than he'll be complaining. Okay, forward into a trot. No, hoss. I said a trot."

"I am!" Andrew kicked Digger lightly in the flanks again to no effect. Digger put his head down in search of something to graze in the yard.

Turning Whip toward the stable, Jessie laughed. Sure enough, the Egghead went bright red.

"Okay, wait." Jake walked up to him. Wanting to hear what was coming next, she slid down and lifted one of Whip's shoes to take a look. Ignoring her, Jake put one hand on Digger's reins and the other on his flank and looked up at Andrew. "Hoss, look. You're doing well. Really well. But your attitude is all wrong."

Andrew flushed again and looked down, mumbling something.

"No, I said your attitude. Toward Digger here. You're...you're treating him like he's your pet Bambi or Cocoa in the house there or something. Digger is a horse. He's not a pet." Andrew looked up at Jake. "He's a work horse, at least he used to be. That means one thing. Between the horse and rider there can be only one master. Now...if you're going to ride Digger, and you are going to ride Digger, let's get that straight...That means he's going to wait to see if you are going to be the boss. Just as soon as he realizes that you're not, he's going to do exactly as he pleases."

"But isn't that...?"

Jessie picked something out of the shoe and grabbed another, hiding her smile and thinking the Egghead was better entertainment than tv.

"Isn't what, hoss?" Jake asked, gently, to Jessie's surprise.

Andrew flashed a quick nervous glance at Jessie.

"Isn't what?" Jake asked again.

"Isn't it mean?"

"No."

"I don't want to...mistreat him."

"I know, hoss. You won't. It's not in you. But I'll tell you something. If you're going to get up on a horse, you're going to have to show him who's in charge. If you don't want to do that, well, it's simple. Don't get up on a horse."

Jessie was impressed. Jake must have been paying more attention over the years than she had thought.

"Here. Get down, and I'll show you." Andrew lifted one leg rather neatly over the horn and slid down. Jake swung up using a stirrup and looked down at Andrew. "Now, watch. He may not be looking at me, but he sure as hell is thinking about me. It's been a while since I've been on his back. So he's wondering which way it's gonna be. Time for me to show him. Left wheel." Jake jerked the reins hard to the left to Andrew's gasp as Digger turned quickly, if clumsily. "He'll get smoother over time. Now, right wheel." Again, Jake jerked the rein hard. Again, Digger turned quickly, with a bit of a stumble. "Okay. Look at him now. Is he screaming? Rolling his eyes or anything?"

Andrew looked at Digger, head up and ears perked, who showed sign of nothing other than waiting for the next command. Andrew shrugged. "No."

"Well, then. Left wheel." Digger turned more smoothly now to Jake's pull, softer now. "You only got to give him a hard jerk the first few times, after that..." Jake slid down and threw the reins to Andrew. "Whip's got the cleanest shoes on the res." Jessie turned red herself, now, and led Whip to the stable followed by Jake's chuckle.

As she turned the corner, she could hear Jake's sermon continuing. "Which way is it gonna be, hoss? Cuz you're gonna have to choose. If'n you don't, one of these days your horse will make up your mind for you and that day will most likely be your last ride. Ever."

***

On another day, as she stomped outside for the mail if only to get away from Jake's pointless droning on to Pop about this day's Pounds Report, swearing up a black storm at Cocoa's latest fur ball, this one delivered right in Pop's chair, and wondering how she was going to get the stain out thinking instead that she'd like to take that cute little purring bundle of joy and slit its belly open from the neck all the way down to its scrawny little ass, she came upon the Egghead on the front porch. He was sitting quietly at the end of one of the picnic benches, his boots placed carefully next to him, his legs crossed over his stockinged feet like a fucking Indian swami or something, his half-closed eyes bent on the galloping glacial horse running up the side of Mt. Adams, polishing Digger's saddle. That Biscuit was lying on the rest of the bench, his head lovingly resting in the Egghead's lap didn't improve her mood. Nor did the fact that Asa's saddle, all freshly polished into dark, shiny leather sat upright on its end, its stirrups lying out like a godawful mess, the bright buckles to adjust their height twinkling in the dying sunlight.

She stomped over to it, startling him out of wherever he had gone, and picked one up, snarling, "See these? They get curled under the saddle so's they dry right." And she showed him. "That way when you're in a full gallop and your boot slips out, it falls right so that you don't have to look down to find it again." Biscuit lifted a lazy eye at her, pissing her off even more, and closed it.

His bright red cheeks stared at her for a nervous moment before he nodded.

"Good. Jake should've told you."

Suddenly, she felt all stupid for ruining their peace and wanted to get out of there. "Now you know."

He looked down and kept polishing Digger's saddle. She stalked across the porch, down across the yard, got the mail, slamming the box's lid shut with a savage snap and, feeling his eyes on her, decided to take the long way back around the house.

Only later when she was cooking dinner did it dawn on her that that was her first real conversation with him and she regretted it. Watching him carefully finish his plate in silence, on impulse she cut the first slice of pie extra large and with a grunt of "Here" held it out to him. Strangely enough, he didn't blush this time. He just nodded a mumbled "Thank you" but not before she caught a glimpse of something like sympathy in his eyes, which pissed her off all over again. Still, she'd made her amends, she thought and let it go, serving out the rest of the pie.

***

Taking in the wash another day, Conk honking after her spring's brood of goslings at her feet, she saw Andrew perched astride the stableyard's fence watching as Jake threw down a few bales from a stack on one of the working trucks. "Forty-seven cents a tie," Jake was saying. "Back in the fifties, I think. From Uncle Willem. Probably the last time those two've talked. You'd think I'd know it by heart given how many times he's told the story."

Andrew was looking around at all the fencing of the working corrals and pastures across the fields. "You mean, all of it's built with railroad ties?"

"No, just the corrals because they're used so much. That and two by eights. See, hoss, a cow will butt her head through just about anything. Calf, too, at weaning time. Probably a brick wall, if we gave 'em the chance. The other spreads are like we saw over on Evans Road and White Swan Road yesterday, just regular posts and barbed wire."

Andrew nodded. Jake starting shifting the bales around to make a mattress. "Some of the newer outfits use cable and weights. Like Halverson's feed lot out on Brownstown Road, remember? We saw it when we came in."

Andrew nodded again, his face screwing up in distaste.

"See, if a cow butts up against the cable she can push it out as far as she likes, then when she pulls back, the weights on the end take up the slack and pull it straight again. Nicer than wood. Cheaper. Doesn't break."

Andrew looked down at the fencing. "Are you going to put cables and weights on the corrals here?"

Jake laughed. "And have Sticks there geld me for suggesting it? No way."

Jessie frowned at him. Jake laughed again. She turned back and began folding a bed sheet.

Andrew said, "Well, I like the wood. It's prettier."

At this sarcastic fling, Jessie spun around to actually do some gelding but only saw Andrew patting the top of a tie as he was looking over the corral. She grunted and threw the sheet in the basket.

"That's because you don't have to paint it. Now. Here's the drill. You're riding along having a good day thinking about one your Buddhist books..."

"Sutras," Andrew corrected him with a slow smile.

Jessie turned slightly while folding some of Pop's jeans, interested, as Jake continued. "...when suddenly a pheasant explodes out of the brush at Digger's feet thinking you're a hunting him. Which spooks Digger and, godawful fat as he is, he rears and because you're miles away in your head, you get thrown."

"Right." Andrew nodded, looking down at hay bales.

"How do you fall? Flat on your back with your head up so that the worse thing that happens to you is getting the wind knocked out of you? Or on top of your head so that you break your neck and wake up in a hospital, if ever, as a paraplegic?"

"I'll take the first choice." Andrew grinned.

"Good man. So the first trick is to raise your leg over the horn and push away. The second is the fall itself. Let's do the leg a few times first. Just pretend you're a dog who's just found a fire hydrant..."

That night, washing up after dinner, she could see Andrew out in the yard practicing his falls. Just as he was told, he lifted his leg for a pee, and pushed away from the fence to fall on the bales, only he was crouched up when he landed. Getting up, he paused, rubbed his back, then climbed back up the fence to do it again. Watching him try it several times in a row without stopping, she never heard Jake come up behind her. She felt the spark of pain on her hip, though, just as she heard the snap of the towel. "Jake!" she yelped. She turned and armed herself with a towel, too.

"Oh, come on, Sticks! Just having fun."

"Yeah, I'll show you some fun." She dipped her towel in the sink water and started twirling it into a twist, suddenly getting a flash of a feeling of happiness from long ago, when they were kids.

"We've got ourselves an arms race, that's what." Jake grabbed a second towel, and twirling both in each hand, crouched at the ready, eyes shining. She watched him, gauging. As he reached out to snap her with one, she dodged it to take the second right in the thigh. She squealed.

"Jacob Van der Vaal, you are going to be tomorrow's mince meat pie."

"Mmmm. Sounds good." They circled around each other, laughing, feinting and dodging each other until Jessie scored a direct hit on his rib cage. "Ow! Damn, Sticks, what the...?"

"Jacob." The voice rang out of the shadows next to the reading light in the living room.

"Yes, Pop."

"You know that I don't welcome that language in this house."

"Yes, Pop. Sorry."

They circled each other, again, quietly this time. But, strangely, Jessie didn't feel up to it anymore. She straightened.

As if understanding, Jake smiled, putting his towel down. "Okay, blood for blood. It's a tie. This time."

She nodded and grinned, then turned back to the dishes. Jake grabbed a plate and began drying it. Nodding toward the window, he asked, "Still at it?"

She looked out to see Andrew fall, badly this time. He sat up, grimacing in the yard's light while holding his arm and looking around to see if anyone was watching. She pulled back. "Yep."

Jake looked out. She joined him as Andrew, shaking his arm a few times, climbed back up the fence. "We never did that in 4H."

Jake nodded. "I know. But we should have. Remember Timmy Stephens?"

She shuddered at the memory. "Yeah."

She went back to her washing, Jake to his drying. The kitchen was silent except for the clinking of plates and glasses. From time to time, they would glance out to see, sure enough, Andrew was continuing. Finally, she asked, "How long is he going to do that?"

"I told him two hundred falls."

"You're kidding."

"Nope. Just setting it in his muscle memory for the day he needs it."

She shrugged. "Looks like he'd make a good soldie--" Jake's flashing eyes cut her off. He nodded toward the living room. She started scrubbing out a pot, murmuring a "Sorry."

Jake put down a spatula and peered out, his features full of thought. "As a matter of fact, Andrew wouldn't. Too independently-minded. Has to know why before he'll do what. In that line of business, there's usually no time to explain."

It wasn't like Jake to speak openly about his new world, so Jessie stopped and looked at him. She waited for more, but he didn't say anything else. Then, looking out at Andrew again, who again was falling, better this time, she noticed, she thought about all the different things that Jake had Andrew practicing these days and asked, "Do you have to explain everything to him?"

"Of course not, silly." Jake's shoulders had grown broader over the last year, she abruptly noticed.

"Why not?"

"Trust."

***

Galloping Whip along a harvested field of asparagus one painfully bright afternoon, the leftover spears poking out of the ground like stubble on Pop's chin when he shaved badly, she saw Angel, Josef and a few hands gathered around a calf with its mother standing nearby in a yellow pasture dotted black with their cattle. She spurred Whip to jump the gate next to the idling truck and trotted up to the hands as they turned toward her, Felipe on his knees holding the calf's rear hooves. "Angel, what's going on?"

He gestured at the calf, bawling away while it tried to break through the ring of men back to its mother who was squirting out a stream of thick brown shit as she chewed her cud. "Señorita, I think it's the pink eye." She nodded and, lifting a leg, like a dog and a fire hydrant, she thought, slid down. She walked over to the calf, seeing it was Fussnut, brushed aside a few flies, knelt and held his head as he bawled louder while she peered into the eye he was holding shut. Sure enough, there was the little white dot right in front of the eyeball. She nodded again. It was summer, after all. Still, it wasn't cloudy, or worse, turning blue yet.

Angel's walkie-talkie squawked. "Jefe," he spoke into it and listened, tucking it to his ear because of the poor range before responding, "Señorita Jessica aqui, Jefe." The radio squawked some more.

Angel shrugged and turned to Jessie. "Señor Van der Vaal wants Jake to look at it."

Her blackness deepened. Suddenly, angry for Angel, she blurted out, "Why? It's only pink eye. You can recognize it as well as me."

He turned up his hands and went over to speak to one of the hands. Turning back, he said, "Señorita, do you know where Jake is?" She shook her head. Turning his hands up again, he shrugged and began moving off to the truck.

She got up on Whip and tore off, jumping the gate again to terrorize a passing car, and turned Whip back up the track. Pounding the dirt, she felt the wind tearing at her hair, felt Whip's exhilaration at the pace, felt all her anger at this fucking world and being a woman in it coursing through her beating, thumping, hammering heart to match Whip's great, flying strides. Three fields and a drain ditch later, she raced past a tractor, clipping the tire with a hoof, and frightened for Whip, she pulled up to a stop.

"Hey, Jessie, hot enough for ya?" Old Ben Yamamoto smiled at her, a bit nervously. She got down without a word and began checking Whip's hooves, only sighing with relief when she could see that no harm was done.

Turning to Old Ben, she nodded, mumbling a "Sorry" and swung up to leave at a canter.

***

Trotting into the yard, she could see Andrew astride Digger, looking leaner and meaner now, she realized with a shock. Both of them, though the Egghead couldn't possibly look any leaner. Still, it looked like the riding was doing its thing, she mused, noting that he actually had biceps now. He was looking at the house when he saw her and colored. Fucking idiot, she swore to herself. Turning the corner of the house, she could see Jake standing, holding the door open, head down listening as he turned a pointed finger round and round as if whatever he was being treated to would not stop soon. "And Jacob, I want that mother led in. I sell pounds!"

"Yes, Pop." Turning, he beamed at Jessie and walked up to her. "So is it?"

"How should I know?" she began bitterly then, biting off her remark, regretted it.

"Because you're my Sticks. And just because Pop..." he broke off.

She shrugged and headed for the stable. "I've got to get dinner ready."

"Jessie, I'm just asking if I should bother bringing a lariat."

She turned at that. The Egghead watched them both, wondering what was up. "Better not let Pop hear you say that."

Jake beamed again. "Come on. Come with us. I'm only going to do one so Andrew can see it. Who knows when I'll get to do it again?"

She paused, considering, blinking away the unwelcome thought that Jake would be leaving them someday, soon. Then, she grinned savagely. "Let's bring two. I'll saddle up."

"You're on."

***

On the way over to the pasture, several halters, the two lariats, and some extra rope on their saddle horns, Jake explained to Andrew all about pink eye, how it popped up every summer, a nuisance, carried by flies from the head of one cow to the next, and the only thing to do was to quarantine the calves and cows that had it and spray 'em twice a day in the eyes until it went away. Worse ones you had to jab 'em in the eyelids with antibiotics. Even sew the occasional eyelid shut for a few weeks.

"Is it infectious?"

"Like a prairie fire. Which can make it expensive. Besides, it hurts 'em, makes 'em upset enough to stop gaining and we don't want that."

"Does it...get into the..."

"No, hoss. You won't get pink eye eating a hamburger."

"Oh."

Hanging back a bit as they talked, Jessie could see that Andrew was handling Digger quite well now. In fact, now that his gloves and boots were looking pretty well broke in, he had lost quite a bit of that shine of the store-bought cowboy. Reaching the gate to the field, empty of the ranch hands off working elsewhere, and feeling a bit foolish now about Yamamoto's tractor, Jessie decided to open the gate instead of jumping it. They all filed in. Andrew even walked Digger the gate closed.

"Pop said he wanted us to check the whole pasture. Good experience for hoss here, I 'spect. So, Sticks, how do you think we should handle this?"

Stunned at the question, Jessie sat there looking at him. The others waited, looking at her. After a moment or two, Jake shrugged, "D'ya suppose we should split up or...?"

Her mind working now, she thought a moment, then said, "Andrew, you've never..." She broke off as his face snapped to her eyes while coloring its usual strawberry red. Wondering exasperatedly what was wrong now, she then realized that it was probably the first time she had ever called him by name. Pushing aside that thought to focus on the matter at hand, she continued, "...seen pink eye, have you?"

His flush almost shining, he shook his head.

She looked around the pasture, shading her eyes in the afternoon sunlight, seeing about forty head, some laying down with their calves in the shadow, others grazing quietly, their calves tagging along behind, always searching out that elusive teat. "Okay, well, Jake, how 'bout you show Andrew what to look for while I get started." Though she tried to keep the skepticism of how much the Egghead would help out of her voice, she said, "If'n it's no more than two or three, you'll have no problem leading 'em in."

Jake smiled at her. "Yeah. I reckon we can handle two or three pairs just fine."

"I'll take the north and work my way back." Taking another look at the Egghead, sitting helplessly atop Digger, she added, "Let's just count up first and then decide."

Jake nodded again. "Okay, hoss. I think I can see one squinting from here. Follow me." He kneed Asa into the herd and Andrew turned Digger to follow.

Jessie walked Whip slowly through the herd. On the far side, she spotted Fussnut right away. Checking his mother and finding nothing wrong, she put a halter on her and led her to the fence to tie her up. Dutifully scampering along, the calf followed them. In the distance, she could see that Jake and Andrew had already split up and were working their way slowly through the herd on their end. Trust, she thought, then irritated, rubbed her sweaty nose and decided to check the calf shelter in case some heifer decided the heat was a little much.

In all, to her vexation, it turned out to be five calves, two heifers and three steers. None of their mothers showed anything, as she suspected, because of their insecticide ear tags. Most of the troubled calves were just showing signs of beginning irritation but one of the steers was already growing cloudy. Ten cattle in all to take back to the corral. With calves you couldn't do much about flies, she knew, but noticing some ridges of tall grass that should have been cut back to help keep this kind of thing away, Jessie asked herself if Pop's money problems were forcing him to start letting things go before shoving that thought deep, down inside her. She frowned, pulling at her ponytail and wondering again how much Andrew was going to get in the way or whether he could manage Digger well enough to take a side. While she was considering, she suddenly felt a jet of anger again that she wasn't asked to help out, not even with this routine task of the summer. Jake threw out a lariat and began coiling it, interrupting her thoughts. She grinned, suddenly ridiculously happy that Jake was home.

"So how d'ya want to do this?"

She smiled over at Andrew. "Would you count for us?"

"Sure." He smiled, confusedly. He had a not bad smile, she thought suddenly. When he relaxed.

"Nah. Let's do it for real. At the same time. We'll rig slip knots, we've got the rope. Opposite sides of the pasture, this end."

"All right," she laughed. Looking over the pinkeyed calves, though, she frowned at the thought of bothering them, knowing they weren't going to like the next week of their lives. Instead, glancing around, she pointed out two steer calves farther down the pasture, butting heads as they capered back and forth together. "Let's use those two. They look about the same size."

"Good idea. They could use a little exercise from the looks of 'em."

"Oh!"

Jake and Jessie both turned at the sound, staring at Andrew.

"I sell pounds! Now, I get it. He doesn't want us to run the...fat off of them."

Jessie screamed out laughing, delightedly, feeling like a girl again. Happy. Andrew began to blush again, then stopped when Jake began laughing, too. "That's right, hoss. If Pop had his way, they'd be born in a stall and stay that way their entire short lives."

"Not if I can help it." Jessie surprised herself blurting this out. Jake only smiled. "Anyway, let's get to it."

"Right."

They led the haltered cows and their pinkeyed calves down to the herd giving them lots of room. Then, acting the clown, Jessie strutted around in front of one of the steer calves, distracting it long enough for Andrew, instructed by Jake, to grab its hind hooves while Jake threw on a shortened halter and, together, they dragged it, bawling, to tie it to a slip knot on the fence in their end of the field. They did the same for the other, tying it to the fence on the opposite side.

Leading Whip over to her calf, she was surprised to see Andrew trotting Digger up to her. "Do you mind if I...I judge?" he stammered out. "Jake said it was...was fine with him."

"Sure."

"Good. The only thing is...I don't...know what to look for. Jake said I should ask you."

"Oh." Laughing with delight again, she thought a moment, then simply said, "Calf is down on the ground all tied up and first hands in the air wins. Oh, and, we'll each start, mounted, about thirty feet from the calf. When you give the signal, we pull the slip knots letting 'em free."

"Okay. Seems easy enough. I'll uh..." squinting back to the edge of the pasture, he pointed, "...be over there. And...uh...throw my hat in the air to start."

"Sounds good." She watched him trot off across the pasture to Jake, wonderingly. Before she knew it, however, Jake and Andrew were already in position. She waited, the end of the rope holding the slip knot to her calf in hand, another rope clenched in her teeth, watching Andrew out of the corner of her eye behind her but staying focused on her calf. Suddenly, Digger reared and for a split second she thought a snake or something and that Andrew was going to get thrown but, no, there he was lifting his hat at the height of Digger's rear. Sonofabitch, she thought, yanking the slip knot free even as she was heeling Whip to explode out of their stance. Pounding down toward the calf, she saw its eyes rolling as it frantically scattered downfield to find its mother in the herd. Whirling her lariat over her head, she saw the calf start zig-zagging crazily across the field, the dusty sunlight picking up brown highlights in its black hide, then suddenly turn around to head right back where it had started. As she turned Whip in its path, making it skirt around them, she swore and wondered if she'd just lost. Twisting in the saddle away from the glimpse of Jake's calf already down as he dismounted, she threw that thought with her lariat out over her shoulder, watched the loop settle neatly around the calf's heaving shoulders and pulled Whip to a sharp, hard wheel, hearing both the steer stop dead in its tracks with a bang and the lariat tied to her saddle horn sing with the quivering strain. Knowing her horse, feeling Whip's stand, she didn't bother looking to see if the steer was fully down, but was already dismounting and turning toward it, tasting salty grit on her tongue, one hand following the lariat to her steer struggling on the ground. Arriving just as the calf was starting to wriggle around so as to get up, she grabbed the two hind hooves, wrenched the rope out of her mouth, feeling something tear, and looped them together, then grabbed a fore hoof and added it to the pair. Panting, she wildly threw up her hands.

And looked over. Jake was just tying the fore hoof! He began to throw up his hands as he looked over at her, then seeing hers raised, stopped. Instead, he pumped the air with a clenched fist and let out a throat-ripping whoop. He jumped up, then started running toward her, with a limp she saw. She ran to him, seeing Andrew and Digger pounding toward them. They met in the field with Andrew managing a running dismount, no less. Jake threw his arms around her and for a moment, she felt like a little girl whose best happiness was her older brother's hand in hers at the fair. Andrew stood back, like he was wondering what to do, until Jake released her and began thumping Andrew on the back. "Tripped! Fucking tripped! Did'ja see that!?" He whooped again and thumped Jessie on the back now. "Fucking bastard kicked me, the little cocksucker! Whew!" He paused and leaned on one leg, rubbing the other. "Ow! Sonofabitch!"

Jessie, still panting, leaned over his leg. "How bad is it?"

"Dunno."

"Try walking it off," she suggested.

He nodded and began limping down the pasture. She watched him for a bit, then turning to Andrew, said, "He'll be all right. Knock some sense into him." She stopped, realizing that Andrew was staring at her, his eyes glowing.

Growing uncomfortable, she felt her cheeks burning and asked, "What?"

He suddenly looked down and mumbled something about "poetry." She didn't want to think about what that meant, so she decided to change the subject. Before she could say anything, though, he managed, "You're bleeding." She reached up to her mouth and felt it, remembering ripping the rope out.

"It's nothing." Seeing the cattle trough nearby, she walked over to it, nudged a cow's head out of the way, and splashed some water on her face and the back of her neck.

Looking back at Andrew, she saw him wincing. "What now?"

"Uh...is that...hygienic?"

She snorted. "So you can make Digger rear?"

He flashed a glance at her, then said, "Oh. I...well...I..." before trailing off. She waited, then shook her head, feeling annoyed all over again. What was it with him, she wondered?

Jake began limping back toward them, a little more easily now. "I showed him. I know you don't like it, Sticks. But I was so proud of how quickly he's coming along, I asked him what he wanted for a prize."

She turned toward Andrew again, wonderingly. "And you chose rearing a horse?"

"Yes...yes," he mumbled, looking away.

She smiled, throwing up her hands. "Well, just be careful with that, okay? He's old. And you're young. As a rider."

He nodded.

***

Herding the cows and their pinkeyed calves along the tractor paths home turned out not to be difficult after all. She took the lead, to keep an eye out for traffic and other whatnot, old Sow right behind her with the others all falling into place, and Jake and Andrew each took a flank. Andrew managed his flank, the fields side, quite well only losing one calf to some alfalfa until she rode back to help. Jake was right. Andrew was coming along quickly. Dinner that night was a light-hearted affair, though she had to rush to fry the chicken, with the three of them working hard not to chuckle at Jake's made-up story about tripping in the shed and smacking his thigh on the baler. Pop only nodded and said, "Farming is the most dangerous occupation..." and asked for another slice of pie. Then he abruptly asked, "What were you doing in the hay shed, Jacob?" Jake looked dumbfounded for a moment until Andrew cleared his throat and asked Pop to tell about the good deal he had gotten, way back, on the railroad ties for the corral.

Pop slapped the table, saying, "Good. So. Willem calls me one day. He says, 'Guess what I just heard about Burlington Northern.'" As Pop wound up into the retelling of one of his favorite yarns, Jake smiled with relief at Andrew and sat back to listen with all due attention.

Jessie felt a bit silly about the rebellious satisfaction that pulling one over on Pop gave her, but she finally decided not to care and to enjoy it. Later, as she took her night ride lying back on Whip, she replayed the sensations of dismounting from Whip and running down the lariat toward the steer again and again, as if it were a dream.

***

The next morning, Sunday, she heard Pop talking to Jake while ironing her dress. "It's past time, Jacob. Everyone's been asking for you and Andrew this last month," he was saying.

"Yes, Pop." She smiled at the thought of Jake finally attending church. He had been able to skip so far, claiming he needed the time to train Andrew. No such luck this morning, she chuckled. Even Pop had noticed how well Andrew was handling Digger bringing in the cattle yesterday afternoon. A few minutes later, Jake looked in, all sleep-tousled. "Catch a ride with you, Sticks?"

"Sure." She turned away trying to hide her grin. "Better hurry. Sunday School starts in twenty minutes."

"Sunday School!"

"Just kidding. I'm only going to the service, too."

"Whew. God, you had me there!"

"Jacob." Pop's voice floated down from the top of the stairs.

"Yes, Pop." He went to stone, his eyes widening.

"Don't make Jessica late."

"Yes, Pop." The door slammed followed by the sound of Pop's old pickup grumbling its own way to a Sunday morning start. Jake growled.

Feeling sorry for him, Jessie stopped ironing. "Tell you what. We've got a good hour or so. Let's ride."

"Now you're talking."

She grinned, feeling again how nice it was to have Jake home and pushed her dress off the board to drop onto the floor. "I still got some batter. I'll put on some pancakes for you both if you get moving."

"Give us ten minutes."

***

At the breakfast table, with the sun painting the room a nice, bright gold, the three of them sat talking and laughing over yesterday's roping. It felt like old times for Jessie, and she relived the stunned silence that day a few years ago that had greeted Jake's request for them to be let off of Sunday School. Pop had kept staring at them, saying nothing then reaching for his Bible when Jake had blurted out, "We promise to keep up with our Bible reading, don't we, Sticks?" She had nodded quickly. "And we'll never be late for service. It's just that, well, Pop, everybody's so...old there."

At that, Pop had smiled and shaken his head before finally agreeing. "You're good children, Jacob. The Lord's blessing in a bountiful life." Then, he had paused, thinking, "I wonder if that is why so few youngsters come anymore to Sunday School and Prayer Meeting." Jake had earlier gotten them out of that weekly Wednesday night gathering, pleading homework to Pop's grudging agreement. "Perhaps you could call all the youngsters for your own Sunday School? I'm sure you could use the loft or Pastor Don's living room."

Jake had gone to stone, looking stunned at the suggestion. Jessie had had to bite her tongue not to laugh at the thought of Jake leading a Bible lesson. Eventually, Jake had mumbled a "It's a thought" before never mentioning it ever again. As it was, Pop had felt it important to break out the Daily Bread's lesson of the day, making Jake read aloud the passage from Jeremiah and take the first whack at explaining it. "Before I formed you in the womb, I knew you." She smiled at the memory, reflecting that it was one of the few verses that she ever liked wholeheartedly. She had never been able to see the worth of church so regular, other than to make Pop happy. She had always figured that God knew all about it, making her that way, and had left it at that.

Suddenly realizing the time, she drank up her coffee and said, "Jake, Andrew, you two'd better saddle up." At the sound of his name, Andrew paused with his fork stuck in his mouth, staring at her. Trying not to roll her eyes, she continued, "Pop'll skin us if'n we don't get there on time."

It was a beautiful ride. In fields along the way, with a hawk soaring high above for company, they could see the lazy ballet of line after line of sprinklers throwing out their morning offering to the parched earth, their great ten foot high wheels rusting quietly in the morning's heat. Pausing to watch a rainbow doing its sparkling dance over a water line, a sight she never tired of no matter how often she saw it, she spotted a coyote in the distance skulking along the side of an irrigation ditch and, glancing quickly at Jake, thought a prayer of thanks that he wasn't carrying a rifle. Whip danced a few steps herself, rousing Jessie from her reverie to hear their conversation.

Andrew was asking about the service. "So it's Protestant, right?"

"Well, I suppose. It's called non-denominational."

"It's not Catholic."

Jake laughed. "Yes, hoss, it's definitely not Catholic."

Andrew looked thoughtful, as if he were looking at something inside of his brain. "That means a longer sermon."

"What do you mean longer?"

"Well, it's not a five or ten minute homily, like Catholic priests give."

"Only five minutes? Shoot, Sticks, maybe we should become Catholic," Jake said, laughing again.

She grinned. Feeling Whip's bouncing energy again, she leaned down to pat her neck and asked Jake, "Race? End of the next field?"

He looked her over, then down at Asa, as if measuring. "Well..." he began, then suddenly heeled Asa into a jumping gallop. Swearing, she caught a glimpse of something like longing in Andrew's eyes as she kicked Whip into a frenzy. Down the tractor path she pounded after Jake, laughing that as young and fit as Asa was, Jake was going to need a head-start to take on her and Whip. Feeling, rather than seeing, the sway of the nearby alfalfa, almost tall enough for its next cutting, she settled into Whip's cheery stride and that delight for which she had no name: a horse and her rider as one, now aloft carried by the air, now returning to the earth to spring forth once more. Asa was doing her best, especially with Jake spurring her on, the edge of this field coming quickly, the tractor path rising to cross over a dirt road and mark its end, but they were catching them. In a flash, Asa was pounding up the rise. And stopped. Jake turned back to look at her.

Jessie snorted. Jake was getting old for his age, she thought and kept Whip going hell for leather bounding up the rise, the stunned anger screwing up Jake's face growing larger with each stride. Just as they began to reach the top, and she was preparing a huge grin for him, he whipped off his hat and waved it in Whip's passing head. Who reared. Up she went, her instincts squeezing her knees to Whip's flanks before she realized she was doing it. Up she stretched, as far as she could, having no stirrups to stand on. Up Whip flung her hooves, throwing out a loud neighing protest, beginning in her lungs to explode out of her nose and strike the air beyond her reach. Up to the height of everything best in this world and Jessie sparked a reckless joy. But they had to come down, too, and as they did, she wrenched Whip hard to the left so as not to hit Asa.

"What the hell are you doing?" Jake's angry eyes flashed at her over his outstretched hat pointing down to a group of hands gathered around a wheel sprinkler, hoes in hand, staring up at them in confusion, their truck parked across the tractor path right in their way.

She shrugged. "Nothing."

Jake stopped at that, the remark she could see half-formed in his open mouth, his tongue curled at the ready, died before he could start saying it. He looked at her. Really looked at her. Almost as if her were seeing inside her.

Jessie turned away, not wanting to feel him cutting her open like that, but said nothing. In the distance, she could hear Andrew trotting Digger down the field. She looked back at him. Could see his confusion mounting as they drew closer and he could see something in Jake that made him concerned. At the bottom of the rise, he stopped Digger. "What's...?"

The hands, shaking their heads, went back to their work, fanning across the field to hoe the mint. She glanced at Jake who was still staring at her, but now with a look of deep sadness filling his eyes.

"Let's get going. Pop will be looking for us." She reined Whip down the path, threaded her between the truck, now starting to reverse back out onto the road, and the handful of workers still standing around. "Buenos dias!" She greeted them with a grin, still feeling the weight of Jake's eyes on her.

***

"Pants, Jessie?" At the top of the stairs, Pastor Don's florid cheeks over his tremendous belly frowned down at her. Biting her lip, she now regretted her earlier rebellion. She felt the grip on her Bible turn sweatier as she wondered what to say.

"Ah, that was my doing, Pastor Don. How you doing? Hot enough for ya?" Jake's cheerful voice boomed out from the hitching post as he took over Andrew's bungling attempts to tie up Digger. "I missed Spring Roundup, you know, and so I asked Sticks to ride with us."

"Jake! It's great to see you. Finally." His wide smile seemed to belie the last word of disapproval, almost. But then, she considered, Pastor Don was never disappointed for long. She began to look past him into the church's parlor.

"We just broke up Sunday School," Pastor Don was saying. "Should be a good service today, we've got--"

"That the women should dress themselves modestly and decently in suitable clothing, not with their hair braided, or with gold, pearls, or expensive clothes, but with good works as is proper for women who profess reverence for God." Andrew's quiet voice seemed to fill the entire yard, drowning out even a passing car. Jessie swore softly, thinking how little she could use the Egghead's help right now. Turning to warn him with a flash of her eyes, she was startled to see him staring at Pastor Don with his mouth half-open.

"First Timothy, chapter two, verses nine and ten!" Pastor Don's smile lit up with surprise and delight. "You must be Andrew, Jake's friend that I've been hearing so much about. Welcome! A man of the Lord is always welcome at this church."

"Thank--thank you," Andrew stammered, almost bowing a bit. Jesus, she thought.

"Andrew's a real Biblical scholar, Pastor Don." Jake was now pulling out a couple of Bibles from his saddlebag.

"Is that so?"

"Yep. He, uh, inspires me to read my Bible more." Jessie stifled a snort.

"That is good to hear! However, as fruitful as the Apostle Paul's admonitions are to us every day of our lives, today's reading is from a different book." Almost bouncing on his toes with anticipation, his belly bouncing in rhythm, she thought, he cocked an eyebrow at Jake. "How about it? Soldiers of Christ! Where are your swords?" Without thinking, Jessie raised her Bible, as did Jake. "Mark, chapter four, verses thirty-five to forty-one."

Jake beamed in response while Andrew began looking inside his brain again. They all waited on Jake to see what would come out, a couple of cars slowing outside the church and turning into the drive. "Well...," he said, mounting the steps to stand next to her. "I 'spect it's got something to say about faith."

"Jacob Van der Vaal, you have not changed one bit!" Pastor Don's chortling laugh rang out as he began pounding Jake on the back. After a few more slaps, he raised his nose at Andrew. "How about it? Care to try?"

Jake turned to Andrew with a smile of grand pride. "I bet he can do it!" Jessie turned to watch Andrew, enjoying the way his eyes scoped the inside of his head.

"Uh...the windstorm?" Andrew frowned in concentration.

"Yeesss..." Pastor Don's eyes were now sparkling as he absentmindedly nodded good morning to other members walking up the steps.

"Uh...I can't do it all, but...He woke up and...re-- rebuked the wind and..." Unreal, Jessie thought, even with his stupid stuttering. "...and said to the sea, 'Peace! Be still!'" Andrew shifted his weight to the other leg, still looking inward, his eyes following the path of another car crunching gravel as it turned into the drive. "The--then the wind ceased, and there was a de--dead calm. He said to them, 'Why are you afraid? Have you still no faith?'"

"Amen. And when the tempests of Satan torment us, we are called upon to deepen our faith in our Lord, our Savior, Jesus Christ...But I'm getting ahead of myself." He peered down at Andrew. "Well, Andrew, I can see that I'm gonna have to be at my very best today." The beginning chords of a hymn from inside startled him. "Goodness!" he said, turning to step inside. "Jake! Bring Andrew to Prayer Meeting!"

"Yes, Pastor Don." Following Pastor Don, Jessie heard a subdued "Ow!" Turning back, she saw Andrew clutching his shin and Jake's cheerful beam bounding past her into the church.

Slamming the tool shed's freezer door shut, Jessie coughed in the dust, grateful for the iciness of last year's corn, put up in tubs, biting into her arms. Sunday afternoons were her prep time for the meals to follow all the next week. Ten mouths to feed at lunch was a lot, not that she minded it now with Jake and Andrew home, so long as she could draw up her lists of what to cook ahead of time. That way, she could spend as little time as possible thinking about it during the week. Pork chops, she suddenly thought. They hadn't had that in a while. She wondered if they still had some in the basement freezer. Sensing something missing while passing by the stable, she stepped in to look around and immediately saw that Digger and his tack were gone. Whip poked her head over her stall door, whinnying a hello. Asa soon followed. Over in the tack corner, she saw to her delighted surprise that Whip's saddle, used for the first time in years the other day, was neatly polished and stood on end, with the stirrups curled carefully under the seat, and the tin of saddle soap next to it with a cloth folded neatly underneath. She smiled at the thought of who had done that for her.

Balancing her bundle of corn, she walked out to the corral and found Jake perched atop the fence reading a piece of paper, his face a stony blank. At the sound of her steps, he jerked around, cramming the paper in his pocket. Then, seeing it was her, he relaxed.

"Andrew took Digger out on his own?"

"Yep. His first solo."

"Where'd he go?"

"Halverson's spread."

Jessie wrinkled her nose in disgust. "Why?"

"An errand. His golden fleece, you might say."

She waited for him to say something more only seeing his sly grin spreading slowly across his face.

"What'd you send him to get?"

"Well. The day we were coming over the pass, I was telling him about how feed lots finished up cattle for the packers, so he asked to see one. We stopped there so I could show him a large one." He paused, his grin growing wider yet.

"And? Did he like it?"

"Well, he was disappointed that I couldn't point out which cattle there were ours." He paused for a moment. "Halverson's gotten bigger since I've seen it last."

Jessie grimaced.

Jake went on, "But he did admire how all the lots were bull-dozed up into peaks at the center, see. He liked that. Until I explained to him they did that so the manure could slide downhill."

Jessie snorted.

"After that, he didn't think so much of how they run things."

"Who would?" She frowned, then sighed. "Well, at least it's better than having to stand all year round in their own shit. Not much. But better." Then, thinking of Halverson's big, beefy face, she glowered. "So long as they keep bulldozing it away from the bunk." In her mind's eye, she saw long lines of cattle stumbling through manure as they bent their heads to the trough at feeding time.

"Exactly what I pointed out to him. But you know Andrew. He whined about it lacking poetry or something..." Jessie giggled, in spite of herself. "So, when he asked to take a solo today, I told him he could so long as he brings me back a handful of Halverson manure."

"Oh, Jake!" She started laughing so hard, she dropped a couple of tubs. After bending to pick them up, she again noticed the paper in his hand. "What's that?"

Looking down at it, he shook his head, the laughter dying in his eyes. "Orders."

She felt the blackness step toward her, from a distance, silently, yet steadily, as if it were hunting her. Off in the distance, the flat, wide cone of Mt. Adams beckoned, its happy, running horse melting as the summer slowly nibbled away at the glacier adorning it.

"How soon?"

He sighed. "A week. They moved up my entry date for Airborne School and everything else slides forward." Looking down at the paper, he squinted in the bright sunshine. "Emailed me this morning. Just got it. Report Ft. Lewis next Sunday to catch the next available transport yada yada yada..."

She carefully set the tubs down and slowly climbed the fence, feeling pain in each step.

"Damn. I thought I'd have more time. Still, when Uncle Sam calls, I gotta respond."

She said nothing, just stared out at the fading horse on Mt. Adams. Jake stared with her.

At last he stirred. "Well, that's what I get for being a good soldier and checking. There's usually a maintenance convoy heads to Lewis from the firing grounds off of Manastash Ridge Saturdays. Maybe Angel'll drive me to their barracks. Have to leave early, though."

Trying to focus on this detail, she asked, "How early?"

"'Bout four." She nodded. "Don't worry about breakfast." She nodded. Straightening up, he looked at her. "Say, Pop said Esmeralda's got two kids now."

Surprised at this new question, she looked at him. "Yeah. Ramon is three. Teresa is almost one."

"Antoine still the world's original fool?"

She chuckled, feeling the cloud recede a bit. "Yes."

"Interesting."

Unable to muster all that much indignation, she softly whistled. "Jacob Jedidiah Van der Vaal, Esmeralda is a married woman with a family."

"Who're probably demanding so much of her she's forgotten what it feels like to be wooed."

Shaking her head, she laughed quietly. Jake's conquests had been far too numerous for too long to do anything but smile. "Antoine still spraying fertilizer for Takeshita's?"

Though unwilling to admit it, she began to feel a certain admiration. "Yes."

"I wonder if he was in that rig we saw over on Lateral C coming back from church."

"Could be."

"Excellent." He stood up and jumped down. "Greet the returning hero for me, would ya? I won't be too long."

"Whatever."

***

Looking up from her choice of a roast chicken and potatoes for, maybe Thursday she thought, she saw Andrew through the kitchen window, trotting proudly into the yard, his sweaty grin happily lighting up his face. Seeing his all too obvious delight took her back to her first ride, so many years ago it seemed, on old Nugget. So long in the tooth, so wide in the girth, Nugget could barely manage a canter, but it didn't matter. She was all Jessie's. After Mom had taken that hoof straight in the forehead diving behind a work horse to snatch Jake from harm, Pop wouldn't let any of his family left near a horse. Until she had got it into her head one day that she needed one and asked, watching him convulsively reach for his Bible as he frowned way up to the eyebrows in silence. It took reading every book the school library had on horses, blue ribbons in caring for other people's horses at 4H, and three Christmases in a row asking for one thing and one thing only to change his mind.

She used to stand for hours it seemed grooming Nugget in her stall. Brushing her dry golden brown hide in long sweeps, arcing over the neck, flanks and rear, wondering what it would be like to groom a horse that could actually work up a sweat, trying to braid her frustratingly sparse mane and tail, checking her shoes to pry out non-existent pebbles and polishing the tack to a high gleam after every single ride, Nugget was Jessie's total happiness in junior high. And when Nugget had suddenly taken ill one bitterly frozen morning, she had gone almost crazy the following weeks with worry, wrapping her with blankets that seemed to do no good, pushing the best alfalfa hay they could get in her mouth only to have Nugget spit it out, pleading tearfully to get her to stand again, even sneaking out one night to spend the night next to her in the stall until Pop, his eyes long and sad peering out at her from the scarf wrapped around his head, found her and made her go back to bed. The next day, Pop had helplessly prescribed the "twenty-three cent pill" but, unable to do it himself at the last, she had slowly took the shotgun from his hand and, with him bracing it, placed the muzzle next to Nugget brains, had took one last look into that deep brown eye looking up at her and pulled both triggers.

She sighed. She frowned, realizing she was pulling at her ponytail and wondering what made her think of Nugget, but couldn't remember. Shaking her head, she put down the pen and decided to make good on her promise.

However, as she drew near the stable doors, she could hear Andrew inside talking, so she paused just outside. "Jake thinks you're old and fat, but we know better, don't we?" he was saying over the rasps of his brush combing the hide. "We even got up to a gallop today, didn't we? Almost. You did really well today, Digger. Maybe we'll even try it without the saddle one of these days." She heard Digger's answering whiffle and though she couldn't see it, she could imagine that Andrew was standing close by, Digger's nose resting on Andrew's shoulder as he breathed in all that glorious steaming horseflesh. After a few moments of silence, accompanied only by the sound of the evening breeze just picking up, she heard a "You can even rear now, can't you?" followed by a few more rasps. "Well, we showed them. Though, tell you the truth, Digger, having done it now, I can't really see what all the...fuss...is about." She smiled at his self-conscious use of the word and tiptoed away.

At lunch the next day, over Angel's faltering explanation for the broken belt slowing them down on the alfalfa cutting, Jessie looked across the crowded table at Jake's smug smile and realized that she knew all there was to know about how Esmeralda was taking his shipping out. She began grousing to herself at the weak stupidity of some women, but stifled it when Pop looked her way for interrupting Angel's confession and dug into her ice cream. Taking Whip out for her daily run, she saw Andrew trotting Digger bareback in the yard, perched helplessly atop, jouncing this way and that with each jolt, his face all screwed up in frustration as he tried to squeeze Digger with his knees. Jake patiently stood nearby, making suggestions.

"God knows why you want to do this, hoss. Other than the chariot, the stirrup has been one of the most important military innovations for all time." She let her laughter dance after her as she took Whip into an immediate canter down the back road.

***

That night, after dinner, as she lay back on Whip's haunches and took in the bright oranges and purples sweeping across the evening sky and its first, faint star, she was surprised to hear Jake stop Asa just outside the pasture gate. "Sticks." She sat up, looking over at him, seeing Andrew astride a saddled Digger waiting next to him. "Do you want to come with us?"

Too surprised to say anything, she simply nodded.

Jake led them a pleasant ride, threading their way, mostly single-file, after the usual roads through hilly peach and apple orchards, making Jessie wonder if they might be Uncle Willem's, working their way toward the hills surrounding the corner of the valley. Jessie was just glad to be invited along, so she didn't break the silence, and focused instead on the deepening hues of the evening watching them slowly turn the hills dark golds and blues. The breeze sang a little more strongly now, particularly through the low branches of the trees with their hard little fruits, their coming sweet fragrance just hinted at, passing them by. Finally, turning out of the latest orchard, he stopped at a gate with those large signs she hated so much saying "Property of the Yakama Nation. NO TRESPASSING." Her school friend, Nora Whitefeather, had once told her why the tribe had changed its name to spelling with it with the third "a" but Jessie couldn't remember, just that, usual for Nora, it was a long explanation full of the Creator's purpose and the elders' dreams that had begun it. In any case, much as she didn't like this new law, she thought it should be respected, at least for Nora's sake and sighed at the memory of Nora telling her at graduation that they wouldn't be walking the same road anymore for a long time.

As he reached out to undo the binding wire, she said, "Jake..."

"What they don't know won't hurt 'em," he said with a beam at her flashing in the fading light and went on untwisting it.

Too right, she thought with a spurt of anger and followed them through, then walking Whip the gate closed. The road slowly rising ahead, smooth in most places, was wide enough for them to ride abreast, Jake taking the middle. After some more silent riding, as they watched the hills gradually meet them, pausing now and then to look at more and more of the rest of the valley left below, he suddenly threw out, "Tell you what, though. Tommy Franks, he'd be the commanding general if it came to that. By reputation, he's no fool. He does his homework."

Suddenly intrigued at the realization that she was about to be let in on what they talked about by themselves, Jessie said nothing and just stared ahead, as if she weren't there.

"Do you think he's going to start working on an invasion plan soon?" Andrew asked, steering Digger around a rock in his path.

Jake chuckled. "Start? It was probably done years ago."

"Really?"

"Hoss, that's all staff work is, laying on military plans. All the possible alternatives for just about any scenario."

"I never guessed."

"Planning, laying on the logistics if such and such happens. Or if something different happens. Hell...," he paused, turning back to look at the lights dotting the yards of the different farms below. "They've probably got a plan for the day that the Canadians try to take Union Gap," he said, nodding over to the far side, where the glow of city lights could be seen arcing up over the hills of the valley.

"Weird."

"Tell you a story, hoss. Six-Day War, 1967. Israel knew that it was surrounded by a bunch of neighbors that just as soon'd push them into the Med as not. So when things started getting dicey, they didn't sit on their hands, began instead calculating the strengths of the different forces that would be coming after 'em, decided that Egypt's air force was a key. So on the morning when all the talking had pretty much ended, the Hebs struck first and took 'em out. Bombed them all as they sat in their neat little rows on the ground."

"And that was it?"

"Pretty much. At seven o'clock the Egyptians had a mighty air force that was going to bomb Tel Aviv into the stone age. By ten, they had a heap of scrap metal. Oh, there was some more shooting and tank battles and such. But everyone already knew which way it was going to go."

"They couldn't have talked it all out, first?"

"Hoss." Jake shook his head, then looked over at Jessie. "Andrew here, despite his first-hand taste to the contrary, persists in this delusion that you can work out just about anything."

Andrew looked down, then off at the hills. Though she couldn't see it in the fading light, Jessie could almost feel the burning on his cheeks, and smiled. Still, she was taken aback to catch this glimpse into Jake's world and felt a little jealous that Andrew got to see it all the time.

"You don't even have to go that far. What do you suppose happened at Pearl Harbor? Same thing. Thank god most of the fleet was out on maneuvers that Sunday morning." Warming to his theme, Jake picked up their pace from the walk into a light trot. "The Germans started it in World War I. High Field Command began laying the first war plans. Caught the limeys and frogs with their pants down. By the time they finally got moving, they wound up in trenches for the next three years lobbing shells at one another to little effect. Tell you what. After that debacle, all the major powers started investing in war plans divisions."

"Well, I suppose it has its value." Andrew allowed, reluctantly.

"Yeah, I know. You hate it all the same," Jake responded cheerfully, leaving the road now to take them up to a spreading level where they could dismount and hobble the horses, Andrew fussing a bit with Digger's.

Jake stood for a while in the night looking out over the valley, and they watched him. Then, sighing, he shook his head and said, "Not that it's my problem anymore. I just hope they give me some NCOs who know their men." She watched him, wondering what to say, when he suddenly beamed, calling out, "Libations!" before walking over to Asa's saddlebag and undoing the buckle.

"Are you serious?" Andrew looked at him, the lights from below floating up to catch his gape of amazement.

"Yep." Jake took out a six pack of beer to Jessie's gasp. "Don't have too many nights left in the valley. Time to make some last memories." Throwing her one, he said, "Don't worry, I've got gum, too. Don't forget to tap 'em!"

He tapped the top of his a few times, cracked it open and sat down to survey the view some more. Andrew opened his and sat down next to him, taking a sip. Jessie stood there, uncertainly, wondering what to do. Beer. She wondered what it would taste like. Finally, feeling Jake's eyes looking for her, she tapped her can and opened it, and sat next to them taking an experimental sip. Thin and sour, she thought, making a face, but making herself drink some more. Then, wanting to feel like she was fitting in, rather than sitting there like a rock, she threw out at Andrew, "So whatever happened to your golden fleece?"

He looked at her in confusion as Jake, mid-gulp, choked and began spluttering and coughing to struggle out a weak, "Bastard."

Andrew laughed.

Jessie began slapping Jake on the back until he lifted a hand to get her to stop. "Son of a bitch stuck it in my bed!"

"What?!" Jessie screamed with laughter.

Jake nodded over at Andrew's huge grin, booming out, "Yes!" He aimed a playful punch at Andrew's arm, then continued, his own grin spreading across his face to catch the new moonlight. "So there I am. All tired out from the exertions of the afternoon..."

"I bet!" Jessie cut in.

He laughed some more, clearly relishing the telling. "I crawl into bed, feeling some lump near the end. So I reach out, thinking it might be Cocoa buried under there but instead I find it's an old rag all gathered up and making me wonder what the hell? I take it out, find out there's a plastic bag inside." He was now laughing hard enough at himself, he could barely finish it. "I open that, and it's...a bunch of cattle shit!"

"Halverson cattle shit!" Andrew crowed, to Jessie's surprise.

" Halverson cattle shit," Jake agreed. "You sure got me on that one, hoss."

"I was going to tell you that I had gotten it, but I could see your mind was on other things." Andrew smiled and they all laughed long and hard to the accompaniment of a coyote's wail far off in the distance. Jessie sat there in almost complete contentment, feeling the last waves of heat rising from the ground around them, marveling only at how different it was to see Jake let a friend talk to him like this, and glad that she got to see it now that he was leaving so soon.

They sat quietly for a few more minutes, until Jake said, "Oh, by the way, Sticks. Had a short talk with Pop after dinner."

"Uh-huh."

"He feels, and I agree, that it would be good for your character development to go along with us to Prayer Meeting."

"Jake!" she wailed.

He laughed, a great thundering laugh that seemed to echo off the hills around them.

"I'm looking forward to it," Andrew said.

"Only cuz you've never been to one." He sighed. "Well, why not? Just for shits and giggles. Hope the pie is good."

"What do they talk about?"

Jessie snorted. "Oh, it's just a bunch of whining about how Satan is tormenting 'em and how good it is that they have Jesus on their side."

"Oh now, Sticks. You're going to give the visiting egghead here the wrong idea about our local culture."

"Yeah, right."

"Well," he said, looking at Andrew. "It does get a bit long at times."

"I'm still looking forward to it. I've never been to anything like that."

Jessie paused in her self-pity to sneak a glance at Andrew but couldn't tell from the night. It didn't sound like he was joking. He actually sounded like he really meant it. She wondered why.

Jake sighed long and loud, then waved his beer across the entire valley before looking significantly at her. "Jardín del Paraíso."

She hit him. Hard. In the face with a good strong fist, throwing her hip into it just like he'd taught her. Jake's beer went sprawling on the slope in front of him.

"What?!" Andrew almost jumped.

She glared at Jake, hating him.

Wiping his face, his eyes serious now, Jake said, "It's okay, hoss. I suppose I deserved it."

"You fucking better did!" Jessie growled at him.

She stared at him, her breath heaving in and out of her, Andrew's alarmed features just over Jake's shoulder, trying to understand, while Jake softly, slowly reached out a hand to her shoulder. She batted it aside once, twice, then finally let him pat her softly on the shoulder. "I wasn't looking to read it. I just found it on the table one afternoon, opened it and read a paragraph before I knew what I was doing. Then, I closed it."

"Mother-fucker."

"Would somebody...?" Andrew's unfinished question hovered in the night air.

"Well, hoss, Pop may think that Sticks here is made out of porcelain, but you're getting the real deal."

Slightly mollified by this, Jessie sniffed, then downed the rest of her beer. Jake opened one for her and one for himself, looking over at Andrew who shook his head, saying, "I have memories of almost drowning in this just before we left Seattle."

"That?" Jake looked at him with a grin, rubbing his eye where she had hit him. "That was nothing." He took a sip, then looked back at Jessie. "Do you mind if I tell him?"

She sat for a while not knowing what she thought, just angry as hell. Eventually, she grumbled, "Why not? Seeing as how you've already half-done it."

Jake smiled quietly this time. Looking over at Andrew, he said, "I read a bit of Sticks' diary..." At the tightening of her shoulders, he quickly threw out, "By mistake. Jardín del Paraíso is her nickname for the ranch."

"It's beautiful."

Jessie started to bridle, but then realized that she recognized what Andrew sounded like when he really meant something. She sniffed again.

"What does it mean? If you don't mind my asking."
She glanced over and saw Andrew looking at her, the
polite expression in his eyes coming through his tone
if not the darkness.

She didn't say anything. She wondered how to
explain it, even if she wanted to.

After a few more breaths, Jake said, "Garden of
Paradise. In Spanish. Put another way, Garden of
Eden."

Jessie looked away again, feeling all undone.
Embarrassed.

Finally, Andrew cleared his throat. "Good name. I
like it. It does credit to the original."

Jake chuckled. "Ah now, hoss here is about to tell
us a pack o' lies about Adam and Eve."

But Andrew didn't. They sat quietly, Jessie feeling
a wave of something like gratitude to him for not
making fun of her. Without really asking one
another, they all more or less decided soon it was
time to be getting back. Jake poured out the opened
ones, crunched them up small and put them in a
plastic bag in the saddle bag, then broke out gum for
everyone to chew as Jessie went around unhobbling
the horses.

Andrew stood looking at Digger while the others
were already mounting up. Jessie, feeling a bit
woozy from her first try at beer, was about to ask
what was wrong when Jake lifted his hand for silence,
watching Andrew intently, who was now talking
softly to Digger. Then Andrew suddenly took one
long step and sprang into the saddle, his leg lifting
neatly over Digger's back. As he slid his feet into the
stirrups, Jake commented, "Nice, hoss."

As if he hadn't heard, Andrew said, "You know, if
there ever was such a place on this planet, it was in
Mesopotamia. The cradle of civilization, they call it.
Where the Tigris and Euphrates meet. Where you
want to go." She watched him slowly look over at
Jake. "That's what you'll be fighting over."

Despite Jake's suggestion that they ride over, in case the youngsters needed to leave early so that the others could talk about anything, Pop had looked thunderstruck at the idea, responding, "I can't see how that would happen, Jake. We can all drive over together." So there they were in Pop's old mustard lime-colored Buick, Jake at the wheel, Pop next to him in front, leaving Jessie sitting next to Andrew in the back. Andrew looked, well, positively excited, his eyes wide as he looked at everything that passed either side of the road. She sighed. After the way he had treated her nickname for the ranch, she supposed she could forgive him almost anything. For a while. Besides, sitting next to him in the backseat, she could smell Digger on him and was pleased at him for it. She turned her mind to how to convince Pop to let Angel's sister Maria cook for them these next few days so that she could spend as much time with Jake as possible.

Walking into the parlor at the Jameson's, they could hear Pastor Don's loud rumble, "...and he looks at me, all proud as a peacock and says, 'Well, Pastor Don, I 'spect it's got something to say about faith,'" dissolving the room into laughter, which stifled as someone cleared his throat and nodded toward them. Looking over, Pastor Don, exclaimed, "Nijs! Welcome! Jake, Jessie, and, of course, Andrew. Welcome!"

"Jake!" Elsie came up to Jake and wrapped him in a big hug, her purplish gray hair hiding her face in his shoulder. Standing back to size him up, she cried, "What happened to you?" as she reached out a tentative hand to his eye, now all blue and yellow.

"I fell."

She smiled. "Same old Jake." Her apple cheeks glistening with a tear, she murmured, "It's so good to see you before you ship out."

Pop coughed. The room grew quiet.

"Oh, Nijs! Get over it! You should be proud of the man he's turning himself into!" She scowled at him.

"A man can do himself right proud taking after his family instead of running around the world solving other people's problems."

"Men! They're impossible!" She gave Jake another hug, then squeezed Jessie, too, in her happy, fragrant warmth. As she saw Elsie turning to shake Andrew's hand, her view was blocked by others coming up to shake Jake's hand and hug her, shouting out their congratulations at Jake's graduation and questions about where he was going next, now that Elsie had broken the ice. Finishing a deep hug from old Milsolm, who always held her a bit too close, she thought, she caught the sight of Andrew looking almost overwhelmed at the number of outstretched hands wanting to shake his.

As if catching this, Pastor Don, cried out, "Now, now! We don't want to drown the boy. Let's get him some coffee and pie and get to our business."

At this the room moved around some more, Elsie grabbing her hand to lead her into the kitchen, saying, "Here, dear. Help me with the coffee cups. Goodness, so many came tonight." She paused, holding a short stack of her best cups in mid-air about to hand them to Jessie, whispering, "I expect they all came wanting to say a goodbye to Jake." She smiled.

Jessie grunted, not sure if she wanted to let herself feel her own stomach's churning about Saturday. Elsie watched her a moment in silence, then squeezed her hand and softly asked, "What are you going to make for him Friday night?"

Relieved at this reminder of the mundane, Jessie shrugged, whispering back, "Well, he always likes t-bones. They're kind of expensive, but I thought I might be able to trade Wallis for something."

Elsie's eyes sparkled. "If I were you, I'd remind him of who they're for and ask him to just give them to you." Jessie almost shook her head, then reflected that there might be something to that. Old Wallis had always liked Jake. Might as well take advantage of that. Then Elsie was handing her more cups and they were pouring out coffee, Jessie threading her way with a tray through all the women in the kitchen out to the living room where the men all sat waiting quietly, save Pastor Don who was in the corner paging through his Bible, muttering something to himself.

After more trips back and forth, and getting herself a nice big slice of Elsie's peach pie, "Just a few more months to fresh ones, but this didn't turn out too bad," Jessie grabbed a perch on the edge of the piano bench, next to sweet old Janet Wiley, her tiny frame holding a shaking cup to take tiny sips from time to time as she smiled a deeply wrinkled happiness at Jessie through her thick, round glasses, saying nothing, but lightly squeezing her knee.

Pastor Don was clearing his throat, subduing the last titters and whispers from around the room. "Let us pray." Around the room, almost as one, like a string of cattle at the trough, Jessie chuckled to herself, the heads bowed over their hands, reaching out to grasp others, or wrists where cups had them occupied. Then she immediately felt stricken, as if she had said something unforgivable. "Lord, we just want to say thank you for Jake's safe return to our fold, and a word of welcome to friend Andrew who is doing good work finding the inspiration we all may find studying the Word you have left us. We also just want to pray for all of our boys in uniform..." and girls, Jessie rebelliously piped up in silence, then just as silently shushed herself, as he continued. "...as they go forth to tame the forces of Satan, meeting him everywhere that he unleashes his armies of darkness. And, Lord, we also want to give thanks for Jessie, who has come out to be with us this evening..." Stunned to hear her name, she tried to squeeze more tightly back into her corner, only to have Janet's grip tighten on her wrist. "...she is blooming into a fine woman, Lord, as so many of our youngsters are, Lord, under your watch and guidance that never fails us, not on our darkest nights, not in our deepest sorrows. For that, Lord, we just want to offer up our praise and thanks to you, Jesus Christ, our Lord and Savior. Amen." A round of amens chorused after him.

Rubbing his hands in delight, Pastor Don looked around at them all, his friendly gaze settling on Andrew who was staring around at everyone, his eyes very alert, as if taking in every word that was said.

"Friend Andrew."

Andrew jerked a little, spilling coffee in his lap. "Sorry!" he cried out, as Elsie handed him a napkin to mop up. "Sorry," he mumbled again.

Jesus, Jessie thought, what an impossible...but never got to finish it, as Janet leaned in to whisper, "What a nice man. Jake's friend from Seattle, isn't he?" Jessie nodded dutifully then went back to watching what happened next.

"Oh, Andrew, we're simple folk out here. We don't stand on ceremony," Pastor Don rolled out, looking around the room. Heads nodded. "Now the other day, when we got to meet just before service, I was pleased to learn that you were able to quote, from memory, parts of the reading." Heads nodded again, looking over at Andrew in friendly interest, Jake's and Pop's faces among them glowing with pride. Here he goes, Jessie thought. And, sure enough, Andrew turned a hot red and mumbled something that only he could hear.

"It was a story handed down to us by apostolic authority that when faced by the terror of his disciples, Jesus woke from his slumber and subdued the storm. Friends, I ask you..." as the thought slowly dawned on Andrew that he wasn't going to be made an example, Jessie was amused to watch relief and even a little smile flicker across his face. "I ask you, what can be more terrifying than that? You are in a small boat, watching the waves grow higher and higher, knowing that at any moment, you will be swamped and go straight to the bottom, wondering which breath will be your last." Heads nodded again, and coffee was quietly slurped as the sense arose that Pastor Don was moving into his stride.

"Now, I know that there are places in this world that do not believe such a miracle ever happened..." a quiet clucking of tongues broke out amid several shaking of heads. "...that there are even schools who choose to call themselves seminaries that teach our young ministers-to-be that...and I have a big phrase for you here...that this passage is only a literary allegory." He looked around the room in triumph as faces turned toward him in expectation. Andrew, she saw, was scoping the inside of his head now. "That it didn't really happen! Well...we are simple folk, are we not?" Heads nodded vigorously, Janet reached out to grasp Jessie's wrist and squeeze again. Pastor Don's voice began to reach upward, "And we don't need fancy gymnastics like that, do we?" Heads nodded even more vigorously as he began to reach toward his pitch. "We believe this miracle happened. That it is the gospel truth." Heads wagged, faces bowed, as a few amens broke out as well.

"Friends, I ask you...how do we know this?" A few faces looked up in surprise, questioning. "Were we there?" Some faces shook their heads, uncertainly, wondering what he was getting at, the room's pleasant atmosphere wavering a bit, just like when Mildred hit a wrong note on the piano during service. A silence descended as Pastor Don turned slowly, scanning everyone's face, some looking a bit uncomfortable as they shifted, Jessie noticed. "Nijs!" Pastor Don's gaze, almost fierce with inspiration, swung to Pop. "Were you there?" Jessie looked at him, wondering how he was going to answer this question of faith.

After a beat, Pop said, "Tain't that old yet." A few titters broke out.

"That's right." Pastor Don was strutting around the room now. "You weren't there. I wasn't there. Jake, were you there?" Jake beamed a shaking of his head. "Tom? Elsie? Maggie?" One by one, as they followed Pop's and Jake's examples, confidence seemed to be reborn and the room relaxed. They really were like cattle, she thought, not shushing herself so strongly this time.

"How then, friends? How, I ask you?" He was parading back and forth across the living room. "How can we know this to be true when oh so learned doctors of exegesis having spent their entire lives studying the text tell us that it is only a metaphor?" Another silence reigned as eyes turned inward in thought. Jessie had to admit that she was stumped herself. So much for blind faith, she thought. Still turning it over, she noticed that Pastor Don had in all his marching ended right in front of Andrew.

Whose quiet voice broke out in a stammer. "Be-- because..." Then, he went a deeply flushing silent.

Pastor Don looked down at him quietly, waiting. Then his voice, so strident and triumphant before, surprised her with its quiet, "Go ahead." She smiled inwardly, wondering what Pastor Don was going to say when Andrew flashed out some Buddhist slogan.

His eyes reaching out to meet Pastor Don's, Andrew struggled out, "Because...we...we experience that same tr--truth in our...lives even now."

Jessie was thunderstruck. Jake beamed with delight. Pop frowned, working it through, then his expression cleared.

Pastor Don smiled and said simply, "Yes." Turning to find a seat on one of the couches, as others squirmed to make room for his girth, he continued, "Irma. Why don't you tell us what you told me after service." The room froze.

Her smoky gray eyes quavering behind her glasses, Irma shook her head, then began to look down. "For heaven's sake, Irma, tell us!" Elsie shot out. "You've got nothing to hide. It wasn't your fault." Heads nodded sympathetically as the room began to slowly turn their attention toward Irma, watching her house-dressed shoulders shaking until she took a big breath and began. Jessie sat back, thinking it probably had something to with Mika drinking too much again down at Four Corners.

"Saturday night..." her reedy low voice began, "I woke up and didn't find Mika next to me. He..." Her voice faltered before going on. "He snores heavily on Saturday nights on account of..." suddenly her eyes flashed an ugly anger, "...that disgusting devil's brew that he drinks...drank so much of." Heads nodded, looking down. To Jessie's surprise, she couldn't see one glint of an "I told you so" around the room. Just quiet faces and, next to her ear, Janet's quietly murmured praying.

"I went into the kitchen, and I found him on the floor in..." her eyes quivered again, and began to well up.

Pastor Don nodded at her to go on.

"I found him in..." A single tear popped out from behind her glasses and began its solitary track down her cheek, losing itself in the wrinkles. "...in a pool of blood." Some gasps and sighs broke out around the room. Irma's eyes moved out, across the room to Pastor Don's who held her gaze without blinking, just nodding slightly. "And there was so much of it...I didn't know what to do...it was everywhere..." Her voice's brokenness began to clear finally and found new strength. "For a moment, I thought the worst." She broke her gaze to look briefly around the room, then down, saying, "Like everybody, I suppose, we have knives for cooking in the kitchen. And Mika had been so upset lately with the way that hay prices had fallen so far. The second year in a row. And the two harvests before that had been so disappointing with the drought, you know. And the bank was saying..." At that, people began to look up at one another, particularly the men, with cynical snorts and shakings of heads. "Anyway, it wasn't that. The doctors told me he had hemorrhaged. That with the way he had been drinking it was only a matter of time." Janet squeezed Jessie's hand again, while shaking her head in dismay to replace her praying.

"Now, I know, that many think that...Mika wasn't a very good farmer." She looked around the room, much stronger now, almost daring anyone to say something, Jessie saw. "Like they say, some farmers are never going to make money, no matter how good it gets." Pop nodded his head thoughtfully but stopped when Irma looked at him. "And I know that many think that he was a bad man because he...drank so much. But..." Her features screwed up, her lips twisting as she struggled to say what was next. The room was held in a hush, waiting. She struggled with a few sounds, then said, "But, he...was..." Suddenly, as before, one single tear popped out of her welling eye to slowly wend its way to its own little death, Jessie thought with surprise, as she realized that she, too, was crying. "He was all that I had."

There was a long silence after that, broken only by the sounds of Irma's quiet sobbing. After a time, Pastor Don cleared his throat, saying. "Please finish it, Irma."

Wondering if she could stand it now, Jessie angrily wiped at her cheeks and looked on. Andrew, to her shocked fury, sat with his eyes almost closed, at peace, almost as if untouched by the pain and grief surrounding him.

Irma slowly wiped her own eyes with dignity, then said, "I know that no matter how...strong Satan's tempests are...I'm supposed to dig deeper...in my faith...to my Lord, Jesus Christ. But, what I..." Her voice briefly failed, then her eyes took on a hard sheen, and she cried out, "What I want to know is why? Why? Mika had his faults...We all do...He deserved better...I know I'm supposed to believe..." Her voice came faster now, as if rushing to get it all out, its harshness scraping Jessie. "I'm supposed to believe that...Jesus just woke up and calmed that storm...Great for them on that day. Where was Jesus on Saturday night? For Mika?" Her eyes darted angrily around the room now before settling on Pastor Don, her breaths heaving her chest. "Where will Jesus be for me tomorrow?"

The room sat in stillness. No one moved. Finally, Pastor Don, still holding Irma's gaze, asked quietly, "Anyone?" No one responded.

Pop stirred. Of course, Jessie thought. No one would speak before him. She sat back, again, realizing both that she had been sitting clenched forward almost bent to her knees and that she really didn't want to hear some bullshit from Paul or Matthew or anybody just now. He rather loudly cleared his throat a few times, coughed, and then said, "When I lost Ana on that...terrible day..." Jessie gasped, realizing that he was talking about their mother and her eyes reached out to Jake's across the room, seeing his jaw tighten in pain while feeling her own eyes damnably tear up again. But Pop was going on. "...I got very angry with Jesus for a very long time. I couldn't believe that he took my Ana away from us just when..." He shook his head in frustration. "Just when the ranch was starting to pay out. When...the Angus herds. Before they became what everybody wants now. Before...the bank...the... All those risks. All those worries...I...just didn't get it. I...still don't." Heads around the room turned to him, then quickly looked away. A few throats began clearing loudly, one a particularly phlegmy rattle. "All I can say..." He stopped and looked at Irma. "I can't speak for you, Irma, for Mika, or for this sorrow. I'm sorry..." The room waited, in anticipation, sensing a conclusion of some sort coming. "But, I...I can say that over the years, as I've watched Jake grow into the man that he's becoming..." Jessie looked over at Jake and saw his own tears running silently down his otherwise grave and silent, almost unmoved, face. "...And, I...especially..." Her breath caught in her throat as she saw Pop's gaze swing toward her. "I...see Ana come to life again in Jessie...I..." He looked down now. His clumsy, gnarled hands, twisted from decades of worried ranching, turned helplessly. "I...have to believe that God is bigger than me...that He knows what He's doing, even if I don't...and..." He turned at Irma's snort of disgust at this and looked at her again. "Most particular, I have to believe that the horse that took Ana would have taken Jake if'n she hadn't grabbed him. And...for that...if she were to...had the chance..." His voice started turning gravelly again and he broke off clearing it. Jessie thought her heart would burst watching him, except she was too tired to do anything but just that. Watch. "...the chance to do it all over again...she would. And God knows that, too." He stopped by blowing a short, hard breath and looking down again. Jessie's eyes swung in turn to Jake's, who sat as before, wet cheeks almost carved from stone, to Andrew's, who still sat like some little fucking Buddha, to Irma's, who sat as if she had been slapped, even reaching up to feel her cheek, as her gaze turned inward, wonderingly.

"Amen." Pastor Don's quiet summation brought them all out of their trance. People began shifting in their chairs, managing a small, quiet stretch here and there. "Friends, we do ourselves a disservice when we look at the miracle in the boat as some movie that does not touch us at all, as if we could never, and never will, know the terrifying fright or pain of His disciples in that boat. We do not know all of God's designs. We may often find ourselves so racked with pain that we fear we may not be able to go on. We may find ourselves so wretched in our anger at God that we fear we may not want to be able to go on. However, one thing is always clear. While God may move according to God's will, at times in ways that leave us at a complete loss, He has also always left us each other to puzzle out why."

He stood. "We have done enough tonight. Irma, I want to thank you for your testimony. Nijs, I want to thank you for yours. But friends, before we go, I want to close with a special prayer of watchfulness..." At this, all eyes closed, all heads bowed, Jessie's too, her mind reeling from what she had just experienced and floating on the comforting sounds of Pastor Don's rumble. "Lord, I just want to give thanks for the heartfelt words entrusted to us tonight by Irma and Nijs and ask that you hold them both, especially Irma, as will this community of faith, in your warm, loving arms. I also, Lord, just want to extend that prayer of watchfulness to our son Jake, and all the boys in uniform, as they go forth to fight for goodness, doing your work. Be with them, Lord, when they find themselves surrounded by Satan's worst storms. Be with them, Lord, when they are torn with despair. When they know almost nothing but fear. Be with them, Lord, as shall this community of faith, carrying them forth to their duties as Americans, as Sons of Christ, buoyed aloft by the strength of our prayers to you, our Lord, our Savior. Amen." Another round of amens broke out, more jubilant now.

Indeed, if Jessie hadn't been in the room the last bit, she would have thought a party had broken out from all the teary, and happy, hugging going on. Feeling Janet's tiny tug, she turned and answered it with a huge hug, feeling so lucky that she had all these wonderful people surrounding her.

On the way home in the car, Jake rolled down his window, saying, "Could use a little air. How about you, Pop?" Strangely, Pop said nothing, just cranked his down, too. As Jake sped along, the wind whistling in the car making conversation all but impossible, Jessie looked over at Andrew who, she saw, looked positively joyful. Wanting to slap him, instead she slid over a bit and whispered in his ear, "What's going on?"

He looked at her, happiness dancing in his eyes. Then, he bent his head to whisper back, "I finally understand Fundamentalism." She sat back, repulsed. Disgusted. What a fucking weirdo, she thought, and turned her head to face the outside and feel the wind rush through her hair.

***

The next morning, she wandered around the nearby pastures by herself playing with Biscuit and avoiding the stable, and then set about lunch as usual, trying to push the thought of Jake leaving as far from her as possible. As Angel and the hands trooped in, swatting dust off their legs and grabbing chairs, she smiled and went to work putting the ham sandwiches on the table in time for Pop to gesture that all should grab hands in time for the blessing. During the quiet eating, Jake gave her an odd look once, but she avoided his eyes and busied herself biting into an apple. Once, peeking over at Andrew, she saw him rubbing his forehead in pain and wondered if they had taken another night ride with libations late last night. After lunch was done, as everyone was getting up, Angel reporting on the mending of a fence that afternoon over on Mill Trunk, Jake made is if to speak to her, Andrew standing patiently nearby still rubbing his temple, she put her head down, grabbed some dishes and all but ran to the kitchen.

And that set the tone. That afternoon, she borrowed Pop's truck, drove into Brickton and sweetly persuaded Wallis to give her the t-bones at half-price. Taking the long way home, she drove out to Fort Simcoe, coming to its oasis-like green lawns and oak trees, stuck right into the middle of the desert, like an emerald one stumbled on at the beach, she always thought, and wandered around its Civil War era homes with their squared white-washed walls and charming little porches all facing the parade ground, and thought again of its history that Nora had told her about walking to the bus after school one day, the day that they had the gotten the usual version of US Cavalry hunting down rogue Indians, and how the ground, with its brook, had been winter quarters for the Yakama until that same cavalry decided that it would make a splendid little fort to which to bring their northeastern ladies. She wondered how it would feel to have somebody just walk up to her one day and say that her ranch was no longer theirs. Kind of like the US Army just walking up to her one day and saying that Jake was no longer hers. She frowned and pushed that thought away. Not that he ever was, she grimaced as the thought teased, nevertheless. He had always wanted this, since they were little. She sighed and thought that she should get back, but the bubbling spring, with its little cemetery just beyond called to her, and so she strolled over and contented herself reading the epitaphs of dead soldiers who had taken the land from friends like Nora and felt a grim sort of satisfaction that they had died here, the thieves, hopefully with an arrow or two in the back until she realized that she was thinking this about US soldiers, Jake's buddies, almost, and gasping in shock, backed away so quickly in confusion that she slipped into the brook.

Arriving home so late that there was really nothing to do but whip up some more sandwiches, she bit her lip and wondered what Pop would say as he bent his head over the blessing. Apparently nothing. He just nodded, saying, "Thank you, Jessie," which caught her by surprise again, so she buried her confusion in a bite. The dinner was a subdued affair, with Pop staring off into space barely attending to anyone,

Andrew rubbing his forehead again, she noticed with irritation, and Jake trying to tell a funny story about a coyote and a hawk fighting over a rat with an injured leg, but no one was paying attention, so he finally just ended it.

That night, as she let Whip wander wherever she wanted, she heard them coming out into the yard, so she slid off and, remembering that first night, let Whip smell an apple she drew from her pocket then threw it far into the pasture and, as Whip trotted off toward it, hid behind hay bales that Jake had stacked next to the stable wall after Andrew's falling practice. Sure enough, as they came around the corner, they stopped to look for her. Peeking out, she saw Andrew looking far into the pasture after the sound of Whip's hooves cantering around that end. Jake, though, again, looked straight at her. Her heart caught as she wondered what she should do. But after a moment, he looked down, saying, "Looks like she's exercising Whip. Let's go." Listening to them ride off, she felt tears on her cheeks. Not again! she thought, angrily wiping them off and walked out toward Whip to continue her own night ride.

The next morning, she felt better and decided to give Jake a hero's farewell this last day, beginning with a hearty breakfast. Rummaging around for some bacon in the freezer downstairs while wondering if she had time to boil some potatoes for hash browns and what she could pack for some sort of on-the-road deal for Jake and Angel tomorrow morning, she saw Andrew wandering around rubbing his head again. For Christ's sake, she thought, what a lightweight! Still, after shouting, "Jake? Breakfast!" she placed a short glass of water with a few aspirin next to Andrew's juice.

Jake, hair sleep-mangled, poked his head a few minutes later around the corner into the kitchen. "If I didn't smell it, I'd be sure you were just pulling my leg."

She smiled back. "Who knows what they're going to feed you? And, if'n you don't hurry, Pop's liable to take your share."

He beamed. "Be right back."

Breakfast was much better. Pop, too, seemed to have recovered a bit, for his blessing went on a bit longer than usual, saying, "And, Lord, you know that the months ahead we will be petitioning you with many prayers to watch over Jake as he continues with his training that he may do Your work the better, but this morning..." Hearing him break off, Jessie opened her eyes to see him looking around the table and then at her with undisguised pride, before continuing, "...this morning, over this glorious breakfast that loving hands have prepared, we just want to say thanks for this bright day to break bread together." Her cheeks burned.

Jake paused after taking a bite, then, breaking the silence, said, "Not bad, Sticks. Had better before, of course, but--"

She threw her napkin at him, saying, "Better watch it, or you'll lose another eye!"

"Hey!" he cried and they all laughed. Pop, too. Then, he murmured with a kind tone, "Let's not waste what the good Lord has provided." They all tucked in.

After breakfast, Pop revealed his surprise of the day, saying that he knew they would want to spend the last day riding around together and that Angel had offered Maria to take care of lunch. Jessie smiled at him, feeling grateful. Then, trying not to look at Andrew, and wondering why she was still irritated with him, she cocked an eyebrow at Jake saying, "Guess you two'd better saddle up. We'll be in the yard waiting."

***

It was a great day. Andrew looked better, too, she noticed, as they trotted into the yard. Asa was positively dancing. "Race?" Jessie asked.

Jake laughed. "You wish. I'd whip the pants off of you. But, no. Uncle Sam owns my ass now, and I'd better take care of it what with where I'm going."

She laughed, too, admiring her handiwork on his face, now a spreading yellowish-brown with specks of purple. "Okay. A quiet ride then."

"Good." Andrew mumbled.

Jake led, by rights, taking them on a tour of all the different places that he had fond memories of. There, behind the pump house off of Brown Road, he had had his first beer. It was the same place she had smoked a cigarette with Nora, she was amused to see. There, in a paddock not too far from the Grange, he had "offered up his virginity to God."

"With who?" Jessie asked, feeling weird.

"Daisy Bennick."

"What?! When?"

"Never you mind," he beamed, leading the way off toward the skating pond.

Following, Jessie was thunderstruck, her head full of Daisy's terrible acne in junior high. There on the pond, he was telling Andrew all about the skating parties each winter when Andrew burst out, "Is that a heron?"

Sure enough, there it was, standing with full dignity on one leg, ignoring them, it's long pointed beak pointed straight into the light breeze. "What's one doing out here?" he asked. They shook their heads.

Jake pointed out toward the center. "Remember falling that one Christmas, Sticks?" At the memory of her head crunching back onto the ice, she reached up to grab it, nodding. "Man, you sure gave us a scare. What were you doing?"

"Trying to skate backward, like Grandpa. I tripped over a chunk of ice."

"That's right." And he went on telling Andrew all about how graceful Grandpa had been, being able to skate, "Pretty much circles around everyone else," going backwards, spinning on one leg, all the moves he had learned on the canals in Holland as a boy.

Jessie's mind flooded with memories of his old, thin face with a red, sharp nose, sticking out from under his knit cap pulled down tight, her thickly-mittened hands grasped in his as he waltzed her around and around and around the pond to the tune of the 1812 Overture playing on Uncle Willem's grudgingly loaned phonograph, set at the side of the rink, running off a car battery. She used to love watching Grandpa, his arms folded behind him, floating with ease over the ice that she found so chunked up and rocky.

"You would have liked him, hoss."

Andrew looked at him.

"He was a free-thinker like you."

Andrew smiled. Then, thinking, he said, "You mean the Christianity doesn't go that far back?"

"Nope, not from Grandpa. That's all from Gramma." Jessie smiled, remembering Gramma's warm bread, straight out of the oven, spread with butter and sugar. "Why, sometimes I used to play sick on Sunday mornings just so's I could run over to Grandpa's and play cards with him." Jessie smiled again, shaking her head. "Jake, he'd say, go down into the boiler room and take out that bottle and deck of cards you'll find behind the water heater. And I would."

They watched a hawk circle lazily over them and then, suddenly, plunge straight into the brush next to the pond, rising again with a squeaking mouse in its talons. Jessie winced, always hating that sight. "The conflictual nature of finitude. Everything fighting for its place." Hardly surprised at this remark, she glared at Andrew stopping, when she saw Jake watching her, to tuck her irritation inside.

As if agreeing, the heron shook out his head, his long neck swaying in large wobbles that grew smaller as they descended, then slowly spread his great wings and took off, leisurely waving them as he flew into the distance.

"Ain't it so? God, I'm going to miss this place." Jake nodded and reined Asa over to the road to continue their tour.

***

Dinner took on a more somber note, as if all were dreading the thought of tomorrow morning, though Jake was clearly pleased at the t-bones. He surprised her, though, when after pie that Maria had baked for them, he asked Andrew to clean up for them. Andrew simply nodded as if expecting it. "What about it, Sticks? One last night ride?" Grateful, she agreed.

Just before they walked out, Jake suddenly turned into the living room and approached Pop as he was settling into his chair, Cocoa jumping up with a loud purr into his lap, and his battered copy of *The Myth of Evolution* already marked with a twisted finger in one hand. Jake stopped in front of him, then, to their astonishment, kissed Pop on the forehead and smiled. Pop smiled back and said, "Take your time leaving and hurry back," then opened his book and sat back. As they left the room, Jessie glanced over her shoulder to see Pop not reading but staring over the page at the opposite wall.

A harder wind was blowing than usual. The moonlight was a beautiful silver, though and it looked to be a nice ride. Jake looking around at some elms swaying, said, "I wonder what that does to you when you're riding the silk down." It took Jessie a quiet moment to realize that he was thinking about parachutes and, horrified at the thought of jumping out of an airplane, she hastily batted the thought aside.

Jake was trotting faster than normal, as if eager to get to wherever he was leading them. Just the two of them, they could ride side by side most of the way. For some reason, he was telling her all about one night at the UW. "Not that you need to worry about this, Sticks, it's mostly sheer boredom there it's so safe..." when Andrew had found himself in an alley surrounded by a bunch of gang members "ready to scalp him sure."

Interested, despite the nervous pace at which he was riding and speaking, she asked what happened. "Well, you should have seen that. Most guys I know would a been pissing their pants, but Andrew gets this whole Zen master look on his face, as if he's taking a walk in the park. At first I wasn't going to do anything, but then, I thought, he's an egghead. Maybe he looks like he doesn't care, but he sure's hell's gonna in a few minutes." Jessie chuckled in disgust. Ignoring her, Jake went on, "So I got him out of there."

Smiling over at him, she asked, "Was it hard?"

He looked at her for a moment, as if gauging something, his head bouncing up and down with Asa's canter. "No. It wasn't."

As he turned into the first orchard, she realized where they were going and settled into enjoying the ride with the scents of the fruit coming on more strongly than they had just a few nights ago. Funny how quickly the summer speeds by, she thought, a bit sad. Jake didn't say anything, either, as if wanting to simply enjoy the moment, the smells. Turn after turn, they finally reached the gate, and after it, as they began to rise once more, Jessie enjoying that feeling of the valley floor being left below again, he started up as if she had asked a question.

"See, the trick when you're surrounded like that is not to lose your head." Jessie nodded, wondering where all this was going. "Any group of jackals who'd take on a single person like that is probably more afraid of their leader and his second than of you." Approaching their landing, Jake turned Asa off the road, and Jessie followed, kicking Whip to keep up so she could hear more. "That's all you got to worry about, their leader and his second," he repeated.

Genuinely interested now, she asked, "How do you know who is who?"

Reining in Asa, he looked at her with a wide smile. "That's the beauty of it. You can always tell from their eyes." She shook her head, not understanding. Leaning toward her, he went on, "Just keep your head, keep breathing, and look around the circle to see who everybody else is watching. And if you're not sure, look for the one pair of eyes that doesn't care. That's the one to look out for. First."

She nodded. "Then what?"

"Act all normal and relaxed, maybe even a bit afraid if you can manage it, so that he thinks you're easy prey. That'll make him come for you. And let him. Let him come at you and when he's close enough, take him down. Hard. I mean take him down. Don't worry about hurting him because he deserves it."

Jessie tried to imagine taking down a man who was bigger than her. "How?"

"Well," Jake paused in thought, then rubbed his eye and dismounted. "You got a good punch on you. I'd smack him straight in the nose. That'll make him reel back for a step, then it's really up to you. Kick him hard in the balls, give him an elbow up the side of the head, even crunch his knee if you're angry enough."

Jessie giggled while sliding down, feeling nervous. "Crunch his knee?"

"Okay, maybe not that. Cuz he'll never walk again." He bent down to hobble Asa. Then, straightening, watching as she hobbled Whip, he said, "Whatever you choose, make sure he's on the ground hurt enough not to get back up. That'll scare the others. Cuz you took their leader down. Makes 'em think." He undid Asa's saddlebag and took out two beers, tossing one to her.

Catching it while following him to where they sat before, she felt the can's welcome coldness and, tiring of this strange conversation from Jake's world, she asked, "Jake, where are you keeping these?"

"What you don't know won't hurt you." He beamed as he cracked his open and sat with a sigh. She sat next to him, absentmindedly tapping the top of hers, looking down at the view and wondering what kinds of conversations others were having in all those barn yard lights down there.

"But remember you're not done yet."

Forgetting for a moment what he was talking about, she looked at him.

"The second. It'll be easier to tell who he is. Because the others will really be watching him now."

Not liking this conversation at all now, she sighed. "What then?"

"Almost done. You don't have the element of surprise anymore, cuz they all just watched you down the one guy that they never thought they could. So, and remember this, there's always a second. As he starts to make up his mind to go after you, he'll be wondering how to do it, so..."

Jessie waited, wondering how she could change this subject.

"You meet him. You don't wait for him to come to you. You go to him and, while he's too busy wondering what to do, you take him down. That's it."

"That's it?"

"Yep, so long as you put him down just as hard as you put down the first asshole."

"What about the others?"

He chuckled. "They'll scatter."

She sat, looking down, her mind in a turmoil. Realizing that this was the last conversation she was going to have with Jake for who knows how long, she felt the need building to say, what? All kinds of things. She just didn't know where to start.

Jake sighed again and said, "Man, this is beautiful." Looking at her, he asked, "Aren't we lucky to have grown up in such a beautiful place?"

"Yeah."

They sat a few minutes more in silence, sipping their beers, Jessie trying to ignore the taste of hers. Then, suddenly, Jake asked, "You going to orientation in a few weeks?"

She frowned. Other than being accepted to the UW last April, she hadn't really given it a thought. She knew that she was supposed to be excited about going away, but it always seemed to be over there somewhere. Outside. She shook her head, then asked, "Do I have to?"

He grinned. "Nope. Just make an excuse of some sort. Or just don't show up. They'll squawk sure enough, but, count on it, not too much cuz they want Pop's money."

She sighed again, feeling relieved that she could push it back even further in her mind.

"What are you going to study?"

At a loss now, she thought for a few moments. Then, grasping toward some strange thought, she threw out, "How about business?"

He laughed, long and hard.

"What?" she growled, feeling stupid.

He only kept laughing, until she punched him in the arm.

"Hey! Remember Uncle Sam! No more bruises!" He rubbed his arm.

"Well, what?"

He paused looking at her, then nodding as if he was deciding something, he took a long gulp, belched and then looked at her again. "You really do want to run the ranch someday, don't you?"

She sat, stunned, thinking only that hitting him did her no good.

He took another sip, casting his eyes out over the valley, and said, "Well?"

Still, she said nothing, feeling nothing, just staring out into the darkness over to where her Jardín lay.

Jake glanced at her. "You know I've never wanted it."

Then, feeling a great wave of bitterness wash over her, she choked out, "Don't remind me," and took a long swallow.

"Hey. Look at me. Jessie."

She scowled at him, knowing she could never hate him.

"I've known this ever since I...saw your diary."

She looked down, then away from him.

"Tell you what. We both know that Pop's got his dreams. Hell, this whole valley..." he paused, waving his beer from wall to wall of the scene below, "...would roll over and die at the thought of a woman running things."

"Tersie Bougoyne runs hers."

"She raises fifty llamas and that only after Ted died. It's her retirement."

Stung, she cursed out, "And Betty Charson runs hers."

"Again, that's just alfalfa, a couple hundred acres of mint, and winter wheat. Not cattle."

"And Betty--"

"Mabton, I know. But only because Charlie's drunk half the time. It's not the same. Anyway, cattle's not their main thing. They raise what, three hundred head?"

"Three hundred and fifty," she swallowed, feeling defeated.

"And Van der Vaal Ranch and Cattle?"

"Nine ninety-seven after the last culling and this spring's calving, give or take a head. Sow's on her last legs. And Magpie, Stretch and Bonnet didn't take this winter. Should've culled 'em right then, but Pop..."

Jake took a sip, smiling. "And we have how many acres of pasture?"

Growing angry now, wondering if he was making fun of her, she spat out, "Including the working corrals, almost seventeen hundred."

"And the main problem facing the ranch is?"

She stopped at that, wondering if Jake really didn't know. She thought about it herself.

He took another sip. "I'm asking because I honestly don't know because, Jessie, I really couldn't give a rat's ass."

"Jake!" she hissed.

"Well?"

Amazed at the turn their conversation had taken, she said, startling herself, "Our falling grades."

"What about 'em?"

She sighed, wondering how to explain the thoughts tumbling in her head. "Our grades, they're not nearly as good as they used to be."

Jake hmmphed in disbelief at this. She sat up, amazed at that, then allowed herself to admit that maybe he really hadn't been paying attention and wondered at that.

"Look, I know that everybody's bitching about packers buying up lots long before slaughter so they can buy and sell however they want to keep the price fixed. But everybody can see plain as day that the country's not producing Choice meat anymore. Shoot, what was it? In the 80s, twenty years ago or so, 97% of the meat slaughtered came in as Choice, now it's something like..." she frowned, trying to remember the number. "Well, less than 60%.

Everything else is coming in at Select or Standard or worse. And all I'm saying is we're no different."

Jake took a long, slow swallow, his eyes over the can never leaving her. Nor the surprise welling up in them. She felt stupid again.

After the swallow, he began, "So..."

Glowering, she said, "So, what?"

He looked away. Then, his voice softer, came, "So what are you saying?"

She looked down, wondering what it was that she was saying. "Maybe...maybe we should be different. Live weight, dressed weight, even that fancy new grid pricing, Pop's tried 'em all these last five years. He gets the same results."

"And you can do better? Cuz I've been riding the whole herd these last five weeks and I haven't seen anything wrong."

At this, she felt a wave of fury rising within her so fierce that she raised her beer can to smack him a good one.

"Whoa! Whoa! Whoa!" Jake cried, his hands in the air catching hers. "I'm on your side, Jessie. Hold on."

Feeling the wave subside, she put her hands down and stared at him, still furious. "Well?"

"How you gonna beat the market?"

"What?!"

"How you...?"

Then, without knowing where she was going, she stumbled out, "You don't. You just do better. Instead of just pounds, cuz that's all we got, you....get better marbling, maybe. Do what you have to do to get that Certified Angus Beef stamp. We haven't had it in years. And I don't know what the price spread is, but it's gotta be huge now."

He saluted her with his beer and finished it. Then he got up to get them two more. At the saddlebag, he asked, "And you discussed all this with Pop? Cuz he sure as hell hasn't discussed it with me."

She snorted.

"Well?" he said, coming back and handing her one.

She looked at him, wondering how much to say. "I can read."

He smiled. "I bet you can at that."

Deciding abruptly that if she couldn't trust Jake, she couldn't anyone, she went on. "Besides...Pop won't say it, but we're in trouble."

Jake set his can down with a snap, a few suds splashing up to splatter the ground.

"I've been...checking his ledger when he's at Prayer Meeting. It's a godawful mess, but...I can see that he had to borrow the last three years to make ends meet. This last one the most. God knows how he's going to afford my school even with the financial aid." At his long sigh, she cried out, softly, "It's the prices, Jake! Our grades are so low, it doesn't matter how heavy they come in. He tried the grid year before last, probably because that shit for brains Halverson talked him into it, but our carcasses came in with a yield grade of 3-4. They discounted our beef a bundle."

They sat quietly, Jessie feeling torn between relief that Jake would let her talk about this...worry that had been growing, she realized now, ever since she had had the guts to look at the ledger and guilt that she was suggesting that Pop wasn't running things all that well anymore. Jake said nothing, just taking a small sip every now and again.

He sighed. "Sitting around's not going make any difference." He nodded. "You do believe that you can do better..." Her head spun at him so fast that he quickly added, "...somehow. Trying something different. Since just going for pounds isn't getting us anywhere better soon. Get our grades back up. Get better marbling, though god knows how you're going to do that if Pop can't. Grades high enough that any market fixing isn't going to hurt us all that much."

Hating herself for what she was thinking, she nodded.

He stared off into the night. "Pop'd never go for it. A girl, even if it's his own daughter, running the ranch."

"I know."

After another moment, he sighed again, murmuring, "The changing of the guard." Then, all at once, he beamed in the darkness and sat up straight. "Well, tell you what. Let's solve both of our problems."

Intrigued at this new cheerful tone, Jessie watched him, waiting but not letting herself hope.

"We lie. Let me do a tour, about two and a half years. Long enough to get him used to the idea of the ranch not dying if'n I'm not somewhere on the continent. You'll have a couple of years of schooling, of...buzanesss..." he drawled out the word, "...under the belt by then. Not to mention plenty of time to think about what we need to do. Write down all your ideas and send 'em to me."

"Will you read 'em?" She found herself grinning, surprised at the lighter feeling washing through her.

He beamed. "For this, yes. I might even write back."

"I won't hold my breath."

Ignoring her, he went on, his enthusiasm mounting, "Then I'll come back and we'll lay our cards on the table."

"Tell him what?"

"Isn't it obvious? He's tired. I'll bet even he knows that. Things are slipping. That's why he keeps on at me resigning my commission, as if I could." He shook his head. "Anyway, we...or me that is, tell him I've been thinking it over and that I have some ideas for improving things. And, that..."

His bouncy tone infecting her, she found a small wave of giddiness building in her that she was having problems fighting as she waited for him to finish.

"That...I want to..." He looked into the starry sky as if trying to find inspiration and, suddenly, found it.

"That I want to keep the ranch in the family and that you're going to help me. That you're going to implement all my...that is your, ideas! Yeah. That'll work. He won't know no different."

A whole host of objections flooded through her. "But, Jake...!"

"No. No. This'll work. See, maybe Pop can't see it, but Angel's as good as they come, can almost run the ranch by himself. Probably has the last couple of years. It's just a change in strategy that we're talking about, not the day to day operations. We focus on that. And then, maybe after my second tour, when we've showed him, not to mention the entire valley, cuz...," he paused, looking at her. "You know they matter. After everybody can see that you're doing well, we just turn it all over to you."

"Oh, Jake!" She wrapped him in a big hug.

"Hey, hey!" He laughed. "Sticks, it's just a chance to prove to him that you can do better."

"That's all I need." Her mind resumed its tumbling over and over, this time with a bubbling joy. She could feel Jake watching her, could feel his confidence buoying her, making her stronger. God, she loved him so much.

"Besides, it lets me off the hook." His comment broke in on her thoughts. "Just keep a room for me, won't ya? When I'm home on leave?"

Grabbing him in an even tighter hug, burying her head in his shoulder, she whispered, "Always, Jake. Always."

***

Late that night, as she lay in bed happier than she had been in so long that she couldn't remember, it suddenly dawned on her that she hadn't set out Jake's and Angel's breakfast where they could find it. Getting out of bed, she pulled on some pajama bottoms in case Pop was up and stepped into the hall, only to hear some murmuring from the living room. Softly tip-toeing toward the kitchen, she could hear Jake talking, saying, "The Screaming Eagles? Well, you gotta apply just like for any job and hope they pick you."

Andrew was responding, "How do you know that they'll pick you?"

"You don't. The only way to get a fighting chance is to make sure I'm in the top five graduating from each of those schools. Top three, if I can manage it." Too right, she thought, happily thinking of Jake kicking ass as she slipped into the kitchen. Scrawling a good-bye note, she set it next to a couple of thermoses and the sack from the fridge. Then she heard, "But, that's not the question you were going to ask me, is it?" She stopped for some reason.

Andrew's voice came thickly, "No, I guess not."

"What is it, hoss?" His voice was gentle, low.

There was a long silence, followed by "I...I...Jake, I..." and then, to her disbelief, some sobbing.

Jake said, even more softly, "You'll do just fine, hoss. I know you will."

Despising Andrew for his weak tears, she decided she didn't want to hear anymore and snuck away.

***

And with that, he was gone. "Until Christmas," he had said. "Really?" she had asked eagerly. He had beamed, "With a case of single malt in the right hands, who can tell?" She woke with a smile on her face then suddenly realized what day it was and felt terrible at how happy she felt, then she remembered why. Jake's parting gift.

Stuffing a couple slices of cold bacon in her mouth, she stepped through the quiet house, hearing a car in the drive. Outside, Angel was just opening the door for Maria. "Señorita Jessica, you want some help today, no?" Grateful, she nodded her thanks and went straight to the stable, not wanting to think anymore about it.

Whip caught her sense of joy and galloped along without any urging on her part. As she bounded up and down, her head bubbled with ideas and questions. Jake had asked a good question. Why were their grades slipping these last years and how did you get better ones? Thinking about how fat the buyers must be getting since the price of beef at Safeway wasn't getting any cheaper, she tried to muster up some disgust, but was too happy today to manage it. Still... Seeing a gate ahead, she jumped Whip over it just for fun and, at the peak of the jump, suddenly thought that maybe that stupid old UW would give her the answer. She reined Whip in, her flanks heaving lightly as she blew, and watched a swather in the distance go about its latest cutting of alfalfa. She couldn't see how. Well, she'd just have to keep her eyes open, she decided. With Jake believing in her, she'd find it. She knew she would. Looking up at the wide open blue sky and feeling Whip's urge to get going again, she let her.

III

Andrew saw her. Again. Knowing it was
impossible, because classes didn't begin for another
few weeks, he still found himself pounding across
Red Square after that ponytail that had turned the
corner of the library. His feet pounding the red bricks
of the great, wide thoroughfare and its open views of
the campus all around, he wondered if this was what
Purgatory was like, running forever, chasing after
some elusive unknown. At least he had good wind
now, he grimaced. And for a moment, he was back
there again, the surrounding fields of brown and
green, a tiny dust devil swirling nearby in rows of
mint, its sweet fragrance pushing up to his nose as the
grand, muscular heat of Digger's reluctant hobbles
shifted into a canter - all far more real to him than the
gray Gothic arches and ginger-colored monuments to
higher learning surrounding him.

Turning the corner of the library, he almost ran into
her as she was doubling back. "Sorry!" he mumbled
and kept on going, catching a disappointing glimpse
of assumed self-importance, draped like a veneer over
the shoulders of the student who has made it through
the first year. No, not her. Definitely not. She didn't
need it, being made of sterner stuff, he thought. So
different from Amber's carefully coiffed beauty he
thought now, as the recollection of running into her
the other day flooded his mind. The same auburn
hair, the same exquisitely drawn eyebrows, one tilted

up in its coy question mark, hinting at so much more and, he knew now, having so much less to offer.

He swore at his foolishness and, spotting a bench under a group of maple trees, sat down. This had to stop, he thought. Feeling himself tear up, he angrily rubbed his eyes, fighting away the throbbing threatening at his temples. Looking down, he saw a smooth, round black stone and focused on it, trying to meditate on the Noble Truth of Sorrow. Slowly, as his thoughts began to suspend their whirling, he was reminded of his breathing and consciously began to slow that as well. Concentrating on the soft roundness of the stone, he let his mind drift, grasping the edges of this Buddhist wisdom and then, further, pondering the Noble Truth of Arising of Sorrow, born of craving or desire.

A stray thought, as surely as an arrow, struck him in the heart as he heard Jake's "If'n..." He smiled with recollection at how Jake's manner of speaking had grown more...rural...he thought, the first days after they had arrived. He had been surprised at it, had thought it a ridiculous affectation until he had remembered that Jake never seemed to have time to be anything but Jake. Over the following days, as he had begun to listen to how others employed language back there, how much more slowly they spoke, how much simpler their descriptions of life events, how much smaller a vocabulary used to get around, it had dawned on him that he was being given a precious insight into the patterns of life there. That...he suddenly jerked his thoughts back to the stone and concentrated on it afresh, reminding himself to detach. Slowly, teasingly, as if on old withered parchment, the teaching of Sakyamuni Buddha appeared in ancient script: Though you conquer ten thousand cities, you shall never be great until you conquer the self.

He smiled, feeling better. Detachment. He breathed out a sigh and leaned back to listen to a wren in a nearby tree, finally feeling at peace with the world.

And thought of her. The pain, so sudden, so intense he couldn't breathe, broke out new tears that splashed onto his cheeks before he was even aware of them.

"Andrew?"

He looked up and saw a girl - Ella! - staring at him through downy, yellow curls - a new hairstyle, he noticed - with concern from the sidewalk, flanked by two girls looking much like her. "What's wrong? Is it Jake? Is he okay?"

He jerkily wiped his cheeks, rose to his feet and fled.

***

Schnoebel's smoky office had proven disappointingly similar to his father's. Her one departure from academic mustiness appeared to be her scarves, such as this one today, in lurid splotches of brown and leaf green that, he noticed, becomingly brought out the green thread of the same shade in her tweed jacket. A forgotten cigarette burned away in an overfull ashtray, its tell-tale smoke trailing up into nothingness.

"Ach, Andrew. Wünderschön." She peered over her round bifocals at him and gestured to a chair stacked with journals and grad papers. He picked up the stack, set it on the floor and sat, waiting for her to finish marking whatever she was reading. She sighed in irritation, made a large red circle with a flourish and scrawled something in the margin. "Das machts nichts," she growled, flipped the cover closed and put her head back. "John, the Gospel in which the infant may paddle, the elephant may swim..." she said, tilting her head to look at him with one corner of her mouth lifted in a wry grin, "...and feckless grad students may drown." She lit another cigarette, then spotting the forgotten one, stubbed it out while taking a long drag.

He shifted uncomfortably.

Watching him for a moment, she frowned, exhaled, then shook her head. "So, cherub, you have done excellent work checking that wretched feminist critique of 2 Timothy." Andrew blinked, feeling somewhat foolish and his cheeks burn. "Come, let us find the limits of your savanted knowledge. Tell me what you know of John. And don't feed me back what we covered in class last fall."

Andrew's mind raced, feeling on better ground now. Like so many times before with Schnoebel, he was being tested. And, as had become his habit with her these last few weeks, he began speaking almost as soon as the thoughts appeared in his head, having grown more comfortable with the expectation that they were heading somewhere, even if he didn't know where they would ultimately end.

"John's co--community of churches, probably originating in Palestine with all the ref...references to witnessing to Jews and Samaritans in the text and....maybe, landing in Ephesus, on the coast of Turkey."

She nodded, taking another drag, her eyes shrinking through the smoke to two shaded hoods as she watched him. "Güt."

He kept going. "Mar...marked by the unusual "I Am" statements of Jesus but also by the...the speeches in the middle..." He paused then, looking at her.

"Yes, cherub?"

"There...it...you can split the gospel into four parts."

She sat back. "Really?"

"Maybe."

"Go on."

"The...lo...logos...hymn at the beginning...then, the...Jesus' public ministry starting with the cleansing of the Temple...different from the other gospels...then the speeches...the symbolic speeches about who he is..."I am the vine, you are the branches"...and the last part, his private teachings just to his disciples."

She watched him for a moment, stubbed out her cigarette, then removed her glasses and set them down. "And the essential truth to the Gospel, cherub?"

"That Jesus is God." That popped out of his mouth so quickly it surprised him.

She waited for more, then smiled. "You have been thinking about this, have you?"

"You..." The words stuck in his throat, then came out. "You said I was a bit light on John..."

She frowned, wrinkling her forehead, the one part of her that was somewhat smooth, he thought. Then her eyes brightened, "Ja, Ja! The Matthew confrontation with..." Her mouth pursed in thought, then, "...mit Herr Hegland of Campus Crusade for Christ fame."

Andrew suddenly found himself thinking of those green eyes and red hair in a scent of vanilla. For the second time in...how long? He wondered. Then, just as suddenly, he caught a flash of faded blue eyes, squinting in the sun over freckled cheeks and the musky smell of damp horseflesh. He breathed out. Detach, he reminded himself.

"Ausgezeichnet, cherub. As usual." She tossed the paper she had been marking up over to him. "Read that and let me know your conclusions." Catching it, he heard her rasping chuckle that "...probably scare hapless young Fraulein Mintz into some tolerable scholarship..."

He looked down. These last weeks had still not taught him how to respond to her compliments. Not that she appeared to mind. When he had ridden Digger into Brickton where no one would hear him make the call that day about three weeks after Jake had left, about three weeks after she had stopped talking to him, stopped looking at him, stopped all notice of him whatsoever, Schnoebel had only chuckled that she was certain they could "find something for him to do..." That morning, he had taken a slow ride back, his last on Digger, wondering whether he had made good on his promise to Jake in keeping up the daily Pounds Patrols, keeping an eye out for calves not feeding, cows looking sluggish, anything in particular looking wrong, even giving the daily Pounds Report to Pop, just as Jake had, though Pop hadn't looked all that interested. It was with considerable pride then, a couple of afternoons after he had been out on his own, that he had found a case of foot rot. Pop's increasing malaise had suddenly given way as he slapped the arm of his chair, saying, "Good, Andrew! Good!" Then, when he had noticed a cow looking out of sorts, kicking her steer calf away from feeding and he had reported it to Pop, it had turned out to be a case of "hardware disease" - the cow had swallowed a coil of baling wire. Pop had begun talking over dinner again that day, though only after they had finished the main meal, of course, telling Andrew old stories about how he had started with pretty much nothing but "Jesus' love and a pair of willing hands," how he had earned the respect of other ranchers with his early successes and had been able to buy out leases, quickly doubling and tripling his holdings. Through it all, though, she had sat there, her mind clearly elsewhere. She had looked happier than Andrew had ever seen her, though in a contained way, as if it were her own secret. And watching her out of the corner of his eye, he had known that he would never learn it.

That sad morning, after a long, slow rubdown of a goodbye to Digger, he had found Pop in his chair and, blushing at the memory, had lied outright saying that a professor had asked him to return to help out on a Scripture project.

"Oh? They read the Bible at that university?" The eyes of that same faded blue had peered up at him.

"Yes, sir. Very carefully."

"Good. Andrew, the Lord's work may be found everywhere."

"Yes, sir."

To Andrew's stammered confession that he should probably leave as soon as possible, perhaps even that afternoon, Pop had only looked down at his Bible, open to Ezekiel, and sighed.

As Andrew was leaving the room, Pop had finally ventured, "Andrew?"

"Yes, Pop?"

"Remember." He had cleared his throat. "Remember that everywhere we go, we are always in Jesus' hands."

"Yes, Pop."

It was with considerable surprise a week after that he had received a check from Van der Vaal Ranch and Cattle, sent him care of the UW's general PO box, for two thousand dollars. No explanation at all, except her note in the memo line "summer hand" and her signature. Not bold. Certainly not adorned. Just small and fierce.

"What do you know of Kuan Yin?" The question, so startling in its direction, confused him, making him wonder where he was - one of the pastures, Pop's living room, or...until he realized that he was staring straight into Schnoebel's eyes.

"Av--avalokitesvara?"

"Genau." She smiled, shaking her head. Then, realizing that he didn't understand her, said, "Exactly."

"Bodhisattva...male bodhisattva of mercy...of the Indian Buddhist tradition who becomes the female goddess of co--compassion Kuan Yin in China and Kannon in Japan after traders along the Silk Route brought word of Her. Him." He paused, not knowing what to say next, wondering where this was going.

Schnoebel chuckled. "Normally, I do not loan out my...finds...to my colleagues, but Wei's in a jam, and I...owe him one or two."

Andrew shrugged in confusion.

"Charles Wei. East Asian Buddhism. His publishers are after him to finish his latest tome of fortune cookie wisdom." She looked him over, holding out a piece of paper with a number scrawled on it. "How about it? He pays the same."

Andrew blinked, then smiled and took the paper.

She suddenly whipped out a bony finger and wagged it in his face. "Don't forget, cherub. You belong to me, first."

He jerked out a nod. She smiled, pulled out another cigarette and lit up. "Ach, cherub. Your habitual reticence is wearing. Auf Wiedersehen." She turned back to another paper.

He struggled out a "Bye" and left.

***

Mounting the two flights up to the Buddhist Studies department, Andrew found his mind curious, even intrigued at the possibilities. He wondered what this Charles Wei would be like and thought, with relief, that he could use a break from Christianity. Reading that critique of 2 Timothy, he found it hard to concentrate if only because he kept hearing the shards of naked suffering in that old woman's voice during the Prayer Meeting. At first, he had been fascinated watching the whole event develop, despite Pastor Don's challenge, the answer to which he still didn't know how he had managed. And as that poor woman's story had unfolded, that fascination had only grown at the realization that he was sitting in on a real conversation about faith, about how Fundamentalism met the uncertainties of life, about how devout Christians witnessed to each other, until at the point - Irma that old woman's name was, he just remembered - he had looked over at her sitting across the room on the piano bench and had seen the terrifying pain in those light blue eyes, growing wider and deeper as

Irma had laid out detail after horrifying detail. He had shut his own and, for the first time in his life, had found himself meditating on the Noble Truth of Sorrow, something that up to then had always been an historical artifact to him and nothing more.

Finding Wei's office, he knocked on the door, heard a murmur inside and opened it. Inside, he found a man squinting over a long scroll laid out over his desk. "Dr. Wei?"

The face, round as a pie pan, he thought, and just as smooth, looked up, framed by a few wisps of black hair. "Yes."

"Umm..." He found himself blushing again and swore inwardly. "Dr. Schnoebel..."

The eyes, a startling pure brown blinked at him, waiting.

"Dr. Schnoebel said...I should...you...needed..."

The eyes blinked again, revealing two fine lines at the outside of each fading off into the smoothness. They sighed then. "Ah. Her Christian wunderkind." The lips protruded out to pronounce the German word like a foot soldier in a comedy. "Please come in." Wei gestured to a chair which, like all academic offices it seemed, served more as a bookshelf.

Andrew set the books, many dog-eared, on the floor, noticing the top title as something about the Mahayana sect in Mao's China. He looked down, then remembering Pop, looked straight up into the brown eyes who were surveying him patiently.

"So. Ingrid tells me that you are exceptionally gifted at finding leaps of logic in her grad students' research."

Andrew tried a smile and failed spectacularly, he thought. He tried to say something but only managed to grunt.

"How much do you know about Buddhism?"

"A little." He felt the dreaded burn score his cheeks.

The eyes watched him quietly without any visible emotion.

"A test?" Wei finally asked.

Andrew shrugged.

"What are the cardinal virtues of the devout Buddhist?"

Andrew blinked, wondering if this were a trick question. Finally, he cleared his throat and managed, "I can only answer for the Th--Theravada tradition."

The brown eyes smiled for the first time. "At least you know there is more than one tradition of Buddhism."

"Yes, sir."

"Well?"

"Friendliness, joy, co--compassion and equanimity."

Wei smile again, a little more deeply. "Not peace and love?"

Andrew hesitated, unsure for a moment. His mind tried scanning quickly through what he knew about Buddhism. Not much, he had to admit. He bit his lip then, wondering what to say next.

"Everything that is not Christian, perhaps?" The eyes sparkled merrily now, the thin eyebrows over them raising in arched hoops.

Andrew abruptly realized that Wei was poking fun at the pop Buddhism of the Northwest which, he had to admit, had struck him as pretty much the same way. He smiled. Nervously.

"Tell me a Jataka."

"On--one, sir?"

"Just one. Your favorite."

So, Andrew told him the story of how, in one of His past incarnations, the Buddha had been born as a beautiful White Elephant King that, finding a hunter lost in the woods, had not only generously showed him the way home but also when confronted by the hunter's claimed poverty, had freely given up his tusks. The hunter, thinking only of his own greed and

169

not caring about the elephant's selfless generosity, had been swallowed by the earth into a fiery hell shortly after.

Wei watched Andrew nervously shifting in his seat, then asked, "And why is that particular Jataka your favorite?"

Andrew felt his mind suddenly empty. Then, as before, the words appeared before he could imagine where they came from. "Because being lo--lost and alone is the worst thing I can imagine."

Wei watched him some more, his eyes growing a brighter brown. Then he smiled. "Hardly the point of the story; however, I can see what you are saying." He stood, walked over to a stack of papers balanced on the edge of a bookcase and began rifling through them. "You know of Kuan Yin? How her shape in art forms changed as Buddhism traveled across Asia?"

Andrew nodded. Hearing nothing, Wei turned. Andrew nodded again.

Wei tossed him a paper. "Art history that one. The same work you do for Ingrid: check the sources, look for gaps of reasoning. One page written summary of the work. One page also of any concerns you have would be nice, though Ingrid tells me two or three are your usual. Enjoy."

Andrew nodded a third time and got up to leave. He had just reached the door when Wei said, "You remind me of a quite talented scholar in the Midwest. A Gordon Worth." Andrew froze, wondering what to say.

"An Indian Buddhist scholar. Because classical Chinese as a language did not lend itself to creating the hierarchies of thought that Sanskrit was capable of, he flatters himself that we of Middle Kingdom Buddhism lack...subtlety. Still, the Buddha's light shines on us all."

Andrew turned to see the pie-face wrinkled into a mischievous grin, the brown eyes twinkling. "As a

matter of fact, now that I think of it, I believe he
mentioned a conference or two ago that a relation of
his was studying here." Andrew tried to muster up a
comment but found his tongue too thick to move.

"I look forward to your insights."

***

Late one night in the small grad apartment on the
far edge of campus that Schnoebel had scrounged for
him, he looked up from the John thesis to stare at the
emptiness of the rooms and wondered how long he
would be able to stay there. He couldn't bear the
thought of a new roommate in a few days. He had
even managed to mention the hope to Schnoebel the
day before. She had only smiled, "We shall see.
Wei's recommendation would prove helpful."

So he had redoubled his efforts to turn in topnotch
work on the Kuan Yin thesis. Academia had its perks,
he considered, stretching. The coin of the realm here
was the quality of thought produced. Quantity didn't
hurt, either. Just like pounds, he thought, feeling his
stomach clench. Not to mention that he was actually
busy enough that pushing her out of his mind was
becoming an almost automatic reaction, as he did just
now. Suddenly lonesome for the sound of passing
cars in their old dorm, he threw on his raincoat, not
that he needed it, he thought, given how clear it was
and walked out.

Crossing the moonlit, deserted campus, he
wondered what time it was and decided it didn't
matter. Then he realized that he might be growing
detached from the concept of time and grinned.
Down the street, on frat row, he could hear a loud
party and suddenly, desperately wanted to join it.
Then, remembering his experiences with house
parties last year, he changed his mind and just kept
walking into the center of campus. Before he knew it,
he was standing outside their old dorm building

looking up at their window. It looked pretty much deserted, except a few lights. But not one in their room. Wondering if the elevator had ever gotten fixed, he stood there, wondering what to do next. Finally, after a few minutes feeling absolutely ridiculous, he spotted a trio of boys supporting each other on the way home from some den of inebriation and decided to simply go in.

It was fixed. And before he knew it, he was standing in front of the door, tracing out the numbers of their old address. His hand automatically reached down to the knob and turned it and, to his surprise and wonder, it opened. He stepped inside, smelling the unaired mustiness, and softly closed the door. There. Finally. He could feel him. Even if through the memories. Even better than when he pulled on his raincoat every day. Closing his eyes, he could almost see the titles lining Jake's bookshelf and the old bayonet lying next to its accompanying wet stone on his desk. Jake's booming laugh and bright beam came back to him. He could remember carefully stepping over the empties strewn around the floor and, suddenly thinking of how Irma's husband had died so terribly, was horrified by the thought that Jake could well end up the same way. Shaking off the thought, he made up his mind to talk to Jake about it when...

When. Christmas, he had said. Maybe. Jake had promised to write, but, Andrew shrugged, helplessly reminding himself again that, so far as Jake knew, Andrew was still at the ranch. He wished that he had thought of asking for some kind of general address to write to, given the complicated timeline Jake had drawled out of the different bases he would be posted at across the country. But Andrew, in his panic at Jake's leaving had forgotten to and now, with the way she had looked at him, or had not looked at him those last weeks at the ranch, he knew that he couldn't ask her.

Instead, he sat on Jake's bed and hoped to...what? Smell him? Something. But there was nothing. Just dust and moonlight and silence. Casting around for something to think about, anything to fill up the emptiness, he abruptly realized how blue the moonlight was in this room and remembered another blue-lit night here. Ella. How beautiful she was that night. Like a goddess. Remembering Ella, and her erotic playfulness that night, he felt himself stiffening and, embarrassed, pushed that thought out of his mind.

Finally, frustrated at what wasn't there yet grateful for what was, he slipped out.

**

Over the last days before the quarter started, he visited the room several times, each late at night. He found himself torn by the paradox that the closer that day came, the closer he had the chance of hearing from Jake but the farther he would be from being able to steal the memories of their room. Each visit as he rounded the corner of the building he found his dread mounting that that night would show a gleam in the window. Or that the door would be locked. Finally, the night before classes began, as he stepped around the corner, he saw the flickering light of a television up there. He paused in the light mist that was falling that night, thinking that it must be around two or three in the morning. He looked around him at the sparkling sheets of jewels falling to the earth and felt his own grief rising, unmatched by anything he had felt yet. Maybe. Then, again - it was almost becoming rote now - he found himself seizing upon a brick in the wall of the building, noting that it had caught his eye because of its slightly different shade of color in the darkness, and meditated on detachment. He stood there, breathing in and out. Breathing in and out. Breathing in and out.

"Yo! Buddy! You gotta problem?"

Looking over at the figure standing in the doorway to the building, he smiled sadly, gathered Jake's coat about him - about the only thing he had left - turned and walked away.

***

And so the quarter began. His classes were not difficult. The combined requests from Wei and Schnoebel, now coming faster that school was in session, kept him busy. And his evenings were quiet. His meditation on detachment continued, adding the desire - albeit a detached one he always reminded himself - for balance. It seemed to work. He got to know his mind so well that before long, he could meditate for many minutes, sometimes as many as ten, without a single stray thought appearing to distract him. Not long after, he got to the point when he could tell the difference between a thought about Jake, a thought about Yakima and a thought about her. He even colored them: black for Jake in his now quieting rage that Jake had never written; an indifferent, he trusted, blue for the skies of Yakima; and, at first, pink for her, because it was the color she would hate most. Then, knowing that he was spending too much emotion on her color, when it changed itself to red during a walking meditation one day on the way to an English Lit class, he allowed it remain red and chose not to ponder why. Nevertheless, his mental discipline grew to the point that he could feel one of the thoughts, identified by its color, before it had even formed and could stop it in its tracks, like a martial artist stopping bullets in a Hong Kong action movie.

Proud of his efforts, he even mentioned it one day to Wei. The brown eyes in the pie-face, really more of a moon shape, Andrew had decided, had sparked with interest. "Yes. I've never heard of color-coding thoughts as a way of harnessing them. However, and you may not know this, but professional therapy is getting interested in that very method to help trauma victims. Cognitive behavioral therapy, it's called, I believe." Andrew's face fell, so Wei added, "Still, points to you for original thinking."

Andrew felt the heated waves of pleasure marking his face, then cautioned himself not to grow too attached to it, then got confused about which way to think and gave up.

Watching him, Wei shook his head before adding with his mischievous grin, "Of course, if you're really daring, you'll go beyond trying to keep track of every single neuron firing in the mind and dissolve the self entirely." Stunned, Andrew didn't know what to say, but nodded and walked out.

Of course there was a price to pay for his newly found balance - further alienation from his classmates. It began when he had noticed interesting parallels of meditation between the Christian and Buddhist traditions. Reading ahead in his History of Medieval Christianity class had sparked his interest in the mystics. A footnote had sent him digging in the library for a battered, seemingly forgotten, copy of St. Bonaventura's *The Mind's Road to God*. Bonaventura's conviction that one didn't need a great deal of knowledge or reason to find traces of God in the universe - indeed, one would do better to simply show up and look around - had reminded Andrew a great deal of a thesis he had been checking for Wei: the development of anti-intellectualism in the Chan school of Buddhism in China - with its great stress on meditation - and its further transformations to Zen in Japan. Emboldened by his find, he had brought it up in the history class because Cohen, a Jew, appeared to be one of the few scholars in the department with sympathy for traditions outside one's specialty. At first, in response, Cohen had simply stared at him. Then, lightly rubbing the spot above his nose with a

finger, he had said, "Yes, that's been observed before,
but no serious work that I'm aware of has been done
on it." Behind him, Andrew had heard the hiss,
"Kid's a monk."

Another nickname. Before long, he seemed to be
hearing it whispered all around him whenever he
raised his hand to ask a question in class. Whether it
implied like or dislike, he couldn't tell. However it
certainly meant that everyone cut him an even wider
swath than last year. Andrew, growing resigned to a
school year spent alone it seemed, tried to like it at
first, but then, sitting in the apartment at night, grew
to detest it. In desperation, he began combing the
aisles of the library for anything and everything on
mystics, reading far into the night, devouring the
books as quickly as he could in the hopes of finding
some way of combating his loneliness, as the mystics
had. All he could find was the same answer: If they
didn't have people, they had God. Well, he grimaced
in disgust, he didn't have either and continued
meditating on detachment. His attempts to color the
thought of loneliness failed him every single time.
Much less stop those thoughts in their tracks. One
quiet Sunday, overcome with exhaustion at the effort,
he gave way to despair, curled up on the couch and
cried himself into a troubled sleep. Upon waking, he
felt better somehow and decided to keep on with it.

It was on just such an evening halfway through the
quarter when, on an errand to find St. Teresa's *Way of
Perfection*, he passed by a table spread wide with
books and magazines on organic ranching, the
business of ranching, grass-fed cattle, the business of
organic farming, the rise and fall of the ranching
industry, all open to certain passages marked with
notes. Pausing by the table, still wondering if Teresa
had really believed one should begin and end every
prayer with self-knowledge or whether he was just
imagining that, he allowed himself the luxury of
riding Digger again, even if just for a few minutes,

something he had not let himself do since that day with the black stone. Meditation had helped steel his mind, and he preferred it that way.

Initially, he was afraid to. He remembered the searing pain of those first weeks back from the ranch. Then, thinking over everything he had learned in his many quiet hours about disciplining the mind, he let himself go. He could smell Digger's foam, could smell the dry, hot dust baking the fields, could smell the rustiness of a wheel sprinkler as they galloped by. Did he ever get Digger to gallop, he suddenly paused in thought? He didn't remember anymore. Bemused, he looked down at all the books and magazines, the penciled and penned notes sketching out graphs on ruled paper, and wondered what field a grad student would be working in to do organic ranching. Economics? Business? Horticulture?

"Andrew?"

He seized up, knowing the voice. He looked down at the sprawl again, shaking his head.

"I thought I'd run into you one of these days. Though sooner." Jessie had paused by a corner of some nearby stacks, another pile of books in her hands, then continued on to her table and set them down.

"Hi."

"Well, aren't you going to ask about Jake? I know he didn't write you."

Andrew's carefully balanced world caved in. "He...he...?"

"Same old Andrew." Shaking her head, she sat down. "The only thing that will make Jacob Van der Vaal pick up a pen is the chance that it will get him between the sheets of some woman's bed someday."

Surprising himself, Andrew barked out one ringing laugh that gave way to a loud chortle, causing students nearby to shush him. God, it felt good to laugh again, he thought. Moreover, Jessie looked pleased that he had laughed at her joke. Pleased that he had made her pleased, he smiled, saying, "Same old Jake."

"You know he is! Been that way since, I don't know, probably kindergarten. I only know that he got through Airborne school because Pop put his foot down and made me email him."

Conflicting emotions crashed within his heart. "You...you've got...he's got email?! He made it thr--through the first school!? How di--did he...?" His vague wondering whether he, too, had an email account and how one used it was quickly overrun by the happiness and pride for his friend tearing up his eyes.

Jessie looked away, saying, "Second in points, he said. With a hairline fracture to the ankle that he hid from them. That's our Jake." Ashamed, he quickly blinked away the wetness as she shook her head then suddenly ran her hand through her ponytail like she always used to when she was about to say something.

"Andrew?" she asked, her voice quieter.

"Yes." He sat down opposite her, lowering his voice as well.

"I can't figure you out."

He stopped for a moment, wondering what she meant, wondering how he should respond.

"What is up with all this stuttering?" Shaking her head in irritation and tugging at her ponytail again, she said, "I mean, I watched you do those stupid practice falls that Jake made you do. From the kitchen. I was washing up. Did you do 'em all?"

Andrew shrugged. "Yeah."

"All two hundred?"

"Of course."

"Why?"

"Jake said it was important. That it could come in handy some day."

"Stay on the horse and you won't need it."

Andrew burst out in quiet chortles.

"What?"

"Same old Jessie."

She scowled at him. "I don't know what that means."

He thought about trying to explain how indomitable she could be, kind of like an unstoppable freight train then, imagining her reaction, decided against it. "It means I'm glad to see you."

"Oh." She looked surprised. Really surprised.

They sat quietly for a moment. Finally, to move the conversation ahead, Andrew smiled and pointed to a book, "Guess we know what your major is."

When she didn't answer, he looked up to see her face a study in frowning. "Andrew. I wasn't very nice to you before you left."

Now it was his turn to be surprised.

"I'm sorry about that. It's just that...you can be a little...eggheady at times. And it pisses me off."

Stunned, he sat as if carved from stone.

"So, knock it off, would you?"

Not knowing what that implied, not daring to hope, and certainly not wanting to discourage it, he quickly nodded. "Sure."

She relaxed and smiled. "Good."

"So..." Suddenly feeling his mind go horribly blank, he racked his brains to think of something to say.

"And another thing."

"What--what's that?"

"Quit your damn stuttering. It's irritating. Any man that can learn to get Digger in shape as fast as you did has no reason to go around stuttering all the time."

"O--okay." He sighed.

They sat in silence a few minutes more, looking each other over. Andrew was about to ask after Digger when, surprising himself, he took the plunge and said, "I don't know why I do it. I've always hated it."

She sighed. "Try making the sentence in your mind first. Then say it."

He started laughing loudly with delight, exciting more shushing around them. Of course! Why hadn't he thought of that?

"It--" He stopped, formed the sentence, then said it. "I'm very, very happy to see you again, Jessie."

Her eyes widened, then narrowed in a scowl as if she were about to blacken one of his eyes to match Jake's that night. He quickly raised both hands and was about to speak, then reminded himself to form it before saying it and felt pleased at how easily it was coming. Just before speaking, he had the flash insight that it was proving simple because of all his recent mental exercising. "I'm serious. Jessie. No joke. I am."

"Oh." Her scowl softened. She studied him a moment, then asked. "Why don't you call me Sticks? All Jake's friends do."

"Because it doesn't fully capture your essence. Jessie does."

"What the hell does that mean?" She punched him in the arm and grinned.

***

Andrew had tried to drag the evening out as long as possible not wanting their conversation, meandering at times, poignant in some unspeakable beauty at others it seemed to him, to end. Finally, when she had sighed and looked down at her books, and the mounting dread rising in him rendered him speechless, she had solved the problem for him.

"Do you like Seattle?"

Knowing he couldn't form a single syllable through the parchedness, he had only nodded.

"I don't much. But, maybe I haven't given it a fair shake, yet. Anyway, I've got some more work to do on this. But on Saturday night, how about you show me something interesting over here?"

He wasn't sure that he had heard right. In any case, he wasn't sure that he could have heard anything through the single, sweet tenor he had heard right then in his head, pouring out a Gregorian chant. Shaking his head, he had wondered at that, knowing that music hadn't ever been a distracting thought before, then had quickly realized that it had to do with the thesis on medieval passion plays that he was checking.

"And I'll show you something I found interesting. Pick me up at my dorm at seven?" Her voice, lower, yet melodious in its own rough way and savoring brusquely, he had abruptly thought, of the harsh gray-green of the greasewood sprinkling the hills of the valley, had cut through the chant. He had nodded, and she had smiled and written down her dorm number, and with that the impossible had unexpectedly became attainable.

Not wanting to ruin this sudden turn of fortune in his favor, he had nodded, managed to find the words, "See you then," and had struggled his way out through the stacks.

On the way home, he had stopped under a streetlight to peer at her hand-writing. Small and fierce, he had grinned happily. Certainly not pretty and knowing she never had to be, he had carefully re-folded it and tucked it close to his heart as a talisman. That under the dorm building and number had looked something like a military email address for Jake had hardly seemed to register. Later, he had taken it out carefully and leaned it against a stack of books on the table in the apartment to sit down and stare at it. Then, fearing a capricious gust of wind much like the one that had taken his hat the first day he had seen her flying past the trellis over the canal, on the edge of life itself, like some sort of Valkyrie charging through a Norse dream, he had picked it back up, re-folded it and softly replaced it in his shirt pocket to pulse against the beating of his heart and had slept that way.

The next morning, feeling as if some sort of requisite act of goodwill was in order, he had memorized Jessie's dorm number then searched out Ella and, finding her amidst the usual gaggle of lycra and cashmere, had stepped up to her, his hand outstretched, holding the paper. The chatting had abruptly stopped. Ella, feeling his eyes on her back, had turned, smiled and asked, "Andrew? What is it?" Then, seeing the paper, she had taken it to read, small lines of concentration cutely furrowing between her eyebrows, her deep blue eyes narrowing. Suddenly, she had gasped and, throwing her arms around him he felt her whispered kiss in a mist of lavender, "Thank you." He had nodded long enough to notice that she had already turned and run off down a neighboring sidewalk, the gaggle all watching her with shock until one voice had knowingly whispered, "Her soldier boy." And then they had all, in unison it had seemed, sighed in a moan. He had smiled and gone on his way before they could press him for details.

And Saturday night had come. She had been waiting for him at the entrance to her hall, jeans and sneakers seen under one of Jake's raincoats, already adorned with its own evening set of glittering drops, probably the only jewelry he would ever see her wear, he had grinned. "Where to?" she had asked. And she had driven, one of the battered cars that he thought he had recognized from the ranch.

Great Gothic arches. Okay, he allowed, not really Gothic. Still, the mounting arches of the bridge standing five or six stories high would do as well as any medieval cathedral, he thought and suddenly stopped half-way out of the car, captivated at the realization that he finally understood the modern municipal obsession besetting the country to outdo one another in building the largest, widest, grandest football and baseball stadia known to humankind.

Much like the 12th and 13th century competition among the cities of Europe where, scratching their heads to leverage their crude technology into flying buttresses, ribbed vaults, and fluted columns to raise the arched ceiling of their cathedral just a few feet higher than the neighboring efforts: Notre Dame, 114 feet high; Chartres, 123 feet; Rheims, 124 feet; Amiens, 138 feet; and so on. He wondered why the engineer turned history student's thesis he was now checking hadn't clued into the modern comparison and decided to mention it to Schnoebel at their next meeting.

"Andrew!" He snapped his gaze back down from the arches to see Jessie's irritated scowl. "Don't get all eggheady on me, again. Remember? You promised."

"Right." He grinned nervously and finished stepping out of the car to close the door. It stuck, unlocked partway, so he tried to open it again.

"What's wrong?" Her impatient tone cut his ears.

Feeling foolish, he didn't want to say and tried heaving on the door, harder this time, but to no avail.

"Is it stuck again?" He felt her come closer to stand next to him, frowning at the door. He tried to think of something witty to say but, suddenly overwhelmed by the trace scent of Digger, but different, he found his mind going blank again.

"Well. Why don't you...?"

He looked at her, wondering.

Exhaling in disgust, she elbowed him aside and kicked the door shut to a satisfying click. He tried to feel embarrassed but could only feel a secret delight as the spot in his ribs where her elbow had hit him took on a rosy, inward glow.

"So where are we going?"

Pointing uphill, where the bridge met the crest of the hill above them, he formed the sentences in his head first, then said, "Somewhere special. Not too many people know about it."

Following his pointed finger, Jessie looked at him, a confused expression overtaking her features. Then she sighed, "Okay. Lead the way."

As they trudged up the steep slope, the bridge overhead simultaneously keeping them dry while affording them the splendid view of sheets of rain cascading down on either side of them, he tried to remember at what point on the rise you could just make out the top of the head. After a few more steps, he thought, here, and stopped.

She was staring at him with a look of...pity, he was surprised to notice, in her eyes.

Not liking what he was seeing, he began talking to see if he could ward it away. "It...I...only ca--came across it myself...by surprise...one night...last year." He tried to grin but felt that he was horribly messing even that up. So, his spirits suddenly sinking, he waited to hear her reaction.

"Andrew. Are we going to see the Fremont Troll?" She frowned at him, uncertainly.

"The Fremont Tr--?"

"Yeah." She pointed the way they were headed. "Just under the bridge up there. Big ol' heap of cement, high as the tool shed at home. With a crushed VW in his hand and hubcaps for his eyes."

No, he thought! Not wanting to meet her eyes, he turned away and looked uphill and felt absolutely stupid. Again.

"Some girls from the dorm took me the first night I got here. They all do it. Some sort of freshman ritual, just to say they've seen..." Her voice faded leaving nothing but the sound of falling rain.

He chanced a look at her and found that same infuriating look of pity on her face, mixed with something else he didn't understand. He looked back up the hill. "It's okay," she said. "It's no big deal. Just a lump of cement."

He shook his head not wanting to think anything other than how quickly they could end this night and he could go back to the apartment. She didn't say anything either for another moment or two.

Finally, she moved as if to speak. Glancing at her, he saw her pulling at her ponytail and, curiously relieved, turned to face her. "Andrew, you don't...have too many friends, do you?"

He grunted, not trusting himself to say anything further. She waited.

Then she said, "Well, we're here. Why not show it to me anyway?"

Somehow that was the worst thing she could have said, he thought.

Brusquely, he turned and trudged furiously back downhill to the car, feeling his clodding footsteps turn into angry stomps. Never, he thought! Never again! Of course she would have seen it already. How more stupid could he possibly be? Angrily, he tried heaving on the door then realized it was locked and, smacking it with the flat of his fist, contemplated just running away out into the rain. It would hide him, he thought.

She was suddenly next to him. "Hey." He didn't dare look at her. "Here," she said and unlocked his door. Holding it open for him he felt her eyes, intrigued, staring at him. Not knowing what else to do, he climbed in and let her shut the door, not needing to kick it, he noticed with a last exasperated wrench of self-pity. She opened her door and sat down, then closed it. She started the car and, without another word, other than swearing when the clutch stuck, pulled away from the sidewalk and drove up the hill, to his surprise, retracing their footsteps. Driving right up to where the road T-ed the side street, the beams flooding the troll in all his glory, she put the clutch in neutral and put on the parking brake.

"Okay. So we're here. The first time you and I have seen it together."

Startled at this thought, he gaped at her.

She smiled. "Now, tell me. What did you want to show me?"

He paused, gathering his thoughts, then suddenly noticing that she was staring right through his eyes, frowning. "And, Andrew," she said. "Keep it simple, all right?"

So he had told her. All about Lao Tze, about the Tao Te Ching, about standing for one's own truth in the face of an uncaring cosmos, wondering if the next generation would even care about the quality of wisdom and the pains it took to achieve it. And how much he liked this troll, stoically weathering the passing of the seasons, carrying its crushed symbol of 60s idealism in its paw for all the succeeding generations to ponder the death of that inspiration. Each sentence, carefully formed within his mind before he uttered it, though at the end, when he began to speak more quickly, rushing to explain how this icon, even seen only once before, had nevertheless become a symbol of the principle of wu-wei, for that was the source of its strength, its--

"Wait a minute."

Pausing, he suddenly realized with a pang of guilt that he had stopped forming the sentences in his mind before speaking and braced himself for her complaint that he stop stuttering.

"Woo-what?"

Surprised, he hesitated a second, then explained. "Wu-wei. It's the Taoist ideal. In the face of a sudden turning of events, you resist the urge to react. You simply..."

"Simply...?" She was looking at him, a frown of concentration on her brow as she tugged on her ponytail.

He smiled, inwardly taking a picture of her to remember forever, and went on. "You simply find the...character, I think we would say...or maybe the integrity of self and become a mountain that may not be moved, no matter what..." Pausing for a moment, he then shrugged silently and thought, why not? "No matter what tempests beat upon you."

She was silent, watching and then, finding herself pulling at her ponytail, she grimaced and pushed it away, to his inarticulate thrill.

"You're telling me that when you're in trouble, these Taoists say that you shouldn't do anything?"

He looked off for a moment, wondering how to respond. Then, as he stared through the windshield, he marveled for a moment at how nice it was to have someone...someone his own age actually talk with him about this. His eyes lingering on the hubcap eyes of the monstrosity in front of him staring back out at nothing of any consequence, he then said, "I think they would say that when you've finally come to understand yourself, you'll come to see that the trouble won't be there anymore," and then smiled with the delight that he finally understood what they were talking about.

Jessie continued staring at him for a long time. Finally, she stirred and said, "I don't think I understand."

"Sometimes I don't think I do, either. Besides..." he swallowed, wondering if he should chance saying this next, then thought, what the hell? "I wouldn't worry about it. You, Jessie, have always struck me as being a lot farther down that road than most people I've met."

At that, she smiled. And even in the darkness of the car, he saw a dazzling light that he thought he would carry with him to the grave.

**

"There." Wondering why she had pulled him into a grocery store, he looked down at the package of ground beef she was pointing at. He peered at it, not noticing anything different than usual, then looked up at her and shrugged.

"$3.85 a pound. For 15% fat."

He looked at the price and nodded.

"Okay, remember that. Follow me." She set off back out of the store, and wondering where they were going next, he did just that.

It was a week later. Like the time in the library, as the evening had drawn to a close after their long talk in the car, ending only when an SUV coming down the side street had indignantly honked because they were blocking the way, he had found himself stricken helpless at the thought that he would like to see her again but didn't know how to ask. And, as before, she had taken the matter into her own hands, saying that he had given her a lot to think about and that her turn could wait until, how did the following Saturday sound? Saturday had sounded just grand.

The ensuing week, as he had tried not to count the moments until it would be over, he had noticed Ella, back in her ponytail again, looking a little distracted in the midst of her ever-present group of friends chattering happily as they gathered on blankets around a large, spreading pine, one extending her wrist to the others to sniff appreciatively, then another following suit. As he had watched them, he couldn't help remarking on the difference in the ways Ella and Jessie wore their respective ponytails. With Ella, it was part of a pleasing picture to be admired, a...knowing Ella he tried to think of a different word than calculated, particularly when he compared her with Amber...an intentional stroke of the brush...the perfect accessory to a carefully thought through outfit...a collaborating part that made up a summed up entirety of beauty. After all, she was picture perfect to look at, inside her clothing as well as...his thoughts had hurriedly run on to the medieval preoccupation with beauty being the proper proportion of the parts to the whole until he had noticed Ella watching him with...a look he had thought reminded him of longing. He had nodded and begun to move on. She had

smiled at him sadly and turned back to her friends as
he felt a pang of guilt that he hadn't warned her that
Jake wouldn't write. Suddenly struck with the flash
of insight that he wanted God's perfect creation to be
marred by the helpless, sinking rage that he had
known, he had quickened his step as if to escape and
then, carefully, had resettled his thoughts on how
Jessie's ponytail was different. With Ella, putting her
hair up was an act of intentional beauty, just as surely
as she had flicked it from time to time when talking
with Jake. Was flicking it now, he had noticed with a
backward glance. And had probably enthralled Jake
with such a simple move. With Jessie, putting her
hair up was getting it out of her way.

In the car, as she threaded her way through the busy
streets of Seattle, he heard her say, "Like herding
cattle." After several turns, then a long stretch along
a gorgeously tree-lined lake surrounded by twos and
threes of runners, walkers, and strollers, she pulled
into the cramped parking lot of another grocery store.
As they walked through the doors and he saw posters
advertising local folk singers, tarot card readings and
other paraphernalia of the spiritually woo-woo, it
dawned on him that they might be in some kind of
coop store. He looked at her, inquiringly, but she
only smiled, "You'll see," and led him into the back to
that store's meat department.

"There." She was pointing at another package of
ground beef. He picked it up and, after finding the
15% fat label, noticed the price and almost dropped it.
$7.25 a pound.

"Wow."

She nodded.

"Why?"

"Keep looking."

He looked at the label wondering if it was some
kind of super-beef or something. But he only saw
that the label, amid the usual FDA prescriptions of
how carefully it had been processed and how

carefully one should handle it, said rather simply, "Certified Organic Beef."

"Organic?" She nodded, a triumphant smile on her face.

"Why's organic so much more expensive?"

"Well, that's the question, isn't it?" She took a step back and folded her arms, scowling all around her at the meat department. "In my Business 101 class, I wrote my first paper about small ranchers struggling to make do with low prices for falling grades of beef, but the bastard only gave me a B, saying that...oh what was it?" She made a move to pull at her ponytail then realized she was doing it and flicked it instead, making Andrew's heart turn right over. "Oh some pompous bullshit that I was over-reaching...oh yeah, 'Your reach has exceeded your grasp.'" She flicked her ponytail again, making his mouth turn dry. "The piece of shit. And that, anyway, I hadn't suggested any possible alternatives. So I was thinking about that when my roommate..."

Andrew felt his eyebrows lifting. She hadn't mentioned a roommate and he hadn't thought to ask.

She waved a hand. "Oh, she's a whining puppy. Still waiting for her prom date to show up. Anyway, she took me here to do some shopping. All the girls do. It's the latest fad, their thing to do when they're bored. Like going to the perfume counter at Nordstrom's to try out...never mind." She snorted. "And that's when I saw it." Her eyes moved from the ground beef to take in the rest of the grocery store and the shoppers strolling by.

Andrew tried to remember what he knew of organic food production. Not much. He had never been interested in it. Of course, in Madison, you couldn't escape it, but... He looked around the room at the people walking down the aisles examining the labels at times, simply picking boxes up and putting them in their hand-held baskets at other times.

And then he remembered. "Isn't organic food so much more expensive because it costs more to produce? Something about having to use natural alternatives to pesticides."

"Yep." She continued watching the shoppers.

"I remember it in Madison, where I grew up." She looked at him now, interested, which made him think really fast so that he wouldn't disappoint her. "It was quite inspiring. You know, people gathering together in...well..." looking around him, he said, "...in cooperatives much like this one, I suppose. Just not nearly as nice."

"Is that where it started?"

"I don't know. But I remember that you could always tell an organic coop shopper. They always seemed to have rasta hair, tie-dyed shawls and sandals, and they liked folk music. Oh, and they were always carrying around their yoga mats."

She started laughing. Pleased that he had said something witty, he looked into her eyes but was surprised to find a hardness there. A...he searched his mind for the right...predatory hardness. "And they probably didn't have much money, right?"

Not following her, and not liking the look in her eyes, he shrugged. "Yeah. It was part of the lifestyle. Live naturally. Eat naturally. Don't die of cancer from pesticides. Don't get corrupted by the Man, so live a simple life. Some of my dad's friends from school were some of the early leaders."

She gestured around them, lowering her voice. "Do they look like they don't have much money?"

He looked around them understanding now what had seemed wrong before. Oh, the sandals were there all right, at least on some. But they were expensively cut ones. He frowned, trying to remember the name of that big sandal-maker that had seemed all the rage in Madison. Others were wearing pricey sneakers. And the shawls had been replaced by...well...there was no getting around it. He saw a lot of fashionably cut work-out outfits. A man next to him reaching for some steaks was sporting a NIKE swoosh on his breast.

Catching his gaze, after having followed it to the swoosh, she gestured with her head back toward the entrance and turned to go. He followed her out.

In the car, staring straight ahead, she said, "I'm still reading up on organic beef production, but I haven't seen anything that tells me that the beef in there..." she pointed at the store with her chin, "...needs to be that expensive."

He looked at her, intrigued at how her mind worked. "You mean it's a rip-off?"

"No." She looked at him for a moment, frowning. "Not anymore than Starbucks is a rip-off."

He didn't follow, so he shrugged, waiting.

"That asshole pissed me off enough that I began to look even harder for alternative ways of raising beef. I couldn't find anything at first. I mean, the small rancher's getting squeezed out, no economy of scale even if they're raising pounds, so who gives a rat's ass?" Sensing something coming, Andrew kept silent, waiting.

"Then I came here and saw their prices and I wondered why. So I started digging, thinking there might be something there. But I couldn't find anything to show me why it was so expensive. Then, one day, 'bout..." she frowned, her eyes looking off. "'Bout two weeks ago, I found a magazine article complaining about how fast organic prices were rising out of all proportion to the market." Andrew smiled inwardly as he listened to her throw out all her new economics lingo, then found himself distracted by the increasing specialization of language and how diversifying, then alienating it can be...but then realized that he wasn't listening and readjusted his thoughts back to her.

"You see, I don't know about the beginning. There isn't a lot of information out there. At least I can't find it. Not yet. But at first, organic food was more expensive because they had to make up new methods of farming. But given time, as the new methods are adopted, the prices should come down. In theory. At any rate, they shouldn't be going up." She looked at him. His breath caught as he wondered if he had missed something important and cursed his wandering mind.

"But they are. Now, maybe the demand for organic beef is growing so much faster than the supply that the rising prices are understandable. Maybe. And your tie-dyed types in Wisconsin? Wanting to make something different? Well, sorry to say, but I'm sure as shit about one thing. They can't afford to shop at that store." She stared at it now. Andrew looked at it, too, with new eyes and wondered what the Rasta crowd would think of it. Maybe fire-bomb it, he smiled, then remembered that they would be the last people in the world to fire-bomb anything. "So I came back and hung out for a while and just watched the people shop to see what their reaction to the price of beef was." She looked at him again.

"Nothing. They barely looked at the price. Still don't."

Wanting to say something illuminating because he could see that this was important to her, he ventured a "So..."

"Didn't you just say it was part of the lifestyle in Madison? Your dad's friends?"

"Yeah."

"Well, I'm starting to think that however it started, pesticide-free beef for a better life...," she said, waving a hand in the air, "...which is about the biggest load of horse-shit I've ever heard of. Whatever. I'm not going to argue with the consumers of any cattle market." She stared at him, that hunter's glint hardening in her eyes again. "What I am saying is that I don't think they're just selling organic beef in there anymore."

And suddenly it clicked. "Starbucks! Oh! You think they're selling a lifestyle."

"To the highest bidder."

He smiled with delight and not a little pride at the solidity of her reasoning. "That's really good, Jessie. Really insightful. He's bound to be impressed because it's going to make a hell of a paper."

She snorted and turned the key to start the car. "Paper? Who gives a shit about a paper. I'm trying to save my ranch."

***

Over a cup of coffee at, appropriately enough, Starbucks, she waved off his questions about the subject remarking that she wanted to think about it before saying any more and turned the subject to the ranch. Only too happy to oblige, he lost himself in happy memories of that summer. They laughed about how fat Digger had been at the beginning and she complimented him again at how hard he had worked the "ol' fat ass." He then thanked her for the check and confessed that he had thought of returning it several times. "Why?" she frowned at him in surprise. "Do you know how much it costs for a good workhorse?"

He shook his head.

"Well, after you left, Digger started kicking his stall, wanting exercise, something we never thought we'd ever see again. Angel rides him now, sometimes. When he needs to cover more ground. He won't touch Asa. You saved us a bundle."

Andrew felt the dreaded blushing scoring his cheeks, but then, happy at her praise, decided he didn't care.

It was a great evening, ruined only when he began an anecdote about how much Jake had hated the idea of going to Prayer Meeting, had given him holy hell after church that day for showing off. He was about to tell her how much he had protested when he saw an ugly glint appear in her gaze and he froze, remembering the cold way she had looked at him after that night. The moment stopped all conversation until, as if remembering something else, she shook her head and changed the subject to Thanksgiving and that Pop had been asking after Andrew hoping he would come.

His heart soared at the thought. He had never in his wildest thoughts expected such an invitation. He stammered out his thanks as best he could.

"Good. And, by the way, it's awful nice not to hear you struggling to put one word after another these days."

He blushed again and, again, not caring.

***

Before starting the car, she paused and laid a hand on his arm, making him stop breathing. She looked at him, pulling at her ponytail, frowned and then said, "Andrew. I'm not used to people listening to what I have to say. That was very nice of you. Particularly because my thinking of how the organic market works might be all bullshit. I gotta think about it some more."

He barely managed to nod as he heard her mention something about "marbling" and "trying to get outside the problem" but all he could of was how much he would give if the God of all gods would only find a way to keep her hand there. Unfortunately, it was all too soon withdrawn, and they were on their way. To his surprise, Jessie insisted on dropping him at his door. At first, he was tempted to lie, if only because Schnoebel, in quietly announcing that he would be able to stay in the apartment so long as he continued the quality of his work for her and Wei, had warned him not to advertise it around campus. "Unter vier augen, Andrew." She had said. "Under four eyes

195

only. What they..." and she had flourished one spidery hand off in the general direction of the admin building, "...don't know will not hurt them." But he decided that he was being foolish and gave her the directions.

As they pulled up to the low-rise building with its parking - limited but parking nonetheless - on the side she whistled softly. Not wanting to know what that meant, he brusquely got out of the car and led the way to the door. Walking inside with her, he realized that she was the first guest he had ever had and, surveying the room, wondered what it looked like through her eyes. Everywhere he looked, he saw books, journals and papers piled in heaps on the table, on chairs, stacked on the floor, even on the meager kitchen counter, some open, the pages held down by half-filled and forgotten drinking glasses and mugs, some turned pages down, referencing some passage that he could barely remember. At least he didn't have any dirty clothes lying around.

Her eyes wide as she took it all in, she whistled softly again, then turned to him. "You even have a kitchen."

"I don't use it, really. Just tea sometimes."

She shook her head again. "And they let you stay here."

"At a reduced rate, but..." feeling the heat in his face, he shrugged, "...yeah."

"Because of the work you do for them?"

"Yeah." He thought about trying to mention Schnoebel's speeches about a university's scholarship being a product in competition like anything else on the market and how his work was raising the quality of their grad research like nothing else recently, was more than...but decided against it.

She wandered the rooms, lingering in the bathroom, the kitchen, and the bedroom, saying nothing.

Finally, not being able to stand it any longer, he asked, "What do you think?"

She paused and looked at him, a new look, he saw. One he had never seen before. Was it admiration? He wondered but couldn't bear the thought of it being anything less.

"No wonder they call you 'the monk.'"

Stung, he felt anger coming into his cheeks. Or maybe it was embarrassment.

"It's okay, Andrew. They call me 'rawhide.'"

Stunned, he found himself choking out some laughter, but afraid to anger her, tried to stifle it, and started choking instead. Smiling, she only shook her head, and got him a glass of water.

"How...how do you know about that?" he coughed out, trying to swallow.

"Well...let's just say that you have a bit of a reputation." He looked at her, hardly knowing what to think. "There are a couple of girls studying religion on my floor and they're always gossiping about what 'the monk' is going to say in class this week. It's irritating." She laughed, that husky laugh of sagebrush that she had. So different from Ella's, he thought, when she's about to...and pushed that thought out of his mind, realizing that he so rarely heard Jessie laugh. She kept grinning but as if amused at knowing something he didn't. "At least it used to be irritating until one day, just before class, I heard them talking about 'the monk' and pointing at you."

Finding himself growing irritated at her grin, he growled out, "What'd they say?"

"Well, Andrew. You have to forgive them." She looked at him, raising an eyebrow.

"What?" He felt the heat rising but didn't know from where it was coming.

She grinned at him again, saucily this time and began wandering the room. "Most of these girls? They're just here for an MRS degree and so they have a lot of time on their hands." He stared at her not understanding what she was saying.

She looked back at him waiting for something, then finally, sighed in exasperation, saying the next three letters slowly. "MRS degree, Andrew. Honestly! In high school, some of these girls were hot after the football stars. In college, they're hot after the academic ones."

Slowly it dawned on him what she was getting at. He blinked, thinking that it was impossible. To change the subject, he asked, "Why do they call you 'rawhide?'"

"Because I've got Whip's saddle blanket in my room. My roommate complains about the smell. What do you expect? She's a fucking twit. Tells the others I sleep in it." Remembering that smell their first - dare he call it a date, he swallowed - he ventured, "I thought I smelled it on you before. The night of the troll."

Her eyes widened, in pleasure, he guessed and felt his stomach do a flip-flop. She nodded without further comment and looked around the room again and sighed.

Encouraged, he asked her again, "So what do you think of it?"

She turned and faced him again, the smile replaced now with her thoughtful frown, he had begun calling it, he just now realized.

"Jake's right. You do have a fine mind."

"Th-thank you." His mind reeled back in thoughts and felt himself, once more, atop Digger rising to the top of their rear.

"So long as it's protected."

***

With a last, almost fond - he hardly dared to think - light pat on his cheek, she had left. The next week or more passed quickly and without significance. Finding that he had lost a lot of his capacity for detachment, and trying not to worry why, he focused on it from time to time, in between mounting work coming from Schnoebel and Wei. If he didn't know better, he would have thought that they were privy to Jessie's visit to the apartment and were punishing him for it. At least they were exacting every last square ream's worth of it from him. The more rational side of his mind told him that this was probably the last, harried, slew of frantic papers being turned in before Thanksgiving break. Who wanted to work those few weeks of school just before Christmas? In any case, the effect on his life was to keep him buried like a mole, scavenging after obscure volumes buried in the dusty stacks in the back, forgotten aisles of the library for topics ranging from the development of the monastic rules of Buddhism's Sangha, which made him think, uncomfortably, of his father, not to mention his own hastily typed paper on Christianity's Benedictine Order - interesting parallels, again, he thought - but realized with despair that there was no time to look into it; the struggles of Pure Land Buddhism in Mao's China, not to mention World War II Japan; a detailing of Martin Luther's trials and tribulations during the Reformation; and one other thesis that he wouldn't let himself look at. In response to his croak at the number of papers she had handed over, Schnoebel had only replied with a lifted eyebrow, "Ja, cherub, it is a lot, even for you; however, you do have the Thanksgiving break, of course." On he worked, as furiously as he could, barely stopping when Ella tried to speak to him one night as he was jogging across the campus to the library, a list of works in hand. It made him feel guilty. He liked Ella, for her goodness and for Jake's sake. A thought whispered that he also liked talking to Ella for his own sake, but he pushed it aside and, as if to prove that to himself and against his better judgment, stopped for a quick hello to see how she was doing. He listened as she complained that Jake hadn't responded, then sighed and confessed the same problem. Which brought her up short. And made her limping ponytail seemingly find new life. She told him how sorry she was for that. Embarrassed, he made an excuse about his research, brandishing his list and moved on, absentmindedly nodding when her voice followed, thanking him for the talk. On he worked, not really eating anymore. Not really drinking, either, which worried him long enough to make another mug of tea using the dinky microwave the apartment had, but not long enough to drink it as soon as he found some questionable leap of logic in a grad's reasoning. On he worked, not sleeping, just closing his eyes for twenty minutes at a time if only to clear out the bleariness. All done so that he would be ready to go in time. Wednesday, she had said. The day before Thanksgiving, she had said. He told himself this over and over and kept at it.

On he worked, barely knowing what he wrote when he sat for the usual pre-break quizzes and tests. Once he found himself dead asleep over the medieval history test, Cohen prodding him awake as the students all, in various states of relief, exultation and fear turned in their papers down at the front. Cohen looked at him a moment, then sighed. "Andrew, you're a real mensch, you know that? Ingrid's working you too hard." Not knowing what to say, and wondering how far he had gotten in the test, but not daring to look, Andrew only looked away. Still, the compliment touched him and he felt his eyes burning. Cohen sighed again, then said, "I want that test in my office in twenty minutes," and walked away.

Jessie, too, didn't seemed to bother about her tests, because passing her for a quick hello in the library, she appeared to be working just as hard at her table on the organic cattle question. Sometimes, as rushed as he felt, he would force himself once each evening for a few precious minutes to stop across the room and watch her work - the way she frowned constantly while turning pages, scanning, he assumed, given the speed with which she was reading; sometimes curling her lips in a contemptuous snarl, sometimes in a curse he could almost feel the force of, if not hear, all the way across the room; snapping books shut and open with a hunger that reminded him of himself at times; popping up out of her chair to chase something down and almost running back with it; bending her head for minutes at a time to draw yet another graph of, he supposed, rising costs of living, the cost of regular beef, the cost of organic beef, and the sales of some conglomerate; every night he saw her, always the same pulling of the ponytail until she realized that she was doing it and flicked it in annoyance instead, as if she would shear it off if it got in her way. Once he was tempted to ask her why she was working so hard on a question so clearly academic, but then her voice cut across him as if she had slapped him for his silliness, "I'm trying to save my ranch." In his exhaustion, he wondered briefly at that, thinking that Jake had never mentioned anything wrong. Turning back to his labors, he made a mental note to ask her about it sometime.

Wednesday morning, she had said. The day before Thanksgiving. Performing at almost super-human speeds, even for him he had to allow, he felt that he was going to make it. Late Tuesday night, as he crawled his way home from the library, shouldering his way through a sparsely attended peace rally outside the library, he felt his mind too numb to listen to the speaker's megaphonic shrieking, to numb to think about anything, really. He was angry or at least feeling some semblance of it, exhausted as he was. The Luther paper - initially so fascinating in its fierce challenge of the argument gaining ground in some circles these days that the Church had not wanted to let its northern brethren go and only acquiesced when it became apparent that Luther had ambitiously wanted to build his own mitred power base - had grown repugnant the moment he realized that the author had plagiarized large parts of it. Shamelessly, too. He hadn't been able to understand why any student would stoop to such callously lazy scholarship until he had flipped the covering page over and had seen Hegland's name. Now he had to make a case for Schnoebel, and he wasn't looking forward to it, given their past. Staggering up the last few steps to his door, he heard running steps behind him and a breathless "Andrew!"

Turning at the sound, smiling in spite of himself, he saw her trotting up carrying a bottle. "Did you finish?"

He nodded, too wrung through to do much else.

"Great! So did I! At least, I know what I want to tell Pop! Let's go inside! I'll tell you all about it while I pour us a couple of this!" Her happiness, bubbling up, almost registered on him, and he squinted in the light at what she was holding. Some kind of whiskey it looked like. He groaned.

"What's wrong?" She looked at him, the frowning lines of disappointment wrenchingly appearing at the corners of her mouth.

He fought to gather his thoughts. Fought to form a sentence, then gave up, smiling at himself that he was probably too tired to stammer. "Jessie. I'm sorry. I'm just too..."

"Oh." She looked away.

"I'm sorry."

"No. It's all right." Now, she looked embarrassed, which, if possible, was even worse.

"Look. I haven't slept in...Tell you what. Why don't we go for a night ride tomorrow night and crack that open then? Okay?" He scanned her face for signs of brightening and, at first, they didn't appear. Then she sighed and smiled.

"Okay. Digger's going to be happy."

"Oh my god. I just hope I can pull myself up on him."

"Get some sleep. I'll come by tomorrow at ten for you, okay? Only..."

Nodding, still nodding even though she had stopped speaking, he suddenly, if dimly, became aware that she was looking embarrassed again.

"I really gotta pee. I couldn't find you in the library, so I was waiting out here quite a while wondering which way you'd walk home."

"Uh...sure." He opened the door. He wandered in, set his book bag down, looked around at all the mess and, again, wondered what - and when, he was suddenly horrified to realize - he was going to say to Schnoebel. Maybe if he got up early, he could write a note and slip it under her--

The bathroom door opened, breaking in on his thoughts for Jessie, her eyes in a tight scowl, stalked toward him while pulling back a fist. Dazed, he watched it cross in a slow arc and had the sudden impression of a beer can tumbling end over end just before he felt the explosion of lights and pain and felt the floor come up and hit him from below.

"Have a good time fucking his girlfriend. I hope it feels good." And a door slammed.

He rolled over, grabbing his head, trying not to touch where she had hit him because it seemed like someone had just placed a burning ring on his cheek.

"Andrew?" A soft voice. He knew that voice. He tried to roll back, tried to sit up as he felt someone kneeling over him. A cloud of lavender. Ella. He blinked, trying to focus.

"I'm sorry, Andrew."

He blinked again, feeling his eyesight come back to something like normal and found his gaze searching out her brilliantly blue eyes, descending to that beautifully drawn neck and, naturally following the line of - was that his blanket - descending downward to a creamy breast of hers with its equally uncreamy, yet correspondingly beautiful, in its own audacity, nipple.

Looking down, she gasped and pulled the blanket more tightly around her, then, as if remembering how ridiculous that response was to their situation, she smiled and let it go.

Which made him hard. As quickly as a heartbeat. He stared at her loveliness, felt his breath catch, then found himself wondering what a curious sensation it was to feel one's penis harden. Much like...he sifted through his swirling thoughts for the right...much like a flexed arm. But one you never knew you had. He tried flexing it. Very much like a flexed bicep, he thought. And, suddenly remembering where he was, who he was with, and who was not there, he climbed to his feet.

"Ella? What are...?" Then, remembering Jessie's bizarre departure, he went to the bathroom and looked in. Across the mirror, in red lipstick was scrawled in loopy, teasing letters, nevertheless certain in their own intent, "Let's make a night for both of us. Ella" with the a in Ella drawn as a heart. He groaned.

"Andrew, was that Sticks?" He turned.

"How do you know Jessie?"

"You gave me her dorm address with Jake's email. At first I didn't know why, but then I realized you wanted me to be as close to him as I could, so I went over to her dorm and introduced myself. Tell me that wasn't her."

He groaned again and sought out a chair.

"Oh my."

Moving some books off a chair onto the floor beside it - much like he did in Schnoebel's and Wei's offices, he thought, completing this surrealist portrait - Ella pulled it opposite him and, to her credit, pulled the blanket more tightly around her and, not without dignity, sat in it to look at him.

"Well, it's not what I wanted, but does it really matter anymore? I must have written him twenty times. No response. I even know that he is reading them and when because I started flagging them two weeks ago to tell me."

He shook his head at her, trying to hear right.

"You can do that?"

She smiled at him. Beautifully. God, she was beautiful, he had to admit. "Of course."

He looked her over. Saw her sweet sexiness; sweet eroticism, he corrected himself, suddenly realizing for the first time what the word meant. Her golden hair, now framing her face in those kittenish curls again, trailed delightfully down her neckline. She had changed her hair back, he saw and reflected on the reasons women change their hair and why. Some women, he corrected, then thought of Jessie and began to get angry.

As if seeing it coming her way, she held out both hands to ward it off, which made the blanket slip. She hesitated, then decided to let it, as she continued looking at him. Feeling the heat rise in his cheeks, he stared at her breasts, even more beautiful in their jutting shapeliness than his memory had sculpted them, and feeling himself stiffen again, he marveled at what a wonderful feeling it was to get hard. Kind of like a god, he thought. The point of the phallic imagery sprinkled all over classical Mediterranean culture all at once became understandable. But then he looked up into her eyes and abruptly, without a doubt, he recognized the searing pain of loneliness that came of being deprived of Jake without reason.

As if he were in the room, Andrew could hear Jake's voice floating into his memory, from a night ride when he had asked Jake more about dating: *Be kind to the ladies, hoss. It's a man's world, no matter how many people say otherwise, and they have to live in it.*

He cleared his throat, smiled at the memory and, deciding that his instinct to hug her without first raising the blanket - at least he told himself so - was brotherly, he stood up, crossed the two steps to her, knelt and did so. She gasped. He held her in his arms, tenderly, yet wholeheartedly, the way that he had wished someone would have hugged him early in the quarter, before he had finally found Jessie. He winced with pain at the thought of her but kept on holding Ella.

Who began to cry. At first tentative shudders, then gulping breaths, then finally, heaving, tortured sobs filling the room with their awful pain. On and on it went. He did nothing at first, just praying out to Jake for instructions. Then, as if hearing a response when the torrent of her moans began to ebb in strength, he began to gently rock her and fill her ear with tender shhhs and "It's okay" repeated endlessly. Finally, she began to subside into quiet sniffles but still not letting him go.

As she began to recover, Andrew suddenly and acutely became aware of the feel of her soft mounds, punctuated by the nipples, now hardening, pressing into his chest. Stalled for a moment in his uncertainty, and certainly enjoying the feeling, even if it did leave him with a sense of...he didn't want to think about that...he sat back on his heels and began to pull the blanket up to her shoulders. Looking up at her, her face whirls of grief, desire, guilt, disappointment, bewilderment, each forming up to the chase the previous from those tear-stained and mascara-streaked cheeks, he suddenly felt the charm of Ella broken.

She wiped a cheek and sniffed a teary "What?"

He chided himself. No layers of makeup added or subtracted could ever veil Ella's goodness. Jake was an utter fool.

"Tea?" He smiled.

She stared at him for a moment as if not understanding then suddenly smiled a cheery, if somewhat trembly, smile. Almost like Ella, he thought. Or maybe the Ella in her essence that he was just now being given the privilege to behold. She nodded.

He got up and moved into the kitchen and, thankfully, found one clean mug that he had somehow missed earlier. He even found an otherwise overlooked tea pot, filled it with water and set it on the stove to heat.

Ella had not moved. Had not changed into other clothing. Had not adjusted her blanket either way. It was actually quite becoming on her, he thought and saw her a moment, in his mind's eye, ascending the toga-clad steps of the Forum in Rome. Definitely. She was crafted for places such as there. Coming back to the kitchen of the here and now, he found that she had been watching him the entire time and that she was about to speak. She pointed over to a fireplace that he had never seen before and asked, "Is that real?"

He didn't know. Without answering, resolutely not thinking about what this portended, he knelt and busied himself pondering the perks - if inexpensive and common ones - of academia. Finding to his astonishment an old, dusty instant lighting log on the grate within and a half-used book of matches on the cheap tiling just aside, he lit the fire. Then, scooting back to watch his handiwork with pride, he heard the steam whistling. Jumping to his feet, he brushed past her, facing the fire now to watch it, and went into the kitchen to steep the tea. On impulse, he grabbed the few used mugs and drinking glasses that were lying around and put them into the sink, feeling the burn of her erect nipples pressing into his chest. Then, ashamed of himself, not wanting to look at her but seeing her goddess-like curving lines in his mind anyway, he paused to right a few books, found his misplaced survey paper on the Zoroastrian tradition for his Ancient Religions class, closed a few others and stacked them neatly on the counter. Satisfied, he picked up the two mugs and turned.

And there she lay, a new blanket laid out in front of the fire, she wrapped in her toga lying on top of it, her sweetly tapered face balanced on one hand, her blonde curls teasing the eye down over her breasts which, while covered, had lost none of their enthralling power. He swallowed.

He crossed the room, wondering how this was all going to end. Nevertheless, obeying Jake's instructions, he knelt next to her offering the tea and then, for want of any other direction, kicked off his shoes, crossed his legs beneath him and sat next to her. She sipped the tea, a look of gratefulness playing across her cheeks, now wiped clean of streaks. Not knowing what to do, what to say, he took refuge in sipping his own.

"I've never had a man make tea for me, Andrew." She looked up at him. The brilliant blue of her eyes almost seeming to smoke. She giggled throatily, "What else can you do?" and setting her tea down, reached up one delicately shaped hand toward the back of his neck to pull him down. It was a soft hand, an inviting hand, so different from the hardness of Jessie's from years of riding, he thought with a pang, and that was where it all stopped.

He resisted the pull. She felt it. And stopped herself. She looked up at him, the smokiness of her eyes withering into resigned sadness. Not knowing what he was doing, he gently lifted her hand from the back of his neck, turned its delicate sweetness over, kissed its palm and, to the astonishment dawning in her eyes he bent and lifted her to a sitting position. She followed his movements, not resisting.

They looked at one another for a few more moments, quietly sipping their tea. Then she put hers down again. She cleared her throat, flicked a few curls behind her neck and said, "I suppose I thought that, like me, you would do almost anything to have something of Jake again."

He nodded, surprised at this insight.

"I ask only one thing: Let me sleep next to you tonight. The world can have you back after that."

He nodded again.

The morning was a brilliantly sun-lit one. He wakened her adorable sleepiness - when did Ella not look charming, he wondered - with the apology that he had only tea, but that he had made it strong. She watched him quietly, still wearing the same blanket, sipping her tea without making any other movement. Enjoying the silence, and trying not to look at the clock to gauge if he could still catch Jessie, he sipped his, too, without a word.

Then, finally, she laughed, a delightful pearl of laughter. "Andrew, you really are quite a gentleman." He felt the old dreaded blush rising and swallowed, wondering what to say. "I can see that you need to go. I know you're not willing to say it, but I can see it in your eyes all the same." He ducked his head now, embarrassed that he should be so transparent.

"She's waiting for you, isn't she?" She reached up to touch his cheek and he winced at the touch, then reached up to gingerly feel his cheekbone, quite swollen now. He wondered how bad it looked, then sighed.

"I hope so." Then he winced at this disclosure.

Her eyes, became even bluer than before, or perhaps he was imagining it he thought. "She was waiting the whole night for you then and you still let me stay?"

Not knowing how to answer, he hesitated and then nodded.

She shook her head very slowly. He watched the curls drape back and forth over the etched lines of her shoulders and suddenly remembered another moon-lit shape draping back and forth over...he refocused his mind on her.

"Andrew, you've been very kind to me." She lifted both eyes to him. "I know that you always see me with the girls, but the truth is that I really have very few friends." Her hand was lifting toward him. "Will you be my friend?"

Quickly running his mind over everything that had transpired the night before, including, he thought with a guilty gulp, the wonderful feelings of her thigh pressed against the corner of his in the middle of the night, of her breasts resting on the edge of his chest, of her hand curled protectively around the back of his head, he reached out his own, finally, to shake hers, thinking lastly of her goodness, a quality he knew to be rare.

"Ella, I will always be your friend."

***

Trapped in dreams. At least one long nightmare. Certainly it had to have been that when he strode across campus, took the elevator straight up to her floor and, without pausing for the towel-clad and dripping squeals scurrying back and forth, made his way to her door and knocked. And knocked again. And was about to knock a third time when a sleepily disgruntled girl opened the door.

"Is Jessie here?"

"Rawhide girl?" She blinked at him, suddenly coming awake. "Who are you? What happened to your face?"

"Is she here?"

"She left last night, for her family's ranch, around one in the morning. Why?"

Without another word, he turned away, hearing her indignant, "This is an all-girl's floor, you know!" Further down the hallway, as he felt his world caving in under him with each step, he heard a whispered hiss, "It's the monk!" He paused, mid-stride, deciding to take it out on someone else, just this once. He turned ready to...not sure what, but...and saw two pairs of awe-filled eyes - he was sure of the awe now, having seen it a few times - staring like a pair of young pajamed owls at him from a doorway. He nodded a tight, polite smile and walked away, feeling their cooing whispers chase him down the hall.

Dreams, or nightmares. Long nights staring at the ceiling, hearing the sweet, throaty chuckles of Ella, feeling the press of her thigh against him, regretting that he never got to see her navel - where did that thought come from, he wondered - and replaying endlessly the moment of holding her, feeling her softness beneath him, knowing that he had had only to lower his face a few inches and do what came naturally to help them both lose themselves for the moment. The moment. Endless moments. Of guilt. Of tortured dreams making love to Ella, or at least it seemed to be Ella's body but with her rough snarl atop it staring down at him, ready to rope him like a steer. Of Ella's golden curls draping, misplaced, across her muscular, bony chest, built for riding Whip full out across a field. Of her hard hips now riding him as they jumped a gate. Of empty staring at the ashes in the fireplace, sitting where he and Ella had lain, wondering vainly where someone bought another instant lighting log, and wishing that Ella had left the tousled blankets lying on the floor, like tangled memories of their shared suffering. All put away now as if Ella had not been there. As if it had all been a dream, after all. Once, on inspiration, he jumped hopefully to his feet and took the few quick steps to the bathroom mirror, only to see that Ella's note, too, had been wiped clean away. Had it happened? He tried to find the mug Ella had used, maybe some sign of lipstick on one of them, but here, too, he met defeat for after shooing him out the door, she had apparently washed up all the mugs and water glasses and stacked them neatly away. Only the cold ashes remained of any sign that the night had happened. That and the charmingly scrawled note, "Here's my number if you need anything! Ella." that he, at first, in his anger upon his return had thrown away, then had dug out of the garbage can and spread out carefully on the table.

Late one night, he thought of calling that number, had even started to, but stopped at the seventh digit, because he honestly didn't know what "friends" meant with someone as captivating as Ella.

Ever so slowly the sun rose and fell. Schnoebel, surveying his swollen red cheek through the blue smoke of her office, had smiled, observing, "Liebchen, I know you are not built for brawling. A little problem, instead, in affairs d' amour?" He had reddened even further than his cheek and looked down. She had chuckled throatily, making him start in his chair, then had put aside her papers and listened as he had carefully ticked off his points as to why he thought that large portions of Hegland's research was plagiarized, her eyes growing ever colder the further he went. At the end, surprisingly, she had said nothing about Andrew's prior encounter with Hegland. She had reached out her hand for Hegland's thesis and Andrew's notes and sighed, "Danke, liebchen. I will take it from here."

Slowly the days turned. He found himself staring at odd colored bricks in walls now, trying desperately not to worry about how recklessly she would have driven over the mountain passes on her way home once the panicked thought had made him sit upright in bed late one night with a cry. Sometimes he found himself breaking into a cold, trickling sweat at the thought that she might be laid up, helpless, in a broken car on the side of the road and that he couldn't do anything about it. Or, even more horrifyingly, given that such a tragedy had occurred, it would be over and done with now, a thought that had felled him where he stood on campus, staring up at a lonely elm. He had found himself abruptly sitting on the wet ground and wondering how he got there. Getting up, he had found the seat of his pants embarrassingly soaked from the ground and, bowing to convention, had made his way to the apartment as quickly as he could, where, disgusted with himself, he had finally done what he thought he couldn't and had called the ranch. She had answered. He had hung up. With relief.

Slowly they turned. His emptiness deepened, taking on the form of a hollow sepulcher. In a moment of desperation while turning in his work to Wei, he asked if the professor knew a good temple he might attend. Wei, looking hardly surprised - but then, Andrew had to allow, Wei hardly looked surprised at anything - simply stared at him, his moon-shaped face giving nothing away, only the deep brown of his eyes slowly looking Andrew over.

"Certainly, I can recommend a few. However, you won't find much there, I'm afraid."

Andrew stirred, feeling an odd ray of hope at his tone. "Why not?"

"Isn't it Martin Luther who said, 'Everyone begins at the milk of the Word. Very few make it as far as the meat.'?"

Andrew didn't know, but he thought it sounded apt. He nodded.

"You will find the same simple piety at a Buddhist temple that you will find at a Christian church. Good souls, most of them; all asking the Lord Buddha or God for the same thing: to solve their problems for them. So it is with all the faith traditions we, in our suffering, invent."

Andrew digested this slowly. Such a notion had never occurred to him. Then, remembering a chance remark Wei had made earlier, he prompted, "I've thought about trying to dissolve my mind, but I'm not doing very well at it."

Wei didn't reply. He just watched Andrew as if waiting for more, saying nothing. The silence stretched from an uncomfortable few long seconds into several minutes without, Andrew realized, even the comfort of a ticking clock to break it and, seeing no watch on Wei's wrists, he wondered how the professor made class on time. Just those same two impenetrably deep pools of brown staring at him, into him.

And still they sat, looking at one another. Andrew was abruptly seized by the memory of how Chan and Zen masters accept new students, even today: the student appears at the door of the temple or school, makes his request and then kneels to wait. And is kept waiting. When his heels and knees can no longer take it, he sits cross-legged, but he still waits. As the day stretches into night and the next day into night, weather notwithstanding, and the next day following that to last, sometimes, a week or more, he receives no answer. All this time he waits, sitting cross-legged in the street, not stirring except to relieve himself and that, it is understood, as sparingly as possible. Finally, after he has proved the strength of his patience, the master allows the penitent in for a short introduction, only. No promises are made. Suddenly, gripped by the angry urge that he had been waiting his whole life, Andrew thought of the old Zen koan, the mystery puzzle that brings greater wisdom and further steps toward Nirvana: Does a dog have Buddha-nature? One disciple had barked his answer.

Andrew barked.

Wei's eyes sparkled. "Nice try." He reached into a desk drawer and removed something, then held it out in a closed fist for Andrew to catch in his open palm. As they sat there with their arms outstretched to almost meet, Wei said, "I am sure that you have noticed that simple stones will work. However, perhaps something with a little more...oomph...might help." He smiled and dropped the object.

Catching it, Andrew looked down to see a circular stone of jade with many striations running through it, some light gray, some deep green. Wei continued on,

"This jade is from the courtyard of the Kuan Yin Temple in Lu Gong, Taiwan. Do you know it?"

Andrew shook his head.

"As I said, any stone will often do. However, you may find this token helpful. Who knows? Perhaps even Kuan Yin shall look down at your efforts with compassion and give you a little push every now and then." He smiled again, his eyes twinkling.

"What do I do?"

"Become the stone."

Andrew thought about that. He didn't know exactly what Wei meant, but he had a pretty good idea how to start. He began to say a standard thank you, but then a memory of something he had once heard a Chinese student say to Wei flashed in his mind. "Thank you, Wei Lao Shr."

Wei's eyebrows raised at the honorific, then his face gravely and slowly bowed. Andrew bowed back.

As he got up to leave, Wei quietly commented, "Your father desires acknowledgment for his scholastic achievements."

Half out of his chair, Andrew looked down, his face burning at the thought of how long it had been since he had talked with his father. He replied, "Yes."

Another moment of silence passed. Andrew, his thigh groaning from the awkward angle, wished now that he had either sat or stood up. Wei seemed not to notice. Another moment lingered.

Wei's voice, finally, gratefully, softly intoned, "You seek something more elusive.   Many seek truth, but I believe you already know many truths. Perhaps you seek your...place."

Andrew, his thigh now cramping badly and not knowing what to do or say, merely nodded again.

Wei's voice came again, more softly than ever. "On the other hand, perhaps it is when you finally discard your quest, no longer having use for it, your place shall find you."

After a following moment in which nothing was said, Andrew finally stood and limped his way to the door and beyond it.

Surprisingly, Wei's Jade - as he began to call it, promising himself that he would return it when he no longer had any use for it - helped. A bit. Rather than distressing himself with his lost sense of detachment anymore, he now simply tried to become the stone. He poured all his grief into it, all his fears, all his desperation; one time expecting it to explode in his face from the power of his toxic pouring. Yet, it did nothing. It continued to sit there on the table in front of him, not winking back at him, not shining, not doing anything, simply continuing to be. It helped. His earlier mental discipline helped, as well, he realized. For, at first, as he concentrated, he kept seeing her wrinkling, freckled nose etched on the surface. Shaking his head in irritation each time it happened, he carefully cleared his mind and plodded on, letting the hours pass, one into another. One day, after a particularly gratifying session, he woke up to realize he had been attending classes again - even that sorely needed Spanish class for graduation - not to mention been working on a few new theses that he must have picked up. There was also the small matter of finals coming in a few weeks, announced with the usual exhortations to study hard. All this, and he had no memory of any of it occurring. Nor of seeing her.

But then, there was no reason to haunt the library unless he had to look up something, for he was tired of reading about what other mystics had done. Now, he wanted to do it himself. He did not trouble himself any longer about his lack of God, nor about the lack of friends. He had Wei's Jade as his beacon. No longer did the evenings stretch out into an everlasting darkness of silence. Now, the stone, as he soon began to rename it, became his sole focus. Yes, he had to admit, it was helping quite a bit, after all.

He was beginning to know peace. One night, he was halfway across Red Square absentmindedly walking through another peace rally - peace about what, he wondered - when it suddenly dawned on him that he may see her in the library. He paused and wondered whether he had visited the library since the quarter had begun but honestly couldn't recall. He suddenly realized that it didn't matter and took a few happy steps, then just as suddenly felt a shiver of fear crawl right down his spine making his stomach turn to water. Stopping again, forcing himself to breathe, he pulled out the stone and stared at it in his hand, the habit of focusing on it overtaking him now, almost as naturally as breathing. When someone bumped into him, he pulled up with a start, just catching the stone before it fell. Maybe it did matter, he smiled. A bit. However, for all his distraction outside, her table was empty. Not sure what he thought about that, he methodically found the sources he needed to check and left, if only granting himself one last look at her table.

Outside, the rally had grown in strength. Standing in the doorway to the library, he could see a speaker standing on a table, stomping it with her foot and screaming, "...back from the imperialists! I say it's time to take our country back from the neo-cons! I say it's..." A number of cheers broke out among the crowd drowning her out. It was of a moderate size he could see, maybe thirty or forty people shrugging off the rain and, wondering what the neo-cons were, he worked his way through them and on his way home.

About a half-block away, he could see a small figure sitting on the doorstep to the apartment. Without another step, he knew it was her, if only because of the freezing shiver working its way down his back again. His stomach...he decided he didn't want to know what his stomach was doing. He thought, briefly, about turning aside, but then saw her face lift and see him. Sighing, and thinking of the stone without taking it out, he continued on. As he drew closer, she stood up, her freckles wrinkled just as he remembered, in concern.

Neither spoke as he came up to her, only her fingers reaching out to gently caress his cheek.

"Are you okay?" Her voice, whisking him straight back to the hot sunny days atop Digger's back, the scent of dusty manure filling his nostrils, staggered him.

She stepped back, her face deepening in disappointment, which made him realize that she was asking about where she had hit him and that he hadn't answered.

Mustering up a grin, he said, "Not even a scratch."

She grinned at that, the light in her eyes blinding him. She lifted her arm for a playful punch on his then, suddenly, uncertainly, she put it back down.

"I'm sorry, Andrew."

This hurt him almost more than he could bear. He raised his own hand then and gently caressed her cheek, watching her eyes widen in surprise. "Really. It's okay."

She scowled at that. "No, Andrew, it's not. I should have known better. It's just that..." her voice faded off into deepening twilight, like a bird taking wing, he thought, then decided that he wanted to take matters into his own hands for once.

"Would you like to come in?"

She nodded.

Turning the key, he stopped and looked at her. "If there's something scrawled on the bathroom mirror, I want you to know, I had nothing to do with it."

She laughed, a hearty, cheerful chortle, her eyes screwed up in pleasure, which made his stomach quiver. He laughed, too, and said, "Come on in."

Inside, she looked slowly around as he put his bag down. "It's cleaner."

He looked at the room himself, and spying the kitchen, seeing its own tidiness, marveled at that.

Then he remembered. "Before she left, Ella..." he began before halting suddenly, wondering what Jessie knew.

She sighed in exasperation. "Oh, I know about Ella." She walked into the kitchen and, without asking, found a couple of clean drinking glasses in the cupboard after setting down that bottle she had been carrying the other night. Watching her in silence, he wondered again what she knew but didn't speak for fear of ruining what few moments they had just had. She opened the whiskey bottle and poured them out two short ones. She handed him one and clinked glasses, saying, "Bottoms up," before swallowing it whole.

Andrew tried to do the same but began coughing as soon as he felt the burning warmth hit the back of his throat. Jessie stared at him in amusement a moment, then began walloping him on the back, which seemed to make it worse. Holding up his hand, he struggled to contain his coughing and, not wanting to wait any longer, struggled out a weak, "Ella."

At that, Jessie sighed again, then grabbed a chair and sat in it, looking up at him. Then, changing her mind, she poured another glass for herself, took a sip, and began. "She came to me as soon as I got back. Practically waiting outside my room. All about how much she missed Jake and how she would have done anything to have a piece of him again." Andrew remembered the phrase and smiled, inwardly.

"All about how she had come over to seduce you, but...after I...left, you had made her tea and a fire, had let her stay the night and had said goodbye in the morning. All the while you not lifting a finger to have at her." Andrew nervously swallowed some whiskey, managing it better this time, at Ella's version of the night and decided not to amend it, particularly when she snorted, "Stupid girl."

"So, I guess..." she smiled crookedly, "...that makes me the biggest horse's ass this side of the Cascades."

"I...uh..." Andrew began before realizing he had no idea what to say next.

She took another sip, then said, "I'm sorry, Andrew. I should have known you would never do that."

His heart suddenly sang as he realized that this was the second time she had said that. Suddenly breathless, he took refuge in another sip, then swallowed the rest and held out his hand for more.

She smiled at him, very prettily, while she poured him another. He felt a bit dizzy and wondered if it was the whiskey or...the realization that she understood he would never, never in an ageless epoch, betray her like that. That she meant that much to him. That from the moment he had seen her...he couldn't finish that sentence. So, instead, loopily happy, he decided to pull out a chair and sit next to her breathing in her essence, or maybe ask her if she knew where they could find a log for the fire and make a night of it, or...

"I should have known you had more strength than a twit like Ella." Looking at him with deep appreciation in her eyes, she said, "You would never betray Jake like that."

And his joy dimmed into the cold, dry ash of the fire that would not be lit, after all.

Mistaking, it seemed, the disappointment that must be mounting in his eyes, she hurried on, "Hey! He made it through Air Assault School, placed first!" Then her eyes clouded over. "One guy, he said, missed the rope on the way out and fell from their helicopter. Paralyzed for life."

Andrew shuddered at the thought of that happening to Jake. Then, seeing she had more news, he prompted, "Is he in Ranger School, then?" Jessie snorted and turned up her hands. "You know Jake. I'll learn it when you do probably."

Andrew grunted in disgust, suddenly deeply angry at the self-absorption of his friend.

"Yeah, I know. Sucks, doesn't it?" He looked up and realized that she had been watching him. "After a while you get used to it. Have to. When you're in front of him, you're the most important thing in his world. When you're not, you don't exist." Then, after a moment's thought, she added, "Almost" and grinned.

He didn't know what to say to that, so he sat quietly sipping at the whiskey, feeling it numb the hollow ache that, he realized now, had begun to fill his stomach.

"Hey, how come you're not in the student directory?"

Surprised at this abrupt change of topic, he had to gather his thoughts, then shrugged, "Schnoebel doesn't want to advertise..." and waved a hand around the room, "...this."

"Oh. Well, I don't even have your phone number." He blinked at her in confusion until he realized that he didn't know what his phone number was.

She smiled as if understanding. "I know you have a phone. You called the ranch, right? On Saturday, over break?"

He blinked again, trying to remember when it was that he had called and from where. Helplessly, he looked around the room trying to find a phone, if he had one.

"I know it was you. Most folks in the valley are still too excited to have phones to hang up without saying anything."

He looked at her, stunned, until he realized that she was joking. He laughed, enjoying it for the first time since the sidewalk.

"Why'd you call?"

He didn't know how to answer that. But, those washed-blue eyes stared at him, waiting for their answer, so he tried. "I was...worried. Wanted to be sure you were all right."

She snorted. "Of course I was."

He tried again, this time not meeting her eyes. "After...that night..." Then, he abruptly stared right back at her, saying, "I've seen you ride when you're angry."

"Oh." And damned if she weren't blushing herself. About time, he thought with satisfaction.

"Well, how about email? If'n you didn't want to talk to me then, you could've at least replied to one of mine."

He blinked again. "Email?" He wondered again if he had an account and wondered further how one got one.

"I sent you two or three these last weeks since break after you stopped coming to the library. Didn't you get 'em? I couldn't tell."

Distracted by a sudden thought, he asked, "You flagged them to see if I read them?"

She gazed at him without the shadow of a blush. "Of course. Ella suggested it."

He smiled at that. Of course. Then, clearing his throat, he ventured, "Well, Jessie, I honestly don't know if I have an email account."

"Honestly, Andrew!" The explosion came with thrown up hands. She got up and walked back and forth. "No cell phone, no regular phone, no email." She stopped, looking at him. "How do you even survive? I mean I'm not into them either, but for crying out loud, the basics!"

He helplessly stared at her then decided to drink the rest of his whiskey so that he looked like he was at least capable of something.

"How about Christmas? You goin' back to Madison?"

Christmas. The question brought him up short again. "I hadn't thought about it."

She exhaled a long, rumbling sigh. "Don't you think you better?"

"What day is it?"

As if sipping from some inner well of patience, she closed her eyes and said, quietly, "Tuesday, December 17th." Then, after a moment, she added, "2002. And, in case you were interested, Christmas break begins Friday night. Where are you gonna go?"

He swallowed. "That's impossible!" Looking around him, he wondered what had happened to the last...month?! He knew that quarters, so different from the semester system he had been brought up with, were always a bit unnerving in the fall with Thanksgiving break chopping up the class schedule. But this?! He started to panic a little at the lost time and then, suddenly, reassuringly he felt the weight of the stone in his hip pocket. Perhaps a little of Kuan Yin's mercy had been showering on him and then he abruptly understood the deeper thrust of that Tang Chinese poem one of the grads had used, artfully he had thought at the time, in her thesis. Inspired, he made up his own on the spot: *The sweetness of your merciful tears washes my suffering into a thousand tomorrows bearable today.* Timeless, he thought. Timeless.

"I repeat for those in the room a bit slow. Where you gonna go?"

He came back to the room and saw her scowling at him. 'Eggheady' was written all over it. "Sorry," he mumbled and shifted in his chair. Then, remembering her question, he said, "I honestly haven't thought about it, Jessie. The..." Casting about him for ideas he saw a stack of journals and lied, somewhat, "...work that Wei has given me these last few weeks has been a bit...absorbing."

She snorted. "I guess!"

She sat back and looked him up and down. "Come back to the ranch. Pop was pretty disappointed you...were tied up with your Bible studies over break." She smiled that new rascally grin of hers. "Anyway, it'll be fun."

After the aborted first attempt during Thanksgiving, Andrew seriously wondered whether he wanted to. Or, maybe he had changed a great deal, more than he realized, these last few weeks...was that even possible, he asked himself, then hastily refocused on the moment.

"I..." he started off with, if only not to sound like an abstracted egghead.

"I promise not to go off on you." She smiled saucily again and, to his great surprise, he found that his stomach was not doing any gymnastics. It felt fine. Just fine. At peace.

"That would be good."

***

"Snow!"

"Yes, Andrew. It may come as a surprise, but there are places in this world other than Wisconsin that have it."

He grinned happily at her as they descended the last ridge into the valley. "It's just that...I thought the valley was a desert. Besides...," he continued, quickly, to forestall her protest, "Jake never mentioned it."

"Yeah, well. We get plenty of it. Could use it in the summer, too. Speaking of which, you probably didn't notice that the fall on the pass was pretty thick, too. Good for us this year."

He shook his head, not remembering.

She sighed. "I know. You went off inside that brain of yours about an hour and a half ago, and I haven't heard a peep since."

He smiled, thinking of the stone. Thinking of Kuan Yin.

"Where do you go, anyway?"

And so he told her. Why, he wasn't quite sure, perhaps because she had listened so patiently when they had talked about Lao Tze and how much those thoughts meant to him, the night of the troll. He told her all about Wei, editing out any connection to his father, and the stone, even showing it to her, and how much it helped him focus his thoughts to be able to...drift sometimes.

"Sometimes?" He snapped a look at her but only saw her sly grin as she squeezed their way in between two unwillingly large semi-trucks and out of the way of an indignantly oncoming SUV. He winced.

"Sometimes."

She gave him a funny look, then a look he couldn't interpret and fearing that she might think he was crazy he stammered out, "Ha--have you ever had anything like that?"

She sighed, chanced one long look at him, then looking back at the road, said, "When you and Jake were taking your night rides, what do you think I was doing on Whip's back?"

He nodded, for some reason not really surprised. And, then, so softly, he almost missed it, he heard her murmur, "Sometimes that was the only thing keeping me going."

He nodded again, inwardly this time. And understood.

***

As they pulled into the yard, Andrew found his heart lifting up to break with joy as he took in all the familiar sights and the, uncharacteristic, hush. Not for long, though, as Biscuit came howling around the corner bouncing around all sides of the car before they even stopped. Opening his door, Biscuit half-bounded into his lap, dowsing him with wet dog-smelling snow, that pink and white nose, with its icicled whiskers, buried happily in Andrew's lap, echoing his joy.

"Guess he missed you."

He looked over to see her face shining brightly as well and said, louder than he intended, given winter's chilled stillness, "I guess!" Hearing it reverberate through the air, his mind cast itself back to the snow-driven years of his own childhood, so long ago. Another age, it seemed.

Jessie held up her hand. "Listen!"

He paused. Over toward the stable, they could hear a thumping. Jessie's happiness took on a slow, beatific smile of contentment, he thought. "Guess someone else did, too."

He stared off toward the noise, wondering what she was talking about, then abruptly realized that Digger was kicking his stall.

She laughed at the astonishment that must have been springing up in his eyes. "Come on and say hi to Pop, first!"

***

Inside, in his chair, next to a lavishly decorated tree, and curiously shrunken from the large presence that Andrew had remembered, Pop set aside his Bible and, a bit shakily, stood to greet Andrew with a thumping pound on the back that was not in the least withered. "Welcome, Andrew! Welcome! You are welcome in this home to celebrate the birth of our Savior."

Nope, he thought, coughing. Not much had changed.

"You got the tree out, huh?"

"Jessica. Come here." He gave her a large, enveloping and warm hug. "You look more and more like Ana every day."

She blinked at that. Maybe a little moistly, Andrew thought. Then, she turned her attention back to the tree. "It looks great, Pop. You didn't do this all by yourself."

Standing back to look it over, as if it were the first time he noticed it, Pop smiled. "No, no. Maria and Angel did it all. Just in time for you to come home. Which reminds me..." he blinked his eyes, still watery, Andrew realized with surprise, but also still their reassuring faded-blue. Pop cast about with his hands a moment as if trying to wrench something from something, then his face brightened. "Maria asked to stay and help out during the holidays. I said, it's okay." He coughed. "I know that you want to do all the cooking by yourself and everything, but..." he coughed again. "She could really use--"

"No problem at all, Pop. I'm glad to have the help." Jessie gave him a quick kiss on his weathered, deeply weathered, Andrew marveled, cheek.

The house looked much the same. He even found himself in his old bed again, Cocoa's milky brown fuzziness still there, purring loudly as soon as he stepped foot in the doorway. Looking over at the other bed, the one that Jake had slept in, he felt a curious lump in his throat, and, for a quiet moment, sat on it and thought about his anger toward his friend, both for his sake and for Ella's. Finally, remembering Jessie's advice, he sighed and decided to simply let Jake be Jake. Then it suddenly struck him that Jake had promised, if at all, he would try to get away for Christmas. He wondered how possible that might be and wondered where Jake was at that moment, conjuring up an image of a helmeted shoulder trying not to swat a mosquito as he carried his rifle wading through some swamp. With the savage hope that Jake got bitten deeply, he decided right there that if Jake should show up they would have a few words about the subject.

**

Digger looked grand, in great shape. He realized that his appreciation for horseflesh had grown. He could see the difference between the somewhat lean and muscular beast nickering at him now, trying to get him to stroke his muzzle, and the somewhat - okay, a lot - fatter and lazy-eyed horse that had greeted him last summer. Whip, too, looked in fine fettle - and he paused for a second wondering where he had picked up that strange word and wondered again at the power of circumstances to shape one's use of language and, by extension, one's way of thinking. As did Asa. He thought briefly about asking to take out Asa who looked a little lonely, but decided quickly that he owed Digger a ride first.

And they did. Every day until Christmas eve. Long, slow rides, just the two of them, the horses plunging happily through the snow, icicles trickling down from their nostrils, plumes of steam rising to contrast them in a nicely balanced picture of rustic beauty, he thought. And, they talked. Jessie seemed much happier. Maria was covering the kitchen, much to Pop's ignorance, even packing lunches for them every day, so they were free to go wherever and whenever they chose. And, they talked. Jessie told him all about her plans to start out with an organically fed herd. They had to keep them separate from the main herd, she had explained. Even had to choose the right ground, because of fear of cross-pollination from pesticides of neighboring fields. Andrew wondered aloud at even the possibility of that given how every farmer used the old tried and true methods. Jessie smiled, "Almost every farmer. Come on."

She led him along tractor paths, beside large, white fields of hushed snow, for several slow miles until she pointed out a small pasture on Lateral F that they leased, and pointed out the organic mint on one side, the conventionally-grown alfalfa running all along the longest side, and the scrub land, chock full of greasewood - that ultimate signifier of uncleared land, he now knew - bordering the other edges. "At first I didn't think it would work, then I remembered that we hadn't used this spread in years. That mint is the key with the way the wind is blowing. The alfalfa...," she said, pointing across the road, "...well, the state inspector I talked to said, because of the wind, the road might be enough of a buffer zone, except for that corner there..." pointing it out. "But then," she smiled brightly at him, "we'll just have to put up some new fencing to keep 'em out of that corner."

He looked it over, genuinely happy for her, then had to pause to remember the right language. "How many head will it support? Without the corner?"

She frowned. "None."

He looked at her in surprise.

She shook her head. "You can tell a Dutchman. You just can't tell him much."

"He refused?"

"Yep." She sighed. "Said, if it were really all that good an idea, which he just can't see, Jake would have come up with it after.." she now mimicked Pop, the slight taste of a tired bitterness lacing her tone, "...four years at that university in Seattle."

They sat quietly for a few minutes. Finally, she roused herself. "Still, it was only my first run at a new idea. Maybe next year I'll come up with something better." Then, she grinned that saucy grin that was becoming, Andrew realized with a jolt, a real staple on her features. "'Ticularly after I leave the buying premiums for organic cattle all over the house for him to find."

He grinned. Encouraged by her change of heart, he said, "At least you spoke your piece."

She looked at him, strangely. "Yeah."

"What?" And he had the odd sensation of their gradual role reversal: she was becoming the one with the hidden thoughts and he the one asking what they were.

She shook her head in response and took Whip off at a canter. He followed her, enjoying the happy lifting plunging of Asa's heat carrying him through the air, so much more vibrant than Digger's, the crisp smell of snow in his nostrils, until she reined up looking at him.

"I knew he wouldn't like it. But I got the idea of talking to him from you."

"Me?"

"Yeah, that night in front of the troll, when you talked about a body being herself so thoroughly that problems get out of the way. You said I was more like that than most people you know."

He remembered now and smiled at the memory, pleased that she had taken what he had said seriously enough to...use it, he decided. And smiled more broadly than ever. Feeling suddenly like a king, he cocked an eyebrow at her, "Race? Field after next?"

"You're on!"

***

On Christmas eve morning at breakfast while Pop said the Blessing, clasping hands as usual turned up for Pop, turned down for Jessie, and mixed for Andrew, Pop had surprised him with the added note, "...and we pray, Lord, that today's Christmas eve service celebrating the birth of our Savior turns out well."

Andrew flashed a glance at Jessie, wondering what this meant for a ride today. She only lifted the corner of a lip at him in silent commiseration. Still, he thought, happily dumping some of Maria's french toast on his plate, it should be interesting. He looked forward to seeing Pastor Don again and wondered what the sermon would be like. Probably retelling the manger story, largely apocryphal Andrew knew, but a captivating story all the same. He found himself suddenly hoping that they would sing a few carols, too, and just as suddenly remembered Jake's description of caroling in a hay wagon and wondered why Jessie had made no mention of it.

In the car, there being no Sunday School this day, as they sat waiting for Pop, Andrew asked her.

"Well..." she began, her eyes moving to the stable. "...I don't think anyone's in the mood this year. But maybe after church I could ask around."

"Why not?"

Not really hearing him, Jessie thumped the steering wheel. "What is taking him so long?" Giving an exasperated sigh, she asked, "Would you go see what's wrong?"

"Sure." Feeling absurdly pleased that he should be trusted with this errand, Andrew set out, shaking the snow proudly from his riding boots - taken the afternoon they had arrived from the basement cupboard, complete with rolled up newspaper wads inside to keep out mice - and paused to pat a panting Biscuit on the head before going inside.

In the mud room, next to the washing machine, he called out, "Pop?" and listened but heard nothing.

Thinking that this was odd, he shucked off his boots and, in his stocking feet, padded around the house looking for Pop, expecting, at every turn to find those wrinkled light blue eyes greeting him. After every other room had been looked in, however, he finally came to the closed door of Pop's bedroom. Feeling now an odd sense of worry, he knocked softly. To his relief, however, he heard a "Come in."

Pop sat on the bed his pants undone, his church shoes, brightly shined, untied, the laces sprawling around them on the floor. His twisted up hands, clenched into fists tight enough that the knuckles showed white beneath the tanned, leathering skin set on the bed either side of him.

Andrew took in the scene at a glance and before he knew what he was doing, knelt at Pop's feet and began tying the shoes. "We'll have this taken care of in a jiffy, Pop."

Pop cleared his throat as he watched Andrew lace them up. "I...uh...my hands don't work so good any more sometimes, Andrew."

Making light of this sudden, unwelcome view of a stout, if badly weathered, oak tree failing, Andrew decided to make light of it. "Well, I have days when I wonder how I tie my shoes myself." He finished the second one and sat back on his heels feeling taller that he could help out in this way. Then, before he moved his eyes to Pop's waistline, he found himself wondering how they were going to handle that.

Instead he found his eyes moving up to meet Pop's, which were glistening.

Pop cleared his throat again. "You're a good man, Andrew....you...are from the city and..." He cleared his throat one more time, rather noisily, then asked, "Are we going to war, son?"

Andrew blinked at the word and, but for his honest cluelessness about how to answer that question, he would have basked in the pleasure of Pop's endearment. But, hastening to answer, he put aside that thought to dwell on another time. "Sir, I honestly can't tell you. Jake would..." and his voice faltered now that it suddenly dawned on him what Pop's question really was. He felt very stupid.

Pop shook his head at the mention of his son's name and mustered a weary smile. "I should never have given him those books."

"Books, sir?"

"Oh..." Pop's hands came up now, their thickly bent fingers flailing around, as he turned them over searching for something. "Those King Arthur stories. He begged me for them. Only God knows where he first heard of them."

Andrew smiled at the thought of a young Jake poring over tales of the Holy Grail under his blankets with a flashlight at night.

"That was the beginning of it. Lancelot did this and Lancelot did that. Lancelot was the best there ever was." Pop smiled, in spite of his mood, and shook his head again. "That was the beginning of it. From then on, all he ever wanted to be was a soldier and...right the...terrible wrongs of this world."

Andrew nodded. It certainly fit with the Jake he knew. "Andrew..." he blinked at the sound of his name and looked back into Pop's eyes peering down at him. "You are a man of faith, I know. Doesn't our Lord work in very mysterious ways at times?"

Andrew was about to nod, then felt some sort of verbal answer was needed. "Yes, Pop. I believe our Lord does. Besides, ultimately, as you told me last time I was here: We are all in Jesus' hands."

"That's true!" Pop's hands came up again, splayed wide in his fervor. And somehow the dim gloom of the room had broken. "Thank you, Andrew. You're a good son. I needed a reminder of that just now."

Andrew smiled. That he knew his smile was stretching his face into a wide beam of pleasure only made the sun rising in his heart all that much brighter.

"Now, let's get the rest of this done. We don't need to tell Jessica. Womenfolk take it hard when their men begin to fail."

Andrew bent his head to hide his bemused expression at that bit of valley truth and set about doing up Pop's pants.

Arriving late at the church, despite Jessie's best efforts, they saw the service was already well underway. Yet, Andrew noticed, Pop's place in the pews was not taken, almost as if a sign of due respect and faith that he would arrive in time. They slid in and joined into a rough-hewn, pell-mell singing of *Angels We Have Heard on High* and smiled at the memory of hearing other, slightly more angelic versions.

To his disappointment, he didn't see Pastor Don anywhere. Raising an eyebrow at Jessie, he saw her gaze narrowed on a middle-aged man, with movie star good looks right down to the dignified graying of the temples, sitting complacently in the chair that Pastor Don usually used. At the end of the carol, a man in a well-worn and badly fitting gray suit stood up and looked over at Pop. Andrew frowned trying to remember his name: Tom? John? The man said, "Nijs? We announced earlier that Pastor Don's mother was taken bad early this morning. He's with her now but sends his prayers to us." Pop nodded. "Earnest Brickton will be delivering the Message this morning." Andrew's ears pricked up at that, and his gaze settled on the good looking man as he wondered if the man's family had originally settled the town. His mind quickly scanned back over the little Yakima history he had managed to pick up: immigrants, mostly, arriving in the 1880s and the following decades, taking up uncleared land with a plow, a set of horses and an unbreakable will, had over the last century wrought this agricultural marvel out of a desert.

Jessie's murmured "Shit!" broke into his thoughts. Pop, in return, cleared his throat, more loudly than usual. Andrew wondered what was wrong. He glanced at her but only saw her gaze, growing harder by the second - he knew that look, he thought - leveled toward Brickton, who was now standing, wearing a vest decorated with polished metal cowboy regalia and strumming a guitar. "I thought I would sing a song before I brought the Message. It's a simple song. But it's one that contains all we need to hear." Pushing aside this bit of arrogance, Andrew decided that Brickton's voice, a solid tenor, was rather pleasant to listen to and sat back to enjoy this bit of rustic novelty.

After a few more strums, then a lengthy pause as Brickton, rather self-importantly Andrew thought, adjusted a few strings, he finally began. It was a simple song, one Andrew didn't know. But he found the accompaniment of the guitar a good choice as well as the plain-spoken riffs between verses.

Open my eyes, Lord. I want to see Jesus.

The only note ruining this picture was the rather pretentious manner in which Brickton did everything, almost as if he were more of a cartoon than a real person. Andrew chanced a glance around to see if others were a bit amused at Brickton's strutting. But, no, all those he could see, even Irma, he could recognize a few pews over, and Elsie one just beyond her, sat in rapt attention, even devotion.

Open my ears, Lord. I want to hear Jesus.

Well, Andrew thought, it was their church, after all and reflected on the various ways that everyone approached the divine, the important role that charismatic individuals had played over the millennia in all the faith traditions as if, no matter how simple a truth, people still needed the example of other people to grasp it.

The strumming had stopped and the echoing voices of the congregation still lay lapping at the edges of the room when Andrew realized that he had, as Jessie put it, gone off somewhere. He looked over at her and found her face a frozen mask. Indifferent and, yet, with a shade of haughtiness cast about it.

Brickton was setting down his guitar. "Thank you for joining in, my brothers and my sisters in Christ. And that is what we do, isn't it? We join together in the worship of our Lord, our Savior." Heads nodded around the room at his question, though Brickton seemed not to notice them. All at once, Andrew was seized with a sudden dislike of this man.

"For he set us free. From that terrible stain. Our inheritance. The curse of Eve." At the power of this last declaration, ringing through the church, Andrew felt Jessie's tightened fists beginning to beat an almost silent thumping on the pew between her jeans-clad, Andrew suddenly noticed with a smile, legs. He reached a hand over and gently stilled them, just as he saw Elsie's smile slightly tighten with disapproval at Brickton's phrasing. But then, Elsie nodded. Brickton went on. "For you see, my friends, what happens when a woman takes a matter into her own hands without the wisdom of a man to guide her." Unreal, Andrew thought, and straightened in the pew, genuinely intrigued now at where this was going.

"In a letter to the editor of a Seattle newspaper the other day..." Here Brickton paused, looking out over the congregation. "From time to time, I like to read what those liberal feminists think, remind myself of what the world looks like to someone who's mind's so open their brain's fallen out." Titters here and there broke out among the pews. "Anyway, this young feminist was wondering what the world would look like now if Mary, our blessed Savior's mother, had taken the Morning After Pill." Gasps broke out now, like a wave of shock and disgust, followed by clucks of disapproval. "Now, now. I do believe that we should hate the sin, love the sinner. I believe this girl, horribly misguided though she may be, may very well be of a good heart. At least capable of improving, with guidance." Heads nodded at that. "And I pray that someday, she shall meet Jesus, open her eyes, her ears, her heart to Him and repent of her question. At that time, even if she should walk through that door right back there..." he said, pointing to the back of the church, "...as loving Christians, we would welcome her. I know that I would be among the first."

He bet Brickton would, Andrew thought, a bit unsettled at how ridiculous this whole sermon was turning out. He found himself wishing for Pastor Don's deeper wisdom, honed by, Andrew suddenly realized, the experiences of moving among the suffering. He wondered for a moment what Pastor Don would make of all of this, then remembered the pastor's praise of Paul - from one of whose letters Brickton appeared to have lifted his entire wacky sermon - and Andrew frowned, allowing he honestly didn't know how Pastor Don would receive it. Looking over at Jessie, suddenly, he saw her gone, her face a veil of bitterness, her mind roaming freely almost, probably thundering Whip through some field. Turning back to Brickton, as he droned on and on awash in self-anointed self-importance, Andrew finally grew bored. His mind cast off, too, pondering Augustine's allegorical interpretation of the Garden of Eden story and the apple and how much of that complex thinking had been crafted Andrew supposed, if he weren't certain, as the gates of Rome were falling to the Visigoths and Augustine's world must have been caving in. How his wonderful insights - even if Andrew completely disagreed with Augustine, he could still respect the honest effort - into the troubles of that time had been boiled down to some sort of boilerplate patriarchy for all time. Convenient for those in charge to stay in charge, while keeping down the other half because, it was claimed, it was God's design for the cosmos. His mind rambled on to the authority that Augustine's writings had enjoyed all through the Dark Ages. Even so mighty a medieval thinker as Thomas Aquinas had had to cite Augustine in just about every novel argument that Aquinas had made, so far as Andrew knew. Without knowing how long he had been gone, he abruptly found his attention returning to the present.

"...my friends, we must always be on guard against the whispered temptations of Satan as that liberal feminist of Seattle surely was not. We must always keep our eyes, our ears, our hearts open to our Savior and closed to the Enemy. We must always, with the choices we make in our lives, honor God's sacrifice of His only Son, that the terrible stain of Eve's wicked curiosity may be wiped clean each day, that we remain justified in the eyes of our Lord. For that I pray for all of us. That we men in these uncertain times ahead may remember to stay strong, turning to Jesus in our travails. That our women may remember

the two examples of their forebears: turning aside
from the ambitions of Eve and embracing with their
whole hearts, in each day, each decision, the simple
goodness of Mary who bowed to God's will and
prepared the way that we may all be saved. Amen."

Blowing out a sigh, Andrew reflected that the best
you could say of this sermon was that it
was...blessedly, he thought with a wicked inner grin,
at least for him...short, though he had to admit that
Brickton's repetitious use of eyes, ears, and heart,
particularly following the song was rather effective
rhetoric. Jessie's look of bitterness had given way to
one of quiet despair, he saw and felt a cold anger
building within him. However, knowing that he had
grown past the point of doing something rash, he only
leaned over and whispered in her ear, "Nothing like a
traditional Christmas sermon to ring in the season."
At that, her eyes flashed, first, in anger again - he saw
with relief - and then dissolving into a quiet smile.

The car was quiet on the way home. They had not
stayed long, though Andrew had been able to say
hello amidst crushingly warm hugs to Elsie, Irma, and
a few of the others he had gotten to know a little at
Prayer Meeting. "Merry Christmas! Merry
Christmas!" Their happy cries ringing in his ears
made him playful. And when the car rolled into the
yard, Biscuit's hollers greeting them, he noticed that
the icicles decorating the house were dripping.
Perfect, he thought. He delayed a little, petting
Biscuit, while the others made their way up to the
house, then knelt down and, as surely as if he were
born to it, he knew before he touched it that the snow
would pack.

Taking aim, he landed one right square in the
middle of Jessie's back as she held open the door,
splattering Pop a bit in the face. "Whoa!" Pop cried
and turned around with a huge grin. Jessie, however,
stood there for a moment. Then, turning, he saw the
eyes of a hunter in her face, spread wide in a savage

grin and, darting sideways off the porch, she was already bent, scooping up a handful as she ran. He ran also, into the deeper drifts of the yard, keeping a careful eye on her, as he massaged his next ball into throwing shape. "You chuckleheads!" Pop cried out, laughing and watching as Jessie launched a fastball right at Andrew's head. He managed to duck, just in time, it came so fast. But then he found himself bent over her as she plowed into him throwing him straight onto his back. God, she was like a tiger! Sitting atop his chest, laughing with delight, she brought down two handfuls of snow onto his head. Coughing and spluttering, he heard Pop say, "I'll have Maria put on some cocoa..." and the door's cheerful slam.

Fierce she may be, she was still small. With a heave he overturned her, surprised and pleased at his strength and thought of riding Digger, but only long enough to realize that she had let him so that she could continue the roll. And on they went rolling over and over each other in the yard, chortling and gasping, Biscuit barking and howling, nipping at their heels wanting to get close, but not too close. Finally, after eating one last faceful of snow, and trying to spit it out, he felt Jessie lying on top of him, panting out plumes of steam, her chest heaving against him. And he suddenly realized that she was not all that flat-chested after all. Indeed, they were not so large as Ella's but they were pleasantly soft all the same. About the same moment that he abruptly found himself growing hard, he realized that she was stretched wonderfully all along him, matching him hip for hip. And there they lay, Jessie's breath suddenly caught, her eyes widening in embarrassment as she felt him growing, pressing against her. But she didn't move. She merely lay there feeling him, he guessed, with God knew only what thoughts. He tried desperately to think of the stone to try to deflate the burgeoning warmth filling his loins, but he couldn't recall its shape, much less its color. All the

could think of was how warm her own hips were
growing and, now, through their sweaters, he could
feel them - the tiny pricks of her nipples hardening,
impossible to ignore, announcing their own presence
with authority. All this time, she looked down at him,
her face a swirl of emotions that wouldn't slow down
long enough for him to recognize any and then,
finally, subsiding into a blank gaze of wonder.
Before she hit him with one last fistful of snow,
breaking the spell. Laughing, she got off of him, just
as Pop walked around the corner, calling out, "Your
cocoa's gonna get cold!"

"Okay, Pop!" She smiled at him with joy, a bit
pink around the edges, Andrew thought, blinking
away some flakes and wondering what his own face
looked like.

***

That evening, he got more of the Christmas he had
been hoping for. Jessie managed to plunk out, rather
crudely and disjointedly, a few carols on the small
piano tucked upright into the corner of the living
room. He didn't care. Pop's large bass, thundering
the glass it seemed at times, Jessie's husky and
scratchy alto, and his own weak tenor all combined to
belt out one song after another, between gulped
fistfuls of popcorn that Maria had thoughtfully laid
out before going home to her own family, her own
celebrations. It was the best Christmas, Andrew
reflected, he had had since being very, very young.
Then, correcting himself, he remembered warily that
joy was fleeting, the craving of which led to all
sorrow. And, all at once, he felt free to enjoy it for all
it was, beyond past, present or future comparisons.
Just one moment of time spent in happiness. Nothing
more. Nothing less. That would die soon enough.
And remain all that more precious for having
happened at all, as a result.

***

Under the sheets that night, he found his mind dwelling on the snow play with Jessie that afternoon and, staring out the moonlit windows whose curtains he always left up that he could suck in as much of Yakima as possible while there, his eyes lingered on the snow angel, of sorts, that they, together, had created. He saw the drifts mounded up each side where it had happened, painted blue by the moon goddess's palette and, at the memory of her hips pressed against his, he grew hard again. After nudging an unwilling Cocoa out of bed because he felt embarrassed, he lay quietly, savoring the moment. Yes, he thought, like a god and flexed his penis under his pajamas.

His door quietly opened. And, as if another one of his dreams, she floated like a spirit without stepping to the edge of his bed. Her legs, he saw for the first time, were quite shapely in their musculature, stretching down in fine detail under the flannel nightshirt she was wearing, a musky heat shimmering around her in the night air. He made to speak, but she put two fingers to his lips, nodding toward Pop's bedroom. Pulling back the covers, she swung her bending leg over his hips as easily as if she were mounting Whip. "Ella says Jake told her you're a virgin. Is that true?" she whispered softly. He nodded. "Guess we don't have anything to worry about then." And she reached into his pajamas, drawing out his stiff penis without a flicker of surprise, as if she had been expecting it, drew it to its height under her raised hips and, in one thrust, plunged down upon it.

Her face arched back, her lips snarling, a hiss of pain escaping between them, as Andrew felt something give way. And then he felt a molten warmth of pleasure enveloping him, her hips brought

down squarely to his, the tangy smell of love wafting
now up to him. And she began to move. Short, fierce
strokes that lost him in wave after wave of mindless
tinglings that ran from his penis and hips all over his
body to his fingertips and toes, his mind dazzled by a
light growing brighter and brighter as she continued
with each stroke, his whole being overpowered by the
rise building within, Jessie's answering soft moans
and sighs of bliss until in the midst of their mingled
explosion, he heard the 15th century mystic Julian of
Norwich's loud prayers to God, her lover, in his ears
and understood her ecstasy.

Jessie lay quietly on his breast, breathing out softly.
Feeling a deep, welling love for her, always, here and
ever after, he was shocked to see on her face a
frightening mask of triumph that she shared with no
one. Least of all him. He felt his penis, so divine-
like in its mammoth intensity a moment before,
shrink into a dispiriting nothingness and slip,
dripping, from within her.

There was a soft knock on the door. "Hoss. You
awake still?" Without a sound, Jessie sat bolt upright
and slid off the bed to the far side from the door.
Andrew managed to grunt out, something, anything.
And the door opened. And there he was, his face
almost in shadow, yet lined with streaks from the
nightlights of the hallway, revealing a harder, gaunter
face out of which peered eyes that, even in the dim
light, revealed themselves to be older, deeper, having
seen much since last laying on Andrew.

He stepped in, the soft tan of his combat boots
making little sound on the carpet, his browns, grays
and whites battle dress uniform sporting a few new
decorations since Andrew had seen it last.

He saw Jake pause mid-step, his nostrils flaring, so
he quickly asked, "Is it really you?" Jake beamed and
sat on the bed next to him.

"Yep. Found one of my sergeants banging the CO's
wife one night, so I wangled a short leave. Tough

though." He sighed, a happy sound, and stretched his legs.

Andrew saw a new patch adorning the shoulder and pointed to it. "Is that it?"

Jake nodded without looking at it. "Screaming Eagles. I made it."

Suddenly, all his past rage at his friend dissolved in the pride washing over him. He grabbed Jake's shoulder and exulted, "That's great, Jake. Just great! God, that's great."

Jake beamed again and cocked his head at Andrew. "How 'bout you, hoss? Find your place yet?"

Andrew barked out a laughter, which Jake quickly shushed, that what Wei, speaking from his inner mountaintop, had finally revealed to Andrew in his great wonder and awe, Jake would have long understood instinctively. He thought about trying to explain Wei's suggestion that in forgetting his quest, it would find him, a suggestion that Andrew had quietly worked on, with the stone, since, then decided it was too complicated to go into. "Almost."

"Good, hoss. You have everything you need, you know. Well, you don't know. That's your problem. But I know it." Jake shook his head. "Hoss, you should see some of the fools given command of situations way beyond their ability. Fools with half your qualities..." And, abruptly, disappointingly, he shut off the tap as he closed his eyes with weariness. "It's been a long trip here. God knows what I'm gonna have as paybacks when I get back." Then, his eyes flashed their old hunter's gaze - it really was just like Jessie's, Andrew thought with an inward smile. "We're mobilizing any day. Detached to the 3rd Infantry Mechanized. Tip of the spear."

"Eden."

Jake chuckled at that. "Yes, hoss, the cradle of civilization. Gonna take it back from one very bad man, his psycho sons and their cronies, put a stop to them gassing their people and burying 'em alive.

But.." he paused, looking straight into Andrew's eyes. "...as to our destination, you never heard me say that. Ever."

"It's already forgotten."

Jake slapped him on the shoulder.

"How long have you got?"

Jake lifted a pager. "Until this damn thing goes off. I was half afraid I wouldn't see the ranch before it began buzzing." He shook his head at it, wonderingly. "Well, I'm in the Army now." Then, Jake-like, he shrugged off any impending gloom. "We can talk more tomorrow. Maybe take out Asa. Tonight, I'm sleeping under the Christmas tree. Don't know when I'll be able to do that again." He beamed and began moving toward the door.

As he opened it. Andrew remembered to say, "Jake? It's really very good to see you."

Jake turned and beamed one last time. "You, too, hoss." He paused before stepping through the door and said, "See you in the morning, Jessie."

Silence descended. For a moment. Andrew felt the blush rising in his cheeks and wondered if he could make up some kind of confused indignation. He was about to open his mouth when he heard her muffled answer. "Good night, Jake."

And the door closed.

***

In the morning - Christmas morning, Andrew reminded himself with a happy grin - Jake was already gone.

Pop was sitting in his chair, a cup of Jessie's coffee in front of him sitting untouched when Andrew appeared. One look was enough to tell him. Jake was already gone. Was it another of his dreams, Andrew wondered, but had only to look at Pop's face for his answer.

"His mobilization call came at three last night. He woke me to tell me and..." Pop's voice, usually so full and strong had an odd quaver in it this morning. "...say goodbye," he finished rather lamely.

Jake was gone and had taken all the Christmas cheer with him. Jessie tried to keep things going, but with Pop's drifting aimlessness and his own redoubled efforts to focus on the stone, almost a reflex now, Andrew knew that the holiday was forced.

One day soon after, taking a slow, ambling ride, Andrew had looked over at Jessie's withdrawn, sad face and, hoping to ease her, mentioned that even if a moment was fleeting, it didn't lose its precious value.

She had bridled at that. Had scowled at him, flicked her pony tail in annoyance and heeled Whip into a full gallop away from him. He didn't try helping anymore after that. And so the days passed, without anyone mentioning what everyone was thinking. And Christmas Eve? Whatever closeness he had enjoyed with her, so brief! was now gone as she steadily drew away from him into her own private torment.

Church the following Sunday was a relief for all, if only because they wouldn't only have each other to stare at. Pastor Don was there, slapping Andrew on the back with great glee and asking after his studies. Taking one look at Pop and Jessie was enough for him, however. He only laid a quiet hand on each's shoulder and prayed so softly that Andrew could not catch the words.

His sermon was thoughtful, a bit sad, as he talked of the struggles each generation must face doing God's work, the inevitable sacrifices, even suffering, that must be faced as a result, and the ever-present reminder that all are in Jesus' hands. While it washed over Andrew like some tract he was studying, he could see it helped Pop quite a bit. For the first time since Jake's departure, the old man began to show a bit more life, even a little spring in his step as he and

Pastor Don got into a conversation in the parlor after service about what the coming year could bring for Brickton Community Church. Jessie remained withdrawn.

***

Having grown used to each other's silences during their last rides, the trip back over the pass passed in a heartbeat, it seemed. Before he knew it, he was saying goodbye to her at his doorstep. He thought briefly of inviting her in but after seeing her closed features, decided against it.

Back in the apartment. Which looked as tidy as ever. Too tidy, in fact, given that he wasn't used to making the bed. But then, he decided, perhaps he had been meditating on the stone while doing it. Schnoebel had little to say other than a smoky "Froliche Weinachten, cherub. Let's get to work..." and handed over some papers. Wei, after handing over his own stack, merely sat looking at Andrew without a word. Andrew looked back, at first unnerved, then, thinking of the stone, he felt its reassuring peace fill him. Wei's eyes suddenly sparkled. Andrew nodded his gratitude and, bowing, left.

***

The campus, however, had changed. New classes notwithstanding, the university had mobilized its own answer to the country's direction. Rallies were scheduled throughout each day, speakers flying in from around the region, mounting that table outside the library and in other places, shoes stomping and megaphones bellowing out cries of "Hell No We Won't Go!" They were so omnipresent that Andrew, trying as hard as he might, could not shut them out. Each time he passed through on one his trips back and forth to the library or classes he thought of Jake. One time, as the weeks passed and the frenzy gathered, he was surprised to find himself praying for Jake's safety. To whom, or to what, he wondered. Then, deciding Kuan Yin would do, since he figured any God capable of creating the cosmos would be large enough not to care, he continued it. Soon, his prayers became as regular as his meditations. Sometimes, correcting his thoughts, casting back in his memories for anything and everything Jake had ever said to him about his specialty - the making of war - and, realizing that if anyone could, Jake would come home in one piece, he changed his prayers for Jake's unit and wished he had had the time that Christmas morning to ask Jake about his men. Were there women in his unit, he wondered from time to time, always resolving the question that it didn't matter and kept on praying for them. Then for Jake, again, when he forgot his friend's capabilities. Then back for the unit again.

Of Jessie, he saw very little. Once, on the day of the president's final ultimatum to Saddam Hussein's government, he looked up from a book in the library and saw her staring at him from across the way. She made as if to mouth something, then turned away. Bewildered at her self-imposed distance, angry at it and her, he soon found his thoughts returning to the stone, its reassurance as familiar now as an old pair of socks he had just donned, and then to the sources he was checking.

The next night, the night of the invasion now occurring halfway around the world, he came back to the apartment to find Ella, fully clothed, and with a mug of tea steeping for him on the table, making his bed for him. Abruptly understanding how the apartment had taken on its own tidiness over time, he went over to her, noticing the yellow ribboned pin she was sporting on her breast under her ponytail - back

247

again, he could see and knowing what it signified - took her in his arms and let her cry.

Later, after making tea for her as well, they sat and talked. He thanked her for tidying up for him. Her tired, drawn features lit up a bit at that. "You noticed."

"Yeah. I couldn't figure out how I had suddenly taken to washing my own dishes, but..." He let his unfinished thought die out, not knowing what to say next.

"Keep an eye on him. That's what he said."

Andrew sat up straight. "You saw him? When?"

"Christmas, two days before. He emailed me, finally! Said he was coming through and would I wait for him? He knew I would." She smiled a dreamily happy beam of her own.

"How did you...?"

"Oh." She smiled again, really quite beautifully, if a little naughtily. "I swiped your key in the library once and had a copy made."

Andrew had to chuckle.

"You don't mind? I asked him what I could do to bring him home more quickly, and that's what he said. Said he worried about you all the time. I...swiped it ...Thanksgiving. That's how I got in." Andrew shook his head, realizing he had never thought to ask. "And just before Christmas break, I thought I would sneak in and tidy up. You know, a little Christmas gift." Andrew nodded, suddenly remembering. "And, so, when he said that if he didn't have to worry about you, he would have an easier time dodging bullets, it was obvious what I should do."

Andrew paused, seeing in his mind's eye Jake's broad beam, and felt a wave of pure gratitude for the love of his friend who, while never writing, had held his eggheady friend close to his breast all the same.

"Do you mind if I continue? It's the least I can do to...help him."

Taking his mind back to the present, he quickly replied, "By all means, Ella. And I thank you and him for it."

"Good!" She smiled her most precious smile yet, so relieved, so serene in its peace that Andrew felt his heart stop at the mighty force of love in this world. Given Ella's heart, that was all the body armor Jake would ever need. "Now, I've gotten tired of seeing your empty fridge." He looked up to see her, brisk as a bee, moving into the kitchen. "So, I've stocked it for you. They're all easy to eat meals. Just microwave them."

His protest, so quickly forming on his lips, failed in wonder at the sight of a new, tiny microwave gleaming at him from the kitchen counter.

"You don't have to pay me back. I've..." She stopped, blushing. "My family's got...well...never mind."

"Okay. Uh...thanks. Thank you, Ella."

"For tonight, though, how about some real cooking? I brought everything."

And they spent the evening over wine, garlic bread, and a savory spaghetti that Ella whipped up, Andrew grateful for her company, her delighted laughter at the many stories he had to tell of his year living together with Jake and that glorious, wonderfully sun-drenched summer a horseback.

On his doorstep, she paused, then asked, "Will he come home safe?"

Aglow with all his favorite memories of Jake fresh in his mind, he raised an eyebrow, "Jacob Van der Vaal? He's going to come with a couple of medals and a battlefield commission for bravery."

She hugged him then. He felt her luscious breasts pressing into him and thought, with a pang, how much smaller, yet equally wonderful, Jessie's had felt. Then, Ella kissed him on the cheek and said goodnight. He watched her supple form, so different from Jessie's angular walk, disappear into the night

before he suddenly realized with a gasp that his
answer to her had been ridiculously cavalier and with
the frightening thought that he had just tempted fate
for his friend, went to bed.

A few nights later, after shouldering his way
through yet another rally, this one, he saw to his
anger, featuring Hegland atop a table preaching of the
coming of Armageddon and how the Armed Services
were God's avenging angels hastening the return of
Jesus, he saw Jessie's tiny form crouching on his
doorstep, her arms gathered around her knees, so
unlike her, her head resting atop them, turned away
from him.   And he knew.

God, he knew. He began running.

One look at her face, its stony toughness not fading
when it turned toward him, was enough. In a dream,
he hoped, he walked to the door without a word and
turned the key letting them both in.

She remained standing. He dropped his bag and
then himself into a chair, forcing himself to meet her
eyes.

"He's dead. We don't know how. We don't know
when or where."

Andrew closed his eyes, thought of his stone and
angrily pushed it away. Her voice droned on. "His
XO pulled me from class to tell me. They're flying
him back. He's on his way now. Gonna arrive at the
airstrip at Fort Lewis around two in the morning. The
Husky Battalion are going to be there to give him full
honors." He opened his eyes, feeling the disbelief
clouding them over, wondering vaguely who the
Husky Battalion were, then remembering with a
piercing stab that it was the campus ROTC unit.

"Andrew, it's worse. Pop's...when they told him he
had a heart attack. Pastor Don's with him now. I
have to go back. Bring Jake with me."

He closed his eyes again. This was too much.
Again, the stone beckoned to him. Again he pushed it

away, but not with so much strength now, his anger at it trickling away, like blood dripping slowly, steadily into Mesopotamian sand.

The moments ticked away in silence. He hardly knew what to say, what to do. Finally, feeling he should say something, do something, he made a move upward as if to hold her.

"No." She stepped back, her stoniness giving way to a fury, almost frightening as it mounted in intensity with each word she spat out. "I'm not like you, Andrew. I don't have your Buddhist...or Taoist...or whatever you call it...detachment." Clutching a fist that pounded on her heart, she said, stabbing his own, "I feel pain, Andrew. I feel suffering."

Stung at how fantastically unfair this was, he tried to speak up.

"I'm not like you." He saw her anger, then, more clearly, and realized that it wasn't directed at him. "I can't watch people in pain and just...meditate on it." He didn't say anything, let her go on, even though he felt each wound, almost having to breathe through each one, she opened in him as she continued. "I can't watch people like Irma cry their eyes out when God takes the best thing they've ever had from them and just...sit there...like some fucking Buddha, finding some sort of...enlightened...bullshit in it."

Crushed to where he could barely breathe, he hoped it would end soon. He thought of trying to explain to her his feelings that night, grateful to think of anything other than this awful present, of how elated he had been to realize that Fundamentalism, in all its quirks so incomprehensible to those of his world, was nothing more than a faith born of desperation, of people who had so few options in life, who knew so much suffering, that the only way they could function on a daily basis was to put all their trust in a higher power of some sort. Later, he had changed that view, of course, he corrected himself. Had realized that it was overly-simplified, that it...and decided that it was too complicated to explain. Vaguely, he wondered how Pastor Don would handle this. He wondered how many times, how many kitchens that gentle, if booming, man had found himself holding newly made widows crying over hemorrhaged husbands lying in their own drunken blood. How many times--

"Gone again! Fuck you!"

He came back to the present, painfully, and saw pure hatred written on her face. "Fuck you and that escaping off to the inside of your head when your own friend, my brother, is dead!"

He started at that, feeling the rush of guilt painting his face for all the world to see.

"I'm going."

She moved toward the door.

Finally, finding his voice, he said, "Wait." He swallowed. She stopped, then turned, flinging something on the table. "There's a badge to get you into the base."

His eyes looked at it, focusing on it, in desperation, to keep from returning to the stone. The door slammed.

He could think of only one word, then. Ella.

Trapped by a sniper. Of all the fucking situations to wind up in. Jake grunted and wiped the hot, gritty sweat out of his eyes. Nearby, the medic crouched over him, McLaughlin lay, his teeth chattering as the blood poured out of both legs. One shot and both arteries. Jake had to give the sniper a grudging admiration. Overhead a copter flew low, its thundering whoomp-whoomps almost drowning out all thought. Following its path, then hearing the medic's expletive, Jake found his eyes resting on Gutierrez's panicked eyes. Reaching over, he slapped him on the shoulder. "Don't worry, Gutierrez. Nobody's going to die. We're too good at this shit, remember?" Gutierrez nodded, shakily, and tried to work up a smile. "Now, lend a hand there before McLaughlin bleeds all over our new BDUs." Gutierrez actually smiled a bit at that, shook his head and, cradling his rifle, pressed his hands down on one of the field dressings.

Then Jake saw her. They all saw her. Some old crone, her frayed shawl bent over her burka, a blue plastic shopping bag banging at her knees as she tried to hurry along the wall of the mosque opposite them, hearing the bullets hit around her but not knowing how to get away from them. As she paused, she looked right at him, peering helplessly through thick round glasses, her thick nose wrinkly pushed out between them. Jesus, he thought, seeing the pure terror in them. She could be ol' Janet Wiley back home. That motherfucker wouldn't shoot his own people. A few more bullets popping small puffs of dust and then tagging her, in the shoulder he thought as she went down with a cry, answered that soon enough. He looked over at his sergeant who looked back at him, then shook his head. "Lieutenant, don't rope a dope us!"

"No worries," he smiled back and lit out toward her. Just push her around that corner and all's well, he thought, taking running stride after stride across the street. The boys will be taking out that motherfucker soon enough. He had almost reached her when he heard a distant cry, "RPG!" and the world collapsed into a hail of exploding hell. He couldn't think. Couldn't see. Couldn't hear except for that fucking...Get a hold of yourself Van der Vaal, he thought. Dazed, he struggled to make sense through the shrill pitch screaming in his ears. He

squinted over his shoulder and saw someone, maybe Johnson, pointing at a window and the squad leveling everything they had at it. Glancing around him, he saw that he was half-buried in what used to be the wall of the mosque. He carefully flexed everything, his toes, his legs, his fingers, his arms, and decided he was okay. Good enough for now, anyway. Then, hearing the moan, he saw her next to him, her lower legs turned into ground beef, like at a packing plant back home, he thought, not letting the appalling shock confronting him to freeze him. He wriggled over to her, feeling, if not hearing the first bullet strike the road a few feet from them. He crawled on top of her. Roped a dope, indeed, he grinned as a second one hit, coming closer. Oldest trick in the book: hit one guy, then take out every one that follows trying to save him. Uncertain fire, though. Not like the last guy, his mind registered. Unused to aiming a sniper rifle. Good. They must have taken out the first son of a bitch. She came to, now, screaming in terror, trying to ward him off of her. A third bullet struck, the closest yet. Okay. He's getting the range. It's a factor. Don't lose it. Just get her out of here. Looking back, he could see his men alternately waving at him and pouring it on into that window. He slid off her, feeling now the numbness in his hips. Mother-fuck! A fourth one landed, close enough he thought he saw it just before it hit. He tried to move her but she was all gone now, muttering something over and over, and then the bullet took her in the head, splattering him with her blood, her brains. He blinked it away from his eyes, feeling the numbness grow across his back. He slowly turned his face toward that window. And knew peace. Except for one thing. He had got someone to look after hoss. But he had forgotten to get someone to look after--

IV

Jessie woke screaming. Her fists clenching the blankets. Her door opened and she realized where she was as she hastily wiped away her tears, staring into Pop's worried face, his hair all disheveled.

Get a grip! She calmed herself, taking some deep breaths and choking back down the further tears she could feel wanting to come up. She looked at Pop, then slid out of bed. "I'm sorry, Pop. It was just...a nightmare. You shouldn't be up. Doctor Heller said that you should rest now."

Pushing aside, gently, his protests, she marched him back into bed. As she was tucking him back in, he asked, "Was it the same one?"

She smiled, trying to keep the sadness out of her face and lied to him. "No, Pop. A different one..." She frowned at the effort of trying to make up something...funny. "A bunch of carrots were attacking me in the kitchen. Mad at me for slicing 'em up."

Pop smiled at that thought. "I'd like to see that."

"Maybe you will someday."

"Maybe I will." He let her plump up his pillow then lay his head back. She kissed him on the forehead, thinking again for the thousandth time how much of a child he was becoming after the heart attack, after...

"Okay, sleep tight."

"You, too," he murmured, the sleep already overtaking him.

She wandered into the kitchen and made some tea for herself, then feeling its warmth as she held it in both hands, tried to stop the shaking taking hold of her. She took a sip.

Battlefield commendation for valor. Whatever that meant. Trying to save an Iraqi civilian from collateral damage. All the jargon, arriving weeks ago in an official-looking packet, written by some asshole who was apparently too busy continuing that fucking war to spare a nice word or two. She sighed. We'll probably never know how. Just that he died taking some place called Najaf, just outside some big holy mosque called Imam something or other, right after the invasion had begun. Andrew would know what it was, she suddenly thought, then angrily pushed that thought away to think of Jake. He never even got to see Baghdad. She tried to muster up the sound of his voice but heard nothing. She felt the tears coming then, and too tired to chide herself for her weakness, let them flow. She stared out into the night, her tears dripping silently into her tea.

***

She was going blind, she thought, looking wearily up from Pop's register, his child-like handwriting barely fitting into the tiny boxes. Flipping back over the years, she had seen that his handwriting had gotten shakier. She was blind, she thought, rubbing the back of her hand across her eyes and sat back to listen to a robin singing from its treetop perch in the sunlight nearby. Distracted for a moment by the thought that she used to never listen to birds, she grunted that she had never had the time going full out on Whip's back and, achingly, missed those carefree rides. She couldn't see how to drive this thing. She thought back to that small business seminar she had taken the first weekend in Seattle, hiding the cost from Pop, and remembered the painful, worrying lesson of an example business that didn't track its cash flow. She didn't even know how much they had in the bank today, let alone three weeks from now, she thought with irritation. Gritting her teeth, she tried tapping out a few more numbers into Pop's aged, cracked calculator, then gave up. Suddenly inspired by the robin's cheery birdsong, she wondered how long it would take her to set up a cash flow in a spreadsheet. A real spreadsheet, she thought with satisfaction, that does the totaling automatically. She wondered whether there was one on their old computer that Pop had bartered second-hand when they, well, she really, had pleaded for some sort of email to the outside world. Getting up to look, she heard the walkie-talkie squawk. "Jefe?" It was Angel and he sounded worried. The calving had started, almost unbelievably, as if to flip the bird at Jake's death, the morning she had arrived. Life went on, she thought with a bitter smile. Angel's voice came through again, "Jefe?"

She picked it up. "Angel?"

"Señorita Jessica. Belle is breeched, I think. And the winch is broken. Señor Van der Vaal..."

"He's sleeping."

"I see." He paused. "Should I call the vet?"

She winced at the thought of more bills. Even given Jake's paltry life insurance, with Pop's bills and the medicine, almost frighteningly expensive, they were just making it, barely. As far as she could tell. She made up her mind. "No. Belle's, where...on Lateral B, near Brouchet's mint?"

"Si." He sounded relieved.

"I'll be right there." Deciding that she could take advantage, Belle being a bit slow, after all, and after Flicker, it being her second calf, she grabbed the obstetrical chains and a couple pairs of gloves from the tool shed and bridled Whip.

Riding along, she felt better, as she always did. She thought again how much she missed her daily rides with Whip. The ranch...well...there was just too much to learn, too much that Pop had seemed to carry around in his head and, afraid of another attack, she didn't want to bother him with the gazillion and one questions she had. Better to let him doze all day, reading his Bible or watching the tv when his eyes got tired.

Drawing near, two fields away, she could already hear Belle's lowing, raising four wavering beats upward in clear distress. Feeling a pang of guilt, she heeled Whip into a gallop and resolved never to do that again. The pickup or whatever was handy would have to do. Reining to in the pasture, she saw Angel and another hand, swollen to ten now that it was calving time she thought with another wince about how much that would cost, standing around Belle, tethered to a fence post, her eyes rolling and foam dripping from her pink tongue questing around the blackness of her hide.

Sliding off Whip, and already sliding the arm-length rubber gloves up to her shoulders, she walked toward them carrying the chains. She didn't bother checking herself. She knew Angel's worth. Slipping a bit in the purplish exploded water sac at her feet, she slid one arm inside Belle's vulva and pushed the calf's rump further back in so that she could find the legs. She found one thin leg with the dew claws up and with the other hand slid in the chain to slip the catch around the leg. Then, the harder part, given how little room. She searched around for the second leg, her arm extended all the way in up to the elbow. Her nose wrinkling with concentration, she kept hunting, wondering where the hell it was, and then found it. Leaning into Belle's ass, feeling the sudsy soap that they had washed around Belle's vulva dripping down her shirtfront, she heaved the leg up. Belle, kicked a leg out in protest, but Jessie kept

258

tugging until, grudgingly, it moved up toward her. Blowing out a sigh, she attached the other catch to that, too, then stepped back leaving the chains hanging out Belle's backside like some kind of an appendage. Just like a pap smear from hell, she grinned. She shucked the rubber gloves and pulled on the rawhide ones from a back pocket. Angel, not needing a word, was ready for her and signaled Felipe to reach over the flanks to gently stretch the lips of Belle's vulva for the coming pull. She grabbed the handles of the chains, braced one boot up against Belle's haunch, let Angel grab her around the waist and they pulled.

Slowly, Belle's lowing getting louder yet and drowning out anything they might have said to each other they pulled. Another hand, probably Josef, she thought, grabbed Angel around the waist and helped. Slowly, the legs, their small cloven hooves bearing the trickling slime of afterbirth appeared, then, their bright blackness striking in their slimy beauty, the first knocks. On they pulled, seeing the haunches come next, with more yellowish slime and the rump following, making the entire mess one generally fucked up affair, she grunted to herself. Then, after the hips popped through, finally, it became a pretty straight-forward process, except that, with that sucking pop, she collided backward with Angel and felt his erection pressing into her own rump. Well, she chuckled, he was going to be saying a few Hail Marys about that one, she was sure. On and on, Angel keeping a very safe distance from her now, she noticed, they pulled out the rest, letting the calf curl gently to the ground, the head and its quickly, almost too quickly, emerging front hooves. Somewhere Belle had stopped bellowing. Josef untied her tether and led her around, as the others stepped out of the way, to see her newborn. Jessie bent and, clearing away the rest of the amnion sac from its head, tickled one of the nostrils with a straw. It sneezed and began breathing. Belle chewed her cud a time or two, then bent her own head, her long tongue extending to clean her calf.

"Jefe. What name?"

Jessie, panting from her exertions, took a moment to register that Angel was talking to her. Then, stunned at what it meant, she looked back down at the calf, pretending to consider until her cheeks stopped their burning. After a moment or two, when she felt she had control of herself again, she looked up at him and grinned, "How about Trouble?"

"Si, Jefe. Trouble it is." Belle already having cleaned the head, Angel bent and, with a punch and a tag, marked the calf's ear, Josef reading off the number and scrawling it in their notepad.

Riding Whip back, she indulged herself in a long gallop, reflecting on the ranch. There was nothing wrong with the way it ran from the bottom. Not with Angel. Jake had been right, she thought with a pang before tucking that deep inside. Feeling the wind in her hair, she sighed in appreciation, thinking of Angel's quiet, polite efficiency. A good forehand, never the leader. Simply not interested in the stress that went with the job. No, the problem with Van der Vaal Ranch and Cattle, she thought, pounding up a rise, and slowing until she could see what lay the other side, was from the top. She wasn't sure yet, not until she had crunched more numbers, but she suspected she was already seeing what she had thought she would find. Pop wasn't doing anything wrong. It was just that he wasn't doing enough right. The falling grades over the last years was simply killing them. Unless. Unless she was reading the numbers wrong. In any case, forget about making a fortune, like Halverson did with his disgusting feeding operation. Given the way they were probably going, they would simply run out of options in a year or two, have to sell off some leases, not to mention some stock, to cover their operating expenses, leaving even less money to be made the following years. And then everybody would know, as sure as shit, as if they had painted a big sign on the side of the house, that the decline had begun. They would lose their best hands to better operating ranches, forcing them to hire and train new ones, they'd get the lowest quality feed available for the same price without anyone being able to prove anything, forcing them to buy new supplements to make up the difference, more visits from the vet, and who knows what else she hadn't thought of, all adding to their bottom line and hastening the downward spiral.

She sighed, wondering what she was going to do and thought longingly of her organic trial idea. She snorted and heeled Whip onward through her thoughts. Big city lifestyles aside, the more she read up on organic cattle raising, the more she was coming to admire what they were trying to accomplish. Clean pastures, cattle in their natural environment, not being stressed, trying to leave as little a footprint as possible, naturally plowing the effects of the raising right back into the ranch. These were all things that she, consciously or not she had realized, had come to believe were part and parcel of effective cattle raising. Besides, the premiums for organic cattle were awfully nice, she grinned. The way she had calculated it, anyway, quite a bit of the increased costs of organic feed would have been offset by the decreased costs of conventional raising since so many of the regular supplements, to begin with, weren't allowed. Give it a few years and then the organic rating would have or might have, anyway, made good on the original investment. Then... she abruptly reined in. As Whip stood there, her withers quivering with excitement, Jessie gave herself a what-for about pissing in the wind. Might have, would have. It didn't make no difference. It still would need money up front and there wasn't any. Hell, she thought, they probably weren't going to make enough this year during the stock sales in August to break even. Bitching about it wasn't going to help anything. And thinking of pie-in-the-sky ideas that she had cooked up in Seattle was only making it worse. She suspected they were in a fix and given Pop's situation, she was going to have to figure their way out of it without being able to talk to anybody.

Not even Nora, and with this thought, as her high school friend's face swam before her, with its dark, cheerful eyes, so thoughtful, staring out of her round face, and getting rounder with every passing year, Jessie grinned through her tears then realized she was crying. She checked around quickly, then decided to let them go just this once. No, not even Nora. She frowned at the thought that her old friend had left another message on the answering machine at home yesterday. They had been able to share everything when they were younger, but not this. Not this. No one. She suddenly felt so alone and tried to focus on a hawk's lazy swirling in the bright blue sky above her, trying to keep the panic from overtaking her. She prayed for Jake to tell her what to do, knowing with a deep pang of despair that she would never hear his voice again. Whip nickered, sensing her distress. Getting some sort of control over herself, she smiled down and patted Whip on the neck. "Yeah, I know. You can't help me much with the ranch, but you are here." She bent and gave Whip a kiss alongside the neck, feeling all her love for her horse wash through her. And then Andrew's face swam through her tears, lessening now. She wiped her cheeks and rode away not liking that thought very much.

***

A few days later, as she was patiently typing away at her new cash flow spreadsheet and trying not to think what unknown bills were hiding in today's mail, she heard Pop say, "That's Andrew."

Surprised, she jumped to her feet and stepped into the living room. Pop was, as usual in the late afternoons before Maria finished dinner, sitting in his chair with his feet up, his Bible in one hand, a remote in the other. Following his marveling gaze, she saw only a commercial. "Where?"

"Just a minute. He's on the news."

Reflecting on his child-like tone of awe, coming so much more often these days, she wondered with a brief moment of panic whether his mind was going. Not that, please, God, she prayed. She couldn't deal with that.

"See?"

He was pointing at the screen again which only showed the anchor looking all dry and professional. "Welcome back. All across the country at major universities, a sit-in is occurring, interrupting classes as our nation's students take to the streets. We go now to Angela Wickers, reporting live from Seattle."

The screen cut to an attractive, in the usual boring way Jessie thought, woman looking all serious as she peered into the camera, her hand held to her earpiece, loud chants of "No War! No War! No War!" almost drowning out her own loud efforts. "Thanks, Frank. We're here in Red Square at the University of Washington in Seattle, historic site of Vietnam War protests and now scene of the largest peace rally they've held to date. The police, as a matter of department policy after 9/11, are no longer issuing crowd estimates, but the rally organizers tell me that it could easily top fifty thousand."

The camera cut away from her to capture images of hundreds of students in the crowd, lingering on different faces, everything from tie-dyed hairstyles to buzz cuts with goatees to tight bobs, many raising their fists as they chanted, switching now to "Hell No We Won't Go! Hell No We Won't Go!" Jessie gasped at the recognition of a girl from class as the reporter's voice cut in while the camera moved here and there. "You see here quite the cross-section of America, all united in protest against this administration's decision to go to war. Throughout the day, there have been speeches from professional peace activists, professors, even a few from regular students."

"He was just there." Pop mentioned, a bit disappointed.

Abruptly, the camera lingered on Ella's beautifully tear-stained face, a small yellow-ribboned pin glinting in the sun, just caught by the camera. The reporter went on, "We can only imagine who they are thinking of--"

His voice quietly cut through the noise. "My best friend died today." And the crowd's chanting began to ebb.

The reporter said something, and the camera fixed on Andrew's pale features, strained, as he stood atop some sort of platform just over the heads of the crowd and the handful of boomed mikes extended toward him. "We're seeing now...," the reporter continued, "what appears to be one of those students, we'll learn his name in a minute."

He said it again, "My best friend died today." As if hearing him fully for the first time, the crowd began to quiet, with only a few diehard chanters on the edges keeping up their cries.

Seeing his gray eyes staring out under that unruly black hair, Jessie felt her heart catch. She felt truly sorry for what had happened the night she had told him. Even after the way she had screamed at him, he had still the guts to show up at the airstrip, bringing Ella along with him. With her there, Jessie hadn't felt able to bring up, let alone apologize, for what she had done, and she had squirmed with the shame of it many times since. She knew he hadn't meant to blank out on her. It was just his way. He had probably been in just as much shock as she had been when the XO had told her...the news in that quiet hallway. She guessed much later that he had understood that she needed to yell for a while at her rage that her Jake had been taken from her without so much as a by your leave. And he had let her. She had been grateful for that. She had wanted to tell him but hadn't known how. As it was, instead, she had left them both standing there next to the airplane in the rain as she followed the marching guards carrying Jake's coffin away.

He said it a third time. "My best friend died today." And, at this, the crowd hushed. "He was a good man. I think...you would have liked him. I know I certainly loved him. He was a good man. He was a soldier..." A few people booed and hissed. Andrew, not in the slightest bothered, looked like he had even expected it, she thought, as he quietly raised his hands in a gentle subduing motion and smiled sadly, she saw with a wrench of her heart.

"I know. I know. We don't like all that many of our soldiers this day. But I think you would have liked him." The hecklers went silent at this, if only because some loud "shhhs" could be heard, including one loud voice one of the boom mikes just picked up, saying, "Let the man talk!" Looking down, as if just realizing what he was wearing, he gave a tug on his raincoat, holding up the edge for all to see. "He even bought me this raincoat, when I didn't have the sense to get in out of the rain." A few chuckles broke out around him, near the podium. "He was like that. He liked to protect others." The crowd grew silent then, again.

"He wasn't...we've all seen those in uniform walking around all...puffed up with self-importance...loud and obnoxious...anxious to get into a brawl anywhere and anytime. My friend wasn't like that. He...oh...he was a soldier. A good one, too. He studied the art of war thoroughly, not..." Some heckles cut him off, and some loud "shhhs" cut them off as he waited again, with that same sad and patient smile. "Not because he wanted to fight, but because....because..." He broke off, looking down for a moment, and then, suddenly, he brought his face straight back up, his eyes growing larger with...she could have sworn...kindness. "Because he believed that there are people in this world who...he used to say...are willing to take power at the point of a gun and that he didn't like them very much..." A few mutters broke out, then a couple of halfhearted chants of "No War!" Still he went on, looking down. "Because he wanted to protect those who couldn't protect themselves from those who would hurt them..." He looked up and out at the crowd, letting his eyes range over its whole. "I'm a Buddhist, I think...and that makes me a believer in nonviolence..."

"What did he say?" Pop's bewildered tone cut in.

Jessie shushed him to hear what came next. "...that makes me a believer that, no matter how bad the situation...you can always talk out your differences..." The crowd broke out in loud clapping at this. Yet, Andrew continued to be unmoved by that as well. He acknowledged their applause by dipping his head in a short couple of nods, but as he ended them, she saw the same lingering smile. "That violence only begets more violence..." The clapping continued now, even louder. Again, he waited until it slowed, then said, "Even if I also know, were that always true...we would still be fighting the Germans and the Japanese." The Square went dead silent. Jessie found herself wondering how long they were going to keep covering this and wished she were there to hear it all.

"But what if he's right? What if there are people with whom we cannot reason in this world? I'm no expert on politics. I'm no expert on war-making. Or peace-making for that matter. I wouldn't know a weapon of mass destruction if I tripped over it. If anything, I'm a religious studies undergrad." There were a few chuckles breaking out at that, friendly chuckles, Jessie realized. "I can only reach out to what I do know... In the Christian tradition, this question of what to do, how best to deal with those who bring suffering to our world, particularly for their own gain, has been argued over in many different ways throughout the millennia. I only want to focus on one: the just cause...I am prepared to believe that my friend who died today, losing the promise of his young life as...his blood dripped away into the sands that gave birth to so many of our faith traditions...I am prepared to believe that while he was wrong in some things...he was right in one respect...that he was sincere in his...selfless desire to right one of the terrible wrongs of this world and that..." He blinked. He swallowed, but just for a heartbeat, then continued on, almost unaware of the tear that was working its way down his cheek, sparkling in the dying sunlight as the camera zoomed in on his face. "...that his life was worth that."

Jessie closed her eyes not wanting to hear anymore but having to, feeling her own heart slowly crack and weep. Beside her, she could hear Pop's clearing of the throat beginning.

"I only want to know one thing...for this terrible war in Iraq in which we are presently engaged...or in any future struggle we find that we cannot reason with the aggressor and...find we must...though we hate it...fight. I only want to know one thing...Is there a just cause? Is there a just cause that killed my friend today in the sands of al Najaf?" Jessie winced, realizing that she had never shared the official news with him and wondered how he had found out. "Is there a just cause that will kill more tomorrow in Baghdad? Is there a just cause when we lay down the olive branch and beat our plowshares into swords in the future? Can someone tell me? Is there a just cause? My best friend died today. I know in my heart he would say that it was worth it. But if I am to agree to with him, I need to know why."

At that he stopped. The crowd stood mute. He stood with them, watching them, the unchanged smile on his long, lean face, waiting. Then a pair of hands began clapping, a strong sound, yet almost forlorn in the quiet. And then another joined. And another. Soon, the crowd in sections at first, and then wholeheartedly the Square itself began applauding and cheering. Andrew stood there, looking so alone, yet so...strong...she thought sadly, wondering why she had never seen him this way before and knowing somehow that it was too late. He stood there, smiling patiently, nodding gently at their accolades and soon a chant began, "Just Cause! Just Cause! Just Cause!"

The reporter's voice suddenly cut in. "And that was Andrew Worth, a religious studies student, and a Buddhist..." she said, laying a stress on the word, "...here at one of the nation's largest peace rallies at the UW in Seattle. Back to you, Frank."

The anchor's solemn face filled the screen. "A young man with a great deal of promise. As you know, we follow the news everywhere, even as it is made right before our eyes. Before continuing our coverage of the Invasion of Iraq, then, we now go to our special correspondent for political affairs, Chuck Talbot, Clinton administration insider and frequent contributor to the *Washington Post*. How about it, Chuck? Has this administration made its case for a just cause?"

The screen cut to a rather heavy man in a blue suit, looking rushed as he tightened his tie while sitting down. "Well, to that young man's mind, I would have to say 'No.' And this is the question, with so much criticism leveled at the White House about its decision to invade Iraq: Does their case, as we in the industry like to say, 'Play in Peoria?' From rallies like this we are seeing around the nation today, I would again have to say 'No.' But what is more interesting to me is how articulate, given that young man's age, not to mention the horrible tragedy he must be suffering, his question: To every single reservation made about the decision to go to war, this White House has taken the gloves off replying that those critics speaking up do not support our troops, even implying a lack of patriotism. Up to this point, the White House has been quite successful with that tactic, but as soon as that young man...what's his...Andrew Worth, or others like him go on a national speaking tour..." He paused for dramatic effect, chuckling, then continued, "...this administration will be in real trouble."

Jessie got up and turned it off. Pop stared at her in silence, his own cheeks bearing tear stains among his unshaven stubble. Not knowing why, she went over to him, kissed him on the forehead, then turned and left the room.

***

As soon as she stepped out into the yard, she knew why. All across the wide sky, the vivid purples and pinks of coming twilight were painted. But, more than that, when she looked up, remembering that single tear being caught by the dying sunlight, she knew that Andrew was sharing this same light.

Later, skipping dinner to go straight to Whip's back, as she let Whip wander wherever her horse-sense took them, she found herself frowning in thought over what she had seen and heard. Then, staring up into the great milky whiteness sprawled across the sky, its widespread galaxies now reminding her of a herd of Charolais cattle with their curly white heads, she wondered what the differences were in raising them instead of Angus, wondered idly if you had to keep their teats from sunburning so that the calves may continue feeding throughout the summer. With a start, she realized she hadn't looked at the Milky Way as flour for tomorrow's bread in some time. She had to smile at that. She was getting what she had wanted, after all. At least for a time. And then a stray thought, almost putrid in its ugliness, tearing down all happiness with it, pointed out that the only reason she was running the ranch was Pop's heart attack upon hearing of Jake's death. Stung into tears, her chest heaving with guilt, she sat up and looked wildly around, waiting for...Whip nickered reassuringly. What was she waiting for, she asked herself? For someone to step out of the shadows and accuse her? Maybe. Maybe that would make it easier. Then she would have an enemy to fight rather than a bunch of stupid guilt and fears, and she hastily shoved them back into the dark corners of her mind.

She let her mind drift again, then found herself thinking of Andrew and, she had to admit, for all her anger at him for escaping into his head that night that...Jake had come home, Andrew was doing a lot better at making sense of Jake's death than she or Pop was. She reflected on that. She knew his mind was powerful. Almost a little frighteningly so. She knew that the girls who had called him "the monk" were only doing it, at least some of the time, because they were afraid that they sounded stupid around him. From time to time on campus, she had seen him in the buildings, in hallways, had seen his abstracted expression and honestly wondered if he would have responded had she called out hello. She had also seen, time and again, the way that students would stop talking as they saw him coming, and wait, watching, until he had passed them before picking back up their conversations. It was as if he moved in a bubble of silence at all times because, surrounding him, it always moved where he did. Once, irritated at the coos of admiration, she had walked up to a group of girls and asked who he was. One had stared back at her with wide eyes, saying, "He's the Monk. He's supposed to be really, really smart. Like some kind of super brain in physics or something." At that,

Jessie had snickered inwardly but had nodded, pretending interest.

And now this super brain had just made a...beautiful speech about Jake. She could only wonder at that. When she had first come back, Jake's coffin in tow, for the simple and rushed, given Pop's state, graveside ceremony, she could barely say the name. Pop still couldn't. Then one day, maybe a week or two later, poring over his life insurance policies and other records, she realized that she had to move on, so she let herself say the name aloud once or twice a day after that, but never around Pop. That, and nothing more. It made it easier. Allowed her to keep functioning. Even Pastor Don's invitations to come by for a chat had been rigorously ignored. She would keep it that way. But Andrew hadn't. Of them all, he was the one who had decided to keep Jake's memory alive with that speech before the entire country. She honored him for that. And, she grunted, she was personally grateful.

***

Raised voices in the yard. She frowned out the window of what had become her office wondering what all the racket was. As it continued, she stopped typing and listened to the voices. She scowled. Andreeson. She sighed. She had seen this coming for some time. They had taken on two white boys the fall before last to work the ranch alongside Angel's team of Hispanics. Up to this spring's calving, Andreeson and that Landry boy had seemed to be doing just fine, pitching in hard when needed, slacking, she knew for she had spotted them on her daily rides, when Angel wasn't looking. But, for some reason, Pop's heart attack seemed to have changed all that. Well, at least for Andreeson, she thought. Several times throughout the calving, thankfully done now with only two stillborns, she congratulated herself at that thought again, she had seen Angel's exasperation as Andreeson began questioning his orders. One time when, and this had really pissed her off when she realized what had happened, Andreeson had been too lazy to bring along the usual jar of iodine for a calving to disinfect the navel after the placenta had dropped off. Their pastures were usually clean enough that they didn't have to worry about that, but she trusted Angel's judgment. If the calf had needed iodine, then it had better get it. Hearing the row outside growing louder, Andreeson's voice claiming, "It's doing good, I tell you!" and Angel's softer mutter answering, she got up and walked out to the yard to put a stop to it before Pop began to notice.

They were just knocking off for the day, a few of the hands come back to drop off some equipment. Angel and Andreeson were standing next to the truck, a few other hands, Landry among them standing farther apart, watching. Angel, she could see was angry, an unusual sight. She couldn't remember the last time she had seen him angry. That Andreeson was standing there with his fists clenched...well, she thought with a spurt of anger herself, what the hell can a body expect? Then, wondering what she meant by that, she pushed that thought aside to focus on what was brewing.

"What's going on?" Her voice rang out across the yard separating them as cleanly as the screen door banging shut behind her.

Nobody said anything. Andreeson was staring at her with a look of contempt, further stoking her fire. The other hands began shuffling their feet. Angel was looking away across the yard. She walked up to them, trying to catch Angel's eyes. Drawing closer she could see that he was turning away from her, avoiding her look. "Angel?" she asked.

"Jefe. It's nothing."

"Jefe!" Andreeson spat, under his breath.

So that was it, she thought with a savage spike but forcing herself to tamp it down. Her voice, however, she let harden. "I asked you, 'What is going on?'"

Again silence sat in the yard. Finally, Angel turned to look at her, unwillingly. Suddenly, she realized somehow that she had just embarrassed him in front of the men. That she should have quietly taken him aside first to learn what was up. That thought made her angrier than ever. God awmighty, she thought, the precious eggshell egos of men! She returned her gaze to Angel and saw him wincing as he looked at her now. She waited.

"Jefe. I asked Andreeson to move the line on the alfalfa lot on Evans and..." That he didn't finish the sentence was statement enough.

She turned to Andreeson. There in the yard, she saw him for what he was. A boy she once knew in high school, no older than she was. Probably felt lucky as the day was long getting a job on Pop's ranch and now chafing at the bit at having to take orders from a wetback and a girl. She saw a red rage.

"Did you?" Her question sliced out at him.

Looking a bit stunned by the challenge, he muttered something under his breath.

"What?"

His voice came, grating in its overly politeness. "I said, it's fine. It don't need moving just yet."

She thought about that for a moment. Feeling her eyes turn toward Angel, but having embarrassed him once, she quickly decided to turn them instead in the direction of the field, about three miles away. She wondered how well watered that plot was. Given May's heat, already coming on in suffocating waves, another evening's watering could hardly hurt the alfalfa. On the other hand...

She sighed.

"Andreeson. You're fired."

"What?!" Everyone else in the yard became fence posts.

"You heard me. A check with your wages through today will be mailed tomorrow. Go home."

Nobody moved. Biscuit, however, came bounding around the corner chasing a bird. As he started up a howl, she stabbed a finger at him, making him sit with a quiet whine and then nothing more. All the while, she kept her eyes fixed on Andreeson's.

"Bitch!" The curse rang around the yard. Jessie could feel everyone tensing at this and thought, with another sigh, about the fragile egos of men and how she could really not use a brawl in the yard just now.

"No, actually. Biscuit's a boy. Now, thank you for your hard work this calving, but I don't need you anymore. "

Shaking his head in disbelief at her, he looked around then found Landry. "You coming?"

Landry, younger by a year and dumber by a horseshoe toss or two, she thought, looked nervously around at the others, then licked his lips.

"You coming?"

"Yeah."

*****

After several nights agonizing over whether she had done the right thing and fretting where she was going to find two good hands and how much it would impact their efficiency while Angel trained them up, she thought of an article she had seen back in Seattle. One about increased efficiency on the ranch using improved communications. She thought about that for a while. As far back as she could remember, Pop had always had eight hands year round, adding two at calving, and returning to eight afterward. Still, she thought, a lot of time had to be wasted in having Angel riding around to give everyone orders day to day, not to mention checking up on them. That was worth one ranch hand right there. Actually, thinking that it was Angel, she changed that to maybe one and a half. She was a little...frightened, she was furious at herself for feeling, at taking the step. However, after spending another sleepless night puzzling it through, praying to Jake for help but, of course, receiving no answer, she decided to grab the bull by the horns.

Having, though, learned her lesson in the yard, she called Angel on the radio, bridled Whip and rode out to meet him away from the others. They met near a pump house not too far from the Evans spread, whose alfalfa she had noticed to her satisfaction, was doing quite well on its way to its first cutting. She explained that she had thought it over and that rather than hiring two new hands she had a different idea. He looked a bit thunderstruck as she went on. On the other hand, since that day with Andreeson, she had noticed that Angel had grown different, more... She couldn't put a word to it. Or maybe she didn't want to. Suffice it to say, she thought again as she saw that expression in his eyes following her continued explanation, she was grateful for the way that he naturally moved to her side now when she was addressing the hands. Kind of like her right arm.

After gaining his cautious approval, she drove into town and bought up several walkie-talkies and a whole slew of batteries. The next morning, she had handed them out, explaining that instead of hiring two replacement hands, they were going to increase their efficiency by communicating with each other throughout the day. That she had figured it through, though she knew she was lying when she said it, and that with this improvement, she didn't believe they needed any more than six good hands to work the ranch at a good pace without anything slipping. Nobody said anything. They just kept looking down at their radios in confusion and, for a couple, not without a little awe.

Finally, deciding that somebody needed to say something, she threw out, "Look. I trust you. You're good hands. Among the best in the valley. You know that. I don't need, and you don't need, Angel running around all day checking up on you."

Somebody grunted at that. Nervous, she felt a bit of anger spiking inside her at the needling question of what she had to do to get them to trust her, but she quickly pushed it back down. Instead, looking around, she saw that Josef was looking a bit uncomfortable.

"Josef."

"Jefe. I just wanted to say that my cousin, working an outfit over near Spokane, said they started using these last year. They like it."

And that seemed to seal the deal. Saying a silent prayer of thanks for Josef, she turned to Angel at her side and said, "Well. Let's get at it."

He nodded, murmuring a "Jefe" with a smile and then began to hand out the day's tasks.

***

Her pleasure at the cost-savings of two less hands, something she had been careful to keep from Pop, evaporated as quick as the morning dew, she thought days later when a long overdue feed bill arrived in the mail. Trying not to think, let alone allow herself to openly curse Pop, instead she grunted about "one step forward, one step back" in a glum mood, pecking at the keys, as she factored that into her growing cash flow, resolutely ignoring the latest unopened bill from the hospital. Make that two steps back, she thought later, feeling her spirits slip further as she stepped around Maria in the kitchen and realizing that she, stupidly, had clean forgot to add in Maria's pay as well. Learning how little Pop was paying Maria had enraged her, thinking of how hard it was to keep up a ranch's kitchen and house, and probably making her chuck the whole thought of paying Maria out of her mind. Still, she groused that she couldn't very well afford to pay Maria any better and tried to be happy about it. That she was grateful for Maria staying on after the funeral went beyond words. And she decided to keep it at that.

Moving aside now, as Maria got something from the fridge, Jessie stepped back and admired one of her new maps. She had regretted lying openly to the men. Thinking it over later, she decided to make good on that so had drawn up large maps of all the spreads and taped them to the two fridges in the kitchen and the two freezers in the basement, marking the herds, the crops, and the hands with magnets that she could move around to help give her a better overall picture of the ranch's operations. In theory. She had thought, too, about designing a rotation schedule for the hands, but then decided that, lucky as she was for Angel's loyalty, she couldn't trespass on that ground just yet. Better to wait a while. At least let everybody get used to the radios first. Look for possible improvements to efficiency later. Smiling at her work, she wondered if this was the "logistics" that Jake had always gone on about. As she thought of his name, and last night's nightmare, tears sprang to her eyes which she blinked away before Maria could notice. On reflex, she let herself say his name aloud. "Jake."

"Si, Jefe. A good man. He watches you now. Very proud of you." Maria's bright smile touched her like a kiss on the cheek as she gathered up the steaks for evening's dinner and moved on. St. Jake, Jessie thought with a bitter smile. Might as well be her patron saint for all the help she was getting from him.

**

Deciding suddenly that she couldn't go back to her cash flow, that it was too depressing at what she was learning, and she gulped at that dark thought, she opted instead for a bit of a holiday. Somewhere away from...Andreesons and Landrys and feed bills and a bunch of men always wondering whether she was making good decisions and... She might be driving out of range of the walkie-talkie. She never went anywhere without it for long, even pooping with it laid on the floor next to the toilet. But thinking that Angel had things well in hand as the quiet rhythms of the valley's early summer took over, she decided she could chance it for a while.

Driving up the road, she could see Nora's home, with its pretty flowers in the neat front yard, the two or three junked cars of her brothers parked along the side. Nora's round smile, perhaps having recognized Pop's pickup, met her at the door.

"I was giving you precisely one more day, and then I was coming hunting for you."

Not knowing what to say, Jessie nodded and then, abruptly, felt tears tumbling down her cheeks to her bewildered fury.

"Oh, sweetie! Come inside! Come inside!"

Luckily no one was there.

"You're not sleeping. I can see it in your eyes."

On the table stretched out a lovely deer-skin dress, Nora's minute beading adorning the breast. Grateful for a change of subject, Jessie wiped her cheeks, feeling the dirt on it smear and not caring, and walked over to it.

"Which one is it? Have you put it in yet?" She sounded a bit shaky, she thought, but managed to finish well.

Nora looked at her carefully, then nodding, grinned. "See if you can find it."

Jessie looked over the sewn patterns of red, blue, yellow and white beads, and easily caught it. Long ago, when Nora had first begun beading, she had explained that in every Yakama beadwork, no matter how beautiful and complex, there was always one bead deliberately set askew, destroying the purity of the piece because, Nora had pointed out, only Creator could make something perfect. Putting her finger on

the bead, a yellow one in a field of blue Jessie smiled
with a small triumph. So few easily won successes
these days, she thought.

"So, sit down! Sit down. I'm so sorry about Jake,
honey."

And at that, the tears began again. Giving up,
feeling so, so tired, Jessie gave herself over to them
and to Nora's big arms, wondering why she had been
so stupid as to not come before this. Nora said
nothing, just cooing softly in Jessie's ear, stroking her
hair and rocking her gently. Finally, gratefully, her
weak tears went away and she sat back, wiping her
cheeks again as she glanced at her friend.

"What..." her voice, rough from the sobbing,
cracked but then she got control of it and started
again. "What are you doing these days?" She looked
Nora over, seeing that she had gained even more
weight than ever. She knew better than to comment
on it, though. Once, in junior high, when they were
watching the Fourth of July parade, seeing, first, the
old chiefs walk their horses in their stately manner
down the main road, Nora seeing only the beadwork
just as she saw only the horses, she had laughed at the
old fat Yakama women elders being pulled in a buggy
by a fiercely sweating horse. Nora had spun on her
with indignation. Jessie had pointed, laughing again,
"They're all so fat! They're always so fat." Nora had
grown silent then until Jessie had asked what was
wrong. Nora had replied, with an assumed dignity
beyond her years, "You don't understand. Their
roundness? It's a sign of power." Jessie had
exclaimed in skepticism until Nora had silenced her
with the comment, "You are talking about a people,
my people, that knows what it means to starve."

Looking at her friend now, she had to admit that
Nora's roundness did carry a sense of power.
Particularly considering how slight her own form was
in comparison.

"Medicine."

"Really?"

"Yep. Started last month."

"Wow." Well, she thought, as Andrew's face flashed in her mind, that made two of them.

"Don't be so surprised. You're the one who got me started."

Jessie popped out a confused "What?"

Nora paused, fishing out a cigarette and lighting it up. "I figured if my scrawny little white chick girlfriend can run a big ol' cattle ranch, then I can study medicine..." She blew out a plume of blue smoke, finishing with a sly grin, "...no matter how many men in the tribe don't like it."

Now Jessie felt really stupid. "Nora, I'm sorry. I should have come by before."

Nora shook her head at that. "Never mind! Never mind. We walk in two different worlds now, even if it's the same valley. You know that."

Jessie had to nod.

"In any case, it doesn't matter. You're here now." She sat back, exhaling another plume, and looked her friend over very carefully again, her eyes narrowing in concern. Jessie felt the probing of her eyes, looking within her, and thinking suddenly, how...spiritual, if you could call it that...Nora had always been.

Finally, growing tired of the poking, she asked, "So, you're studying medicine."

"Yep."

"Good, cuz I think I could use some."

"I can see that."

Jessie paused at this, wondering what her friend saw, wondering how to continue. "So, should I...I don't know...go to a sweat lodge or something?"

Nora cracked up at that, laughing her head off, much to Jessie's annoyance. Finally, seeing the flickering anger, Nora stubbed out her cigarette and patted Jessie on the arm. "No. No. I don't think a sweat lodge would do you much good, Jessie."

Her indignation growing, wondering if Nora thought she was stupid or something, she asked, "Why not?"

"Calm down. Calm down," Nora said, smiling. "Your white hot temper certainly hasn't changed."

"Well?"

Nora tilted her head at Jessie in thought, then sighed and said, "It's like this, honey. You can go. You can certainly go, when there is a mixed ceremony for women as well as men, but..." She looked around the room like she was trying to find the right words. "But, I really don't think you'll get much out of it." At Jessie's anger, bridling anew, she waved a hand, "All I'm saying is that you'd spend an evening getting sweaty listening to old men singing songs and chanting prayers in a language you don't know, even I don't know half of them yet, and you'd go home none the wiser, wondering why you had put yourself through it."

"Well..." Jessie paused, suddenly feeling helpless. "What should I do?"

"The point is that you were raised a Christian and you should find your answers there."

No help at all, Jessie thought, with a sinking heart.

"What I'm saying is that you've spent your entire life going to church, listening to sermons, singing hymns...Look, Creator is big enough for both that and sweat lodges. So, go back to Christianity and you'll find Creator there because that's what's going to make the most sense to you."

Jessie felt the stirring of understanding, maybe a single ray of hope.

"If you had more time, and I know that you don't, I'd even say that whatever your beef is with Christianity, change it. Get involved enough to change it. But never mind that. You've got enough on your plate as it is."

Great. Just what she needed, she thought. More work. Still, Jessie had to smile at Nora's suggestion,

thinking that was exactly what Andrew would say.
Then she paused in thought. Would he? And, for
that matter, what the hell was he doing in her
thoughts again all of a sudden? She hadn't thought of
him for...well...days. Nevertheless, she also suddenly
better understood Andrew's Buddhism. Maybe Pop
freaked out at the thought, but that was what Andrew
grew up with. Of course he would reach out to that in
trying to deal with...

"That's it?"

"That's it."

"Well..." Still feeling disappointed, Jessie made
one last try. "Couldn't you at least smudge me or
something?"

Nora smiled. A slow patient smile. "You want me
to smudge you? With burning sage."

"Yeah. We used to do it in junior high, remember?
And some of the twits at school do it because they say
they are trying to...never mind. Can't you smudge
me? I could use something like that. Something in
my corner," she said, hearing her bitterness, "for
once."

Nora tilted her head again, considering. After a
moment, she said, "All right."

They moved Jessie's chair away from the table into
the center of the room. Jessie sat in it and closed her
eyes. She could hear Nora flicking a lighter, then a
soft sound of hissing crackling, and then listened,
trying to clear her mind of everything, particularly
and disturbingly, Andrew's sad, patient smile that
kept floating up, as Nora walked around her
murmuring something softly, around and around and
around, filling the air with thick clouds of sage smoke
that burned Jessie's nose.

Eventually, Nora stopped. Jessie heard her sit
down at the table and light up. She opened her eyes
and looked over, feeling somewhat more peaceful.

Nora inhaled deeply then exhaled just as deeply
and glanced at her. "A few years ago, I never told

you about them, I began to have visions. We don't have to go into that now. If you really want to know, I'll tell you about them someday. This afternoon, let's just say that I had one about you."

Feeling weird, Jessie could only nod.

"You need a lifegiver, Jessie. Right now you are surrounded by those who are taking your life. I could see them, their spirits hanging all around you. You need a lifegiver to balance that."

Shaking her head at the odd turn of this conversation, she said, "Okay."

Nora gazed at her, squinting through her own smoke. "Do you know any?"

***

Yes, she thought sadly, driving Pop's pickup home. She had caught one, but she had thought he was too small and had thrown him back. She winced at the memory of how she had avoided him after Christmas. All at once, she ached for him then, for the feel of his hips meeting hers, for the heaving gasps of his chest pressing into hers. It made her furious with herself. She felt ridiculous. No matter what she might, or might not, think of him, she swore, he was gone and after that speech, he was probably never coming back. After all, hadn't that politics guy said something about a national speaking tour? Overwhelmed with tiredness all over again, she pulled over. She stared out the windshield at the fields running along either side of the road as far as the eye could see until it ran straight into the valley walls in the distance. He was out there, she thought. Outside the walls running free and, she was startled to think, she was trapped inside. Alone. Which made her think of Ella standing near him in Red Square instead of...what? She didn't know...crying over Jake's grave or something. She found herself thinking of Ella's big-breasted, blonde-headed pouty tears and hating them. She didn't know what the relationship was between the two of them, and she didn't want to speculate on it. The memory now of that bitch cooing her admiration for Andrew when Ella had tracked her down after Thanksgiving break made Jessie pound the steering wheel a few times. Feeling better then, she decided to luxuriate in hating Ella with every ounce of tired bitterness she could muster.

***

She slammed the phone down. Then, not knowing what else to do, she began pacing back and forth in her office. Numbers didn't lie, she thought, going back and forth, back and forth. Unless...her formulas were wrong! With that thought, she almost dove at her computer, but forced herself to stop, take a breath, and go into the kitchen to pour herself a fresh cup of Maria's coffee. Maria's usually bright smile looked a bit worried at her as she asked, "Jefe?"

Another lie, she sighed inwardly. "Oh, it's nothing, Maria," she said, forcing a grin. "Just some stupid telemarketer." So many lies these days.

Back at the computer, as she stared at the spreadsheet, she recounted her conversation with the bank. No more loans. That was what it amounted to. After all the nice talk, in that strange tone she couldn't identify, about tightening interest rates after the long years of easy credit because the government was spending money right and left over the war. Not until her stock's grading bettered. With Pop's existing loans, well... She had almost passed out when she realized last week how much in debt Pop had gone with the original Angus purchases twenty years ago. And here they were still paying it down, along with the usual run of yearly operating debt until they sold the year's finished stock in August. They were making their bank payments, just. She frightened herself for a moment with the thought of what happens when you could no longer make them, then shoved it away. No more loans. She had to sink or swim with this year's showlist prices. Well, she thought, she'd better swim and turned her attention back to her spreadsheet, pushing aside also that quietly forlorn whisper that her work was careful. That her numbers were right. Nevertheless, she doggedly went through them all, using the auditing tool she had taught herself about, checking every single last, damn one of her formulas. Nope. They were right.

Looking down, she decided that it didn't really matter a damn anymore and opened yet another bill from the hospital. Whistling at it, she threw it down in disgust, wondering where the money was going to come from. All those damn tests that Pop needed. Or so they said Pop needed, she thought with a cynical gloom deepening despite the bright sunshine outside. Swear to God, all she could see was a man who had grown oddly child-like, years before his time. But, no, whether their insurance would cover it or not, Pop's doctors insisted it was necessary "to be sure." She wondered when it would end. Wondered if she had the guts to tell the doctors to shove it up their ass. Wondered whether she would ever get a handle on the anxiety she could feel gnawing at her guts again.

Frowning at her cash flow that, despite its news, she was proud of, she prayed for a miracle and, reflecting that the Lord helped those who helped themselves, began a new spreadsheet, a test case, that would record the startup costs of a trial organic herd. Small, no more than twenty or thirty head. Put out on that unused spread on Lateral F. She had a time of digging out her old notes and the brochures she had gotten from the Washington state Organic Food Program and the federal's National Organic Program standards. Still, once she got going, she started to make good headway and even though one part of her mind told her that it would never happen, it lightened her mood.

For a while. Then, actually not too long before she had gotten into it, she realized that she had been hopelessly optimistic in her projections because she had assumed early certification of the herd. A sudden, anxious worry that they wouldn't be pinned her. As did the following thought of all the records the state required. Seen from Seattle, the daunting paperwork mandatory for annual certification had seemed easily accomplished. Now, what with the day to day worries of the ranch on her hands, even with Angel's steady help, she knew that she didn't have the energy to attempt a tenth of the forms.

She gave it up. Hell, she thought, with her projections staring at her in the face, not to mention Pop's mounting medical bills, she realized that she would be lucky not to have to sell some of this year's calves after weaning to make ends meet, which meant, of course, less money from next year's cattle sales. Let alone, sell off the lease for Lateral F. And then everybody would know, everybody watching her, that the decline had come. For a moment, in desperation at that thought, she let herself pray to St. Jake. Nothing. She swore. Felt herself growing harder. She decided to put off that decision. She would hold onto Lateral F as long as she could. Miracles did happen. In stories at least. Once she sold that lease, her organic herd was a puff of smoke gone with the next breeze. None of the other pastures would have a snowball's chance in hell of passing certification.

She walked out to the stable wanting to nuzzle Whip. They were making do, she reminded herself. Just. Unless Pop's bills kept on for very much longer. Reaching up to Whip's welcoming nicker, she further vowed that she wouldn't let anything of the ranch get to Pop. Let him rest. Let him get better, she thought.

They were making do. Just. Unless their stock didn't do well this year with the buyers. And, about that, well...there wasn't really much she could do. Pop had made those decisions long ago. Her stock's grades would come in, probably, just as disappointing as the last few years' had. Deciding to take an afternoon amble in the pasture on Whip's back, she mused on that. That had been the original question, after all, that Jake had asked her. What about the marbling? People complained about having to slice extra fat off their steaks, feeling gypped, but buyers knew, and she knew, that marbling fat was what gave a steak its flavor. That's what Prime and Choice grades of beef were, wonderfully marbled beef. And Van der Vaal cattle had not scored that in years. Jake had believed in her, even as he had pointed out that he hadn't known how she could raise cattle with better marbling when Pop hadn't been able to.

Why was that, she wondered? She had heard of long-term breed failures before. Some trace genetic flaw that showed up generations after the first high quality breeding purchase had been made. Frowning, she also knew that there was nothing she could do about that and decided to focus instead on the two other possible explanations that she could think of: slipping management of their own cattle that, despite the consistent poundage gain over the years was showing up in poor later grades or, and what she suspected was the true answer, Halverson's slipping quality. No matter how well they treated their calves, soon after weaning, too soon she had always thought, they were shipped off to his feed lot to be finished for the buyers. She knew that he stressed his cattle. She suspected that acidosis, as the stock ate their grain too quickly, was more rampant than he let on, given the few staff he spread out to watch over his large pens. After that, aside from standing in shit at the trough, she had seen heifers get bullied by rambunctious steers in the pens while Halverson's men stood idly nearby, hands in pockets, watching without doing a damn thing. Then, there was her personal piss-off. The way that his hands raced their bulldozers around the large lots, scooping manure out of the way, backing right into usually placid steers and heifers, panicking them, setting off their lowings of distress and, she suspected, frightening any head within hearing distance. Halverson's hands thought it was fun. She thought she knew better, even if most ranchers didn't give a damn. But knowing that no one was going to listen to a girl, new to managing her ranch, she sighed, deciding to make sure that her end was solid first, before she spoke up. After all, Halverson had cornered the market on Angus feeding and his death loss had never gone above 1%. Finding another Angus feed lot meant hauling her cattle several hours more which meant higher transport costs, not to mention the transit shrink knocking down their weight, giving her fewer pounds to sell, getting them to market later. No, she decided, better to focus on her end before she talked to Halverson.

What that might look like, she wasn't sure, though she thought that Whip's lazy rocking was doing a good job of helping her take a nap. Sleep, she thought hazily. How long had it been since she had gotten a good night's rest, she wondered. And then sat bolt upright at the thought that they were not in a strong position. Any storm, big enough and long enough, could knock them down for good.

***

It was in the morning, the sun up high and already warming the day nicely and burning away the memory of her nightmare. *He grinned as a second one hit, coming closer.*

"It's Andrew!"

Beside herself with surprise and joy, she tried to frown down the little concern also springing up at

288

what this might mean. She walked into the living room and found Pop, in his chair as usual and, on the screen, Andrew standing behind a podium, wearing Jake's raincoat, surrounded by other people, shaking hands. At the bottom of the screen, she could see the words "Peace Rally - UC Berkeley" and just above them, with a sinking heart, she recognized Ella standing next to him looking out over the crowd with pleasure. As Andrew stepped forward, his hands raised in that subduing movement that he had used last time, Pop turned it up. Seeing that old raincoat under those same sad eyes, Jessie was a bit amused to find herself thinking of a prophet in one of the cheap paintings on the walls in the church basement.

The chanting grew louder, typical rally favorites she was starting to grasp but with the additions of something that sounded like "No Bush! No Bush!" and another one that she couldn't make out at first and realized later was "This Is What Democracy Looks Like!"

Through the chanting, refusing to die out as students enjoyed their day out of the classroom and the chance to make a difference, Andrew stood as before, alternately waving his hands to quiet the crowd or resting them on the podium, his patient smile in place. Finally, the crowd died enough for him to bend his face toward the microphone.

"My best friend died today." The crowd went wild. As if he had hit a home run, for crying out loud, she thought. They began screaming, dancing, and jumping up and down. All at Jake's death. The thought made her sick. When the camera cut back to Andrew, he still stood there, looking much the same as always, his hair in a mess, Jake's raincoat hood bunched on the shoulders, Ella's openly sobbing beauty pageant tears, she thought with a jet of fury, at his side. As the crowd continued its wild acclamation, Andrew remained just the same, only nodding from time to time. He looked so...unmoved...she thought. She also realized that she didn't want to watch anymore.

She got up to go when Pop muted the sound, asking with a look of plain disappointment written on his face, "Where you going? It's Andrew."

Deciding to distract him, she replied, "I'm going to get you some biscuits and gravy from the Brickton Bellagio."

Delight pulsed out of his eyes. "Good! Hurry back!" So child-like, she thought with an inner sob of her own, then pushed the thought aside and left.

***

Through the big picture windows, driving up, she could see that they were doing a good business this morning and thought that the spring planting must have gone well. Stepping inside, the bell ringing over the door, the long line of tables cutting the cafe in half, full to bursting with farmers and ranchers, some tilting their chairs back, toothpicks being chewed under John Deere and feed store caps, some tilted back just as far, others pulled down low, exploded in laughter at someone's joke and then, as they began to notice her, gradually, they went silent.

Stepping across the tiled floor, hearing her boots snap with each step, she ignored their stares and went to the counter.

"Hey, Jessie!" Clarise's fat smile grinned at her, a bit uncertainly.

"Hey, Clarise. You got any biscuits and gravy for Pop?"

Clarise's smile lost its tentativeness and deepened. "Sure. Fresh batch just this morning."

Jessie pulled her wallet from a back pocket, but Clarise put out a hand stopping her. "This one's on the house. How's Pop hanging in there?"

"Still hanging. Thank you. And thanks for the free meal ticket."

Clarise grinned. "No problem. It'll just be a minute." And she waddled back into the kitchen where Jessie could hear her bustling about lifting lids and other whatnot.

The silence in the cafe continued however. Until she could hear someone crossing the floor toward her. She ignored him as long as she could.

"Jessie."

Turning, she saw that his hair had gone all white since Doty had died last fall. Still, he looked as beefy as ever. The picture of the prosperous rancher, envy of many in the valley. His hooded eyes, wrinkled, yes, but still full of many years of labor ahead, peered at her.

"Mr. Halverson."

"Oh," he said, suddenly pulling his riding hat off his head. Jessie wondered how long it had been since he had gotten on a horse. "Call me Dick."

Thinking of his large cattle pens and his bulldozers, she thought, okay, she would. Outwardly, however, she just nodded, careful to keep a polite smile on her face. Over his shoulder she could see the Rogue's Gallery, a photo collection of the top farmers and ranchers in the valley running almost the entire length of the opposite wall. She hadn't looked at it for some time, but for some reason, thinking about it now, she knew she wouldn't find one woman's picture in there.

He cleared his throat. "I was sorry to hear about Jake. Good man. Did us all proud."

She felt tears starting in her eyes, but she blinked them away before they could form, only allowing herself to murmur a "Thank you."

"And, Nijs, too." He paused, rotating his hat in his hands, then suddenly popping out with a "Damn, Jessie. It's just not right. Nijs was a good rancher. One of the best I've ever known."

Stung at this, she smiled, feeling her features harden. "Still is." She turned back to the counter.

"Uh-huh." He didn't move away. Beyond them, she could hear a few subdued whispers and mutters.

"Angel tells me you're running a real tight outfit there."

Spurred suddenly into anger, she turned back to him. "Talking around town is he?"

Halverson took a step back at what he saw in her face, his own registering shock and surprise. "No! No." He stepped back toward her then, his hat still rotating. "Now, look here, Jessie. I've been trying to steal Angel from your outfit for years. Didn't Nijs tell you that?"

She shook her head, hardly surprised at this revelation and making up her mind right there to see whether she couldn't squeeze out a small raise for Angel somehow, even with Pop's medical bills. Then, she felt the long table of feed caps stir and realized that she was pulling absentmindedly at her ponytail. Slowly she put her hand down, inwardly savaging herself for such stupidity. It was the worst possible thing she could have done. Never, never again, she told herself would she do that. Trying to get past the moment, she looked down, watching Halverson stop rotating his hat and begin twisting it. He cleared his throat again. And then she saw it. There was only one reason in the world that Halverson was standing in front of her just now and the very thought made her sick. Only now did she finally recognize that bank manager's tone as the one reserved for "the little ladies." The bastard must have talked, or somebody must have. They knew. Everyone knew. He knew. Thankfully, Clarise appeared from the kitchen just then with a styrofoam container. Jessie turned her attention to that.

"Thanks, Clarise. He's going to love it. You know he always says yours is the best in the valley."

"He's a smart man, Pop."

Jessie grinned at that and turning back to the rancher said, nodding, "Mr. Halverson. I'll give your best to Pop."

He nodded.

As she walked back to the door, again hearing the snap of her heels on the tile, she could feel his eyes and everyone else's following each step.

***

A few nights later, atop Whip's back and losing herself in the stars, she heard a car slow out front and then the shout, "Fucking cunt!" She sat up and slid down, hearing the car peel away down the road. Clambering over the fence, she ran down the drive out to the front of the house and saw a pile of something burning on the lawn. She ran forward to stomp it out, before Pop could peer through the window, stopping only just in time as she remembered that prank. Looking around, she spotted a fallen branch and, picking it up, beat out the fire. As the sour smell rose to her nose, she wrinkled it, thinking, so that was what roasted shit smelled like. She chuckled, trying not to feel the anxiety rising in her again. Deciding she would bag it up in the morning, she walked back down the drive toward Whip's answering nicker. Climbing back over the fence, feeling the anxiety wring her stomach into knots, she reflected that she was getting a little tired of this, but didn't know what to do with it. It was always there now. Getting to the point that she couldn't remember a time when it wasn't. Just stronger sometimes and, thankfully, weaker at others. But never going away.

She wondered how much poetry he would find in a bag of burning shit. Probably some, she chuckled with bitterness. "I could use a little of your detachment right now." She looked around to see

who had spoken before realizing with a shock that it
had been herself.

***

*The third bullet struck, the closest yet. Okay. He's
getting the range. It's a factor. Don't lose it. Just
get her out of here. He slid off her, feeling now the
numbness in his hips. Mother-fuck! A fourth one
landed, close enough he thought he saw it just before
it hit...*

Jessie woke with a gasp, screaming down her
shriek before it could pass her lips, careful of Pop.
The house was quiet. Sighing, she sat up in bed and
looked around the room. "They're coming for me,"
she said aloud, knowing it was true. However, she
received no answer but the closing click of Cocoa's
wide yawn. Then, starting a loud purr, she stood up,
stretched her long, matted brown legs in front of her
and padded her way up to Jessie's lap. Settling in it
after turning around once, then twice, she lay her
head on her forepaws, closed her eyes and
immediately fell back into a deep sleep, the purr
slowly subduing into long, trickling moan and then
silence. Feeling the weight on her lap, she suddenly
remembered that day in the snow with Andrew. With
gladness. It had been so unexpected, almost sweet.
Their rolling over and over through the snow,
grabbing drifts to pound into each other's mouths
gasping for breath, each other's hair. And, then,
laying atop him, feeling how trustworthy a man he
truly was, she had felt it. Had felt him. Growing.
Feeling her own, answering heat, responding no
matter how she may feel about it, she had looked up
into his embarrassed eyes, watching the blush of his
cheeks build in rhythm with the pulsing of his cock.

She had known right there that she could pluck him
like an over-ripe peach from one of Uncle Willem's
orchards. Men, she had thought, they're so

predictable. And so, that night, Brickton's hateful words still ringing in her ears, she had. She didn't like to think of that night. Didn't like thinking of it now, but did long enough to admit, again, that she knew she had used him, and felt sorry for it, especially when she had caught that look of desperate longing on his face before it had been chased away by Jake's quiet knock on the door. She reverted, instead, to the happiness of that afternoon in the snow. Thank God, she had thought afterward, that she had still had that morning after pill, gotten along with some condoms and "love oils" from her one and only girls party in the dorm. That, she shook her head with relief again, was something she didn't need now. Then, too, she had savored the swallowing of it after leaving Andrew, knowing what the effect would be in the morning, laughing with a bitter delight at what Brickton's face would have looked like if he had known. But, then, she realized she was thinking of that night again instead of what she wanted to. She redirected her thoughts back to rolling in the snow with Andrew, the heat of his growing hardness pressing into her, and sighed, lingering on the...innocence of the moment.

***

The next day, she learned Halverson's first move while she was busily trying to figure out how to give Angel a raise. The large bill, for a nutritionist's services the past year, the accompanying note explained in his bold handwriting, had been uncovered shortly before Jake's funeral. Out of respect for her family, he had held on to it. However, now that he could see that she had things well in hand, he felt free to send it knowing that she would pay it in good order. She gulped again at the cost and, for a moment, sat before her spreadsheet with her hand over her eyes. Finally, knowing that bitching was no recourse since the bill looked legitimate, she wrote out the check and entered it into her cash flow, forcing herself not to think of Lateral F and not to look at the final totals.

His second move came a week later. Looking at the unopened letter, she moaned, then stifled it in case Maria could hear. The notice from his feed lot informed her that she had missed the deadline for pre-purchasing feed stocks for the coming winter. Therefore, she would have to pay his regular feed prices. Christ awmighty, she thought, wondering what the price spread was and, further, with a sinking heart, how to factor that in. After a moment or two, she felt her hardness returning and, deciding that it couldn't be more than 5 or 7%, came up with the revised number and entered it in. That it wouldn't hit her until December was a shallow victory but, she sighed, at this point she was living month to month.

***

Arriving home after a roadside meeting with Angel one afternoon, to the smell of something savory that Maria was whipping up, she felt the hollowness of her stomach and wondered when the last time was she had eaten. Finding Pop in his chair, just turning a page of his Bible, she felt a bit relieved, and tried telling herself that he was starting to look something almost like normal. As she kissed him on the forehead, he said, "Andrew was on again."

Hardly caring, she asked, "What'd he say?"

"Same speech. Same raincoat. I like it." Nope. This child-like tone, bewildering in its wonder, was most definitely not like Pop. Her heart, so briefly lifted, sank again.

Trying to change the subject in her mind, she asked, "Where this time?"

"Dunno. Think Chicago. Another big university. Another big rally."

"Well..." she said, abruptly feeling a bit lighthearted, thinking now she could hate them both. "Guess he's making a career of it."

Pop was frowning at her. She wondered whether he didn't like this last tart remark when he asked in a lower voice, "Do you think he's really a Buddhist?"

How simple his world had become, she sighed, wondering what to say, anything to say, to placate Pop. The last thing she needed right now, she thought for the thousandth time, was another heart attack, even a small tremor. She couldn't afford one. "Well...he's a very thoughtful man. But..." She suddenly smiled, realizing how easy it would be. "Remember our first dinner together, when Jake brought him home?" She paused in fright for a moment, wondering whether the sound of Jake's name would upset him. He had only looked down, though, his face creased in thought like he was trying to remember. "He told us his testimony. When he was ten or so. He accepted Jesus into his heart."

Pop's face brightened. "That's right!" His gnarled fist pumped up in exultation.

"And Jesus will always be there."

"Amen."

She realized that she wasn't hungry after all and went out to the stable to get Whip for a long, ambling night wander in the pasture, thinking how much she hated both Andrew and Ella and all the troubles they were causing for her. After a while, though, her hatred, so refreshing at first, grew tiresome. Instead, laying back, feeling Whip's quiet plod through the deepening twilight, she turned her face up and tried to find the first star of the evening.

***

The next morning, she felt better. More hopeful. There had been the usual nightmare during the night, of course, but those, too, she was somehow growing accustomed to, almost like a daily chore. Sitting up in bed, Cocoa eagerly making her way over to her midnight lap, it becoming an almost nightly occurrence, Jessie had startled herself by saying aloud, "What I need is capital." Only the house's emptiness had responded. But, feeling better that she had put a name to the problem, even an unsolvable one, she had soon found her eyelids growing heavy and had slipped into a blessedly dreamless sleep shortly after.

"Jefe."

She absentmindedly reached out for the walkie-talkie, still trying to hold on to that good feeling from last night and knowing it was already slipping through her fingers. "Angel?"

"Si. The work truck won't start. I think it's the starter."

Good God! Another fucking goddamn bill! Taking a slow breath so that it wouldn't show in her voice, she replied, trying to inject a nonchalant tone, "Do you know any good mechanics?"

"Si, Jefe. My cousin. Works in Union Gap. He's good and he's cheap."

"Good. Go ahead and give him a call and...thanks, Angel. Good work."

"Gracias, Jefe."

***

She tore out of the house, bridling Whip in a flash and thundering down the back road. Whip, excited at this unexpected burst of a ride, lay her ears back in joy and pounded along under her. Feeling the powerful strides, she heeled Whip even faster, trying to escape the deepening blackness that was pursuing her. Seeing a field that they hadn't galloped in for over a year, she turned Whip into it and, suicidally she knew, she took Whip at a headlong gait, daring any holes in the ground to show up and caring even less. Finally, at Whip's first stumble, her better sense prevailed, thinking Jake would be angry, and she stopped. Looking around, seeing no one as far as the horizons, she slid down to her knees and cried. Whip stood patiently by, leaning down to feast on the alfalfa, already springing up high enough that the second cutting would be coming in the next week or so. She had never felt so alone, so hopeless, for so long. Eventually, tiring even of crying, she stopped, wiped her cheeks with the back of a hand and found herself wondering what a lifegiver looked like and how you found one.

***

The following Sunday, much to Pop's surprise Jessie had told him to get ready for church. Not Sunday School, thank you very much, she had thought with a wry grin. Just the service. Pastor Don, whose bulging belly seemed to have grown since the last she had seen him had beamed with delight, grabbed her in a big hug, whomped Pop, gently, on the back and welcomed them in without a word at their absence. The service had been a typical one. She hadn't been really paying attention anyway, finding her eyes drifting continually down to where Andrew had sat before.

Afterward, Pastor Don had grabbed ol' John Larsen, saying, "John? Take Nijs home would you? Jessie, come with me." And, without thinking too much about it, she had followed him, almost grateful that he had taken charge. He led her upstairs into his tiny study, its bookcases jammed full of books, turned every which way. With a jolt, she found herself thinking of Andrew's apartment. Pastor Don groaned, easing himself into the heavy chair beside his desk and pulling around one for her to sit in.

"Doc's talking about a hip replacement." He said, rubbing one ponderously large side of ham. "Course, he says if'n I cut off 'bout two thirds my belly, I wouldn't need it." Rubbing his face with both hands for a moment, he then asked, "Is Andrew...?"

God knew what he saw in her face for he quickly looked away out the window. After a moment, he sighed, saying, "I may be the shepherd, but I do appreciate a thoughtful conversation every now and again. Still..." He looked back at her. "That's about me and not about you. For starters, Jake."

Well, at least she wasn't crying already, she thought. With a tired inward grin, she marveled for a second how her life was narrowing to such a small series of petty victories to be enjoyed. She nodded at him. "Jake."

"Well? What do you think?" He sat back, easing his girth between his legs.

"I..." She gathered her thoughts. "I think that no matter what Pop wanted, Jake always wanted to be a soldier. Ever since we were kids."

"Uh-huh."

"I think that he died for something he believed in."

"And you?"

She stopped, thinking of Andrew's speech, feeling her hatred for him clouding everything she could see until, blinking, it went away a bit. Enough, anyway, that she could see that, no matter what she thought of him and what he was doing now, she pretty much agreed with him. It was a startling thought. "That I...don't know if I believe that."

"Okay." He waited, looking at her. "Anything else?"

"That...I..." Her voice began cracking and, hating herself for it, she let it. "That I...miss him. I miss his...smile. His jokes...his stupid behavior...his..." The tears, at last, were coming. Again. She sighed and let them. "His...confidence. His...belief in me." Another new thought. "I need him right now. More than ever."

Pastor Don nodded thoughtfully, pulling at one full lower lip. "Let's pick that one back up later. I'll only say right now that Jacob may have been killed, but his confidence in you hasn't gone anywhere."

She looked at him, wonderingly.

"As to the war, well...I'm right there with you." As if warding off a complaint she had no intention of making, he lifted his hands waving them around. "I know! I know. We're both surrounded by people who've been setting back half-racks of ribs to barbecue the day they catch Saddam. I mean...sure...be glad...be grateful, even...that he was stopped by young men, like Jake, who gave their lives doing so. But..." He peered at her, his eyes full of disgust. "...to take joy in the fact that they're probably going to string him up the nearest flagpole as soon as they find him, well...that's just plain...that's wrong."

She nodded, agreeing with him, pleased at what he had said.

"Now, next. Your father."

Surprised at the brevity of this conversation, she looked a question at him. "Jessie, I know you are a very busy woman with very little time these days."

She nodded at that, then asked, "What's wrong with him?"

Pastor Don pulled at his lip again. She had never seen him do that before today and wondered, briefly, where he had picked it up. Then he stopped, eased his belly again and said, "Your father loved three things in this life: his wife, his kids, his ranch. He lost first one, then half of another, and..." He paused, considering her for a long moment. "I don't volunteer the confidences, ever, of my flock, but..." He frowned again. For another long moment. "Let's just say that over the last few years your father has asked for help, for prayers, about his ranch more and more often, I've noticed. That's usually not a good sign."

She looked down. So Pop had known all along anyway. How long she had been telling herself that, somehow, he had been blind, she did not know. That he hadn't made any moves that she could see to change things...well...she didn't know what to think about that.

"Regardless, it's not unusual for a person to have experienced such a heavy series of tragedies to want to...escape for a while."

"Is that what's he doing? Cuz I can see that--!"

He cut her off. "I'm no doctor. I'm just saying that I've seen it before. Many times." He paused, letting her consider that, then continued. "There's no criticism. Nijs started with almost nothing and built that ranch to be the large concern that it is with his own hands. That's tiring work."

She smiled, sadly.

Catching her smile, he asked, "What can I do?"

She frowned, not knowing what to ask for. Then it hit her. "I agree with you. Physically, he seems just fine, only more..." She had to take a breath at her disloyalty before she said it. "...child-like."

Nodding, Pastor Don said, "And that will always remain forever and ever between you, me and that lamp."

Encouraged, she tried further. "His doctors. They keep claiming that he needs all these tests, but I..." And then it came out in a rush. "Our insurance won't cover half of them, and I've told them that but they keep claiming that it's the only way to be sure. But, if that were true, I think I would see some signs of trouble. I mean, he's so quiet all day long. I won't let anything of the ranch come within a valley mile of him. He just reads, watches tv, sleeps a lot, and eats Maria's cooking."

"He is eating?"

She snorted, "Like a horse."

"No problem with bowel movements or anything like that? No complaints hidden or otherwise about pain?"

She cast her mind back, carefully, for any of that. She shook her head.

He smiled, a rather grim smile for Pastor Don. "What's the doctor's name? Just one of them."

She told him and he wrote it down.

"Hospitals do a lot of good work, but sometimes they get a little over-excited about their ability to squeeze a few more dollars out of their patients." He slapped his pen down. "Right. I'll give this joker a call and..." He smiled that grim smile again. "...put the fear of God in him."

"Thank you." She felt a wave of relief sweeping through her, making her very, very weak.

"Last. You."

The wave stopped. She looked at him, wondering what to say. He watched her, waiting. After a moment of silence, he sighed, and ran both hands through his hair, scrubbing his scalp. "Jessie. I'm not going to waste your time telling you to come to church, or pray, or put all your faith in Jesus' healing power."

She grinned at that.

"God knows I've spent a lot of years raining that down on you in youth group, long enough to know whether you'd find much use for it. Here's the thing, though: If coming to service is just one more thing to check off your list or saying your prayers at bedtime is making your mind wander, don't bother."

Surprised at this direction, she wondered where he was going.

"Of course, you don't have to tell your Pop that I said that. I have too much faith in God's will and Jesus' love, not to mention my teaching, to be worried about whether you're missing the boat here. God is always there. Jesus is always there. On the day you need them, just ask. They'll come running with a bucket and a fire hose. Metaphorically speaking, of course." He grinned. Then, his gaze turned serious. He sat back, rubbing his face again for a moment, his hands obscuring what he was saying. "Here's the thing. If'n the regular stuff isn't going to help you, maybe I can in another way." He stopped massaging his face, his eyes all red, but looking straight at her. "One question, first: Your Uncle Willem? I ask since he didn't come to Jake's funeral. That's usually not a good sign."

She shook her head. "They haven't spoken in years. You know what he and Pop are like."

"Don't I ever." He nodded, then looked at her again. "You're eighteen."

Feeling a spurt of anger jet up, she shot out, "Nineteen."

"Whatever. I don't care if you're thirty nine, or fifty nine. No one woman..." Hearing her hiss, he waved a hand in front of his face. "Don't bother. Or one man can run that outfit single-handedly."

Still nettled, she said, "Pop did."

"Not with an ailing father to take care of. Besides, he had Ana to turn to and it wasn't nearly so large back then. After that..." He spread his hands wide, deprecatingly. He didn't need to say it.

She snorted in disgust.

"Oh, I know! You had a good spring. Calving went through just fine. You're having a quiet summer. You're running a tight operation, some say more efficiently than your father."

She looked up, surprised at this.

"And you've got probably the single best forehand in the valley personally dedicated to you." He ran a hand across his eyes. "Between you, me, and that lamp...thank God the man's happily married."

Her mouth dropped open in dismay as she felt a mounting rage at even the suggestion of such bullshit.

He shook his head. "Don't bother. You know what people are thinking just as good as I do. You're going to have to get married."

She stood up, kicking her chair back. "Did that sonofabitch talk to you!?"

He cut her off again, waving his hands and shouting, "No! No. No! No names! I don't want to hear even one. I've already heard enough gossip about who's salivating at the possibilities."

She stopped, feeling foolish then, staring at him, her angry breath heaving in and out. Finally, she pulled her chair back, but didn't sit, instead crossing her arms and looking away from him.

"One of these days, you'll come to realize, I pray, that I only want to help you achieve two things in this life: your happiness and your relationship, even if you wait until your deathbed, with Jesus." His words slowly made their way through the darkening fog of her disgust and, welling, helplessness. "It's that or sell, Jessie. You can keep on. That's true. For a while. Though, if I can take the risk of being candid with you, from the increasing number of your father's prayer requests, almost all of them confidential, I don't know for how long. Even in the best of circumstances, running something that large by yourself would kill you. You know what they're like, Jessie." She looked at him then, seeing him jerk his head toward the window. She didn't know what to say to that. He continued, "Yes, they're Christians. They're also human. Get over it."

Finally, not caring what happened anymore, she sat, saying dully, "What do I do?"

"Marry. Someone with the cash or assets to get you back onto a growth cycle. That or sell."

They sat there in silence for a while.

She found herself speaking. "It's not fair...when I was younger...this was all that I had wanted...now I have it...let alone the guilt I feel about how I--"

"Don't!"

She looked up, startled. He was leaning forward to her now, his eyes burning, his hand cutting the air. "Don't. Don't...ever...go there. Or, if you find yourself there, get away from there as fast as you can and don't look back. You didn't kill Jake, Jessie.

Saddam's soldiers did. You didn't give your father a heart attack, Jessie. His guilt at letting his son go off to war did."

She blinked at that and began crying all over again, wishing she could just stop it someday. Pastor Don sat, saying nothing, just staring at the floor for as long as they lasted. Getting herself in hand again, she sniffed, going on, "...now that I have this dream, I don't even want it anymore."

"Yes, you do."

She looked at him, her heart opening to him then, for understanding her.

"You always have."

She nodded.

"Good, now that that is settled. Goodness, Jessie..." He rubbed his face again. "I will say this...I don't miss your hair-trigger temper."

She giggled at that and wiped her cheeks.

"God's handed it to you for reasons God alone best understands. Point is: How you going to make good on that gift and keep it?"

She nodded, feeling more peaceful now. "Marry or sell."

"You won't sell."

"No."

"Well, then."

The next few weeks passed uneventfully as the summer wore its way toward August and the showlists. The truck's bill, for all her fears, turned out to be only just over one hundred and fifty dollars, including the labor. She set about with renewed determination to find some way of giving Angel a raise, but despaired after a few days of finding nothing. Instead, she set about making sure that Angel had everything he needed, particularly hot meals from Maria's kitchen for their next cutting of alfalfa now at hand and set about praying for a good harvest, knowing that she couldn't afford to buy

306

replacement feed. She was also careful, particularly in front of the men, to praise Angel for his work, keeping a safe few feet from him that couldn't possibly be misinterpreted. Sometimes drawing a gratifyingly pink shy smile as he looked down. She could see that he really appreciated that.

On the other hand, the calls from the doctors stopped, mysteriously, all at once. She made up her mind to give Pastor Don a big, gooey kiss on the cheek next time she saw him. She thought about Jake a lot now. She prayed to him frequently, still hoping to hear his voice, even if just in her memory. But nothing came. Still, she reminded herself what Pastor Don had said about Jake's confidence in her never dying and kept on with it. At his suggestion, so she wouldn't be caught flat-footed when the offers came, and there would be a few, he had chuckled, she began drawing up a mental list of what kind of arrangement she could live with. "If a knucklehead pastor like me who has never bent his head behind a plow can read your situation right, you know the others can." She thought about it, idly at first, then more angrily, then resignedly. One day, thumbing through one of Jake's old King Arthur books that she found in the basement, she found a story of a woman whose knight had died in battle and had had to settle on a new marriage to keep her lands intact. Feeling a ridiculous kinship with a woman in some made-up story, who certainly bawled a lot for her tastes, nevertheless lightened her burden somehow.

That Halverson would be among the first of those hoping to fold Van der Vaal Ranch and Cattle into their operations she finally admitted to herself, even if she had implied as much shouting at Pastor Don, when she received his notice of a half penny yardage increase per head per day for his feed lot services next year. Though she had felt his gaze lingering on her breasts at the Brickton Bellagio, she couldn't believe that she was worth his attention, other than as sport.

He was just a man who liked to hunt, liked to collect trophies and who already had far too many to over-fill that big-game hunting room he was famed for. Why he would see her as a prize for his wall, though, was beyond her. It had to be the ranch. He was known for his shrewdness, for his unexpected purchases of other outfits who, only later it was learned, had been struggling. He prided himself on it. That he usually sold them off after a year or two at a healthy profit didn't make her feel any better.

On the other hand, she had learned these last months that she was tough. She also knew, saying a prayer of thanks for Pastor Don's honesty, that she could let herself fully believe what she had suspected, that she had the loyalty of her men. At least for now. So, unless Halverson had something up his sleeve other than these petty annoyances that, true enough, were bleeding her when she didn't need it, making her weaker, she knew that she could hold out against a fat pig like that. Knowing that he wouldn't settle for less than winning, though, she swung up on Whip's back one evening to take in the stars, the place she was coming to realize that she did some of her best thinking, and pondered Halverson's next move. She couldn't see him continuing to harass her with these new bills for very much longer. Word would spread and the valley would turn against him. On the other hand, she sat upright at the thought, the valley wouldn't bat an eye when he came after her hands. How would he do it, she wondered? Thinking about it, barely seeing the Milky Way above her as Whip ambled back and forth, she guessed that he was the kind of fighter who liked to use sticks before the carrot. Remembering some of Jake's schoolyard scraps, she wondered if Halverson was the type to punch around until he found the weak spot, then kept single-mindedly jabbing at it, knocking you off balance by hurting you, continuing at it to tire you, keeping it up until you were about ready to throw up,

then finally offering the killing blow as a relief from
it all. Yes, she thought, curiously relieved. He knew
her weak spot. The hands. He had told her himself
that he had been talking to Angel. He had to know
that they were underpaid. He also had to know about
the bank. And all these extra fees had to be then, she
realized, his way of keeping her off-balance, keeping
them underpaid. She could depend on it, she decided,
finally. A man like that didn't wait in line. He
wouldn't wait until she was forced to sell some leases
or stock. The day that he was able to bleed her of
hands with offers of higher wages was the day that he
would move in for the kill. All at once, she felt
herself relax. It was comforting, she thought, to
know how he would come at her even though there
wasn't a damn thing she could do about it. She even
had to respect him a little. If it wasn't her ranch on
the chopping block, she thought she might admire his
tactics. Then, reconsidering, she decided that she
could never admire somebody who liked to profit by
another's suffering.

Besides, she reminded herself with a lifting heart,
with Pop's bills now slowing down, they might be
behind, but they were still standing. And next
month's coming buyers would...well...they would
bring what they did. For now, she was still standing.
And she still had Lateral F, a simple plot of land that
had become, she realized, a beacon for her. A symbol
of not just making do. Of getting ahead.

Which made her design the marbling patrols. After
thinking it over for a few days, she carefully had
Maria invite Angel over for a large dinner. While not
much was said, and Pop clearly confused by the
whole affair, she bided her time until after the coffee
had washed down Maria's pie and Pop had turned on
his tv. She took Angel around showing him the
maps. That he had glimpsed them before while
passing through the house she knew, but now she
wanted him to take a long look at them with her.

Supplied with fresh coffee by an ever-pleasing Maria that Jessie was careful to keep near them, she explained to him that she wanted to tackle their falling grades problem. As he listened, committing nothing, she explained that she believed that marbling patterns set in at an early age. She had flirted with telling him where she had gotten the idea, from a white paper she had come across last fall but had forgotten in her eagerness to pursue the organic premiums, but had decided against it knowing that if he wouldn't trust the owner whose cattle were in question, he certainly wouldn't trust a bunch of eggheads from Iowa. Instead, she simply told him that she believed that, no matter what happened to their stock at feed lots, they could establish the foundation for a good marbling here at home. Together, then, they worked out a rotation schedule over the next few months until weaning so that the hands would have as much time as possible with each herd, looking for anything unusual, making sure that no calf was in trouble, no signs of scours or pinkeye or distress of any kind, spending extra time with those calves that were sick, and that the pasture was rich and full for the cows to feed on. Angel chuckled at her next request, but said he would order the men to spend time talking with each of the calves, scratching them where they couldn't reach behind the ears, under the chin, and at the base of the tail.

She also told him that while they could work out the plans in detail later, she planned to delay sending this year's weaned calves to the feed lot by a couple of months so that they would be stronger by the time they got there and not fall prey to the usual host of feed lot pneumonia and other ills that newly weaned calves suffered. She also planned to put off installing the growth implants for a bit to let them gain on their own, in her pastures. She wanted to look at their creep-feeding, too, but needed to think about it some more. To all this, Angel nodded, his dark eyes quietly thoughtful but, she could see, approving.

Riding Whip around herself in the following weeks to look at the ground in particular, she began to learn which plots were better for grazing and, soon after, got together with Angel to schedule rotations of the herds on the choicest pasture. Also, after the hands' marbling patrols began to settle in, she asked Angel to pull Josef from it to roam around on Digger, since Asa scared him, taking more detailed records on each calf. The hands, feeling that something new was afoot, seemed intrigued. Certainly, there wasn't any sign among them of the anxiety she always carried. In any case, after a year or two of marbling patrols, she hoped a pattern would emerge to settle the grades question. If she was still running things in a year or two. Surprised one day at this thought and how fatalistic she had become, she shrugged and kept at it.

As her pride in the marbling patrols grew, she decided she couldn't see giving up management of the cow-calf operation. And she hoped that she would never have to sell off the lease to Lateral F. Remembering Pastor Don's advice to come up with a livable arrangement, she tried to think about it, but got no further than that.

In the evenings, though, she found herself spending time with Pop letting him idly click through different channels watching whatever interested him. After her talk with Pastor Don, she slowly realized that, while not able to admit it to herself, she had been growing steadily angry with Pop for running the ranch into the ground. Of course, she repented of that now, looking at his faded-blue eyes staring in wonder out of his wrinkled face at just about everything he saw, and saw the man for who he was, beaten down by the misfortunes of life after he had built the ranch of his younger dreams. It was an easy time letting Pop watch tv. She could always let her mind drift on to the subject of what kind of arrangement she could live with even though she never got farther than the first two conclusions.

One night, as Pop was clicking through channels, they heard a talk show host, she didn't know which one, say, "Next up! Peace activist Andrew Worth whose inspiration is sweeping the nation. Right after this." And she gleamed into the camera.

Jessie felt confused. She was startled to feel that she wasn't angry at him anymore. Surprised even more that she hadn't really thought about him all that much. Just passing references in her mind lately. But always quickly passing. Before she could figure out why, there he was, walking across the stage to sit down at the usual chairs gathered next to the host's desk, the studio audience enthusiastically thumping their applause. After shaking hands with him, the host sat down with her gleam shining in the lights.

"So! Andrew. You've made quite a name for yourself across the nation these last months."

He laughed but didn't say anything. Jessie saw his same patient smile, though she thought he looked a bit uncomfortable through it. Other than that, he looked much the same as always, even wearing Jake's raincoat inside the studio. She recognized the sweater and thought it odd that he wasn't better dressed for all his success.

"I know. You're famously shy." She gleamed at the audience. "Isn't he wonderful?" The audience applauded again, with a few cheers added in.

"You started by giving a speech about your best friend's death in Iraq, at a rally last April at your school in Seattle."

He nodded.

"And then the world discovered you! Isn't that amazing?" The audience applauded again.

Andrew looked at her, his smile never really wavering, still saying nothing.

His host looked a little put out that he was being so silent, then gleamed. "I hear you have a book deal in the works."

He shifted uncomfortably at that. Unreal, Jessie thought. A book deal!? About what? Jake? Still, she tried to let her anger at him go, tried to be happy for him, tried to look at him like he were someone she barely knew.

"Well," he was finally speaking. "There's been some talk of that. It would be a collection of conversations I've had visiting different universities--"

The host cut in, "Speaking at different universities, isn't it?"

He shifted in his seat again. "Yes. Speaking at rallies protesting the Iraq War."

"How many cities have you visited?"

He shook his head. "Well, there have been quite a few. I'm not sure why--"

"People! Isn't he wonderful? I give you Andrew Worth!" The audience started cheering, even more loudly than before. As the clapping started to fade, she said, "Next thing we know, you'll be running for president!"

Jessie had seen enough. She stood up, kissing Pop on the forehead and saying, "I forgot to pick up some milk for Maria today. Back in a bit." His eyes never really wavered in their honest delight seeing Andrew up there.

**

Driving into town, figuring she had better make good on her lie, she found herself swearing furiously. President?! The whole thing was ridiculous. Because Jake got killed and he made a speech about it!? Spinning the wheel of Pop's pickup to slide onto a side road, she cut loose a string of loud and impressive, even for her she knew, obscenities. She wondered if Ella had been standing backstage watching him, her big tits bouncing up and down with every word that he said. They'd probably go back to the room tonight and fuck, she thought, savagely. Then, remembering that the show had probably been taped, she raged that they had already fucked long before she even got to know about it.

Screeching through the gravel to a halt before the small grocery store in Brickton, she stomped inside and, slamming fridge doors open and shut as she looked over the labels, she tried in vain to remember the special milk that Maria had been feeding Pop. After a while, catching the owner's frightened glance while she snatched up a gallon of 2%, she saw with a jerk that it was Mrs. Rodriguez. Slowing down, she apologized for her behavior and, feeling guilty, grabbed a second gallon and walked quietly up to the front. There, as Mrs. Rodriguez hurriedly rang up the bill, she sought to calm her by making a few remarks about the weather they'd been having and asking a few questions about how Mr. Rodriguez was doing. Eventually, the poor old woman calmed down. Jessie leaned over just before leaving and said, "I'm sorry. It's...my time of the month...I get a heavy flow sometimes."

At that the old woman smiled, knowingly, and asking her to wait a moment, walked over to an ice cream freezer, pulled out a snack and giving it to her, said, "Please say hello to Pop for me." Jessie smiled sweetly and slipped it into a back pocket. Well, as sweetly as she could as she thought of skewering Andrew alive the next time she saw him and, opening the door, entertained the delightful thought of grabbing his cock and slicing it clean through with one of Maria's big knives.

Outside in the night air, she paused and took a deep breath. With the road's streetlights she couldn't see many stars, certainly not as many as from Whip's back, but she could see a few and smiled at them.

After a moment or two, she felt herself quiet and turned toward the truck.

"Hey, sweet thing! No big man to hold you at night?"

She looked across the street at the group of boys walking toward her. She could smell the beer already. She shook her head in disgust, thinking just some country boys with too much time and beer on their hands, and walked around the front of the pickup, her milk gallons in each hand. Just as she turned the corner on the fender, however, one of the boys, in pretty good shape, she thought, wearing a sleeveless t-shirt that emphasized his biceps, sprinted up and leaned back against the door handle.

She sighed. She wasn't in the mood for this. "Get out of the way."

"Why?" He smiled at her, a widely innocent smile that she knew hid everything.

She felt her anger spurt. "Enough's enough. Let's go."

"Great! Let's do it!" And without warning, he pushed her back a few feet. She found herself stumbling, trying not to drop the milk, trying to catch her balance. Finding it, she stood up to see, as she turned around, that she was surrounded. Her anger sputtered then suddenly went out to be replaced by a whisper of anxiety, pulsating in her breast, making her breathe faster.

"Oh, now look at that! Poor little Sticks is afwwaid." The t-shirt drawled out the word.

She turned at that, finding him in the circle, wondering who he was and how he knew her nickname, feeling her anxiety grow.

"Come on, Sticks. Show us what you got. Think you're man enough to run your ranch all by yourself. Show us what you got!" he sneered. The others laughed, loud guffaws of drunken glee. A few still sipped from tall beer bottles, watching him, watching her. She turned around and around, not liking where this was going. She thought, to hell with this, and decided to just push through to the truck but got no further than a few steps before the ones in front of her bunched up to push her roughly back into the circle with a few more shouts. She looked around her at the deserted streets, thought briefly of running but knew they would only chase her down. Besides, she thought, her heart pounding faster and faster making her dizzy, where could she run to? She looked over at the grocery store door, knowing it was the only place open, but saw the boys in front of it leering at her, inviting her to try it. Then she tried searching out a pair, just one pair, she prayed of friendly eyes, but saw only drunken anger staring back at her. As she was turning one last time, she felt a harsh pain in her chest and caught the glimpse of the t-shirt twisting one of her breasts before jumping back.

"Yeah! She's got 'em, boys. I told ya!" They laughed at this, jeering her. "Not much, but she's got 'em. They'll do!" At that, they all started shouting as they cheered, "Do her, man! Do her!" Jessie started feeling sick. One she could care less about, she knew, but this many? How was she going to get away? The thought, scaring her that she wasn't made her swallow several times. She gulped for air. She started to feel her mind go numb.

And then she heard it. His voice. At last. His warrior's voice.

See, the trick when you're surrounded like that is not to lose your head. Any group of jackals who'd take on a single person like that is probably more afraid of their leader and his second than of you.

And through the loud yells of their hooting and catcalls, she remembered that strange conversation that she had never understood Jake's obsession with. Well, she smiled inwardly, so glad to hear his voice at last, now she did.

Act all normal and relaxed, maybe even a bit afraid if you can manage it, so that he thinks you're easy

*prey. That'll make him come for you. And let him.
Let him come...*

So she did. She even one-upped it. Remembering Jake's direction to look at the eyes, she said, "Wait a moment." Which gave them pause. She took advantage of it to take a slow measuring glance out of the sides of her eyes, lowering her lashes to make her look more sexy, of the entire circle watching to see which one they followed. Just as she thought. The t-shirt. Not worrying yet about his second, for she knew that was coming, she turned and faced him, tilting her head.

"I know you don't like the idea, but I can run my ranch, and it is my ranch now, all by myself." She heard mutters that took on a darker tone, including a "Fuck you, bitch!" She went on, fluttering her lashes at the t-shirt. "In fact, I can probably even run it better than some of the other ranchers in this valley..." At this, the mutters gave way to loud cries and curses. She ignored them all, even the ones at her back, keeping her eyes on the t-shirt, who was smiling big, saying nothing, expecting what was coming if the others were too stupid to, and liking it. "But what I can't do..." and here she set down the milk, "...is find..." and stood again, slowly unbuttoning her shirt, "...a good thick cock..." They stood, spellbound, not moving, barely breathing, trying to believe their eyes as she slowly slid her arms out of the sleeves, letting the rest of the shirt dangle at her waist. She continued, "...to satisfy me." She let t-shirt and all those on that side of the circle stare at her breasts that, skimpy as they were, given the circumstances, t-shirt would think them quite large. She saw his eyes glitter with hunger as he stared at them. Then, adopting a sweet tone, she asked, "Can you?"

Looking as if he could hardly believe his luck, he started toward her, actually licking his lips with anticipation. As he drew close, she bent slowly, turning away to keep him on her right side, lowering

317

her lashes again, like she was suddenly shy. "You won't hurt me, will you?" She kept her voice small, even a little frightened, as he drew near to her.

He started to grunt something and she finished his sentence for him. Spinning back, she landed a good punch, just as Jake had suggested, to the nose, not enough to land him, just to hurt him. The pop was so satisfying, she thought, watching him rear back, the eyes of the crowd she could see, or sense, widening likewise. T-shirt bent over cradling his nose with his hands, a loud "Fuck!" shrieking from him. Taking one step forward with her right foot, and imagining he was Andrew, she came down with her all her weight on her left bootheel to the side of his knee, driving it fast and hard, hearing it crack sickeningly as he went down. He was screaming now, rolling on the ground clutching his knee. Remembering it wasn't over yet, she spun quickly around, seeing the gaping mouths staring at t-shirt on the ground, back to her, back to t-shirt, on to...him. She saw him, barely registering that it was Andreeson, and came right at him so fast that he didn't know what to do. He started stumbling back away from her, his eyes stretching wide in panic. She could feel her tiny breasts swinging with each step, her eyes ablaze, and still she came on. Faster and faster and, remembering how sick and tired she was of all the speeches that had been made lately, she delivered a hard right to the base of his throat, hearing his gasp cut off short as he went down at her feet. Thinking of Andrew once more, she added a quick, hard stomp to his balls, feeling her heel make solid contact with the gravel, whatever was left of his testicles, and hearing his shriek added to the din in her ears. She whirled around, actually liking this now, hoping for a third, and started back toward the circle that was quickly shredding its shape, running for the darkness. She stood there a moment, her breath heaving her breasts up and down in the chilling night air, watching their backs retreat from streetlit shapes, into gray shadows, into nothingness. All alone, except her two victims mewling out pitiful moans as they rocked back and forth and, as she drew her shirt back up, Mrs. Rodriguez's frightened, staring, round eyes watching her through the glass of the store. She finished buttoning up, picked up her milk, nodded at Mrs. Rodriguez who managed a little smile, finally, and, stepping over t-shirt, drove away.

***

Arriving home, she found Pop sitting quietly with his Bible. As she was kissing him hello on the forehead, she heard his muffled comment, "He walked off the show."

Confused for a moment, she abruptly remembered what had set her off. "Andrew?"

"Yep." He shook his head.

"Why?"

"Dunno. Except..." Raising his eyes, his whispy white eyebrows shooting all the way to the top of his forehead, he cried out, with all the special contempt he reserved for those on her side of the gender fence, "...that woman kept badgering him!" forgetting entirely that he was talking to one. "Wanted to know what he was going to do next, what he wanted to be someday..." Shaking his head, again, in disgust, he muttered. "All he wanted to do was talk about Jake."

The first time she had heard Pop say the name since... She found herself anxiously scanning his face for signs of trouble or sickness or stress or something. Nope. He was just shaking his head, muttering, "Just like a woman. Jab. Jab. Jab."

She had to grin at this. Then he unexpectedly looked up at her, his face frowning with worry. "I hope he's okay."

"Andrew?" She sighed inwardly, trying to think of what to say. "He's a smart man, Pop. He'll be okay. Now, let's get you to bed."

"Okay." She slowly pulled him out of his chair and herded him, still muttering with indignation about "All the fuss a woman can cause!" gently into bed.

***

She wasn't sorry about it. Not until later. Over the next few days, deciding that she could better figure out what kind of arrangement she could live with if she rode over the pastures with that thought in mind, she began taking Whip out. Trotting her one sunny afternoon along a tractor path, feeling the gorgeous warmth of high summer taking hold of the land, she spotted Angel and the hands sitting under a spreading oak tree eating lunch. She smiled at the idyllic sight and wondered if that was one of the "efficiencies" she had introduced that Pastor Don had heard about. She knew that Pop liked the old ways, but she had always suspected that the daily lunch gave him a sense that he was controlling the men better even though it meant a lot of work time was wasted traveling back and forth to the house. She didn't need that. She trusted Angel. She trusted the hands. She also knew that they had taken to lingering around Pop after lunch, so one day shortly after handing out the radios and after checking with Angel, she had asked Maria to make up sandwiches for the men's lunch the next day. The next morning, as Maria was handing them out with bottled water, Angel had explained to the hands that during the summer and fall months, they were to lunch outside wherever they liked. It had worked. Just as she had expected. Trust the hands to do right by you and they did, never really straying far from where they were working when they stopped to eat and getting right back at it as soon as they were done. Besides, she thought, watching them sit in the shade with the wind blowing through the branches above them, it was prettier out here.

But then, drawing nearer, she saw Angel and one of them, Felipe, stand up, pointing fingers at each other, the others standing around them. She rode into the pasture toward them, galloping between the cows lying here and there on the ground, their eyes half-closed in the sun and their calves, those not able to get at the teats anyway, lying in the shadow of their mothers. Hearing Whip's hooves, Angel and Felipe broke away from one another.

She reined Whip in, about to ask Angel over to the side to find out what the hell was going on, and then she knew. Word had spread. It was the valley, after all. A few of the men looked up at her with honest fear, Felipe even making the cross at her, his pursed fingers tracing it out in the air between them. Off to the side, Angel watched, a look of pure disgust on his face. She looked at him and jerked her head pointing off to the left. He nodded and, with a last shake of his head at Felipe, began moving that way. She slid down to meet him, leading Whip by the reins.

"Angel?" She looked into his face. He was angry. Angrier even than with that bullshit with Andreeson and, as she thought his name, she relived the satisfying smash of her heel into the ground. Angel shoved his hands in his back pockets though and stared off into the distance. Remembering what she had learned about Latino machismo, she waited patiently, turning the reins in her hands wondering what he was going to say and knowing that it wasn't going to be good.

Finally, he sighed and looked at her. "Jefe."
She nodded.
Jerking his head back at the hands, he began, "The men..." then stopped. He looked off in the distance again and said it. "Señor Halverson is opening six new pens. Offering three dollars an hour more

than..." He looked at her. "He stopped by once last week, himself, asking the men to come with him."

She nodded. She had been expecting it, after all, she thought. Though maybe not quite this soon.

"Are any going?" she asked and forced herself not to look at the men, but already knowing with a sigh the answer, at least for one.

"Last week? No."

Well, she thought, she could expect a visit soon. And those hands, not badly-formed, big and strong, yet oddly twisting his riding hat in nervousness the last time she had seen them flashed into her mind. For some reason, she found herself pondering the strange ways of the world, how it was preferable in the valley to have a sixty year old man marry a nineteen year old girl than it was to let that girl run her own ranch. "And now?"

"He stopped by again this morning after..." He looked at her again, this time a little uncertainly, as if he didn't know her at all.

She was stunned. "How many are going?"

"Just Felipe for now."

She blew out a sigh of relief. At this, he turned to fully face her, his face clouded with concern. "Jefe. I let him go. He's a good hand, a bit lazy sometimes. I don't care about him, but the others...He called you a she-demon."

At that, she felt a jet of white hot anger coursing through her and thought about walking over to Felipe and...

"I don't know why, Jefe."

His comment cut into her thoughts. She snapped a look at him then, but only saw him trying to smile, the corners of his lips trembling as he watched her.

"What was I supposed to do, let 'em rape me?"

He shrugged, his hands lifting out. "Jefe, they are simple men. They like the old ways. The old traditions."

Fucking unreal, she thought, shaking her head, then forcing herself to find some sort of calm. Andrew's stone flitted into her mind for a moment, gentling her, and she smiled. "How about the others?"

"They say that boy will never walk again, Jefe." He paused and squinted into the sun. "Tomas and Leon are thinking Halverson is looking pretty good now."

And then it was gone. Just like that, the calculations springing quickly to mind. She'd have to sell that lease on Lateral F. "Tell them, all, that I'm giving them a dollar and a half an hour raise beginning this morning." She smiled her prettiest smile and tried to look harmless. "Oh, and remind them that at Halverson's they'll be standing in shit up to their knees all day long." And, then, an added touch: "Their ladies won't like the smell all that much."

Angel smiled. A big smile. "That will help, Jefe. That will keep them."

And then, why not, she thought? The organic herd was gone forever. "I almost forgot. Two dollars more an hour for you."

His mouth dropped open.

"Well, come on, Angel. I looked back through Pop's records. You haven't had a raise since the culling in '99."

He ducked his head at that, the pink building in his brown cheeks.

She stood there, twisting the reins in her hands, trying to look sweet and gentle and made of fucking porcelain and wondering how long she would have to keep up the act.

Angel had gathered himself now. He cleared his throat, looking up, his face blank of emotion. "Jefe. The money is good. Thank you. But..."

What now, she thought, the pinpricks of despair forming in her stomach.

He squinted into the sun again, holding up one hand to shield his eyes. "Jake was a good man, Jefe. He was good to me, to Maria, to my family. He...made me promise to stay with the ranch until he came home."

"He did come back." Her statement, baldly flat as it was, barely hid the thanks to Jake she felt welling up in her, lifting outward to the sun, to him wherever he was.

"Si. He did." He looked at her.

They stood there a moment, Jessie biting the inside of her cheek to keep from screaming.

He sighed and looked all around them. "Jefe, I live in the valley. Can you show me where I can find a better boss?"

Through the relief dizzying her that she was careful to keep from her face, she wanted to hug him. Instead, she smiled again. Not the doll's smile, her real smile. "Just as soon as you show me a better forehand. You still get the raise."

He nodded at that with an answering smile and turned back to look at the tree and the others.

***

Angel had compounded the goodness by suggesting a cousin of his, the same one who had fixed the starter on the truck. And now she knew why the cost had been so low, she smiled, riding on to the herds on White Swan Road. Call that one a draw, you fat fucker, she exulted. Then, recalling the loss of Lateral F, she grudgingly admitted that Halverson had won that round. She wondered how many she had left in her. With the sale of Lateral F, the decline will have begun.

She suddenly wished she were back outside Mrs. Rodriguez's store, surrounded by a bunch of dumb, drunk boys coming at her. That was easy. Jake had been right, you could not only tell your enemies by their eyes, you could even tell when and how they were coming at you. This was so different. So much harder. Christ! Might as well have a few cows start dropping dead of black leg and, in her mind's eye, she saw the flesh of their legs crackling to the touch, their stiff, dry tongues lolling on the ground. And suddenly horrified at what she had just imagined, like she were tempting fate, she reined Whip in for a moment to say a small prayer to Jesus asking forgiveness for swearing before riding on.

***

He didn't wait long. The next afternoon, as she was frowning over the spreadsheet and wondering who she should talk to about Lateral F, reminding herself that good ground was hard to find in the valley and that there would be no shortage of takers, she heard a truck pull up in the driveway followed by Biscuit's greeting howls. Glancing out the window, she knew the truck, one of those huge, dieseled six-wheeled pickups. Big man, big truck, tiny...she thought and rested her forehead in her hand. It had come so quickly. She knew that she should at least put on some makeup, if only to help negotiate better terms, but couldn't muster up the effort. Instead, she stood at the knock on the door, Maria's answering hello, and re-slung her ponytail.

After Maria had given them both coffee and retired, he took one sip and began. "Jessie. I won't waste your time. What happened the other night was...terrible. You could have been seriously injured...or worse."

The shrieks and moans came to her ears, the fleeting memory of chasing down Andreeson and seeing the terror in his eyes lit a tight smile on her face.

Halverson, seeing it, sat back shaking his head for a long minute before continuing. "Now, look here.

The community won't stand for any more of that. They want it to stop. Brunner's boy will be walking with a cane the rest of his life and the other boy, well....They want it to stop. They don't ever want to see something like that again...I've...I've come on their behalf."

She coughed at that, thinking, damn this man was shrewd. She had never expected an attack from this angle. She heaved an inner sigh and kept her face polite. She nodded.

"What are your terms?"

His eyes widened at that, his mouth hanging open. Clearly, this was not what he had been expecting either. Score a draw on this round, she thought, pleased, and sat back, watching him carefully, crossing her arms over her chest.

He watched her, too, for a moment saying nothing. Then a slow smile of respect crossed his beefy features. "You may be a girl all of nineteen, but you've been fighting a good fight. It's not your fault. This was over before it began. I've already taken one of your hands. I will take the others. Goodness knows, if our situations was reversed, I couldn't have done any better."

Praise, indeed, she thought with an inner chortle of bitterness.

"What's more, you're running a good outfit. Everybody can see that. Got a few of them eating their hats, too." He smiled with a twinkle in his eyes. "Oh, I know. You can hold on for..." he frowned a moment, rubbing one finger on his chin before going on, "...a year, maybe two, before the herd starts eating itself. At that point, every fool in the valley will be lining up with offers. I'm not waiting for that day. I don't have to. I can see the signs, think I'm reading 'em right. I think you..." He looked her over for a moment, shaking his head again with that rueful smile of respect. "...are hiding it well, but I think what with your Pop's medical bills and the last years' performance, I think you're in trouble. We both know you can't expect any better in the showlists this year."

She looked out the window, trying to look bored by the conversation, trying not to give anything away.

"Oh. One more thing. Something only you and I in the valley will know this morning, though it'll be spread all over the country by nightfall." He paused, not trying to keep the satisfaction out of his eyes. "Buddy of mine is in the state inspector's office. They found a case of mad-cow at the packing plant in Mabton."

She closed her eyes. It was over.

"Just one, a dairy cow. But one's enough. You know it as well as me. God knows your stock hasn't been bringing in all that much the last few years as it is. With dropping demand, we can expect prices'll hit the basement this year and the next, maybe two, as people start eating chicken and pork instead."

A bird, she couldn't tell which, began a slow, plaintive song in the yard.

"You won't be the only outfit scrambling for every red cent to weather the storm. Those of us with deeper pockets, well...we might even clean up. Make an honest penny or two."

***

And then he had laid out his terms. Looking out over the spread on Lateral F, thinking how beautiful it was, Whip's reins in her hand, she wondered what to do with it, idly thinking that the terms hadn't been all that bad. Certainly better than she could expect elsewhere. He had offered her hands-free management of the cow-calf operation, so long as it turned a decent profit after Pop's bills were cleared. She wondered how he defined "decent" because she had forgotten to ask. She wondered if she cared. It could stay in her name, but he would own it, too. Oh, and her hand in marriage, commenting that he had a few sons, yet, he'd like to see in this world as he tried, unsuccessfully, not to stare at the breasts he must have heard about. He would wait six months for her answer and, if she declined, he would put back on the heat, in ways that she hadn't dared dream of yet.

She knew she didn't need the six months, not after the Mabton news, but she was going to enjoy it as long as she could. Jardín del Paraíso. It sure came at a high price, she mused sadly and wondered what it was going to feel like being nailed to someone's wall, just one more trophy among all the others. Behind her, Whip neighed a greeting, interrupting her thoughts and, faintly, on the breeze now whispering gently through the trees, she heard Digger's answer. Surprised at what that meant, knowing that Josef was in the truck with Angel today and not even daring to acknowledge the faintest of hopes just stirring in her heart, she turned to look.

There he was, trotting Digger at a nice clip, bareback. Good form, she could see even at this distance, his hands gently holding the reins, his knees easily clutching Digger's frame, wearing one of Pop's old jean jackets under his unruly black hair and thin cheeks. She just watched him. Before long, he was turning Digger into the field and, his eyes scanning the ground ahead of him carefully, he trotted up.

They looked at each other for a long moment, saying nothing, both checking the other for changes. He had found his riding boots, she could see. He slid down and, looking around, said, "Nice spread. Should do well for your trial herd."

She snorted.

He looked at her, surprised.

She thought about trying to explain Halverson's offer, then decided against it, opting only for a "Can't afford it. Not with Pop's bills."

"Oh. As for that..." He paused, digging around in his pockets, mumbling a "...where did I...? Ah."

Then, out of his shirt pocket, he pulled a neatly folded

328

slip of paper and handed it to her. "In Jake's memory."

She unfolded it, and through her swimming eyes, she saw a check for thirty-eight thousand dollars written out to Van der Vaal Ranch and Cattle. "There should have been more from a talk show last week, but I...uh...walked off the set during the interview. Sorry."

She laughed at that, a crazy laugh, almost hysterical. Staring at her, as if he was concerned for her mind, he went on, "Still, you never know. Ella was pissed to beat hell and sicked her father on them. Apparently he's quite a good lawyer. Anyway, he's threatening to make a fuss so they just pay us to go away and...well...we'll see. He's even doing it pro bono."

She laughed even harder at that, wiping away the tears that were flowing down, then, realizing he had said that hated name, she stopped.

He was watching her, those gray eyes shining with kindness.

Which made her ashamed of herself. "Well, thank her for me, will you?"

"You can thank her yourself."

Startled, she looked over his shoulder back down the road.

"She took the car, visiting Jake's grave."

She nodded, in wonder.

"Said she knew that Jake is gone, but she still wanted to see where he grew up, meet his family, see his memories for herself."

That faint ray of hope began dawning again. She tried to push it down but couldn't.

Andrew just kept on talking, slowly, gently, watching her face. "She's a good organizer, Ella. Actually, that..." he said, pointing at the check, "...is really due to her."

Jessie frowned, trying to understand him.

"I mean...well...you probably don't know...oh! Of course you do! Pop told me he got to see a few of the speeches. Well...I got this invitation to speak at UCLA and another at Berkeley...and...well...I turned them down. I didn't want to...make his death a...sideshow or anything like that. But then they called back asking what they could do to convince me, followed by all their own speeches about standing up for justice, taking on..." His eyes went inward and he stopped talking.

She gently reached out to touch his arm which brought him back, instantly. "...taking on the administration's arrogance and all these other...well...maybe I'll tell you about it sometime. And that's when Ella had the idea: make them pay me. And they did. Two thousand dollars for a few minutes in front of a crowd." He shook his head at the memory, clearly still marveling over it. "To make my trip around the barn short..." he paused and Jessie smiled at the realization that he was actually reveling in saying that phrase. "Ella took over then. I put my foot down at ten speeches until..." He sighed with a chuckle before continuing, "...she browbeat me into another five, scheduling them all over the country, negotiating as high a price as she could get, even free flights, sometimes, room and board for me. Her dad paid her way. She's really wonderful, Ella. Wouldn't take a dime for the work. Said that it kept Jake's memory alive for her."

Jessie finally thought she should say something. "She must have really loved him."

"Yes." He looked at her, his concerned smile dissolving into his look of peace. "Yes, she did. In ways he never knew, I suspect."

She shook her head, frowning over the check. "Andrew. I'm really grateful for this. God knows I need it. Not even for the organic herd. But for a storm that's coming soon."

"Okay."

"But..." Taking a deep breath, she held it out back to him. "I can't take it."

Andrew snorted. "Okay, but you better not tell Ella." He sighed. "I've seen the way she negotiates. She may not look it, but she's tough. Daddy's girl." And, at this, he started laughing.

Which made her laugh, too.

Then, all at once, he gently closed her hand over the check. "Take it, Jessie. It's yours. Jake got to fight for his Eden. You should be able to fight for yours, too."

She shook her head, feeling the hated, weak tears come again.

"Don't you think that he'd want it that way?"

And, suddenly, her opposition dissolved. She looked back down at the check, her eyes swimming again, just as fast as her mind swam through the array of possibilities that Andrew had just handed her. Take that, she thought, you bastard of a pig, Halverson!

"How bad is this storm that's coming?"

Her joy dimmed. She sighed, "Bad."

"Well, there's more if you need it. I think. I mean...I don't know what they pay for a book but...anyway, Ella's handling it. Her idea, again. Actually, it's a good one, too. Just the speech to begin with, then all the conversations I've been having with different people across the country, my thoughts following each one. Then, too, there are always more speeches to be made. Schnoebel says I should milk it while it lasts, before they get tired of my face. Strange..." She saw his eyes turning inward. "I only did it because I got fed up with Hegland spewing all his...and, yet, this damn war isn't going to go away anytime soon..."

Not wanting to hear anymore, not now, not with him disappearing into the reaches of his mind, she suddenly blazed out the question that she realized had been forming from the moment she had heard Digger's answering neigh.

"Enough about that! Enough about Ella, about Jake, about me. What about you? What's your Eden? Have you found your...?" She frowned, trying to remember what Jake had said Christmas Eve. "...place yet?"

"No, I never did." He smiled, drawing her toward him, letting her resist one final time then come. "But it turns out I didn't have to for..." she heard him say as she lay her head on his shoulder, enjoying the feeling at last, wishing it would never end. "It found me."

Book Club Questions

1. It is often said that opposites attract. How are Andrew and Jake attracted to one another? How are Jessie and Andrew attracted to one another?

2. What is each young adventurer's Eden? How is he or she fighting for that Eden?

3. What is your Eden? How do you fight for it?

4. Have you ever experienced such a great cultural divide such as we see between Seattle and the valley? Describe that divide?

Author Bio

Jeff Stilwell excels at the unexpected. Not content with his Midwestern roots, he found ways on the cheap to explore the wider world including selling gummy bears in high school to visit the Alps of southern Germany. To pay for college, he worked a slime line as a head chopper in the clammy tundra of Alaska.

His thirst for adventure next took him to Asia where he studied the martial arts and Asian philosophy while exploring exotic locales such as the Himalayas and the lands of *Lord Jim*, even surviving a squall in the Gulf of Siam.

Attracted to strong women lifelong, he met and wooed his wife, jewelry designer Manya Vee there, winning her heart by following her to Java. Upon returning to the States, they founded an art gallery just north of Seattle. She taught him to gallop bareback at the family farm in the storied Yakima Valley, the inspiration for his first novel *Fighting for Eden*.

Together, they became award-winning artzos, creating numerous public service events in the arts including one of the largest art walks in the Pacific Northwest, a celebrated murals collection, and a live music scene where Stilwell performed stand-up comedy every Friday night.

His flair for the dramatic led him to write and stage fifteen plays in and around the Seattle theatre scene. His works earned numerous laurels such as "an intense dramatic comedy you don't want to miss...an uninterrupted 90-minute power pack with something to say," for his *One Tile Short* and "a trip and a half in a little more than a hour and a half through an Alice-

like wonderland and a half; ground-breaking in ways
more than one," for his *Teacup Tipsy*.

Too restless, however, to merely sit behind a
computer, he recently completed a solitary 750 mile
hike from Stevens Pass in Western Washington to
end, a Biblical sounding forty days later, at Old
Faithful Geyser in Yellowstone National Park. Once
upon a time, he even ran for Congress. If it's big,
Stilwell has dreamt it, attempted it, or achieved it.

What's next?

Toni's Smile

Here I stand.
These words flash in Toni's mind as she enters the final presidential debate opposed by a man who represents everything she believes is wrong with America. Ten points behind in the polls, humiliating defeat beckons days before the election, yet this fiery Blatina refuses to surrender.
She can do no other.

Author note: *Toni's Smile* is now available in both Kindle and Print formats on Amazon at getbook.at/tonissmile.

Other books by Jeff Stilwell

Here and Now: A Whimsical Take On God
Author and illustrator Jeff Stilwell takes us on a
journey through time with words and his own
illustrations. When did we humans first conceive of
God? What forms did that take? What have we done
with that concept over time?

Join his delightful skateboarding adventurer
Thrashin' Jack and the faithful feline Lotus as they
cavort across the ages looking for insights into these
intriguing questions.

Available now on Amazon at getbook.at/hereandnow.